THE TEACHER OF
AUSCHWITZ

ALSO BY WENDY HOLDEN

Shrink
In the Name of Gucci
Born Survivors
The Sense of Paper
Mr Scraps
Shell Shock
5 Minutes of Amazing
The Beat of My Own Drum
Haatchi & Little B
Uggie the Artist
10 Mindful Minutes
Lady Blue Eyes
Kill Switch
Journey to the Edge of the World
Tomorrow to Be Brave
Heaven and Hell
A Lotus Grows in the Mud
Memories Are Made of This
Behind Enemy Lines
Smile Though Your Heart Is Breaking
Till the Sun Grows Cold
Footprints in the Snow
Love and Fashion
Waking Ned
Central 822
The Full Monty
Biting the Bullet
Good Vibrations
Unlawful Carnal Knowledge

THE TEACHER
OF AUSCHWITZ

by

Wendy Holden

Based on a true story

HARPER ● PERENNIAL

NEW YORK ● LONDON ● TORONTO ● SYDNEY ● NEW DELHI ● AUCKLAND

Originally published in Great Britain in 2025 by Zaffre, an imprint of Zaffre Publishing Group.

FIRST US EDITION

Library of Congress Cataloging-in-Publication Data

Names: Holden, Wendy, 1961- author.
Title: The teacher of Auschwitz : a novel / Wendy Holden.
Description: First U.S. edition. | New York, NY : Harper Paperbacks, 2025.
| Includes bibliographical references.
Identifiers: LCCN 2024044957 | ISBN 9780063398214 (trade paperback) | ISBN
9780063398252 (hardcover) | ISBN 9780063398221 (ebook)
Subjects: LCSH: Hirsch, Fredy, 1916-1944--Fiction. | World War, 1939-1945--Concentration camps--Poland--Fiction. | Auschwitz (Concentration camp)--Fiction. | Holocaust, Jewish (1939-1945)--Poland--Fiction. | LCGFT: Biographical fiction. | Historical fiction. | Novels.
Classification: LCC PR6108.O43 T43 2025 | DDC 823/.92--dc23/eng/20250211
LC record available at https://lccn.loc.gov/2024044957

ISBN 978-0-06-339821-4 (pbk.)
ISBN 978-0-06-339825-2 (simultaneous hardcover ed.)
ISBN 978-0-06-344794-3 (international ed.)

25 26 27 28 29 LBC 5 4 3 2 1

Dedicated to Zuzana Růžičková,
who first told me about Fredy

Preface

This is the story of a remarkable human being whose light illuminated some of the darkest corners of the Holocaust.

Founded on rigorous research, a few scenes and characters have been created for narrative and dramatic purposes but the timeline of events is faithful to the records.

A person is not forgotten until his or her name is forgotten.

The Talmud

Prologue

MY NAME IS ALFRED HIRSCH, *although my friends call me Fredy. Please, be so kind as to remember my name. The word 'hirsch' means stag in German and, like a deer, I've been on the run for much of my life.*

Today, the hunting of Fredy Hirsch will end in a kill. I am not afraid for myself but for the children in my care. They are all I've focused on since the world started burning and I shudder to think what might become of them.

My name is Fredy Hirsch. I am twenty-eight years old. I am a teacher. I am a dreamer. I am not just a number. Nor will I be identified by the yellow triangle I've been forced to wear.

My name is Fredy Hirsch and I've fought to maintain a vestige of normality and decency in this hellish world. I have loved and laughed, cried and almost died a thousand times.

My name is Fredy Hirsch. I am a good man. Please, be so kind as to remember my name . . .

1

September 1943

'*ALLE RAUS! RAUS!*' Nazis with fixed bayonets bawled at us to get out the moment the heavy wagon doors slid open. A blast of air into our fetid wagon made us dizzy. Their attack dogs were foaming at the mouth, straining on their leashes and leaping up as if to bite.

Senior SS officers glared at us as we surged, squinting and gulping towards the morning light, pleading for water. '*Voda! Wasser, bitte!*' Pushed from behind, dragged to the ground, we jumped or fell as knees buckled and we were greeted not with water but pandemonium.

After three tormented days and nights since leaving our ghetto in Czechoslovakia we had finally arrived at our destination. During that desperate, claustrophobic journey we had to relieve ourselves where we stood, as people wept or clung to each other in silence. Old people died. Mothers sang lullabies to wailing babes and adults lost their minds.

Bumped along the tracks in our hateful coffin-on-wheels, I had done my best to keep the children distracted with stories and songs, but only a few appreciated my attempts. I eventually gave up when an old lady started screaming, 'Shut up! Just shut up!'

Our train slowed to a stop many times, pulling into sidings to allow military cargo to speed past. People taking turns to stand by the window read out the signs of stations we passed, yelling, 'We're at Kolin!' or 'We're approaching Olomouc!' The name of every town triggered fresh wails for those places and the lost families and lives.

When a voice called ominously, 'We've just crossed into Poland,' the carriage fell horribly silent. No matter how bad things had been before, we'd at least been in a land we knew and loved. Yet still we rolled on.

When the train finally jerked to a halt and we heard German voices, someone else cried out, 'It's a huge camp. Watchtowers and fences everywhere.'

Before we could take everything in, we fell from the wagons and were pushed into rows by shaven-headed men with cudgels and bamboo sticks. They wore what looked like blue-and-grey striped pyjamas made of rough cotton cloth. All our luggage was left behind on the wagons with the corpses of those who hadn't survived.

Men, women, and children were loaded together onto trucks and driven some distance before being efficiently funnelled along a corridor of barbed wire towards a building that stood alone on the barren plain. Still pitifully thirsty and with limbs stiff from the journey, we were marched at a pace.

My teenage companion Miloš and the few children I'd been able to keep together remained glued to my side as they gazed up in fear at the sinister watchtowers on wooden stilts. Each one was manned by soldiers with a machine gun.

'Where are they taking us?' one orphan named Tomáš asked, his voice as small as he was.

'To be processed and registered, I expect,' I told him, fear sabotaging my voice.

We'd been in the camp less than fifteen minutes when we first became aware of a pestilent stink that was like nothing we had ever smelled before. It was overpowering, almost animal, with the added acridity of something scorched. Up ahead in the distance, tongues of flames two metres high and rolling coils of dense black smoke were spewing from one of two immense tapered chimneys. Fat flakes of ash fell all around us like snow.

'What on earth are they roasting?' a man at my side asked, wrinkling his nose at the sickly odour that lodged in the back of the throat. 'Whatever it is, it smells rancid to me.'

One of the men in stripes shepherding us muttered, 'Rotten flesh usually is.' I thought he was referring to the poor quality of the camp's food.

Arriving outside what they called the *Sauna*, an SS officer shouted, '*Zieht all eure Kleidung aus!*'

I translated for those who didn't understand, 'He's ordering us to take off all our clothes.' Several asked, horrified, 'What, all of them?' A few of the women tried to run away but were beaten with rifle butts or thrown to the ground.

Bending as if to take off my boots, I quickly unhooked my whistle from its cord. Slipping it into the pocket of my cheek, I prayed that I'd be able to hold on to my last and most treasured possession. '*If ever you get into difficulty, you'll be able to use it to summon help, Fredy*,' my beloved uncle Alfred had told me, what seemed like a lifetime before. I only wished I could summon help now.

All around me, people peeled off their clothes in embarrassment. Miloš and I helped the little ones undress. Naked and shivering with shame, we queued to be processed by blank-faced clerks who took our numbers and occupations before ordering each of us to sign and date something. The forms were removed so quickly that I hardly had time to read what I was signing, but I did see something about accepting my sentence for committing 'anti-German activity' along with the code 'SB6'.

Driven into the next room, we were pushed into communal showers as male and female SS officers with riding crops looked on. Keeping Miloš and the others close and forcing myself to take slow, deep breaths, I stared up at the showerheads and told myself that not all of them dispensed poisoned gas.

'Just think. In a few minutes we'll all be clean again,' I told the children. Their fearful eyes reminded me of my childhood working in my father's abattoir. I'd wondered back then if I'd be as frightened as the animals about to be slaughtered when my time came and the memory sent a new shiver to my soul.

Tepid water trickled from above. Like everyone around me, I opened my mouth like a baby bird hoping to quench my raging thirst, only to splutter and cough as the undrinkable liquid hit the back of my throat.

Without any soap, we were given less than a minute to rinse off the stink of the wagon before being pushed out of the room, still wet. There were no towels but instead a group of shaven-headed female prisoners stood over huge piles of random clothing and flung at us whatever garments were to hand, regardless of size.

Wondering why we weren't given striped uniforms like those worn by our fellow prisoners, I was thrown what looked like a woman's shift dress. Looking around, I swapped it for a pair of baggy trousers that a girl nearby had been given. Next, I was passed some ugly wooden clogs and an oversized green huntsman-style jacket, into the pocket of which I dropped my whistle.

'Make sure all the children have shoes and something warm to wear, Miloš,' I instructed, as I wrapped a jacket around a shivering teenager before escorting others into the next queue, not realising what it was for. It was only as we neared the front that I saw prisoner after prisoner being tattooed by men stabbing dirty needles into the flesh of each forearm.

'I don't want an injection!' Tomáš wailed, his tears falling thick and fast as he clung to my legs.

'Me neither!' cried others, terrified by the prospect.

Desperate to calm them, I said, 'It won't really hurt and, see, it's over ever so quickly. Besides, just think, you'll have something to show your friends and family after the war. It will be your very own number, special only to you.'

A small part of me was secretly relieved: I didn't believe the Nazis would go to the trouble of issuing tattoos if they planned to murder us. Few others had the same reaction, though, and they stood sobbing and trembling. Up ahead, I heard a man ask, 'What is this place? What will happen to us here?' before he was slapped by a guard who yelled, '*Ruhig Sein!*', ordering him to be quiet.

When the guard stalked off, I heard an older tattooist tell the man, 'You are in Auschwitz.'

My mind racing, I tried to make sense of what he said. In German, *Aus* meant 'out of' and *schwitzen* meant 'sweat'. Were we in a labour camp, or was it merely a Polish name? Either way, I thought it strange that in all my years as a prisoner of the Nazis, I had never heard of it.

Looking around me, I scanned the numb expressions for a familiar face. I spotted several, including a young artist I knew from Brno named Dinah and kind Dr Heller and his family. My friend Leo Janowitz was being tattooed three columns away, his face as white as chalk. In a long brown overcoat with a collarless white shirt, he looked like a monk.

When it was my turn I rolled up my sleeve in readiness and stared into the craggy face of the prisoner about to brand me. In a defiant voice, I declared, 'My name is Fredy Hirsch.'

'You're German?' a nearby guard asked, prodding me in the ribs.

When I nodded, he snapped, 'Germans exempt. Step aside,' before turning to the adjacent line. Fearing that this meant I was to be killed, I stared at the man whose needle was poised and hissed, 'Where are we?'

Barely looking up, through almost motionless lips he said, 'Auschwitz. The place where we will all die.'

2

December 1941,
Terezín, Czechoslovakia

A SNAKING COLUMN OF children wrapped in coats and scarves trooped in chattering pairs to the Kindergarten, leaving tiny footprints in the snow. Holding hands, rosy-cheeked, they seemed oblivious to the cruelties of the world.

Stopping to watch them pass, I cried out as a rifle butt suddenly slammed into the back of my head, felling me like a tree. '*Bewegen, Juden!*' An SS officer bellowed at me to move on, as another pressed the barrel of his rifle to my chest. Winded, I scrambled to my feet and got back in step with the other prisoners being marched from the railway station.

Touching my neck, I saw that I was bleeding and that two of the children had frozen in their tracks at the sight. Smiling, I held up my unbloodied hand and mouthed, 'I'm fine,' before remembering that they spoke a different language to me.

The sight of those joyful toddlers gave me faint cause for hope. They were the first residents I came across in the garrison town of Terezín, sixty kilometres north of Prague. Designated a new ghetto and renamed Theresienstadt by the Nazis, this was to be my home. I wasn't sure what to expect as we passed under the town's arched main gate but it was a comfort to now see children.

That glimmer of hope faded the minute I saw where I'd be sleeping. Neglected for decades, the military buildings we were taken to had no heat, no washing facilities and no beds. Nor was there any of the hot food we'd been promised.

Realising how much work needed to be done to prepare the ghetto, I immediately offered my services to Jakob Edelstein, the head of the Jewish Council of Elders; a visionary I admired. Thirteen years older than me at thirty-eight, he was a tireless leader who shared my dreams of a haven from persecution for every Jewish child.

'Ah, there you are, Jakob,' I said, having found him settling into one of the largest barracks, named Magdeburg. It was built around four sides of a huge courtyard that doubled as a drill ground. Pleased to be reunited with someone who'd entrusted me with responsibility in the past, I added, 'Tell me what I can do to help.'

Surrounded by packing crates and paperwork, the fleshy-faced man in round spectacles let out a hollow laugh. 'Most people come to ask for my help, not offer it, Fredy, so bless you. But where to start?'

'Well, from what I've seen, the buildings are vermin-infested and many have been abandoned for years. What is this place?'

'It was a citadel built a century and a half ago by Emperor Joseph II to defend against the Prussians. Ironically, its octagonal shape resembles the Star of David. It would be just like the Nazis to find that amusing.'

'And the red brick complex that we saw across the river on the way in?'

'That's the Small Fortress, the Gestapo prison and home to the SS. No one knows how many political prisoners and members of the resistance have been imprisoned and tortured there since the Germans invaded. Untold numbers have been killed or sent to camps.'

I shuddered. 'Then I'll be sure never to be sent there.'

'We've been given a near-impossible task in turning this town into a ghetto for the Jews from Prague, Fredy,' Jakob added with a sigh. 'None of us expected it to be this run down, and it's not as if any of us have ever done this before. Even with 1,500 fit young men chosen to form the AK *Aufbaukommando* to work on the town's reconstruction, there isn't enough wood and the water is drawn from primitive, polluted wells.'

'When do people start to arrive?'

'In a week, so we'll never be ready in time. Entire roofs have caved in with the weight of snow and we need to establish kitchens to feed thousands yet our men are struggling to update basic sanitation and electricity supplies.'

I shook my head. 'How do they expect so many to survive winter here without heat and only contaminated water to drink? And what about the children?'

'That's where you'll come in, Fredy,' Jakob assured me. 'I'm assigning you to the Housing Department. There's no one better to calm shocked and traumatised people. I know I can trust you to help the new arrivals – especially the little ones.'

Sleep eluded me that first bitter night, lying fully clothed on an uneven brick floor in a dank room. Squashed in alongside several members of the 'AK' crew snoring in tandem, I used my rucksack for a pillow as I lay on my bedroll and watched my breath puff skywards in clouds. Rising in the milky light of dawn, I stepped outside to stretch stiff limbs. After warming myself up by running on the spot, I set off on a solitary stroll.

Terezín was laid out in a grid and each street led to a large central square dominated by a white church. Alongside it stood an imposing town hall, requisitioned by the German High Command. Beyond the square lay scores of shabby, windowless buildings that reminded me of toothless old men. Walking the perimeter, I took note of the number and locations of gates and guardhouses within the impregnable thirty-foot escarpments and broad ramparts surrounded by a deep moat.

'Only a gazelle could escape from here,' I told Jakob later that morning and he laughed.

'But I thought you were a champion pole-vaulter and high-jumper, Fredy?'

'When I was younger, fitter and hadn't been living on wartime rations for two years!'

'Well, enjoy your freedom while you can. Once the deportees arrive everyone will be confined to barracks unless they have an escort or a pass. We administrators will be allowed out, but there are no guarantees for how long.'

*

'*Guten morgen*,' I cried cheerfully, standing in the middle of the overcrowded hall, determined that my smiling face should be one of the first that the new arrivals saw. 'Welcome to Terezín. My name is Fredy Hirsch.'

Any who didn't understand me turned to others to translate. Groaning inwardly, I wished I could have spoken to them in Czech but my rudimentary grasp of their language was frustrating so I found myself in an occupied land speaking the language of the enemy.

Just as Jakob had predicted, the first trainloads of deported Jews had arrived a thousand at a time, each with their permitted fifty *Reichsmarks* and fifty kilos of belongings. Even though they carried so little, it was still a struggle to process everyone as places had to be found for them all.

'I know everything must seem very confusing right now,' I continued, 'but you'll soon be assigned places to sleep and given something to eat.' Looking around, I could see that many were close to collapse after their two-kilometre trudge through the snow from the station, their figures misshapen by so many layers of clothing. Most slumped onto their suitcases as soon as they entered the processing block known as the *Schleusse*. Too tired to take another step, they rubbed aching backs and peeled off shoes to tend to blisters as their children sobbed.

Scanning the crowd in that airless space, I sought out the most vulnerable first and, within minutes, came across one little lad standing alone in the mayhem, biting his bottom lip. A memory swam up of a boy named Sparrow, but I batted it away. 'What's your name, lad?' I asked, but he simply stared up at me with big brown eyes, too frightened or exhausted to speak.

'Drink?' I gestured and, taking his hand, I led him to a wooden pail. He sipped the suspect ghetto water cautiously to begin with but then grabbed the ladle in both hands and gulped so greedily that it spilled down his chin. After I'd given him a little beet jam and handed him over to a couple with a small child, I heard another of the town's funeral carts pull up outside. It bore more live cargo and I went out to help those too weak to walk to the ghetto. The ornate black wagon had once been pulled by plumed horses. Now it was hauled by human beasts of burden, the *rollwagen commando*, whose bodies were curved like bows. Expressionless, they ferried the dead and dying, luggage, firewood and loaves of bread, never washing the cart down in between.

'This way, my dears,' I told an elderly couple as they staggered inside. 'Be sure to bring your belongings with you.' Taking the old lady's arm, I watched her ashen face as she took in the scene, her watery eyes hungry for how her life used to be. Looking at what they were carrying, I wished that they'd been better forewarned. Arriving in a place where there was never enough food or warmth, they'd brought linen and silverware instead of clothing, pots and pans.

Bombarded with questions from all sides, I raised my hand to announce, 'Once you've been registered, you'll be issued with ID cards and ration coupons.' I omitted to warn them that experienced hands would comb their luggage for cigarettes, alcohol and medicines, all of which would be confiscated along with cash or valuables.

'Each of you will be inspected by trained medical staff to prevent the spread of disease,' I added. Not wanting to cause panic, I left out that those with fleas or lice would be roughly shaved and doused in disinfectant that would leave them coughing for a week.

'Anyone with practical skills can start work straight away so please speak up if you can assist with construction or repairs. We also need cooks, cleaners, doctors and nurses.' Keen to find those who could help me with the children, I called, 'Do we have any singers, artists, or teachers?' When a few weary hands were raised, I picked my way over to them, dipping into my pocket for small squares of the black ghetto bread to hand to the hungriest children.

'When's dinner?' several clamoured.

'Soon.' With the kitchens barely functional, 'dinner' would comprise bread and a bowl of soup made from lentil powder or turnips, plus a cup of hot water with a faint taste of tea or coffee. They'd receive nothing until a similar breakfast, then at noon more soup and a baked potato and if they were lucky some noodles, salami, or a little horsemeat. None of it would silence the ghetto's cruellest enemy – hunger.

Hearing a commotion, I hurried over to where a skinny teenager had collapsed in a faint while queuing for the latrines.

'Whose child is this?' I called, as I knelt beside her. Cradling her head in my arms, I reached in my pocket for some smelling salts. Spluttering, she gradually came to her senses with a cough that almost choked her. 'Well, there you are,' I told her with a smile.

'*Tata*. Where's *Tata*?' the girl asked, her smoky eyes spilling tears.

'Your father will probably be settling into one of the men's barracks, my child. You might be allowed to visit him on Sunday . . .' Stopping, I asked, 'Tell me, what is your name?'

'Zuzana,' she replied, weakly, sitting up and adjusting the ribbon in her tousled brown hair.

'*Wie alt bist du?*' I tried in German. She looked about eleven.

'Fourteen. I've always been small for my age.'

'Well, your German is perfect,' I told her, whereupon she proudly informed me she also spoke French, Slovak and Polish. Once she was well enough, I helped her to her feet and into the arms of her concerned mother. Congratulating myself on having found myself an interpreter, I returned to my tasks.

*

Escorting the arrivals to their accommodation after they'd been processed was especially difficult and took all my reserves to try to keep spirits up. Seeing their stunned faces when confronted with a bone-numbingly cold room without beds, I'd tell them brightly, 'Sacks will be coming in a day or two to fill with straw for mattresses.' As if that would make much difference.

The prospect sent many women into hysterics. Once they realised that they'd be allocated just a few metres of floorspace each, lying side by side like herrings with only their bedrolls to soften their discomfort, their complaints began.

'This isn't right!'

'You can't expect us all to squeeze in here!'

'There's been a terrible mistake.'

It was all Zuzana could do to translate fast enough for me. Even her elegant mother in her tailored suit looked close to collapse when she saw their room, paling when she realised that they were expected to live, sleep, wash and undress in front of strangers.

One pensive little boy was dumbstruck by the cacophony all around him. Solemnly rubbing the toe of each shoe on the back of his calves to wipe off any scuff marks, he looked up at me and said, 'I'll get ever so dirty on the floor.'

Bending to pat his head, I told him, 'It'll only be like this for a little while, I promise you. We'll have this place spick and span in no time. Just be a good boy for your mother.' Lifting a toddler onto my hip, I blew my whistle and began to herd the youngest children outside to play. Leaving their mothers to compose themselves, I led them into the snowy courtyard, asking, 'Who knows how to play *Bogey Man*? Whoever avoids being tagged the longest will get an extra spoonful of jam.'

3

June 1924, Aachen, Germany

THE BLADE GLINTED IN the morning sun, temporarily blinding the man sharpening it. Satisfied that he'd given it enough of an edge, he made a sudden slash across the throat of a wide-eyed lamb suspended from a hook by its hooves. As the creature gave a sickening gurgle, I abruptly regurgitated my breakfast.

'Alfred!' my father exclaimed, disappointment contorting his features. 'Get a hold of yourself, boy. You'll never become a master butcher if you do this every time.' Wiping my mouth on the back of my hand, I stumbled away in shame. At eight years old, I so wanted to please Father but could never do anything right, unlike my handsome, charismatic brother Paul, the apple of the family's eye.

Running the two blocks back to our house in Aachen, the westernmost city in Germany, I found Paul in his room with his Hebrew books, studying to become a rabbi. Mother encouraged his chosen vocation but Father secretly hoped his eldest son would take over the family business – as did I.

'I vomited again,' I told my brother, sitting on the edge of his bed, swinging legs too short to reach the floor.

Sighing, he looked up at me with a sympathetic gaze. 'Oh, Fredy. What did Papa say?'

'He was cross,' I replied, staring out of the window dolefully.

Paul put down his fountain pen. 'He's not really angry. It's just that he wants sons he can be proud of. You've seen the notice he placed in the newspaper when you were born.'

'Of course,' I replied, thinking of the framed clipping on the parlour wall declaring my arrival on 11th February, 1916, as his *zweiter Kriegsjunge* or 'second war child'. In the middle of a bitter military conflict that my father's trade exempted him from, I was hailed as another son for the Reich when thousands were dying in trenches across the border.

'It's not just that I'm squeamish, though, is it?' I moaned, thinking of Father's expression each time I recoiled from another helping of meat slapped onto my plate. 'He still thinks I'm too small for my age.'

My father's most frequent complaint was that I should be as fat as a butcher's dog. It reflected badly on him that I was so skinny. 'Your brother has an extremely healthy appetite,' he'd tell me. 'What happened to yours?'

'Then why don't you tell him how you really feel about meat?' Paul asked, returning to his books.

Still kicking my legs, I couldn't begin to explain how wrong it felt to eat a calf whose velvety nose had nuzzled my hand as it gazed at me with trusting eyes. Knowing in my heart that I could never run the abattoir or be a master butcher, I resolved to find some other way to impress him.

*

The answer came to me on one of my many hikes in the forests of our mountainous Eifel region, where Paul and I went almost every Sunday with our synagogue's youth association. Walking verdant trails or running cross-country along the banks of rivers and lakes, I was surprised to discover that I had much more stamina than other boys.

I was even tougher than my brother, which was the first time I'd been better than him at anything. 'These hills are where you belong, Fredy,' Paul told me wistfully that day after a five-mile hike left him in searing pain from an old sports injury. Taking his rucksack as well as my own, I grinned when he added, 'On the Almighty's good Earth is where you'll find yourself closest to Heaven.'

Looking around me, I knew that he was right. Being in that leafy wilderness had always filled me with grace. The iridescence of a butterfly's wing could make my heart sing, as could the discovery of a bird's nest – especially if it was lined with fluffy down. Spotting wild boar through a clearing was more of a thrill for me than any comic book I'd read and camping overnight alongside a waterfall left me breathless with gratitude. At one with Nature under the stars, I'd think nothing of stripping off and plunging into the icy water to emerge reborn.

Aside from the feeling of liberation being outdoors gave me, I had an ulterior motive. I might never resemble a butcher's dog but if I could make myself as strong as an ox then I knew I'd please my broad-shouldered father, who cut a traditional figure of masculinity.

Walking back down the hill that day as Paul limped along behind me, it occurred to me that Father hadn't seemed his usual self recently. I put his lack of energy down to the lingering disgrace of our country losing the war two years after I was born, a loss that seemed to suck the marrow from his bones. *How can we survive such humiliation?* he would rail. *What can Germany build on if we're forced to pay out millions in reparations?* All I knew was that when we were forced to cede territory it created civil unrest, some of which I'd witnessed on my way home from school.

Rounding a corner on Jakobstrasse, I came across a group of workers being addressed by a strident union leader. 'Our Imperial Army didn't lose this war on the battlefield,' he hollered through a metal cone. 'We lost it because we were stabbed in the back by communists, socialists and Jews!'

Feeling the blood rush to my cheeks, I lowered my head, picked up my pace and hurried past the enraged crowd, wondering what on earth we had to do with Germany losing the war. Up until that moment, aside from one boy in our neighbourhood, no one had ever said anything nasty about me or my family as far as I was aware, so the shock felt palpable.

Safely back home, I asked Paul what the union leader had meant. Shrugging, he replied, 'Jews have always been oppressed and we probably always will be.'

I was thunderstruck. 'But why, Paul? What have we done?'

How could I not have known such a thing or was I simply blinkered? 'There isn't a straight answer to your question,' Paul replied, his expression sombre. 'Nervousness about our beliefs, maybe. A lack of understanding about our traditions, certainly. Some may even see us as a threat. Whatever the reason, difference creates fear and fear can turn to hate.'

His casual explanation shattered me. Up until then, I'd thought of myself as German first and Jewish second, believing my family to be an integral part of a wider community. I'd even attended Christian processions, which I'd loved for their costumes and drama. It never occurred to me that other people might feel differently.

I longed to talk to a grown-up about it but my mother was too busy flicking through her glossy magazines while complaining about having to curtail her spending and my father was increasingly sullen as his customers dropped away.

'There were only five people in the shop today,' he told me when he arrived home after work one night, his jawline hardening as he slapped a pack of meat onto the kitchen table. Seeing my face fall, Father attempted a smile. 'But we mustn't let worry get the better of us, must we? As the proverb says, Fredy, *He that cannot endure the bad will never live to see the good.*'

*

'I'll tidy the books away tonight, *Herr* Steil,' I volunteered at the end of class, as my friends glared at me for being a '*goodie-zwei-schuhe*'. Winking as if I had a secret motive, I pulled a face behind our teacher's back but he seemed to have eyes everywhere and, spinning round, caught me mid-grimace.

After Paul's warning, I'd decided that the best way to get people to like me was to be helpful. *Herr* Steil was the first person I tried this out on. My favourite teacher, who taught us religion and poetry: he was a gentle, sensitive man who called me '*mein Junge*' and was the only one who didn't rap knuckles or wield a cane. Stacking books as he sat at his desk marking essays, I began to hum my father's favourite tune, Beethoven's 'Ode to Joy'. Its words about being optimistic had always struck a chord. I'd inherited my musical ability from my father, who encouraged me to learn the guitar in school and then the flute.

'Did you know Beethoven was deaf when he wrote that piece?' The voice from behind snapped me from my reverie. *Herr* Steil was watching me.

'He was, Sir?'

'Yes, Alfred. He composed music based almost entirely from memory. Isn't that incredible?'

'It is, Sir.' When he didn't say anything else but remained seated, I realised he might be a good person to talk to – if I could only pluck up the courage.

'Is something troubling you, Alfred?' he asked and I looked into his pale blue eyes and wondered how he knew.

'Well, yes, Sir, a bit.'

'What is it?'

I took two paces closer and sat on a chair before blurting, 'My brother says everyone hates us.'

Herr Steil frowned. 'Hates who? You and your brother?'

'Yes and all Jews.'

He nodded, suddenly understanding. 'And why does he think that?'

'Because we lost the war and because we lend money and – oh, I can't remember the other reasons, but there seemed to be a lot of them.'

He smiled inscrutably. 'Well now, Alfred. I'm not sure about that, but I do know that we all face prejudice at different times in our lives. The only thing we can do about it is to decide how to respond.'

I frowned. 'Pre-jew-dice?'

He stood up and reached for a large book. 'Let's look it up in the dictionary, shall we?' Beckoning me over, he watched as I ran my finger down the page searching for the word and then struggled with the definition.

'Pre-ju-dice is a pre- pre- . . .'

'Preconceived.'

'Preconceived opinion not based on reason or experience.'

'Do you understand?' I shook my head. 'It means that sometimes people decide if they like you or not, even if they've never met you or know what you're really like.'

'But that's not fair!'

'No, it's not. And when something isn't fair, it hurts people's feelings and makes them sad or angry. Do you know the nursery rhyme "Stock und Stein"?'

I nodded. *'Stock und Stein brechen mein Gebein, doch Worte bringen keine Pein.'*

'That's right. Very good. "Sticks and stones break my bones but words bring no pain." And why don't they bring pain, do you think?'

Bringing my hand to my mouth, I hesitated. 'I don't know, Sir.'

'They don't bring pain if the person decides not to let the words hurt them. Do you understand?'

'I think so, Sir.'

'As you grow up, Alfred, you'll meet all sorts of different people and not all of them will like you. But that doesn't matter. You can stay loyal to the ones that do and ignore the rest.'

'Ignore them, Sir?'

'Yes, or better still, stand up to them, shake their hands in a friendly manner and smile. Show them that their words or actions don't hurt you. That takes away their power.'

Thinking hard, I nodded. 'I understand, Sir. Thank you.'

*

From then on, I did what most children my age did and focused on the things that I cared about most. Ignoring any hurtful comments, I threw myself into drama and sport and my love of being outdoors which saved me from the tedium of learning by rote.

Another joy was tending to the school garden that provided fresh produce for poorer local families. I was always happier with soil beneath my fingernails than entrails, feathers and fur. An unforeseen advantage of spending more time outdoors was that I developed strength and muscle mass that improved my skills in games lessons.

'Another medal, Fredy!' my father enthused at my school Sports Day when I collected six awards. 'Bravo, my boy. We'll display these in the parlour with the rest.'

'Thank you, Papa,' I gushed, happy to have redeemed myself.

In the communal showers afterwards, I compared my physique to the pallid, flabby bodies around me, jokingly referring to them as *kleinen Würstchen*: 'little sausages'. Later that night, studying my reflection in the bathroom mirror, I decided that I liked the way I was beginning to look – suntanned, fit and healthy.

So pleased was I with myself that I burst into my brother's room to announce, 'I'm going to compete in the Olympic Games one day.' I had it all figured out in my head, reckoning that I'd be in my prime by the eleventh Olympiad in 1936. Eighteen years after the war would be the perfect moment for me to restore the nation's pride. I could see it all and most especially the look on Father's face as I stood on the podium with a gold medal glinting at my neck.

Paul laughed, but I wouldn't be discouraged. 'You may have your opinion, brother, but it doesn't hurt me. Trust me, I'm going to be a Jew this country can be proud of.' Feeling as if I finally had a purpose, I was even able to quell my queasiness working with Father after school. And for the first time, I realised that he needed my help.

I'll never forget the day I looked up and realised that something far more serious was wrong. He was lifting a side of beef to a hook on the ceiling, a task he'd done a thousand times before, when he almost collapsed under its weight. Never before had I seen him falter and the sight made me gasp. 'Papa?'

Bent double with sweat dripping off him, he twisted his head to peer up at me through deep-set eyes and yelled, 'What are you staring at? Get back to work,' before summoning the strength to finish the job and stagger breathlessly from my gaze.

Within a few weeks, the man I'd thought of as invincible was confined to bed, suffering from a disease no one gave a name to. 'There must be no noise or disturbance in this house,' instructed our family physician, Dr Klender, as he closed the door on the spare bedroom where Father lay in darkness. 'It's vital that he rest.'

'What about the shop? How will we manage?' my mother cried, wringing her hands.

'Could you not prevail upon your brother: Alfred?' the doctor asked. 'He's a successful businessman, after all.'

The man after whom I'd been named, forty-year-old Alfred Heinemann, was a tailor who ran a textile company in a nearby Rhineland town. I didn't really know him but when I was born he'd sent me a toy dog that I named Emil. With grey fur, he had black eyes made of glass, and the trademark Steiff button in his ear. I couldn't settle at night without him.

*

When Alfred arrived in Aachen like a summer storm breaking the heat, I was immediately drawn to him. Tall and handsome, he had what was known as 'Prussian bearing' and was well travelled, filling my head with stories. 'New York has the tallest buildings in the world,' he'd tell me, his glossy brown hair slicked down with Brilliantine *Haarpomade*. 'They're called skyscrapers because they look as if they scrape the sky.'

'Which is the tallest of all, *Onkel?*' I asked, agog.

'The Woolworth Building in Manhattan. It cost more than thirteen million dollars and stands at two hundred and fifty metres. It has fifty floors of offices and its elevators can travel at two hundred metres per minute. The one that took me up to the observation deck almost gave me a nosebleed.'

Closing my eyes, the thought alone made me giddy. I wanted to learn all I could from a man whose life seemed so compelling. An imposing figure physically, he also had an impeccable fashion sense that went beyond the need to impress his customers.

'Be sure to always look tip-top, Fredy,' he told me as he measured me for my first pair of long trousers with a matching jacket. A tape slung around his neck, he stood back for a moment and examined me with a critical eye. 'You're a handsome young fellow, you know, and if you carry on minding your appearance and improving your physique, you're sure to make a positive impression on everyone you meet.' Sticking pins between his teeth, he added with a wink, 'And by that, I mean girls.'

Feeling my cheeks burning, I caught my horrified expression in the mirror and quickly looked away.

Eager to impress my uncle, I took him on my favourite forest trail and showed him all the places I'd longed to show Papa. Crouching in my shorts and long socks, I crept up the brow of a hill looking for the white hart I'd once spotted drinking from the lake, its long, pink tongue lapping thirstily at the water. 'The hart is a rare and legendary creature,' I explained. 'Its purity is said to prove the existence of the Underworld and act as a kind of messenger. I've only ever seen one but it took my breath away.'

It eluded us that day but we did spot a rare Eurasian wryneck, a type of woodpecker that can turn its head almost one hundred and eighty degrees. And as we continued our journey, a passing hiker mistook us for father and son, telling my uncle, 'What a fine young man. You must be a very proud *Tato*.' Alfred said nothing but my chest puffed up like a wood pigeon's.

'You must buy yourself a decent pair of binoculars, Fredy,' he insisted later, as I cupped my hands over my eyes to squint at a sparrowhawk wheeling through the sky. 'You'll be amazed by how much more you'll be able to see. Oh and a whistle. If ever you're alone or in difficulty, you'll be able to use it to summon help.'

He wasn't to know that I wouldn't dream of asking my parents for such gifts. Instead, for months afterwards, I practised whistling through my thumb and forefinger as I'd seen Alfred do, although I only ever made a disappointing whooshing sound.

With my uncle in charge of our business as well as his own, Mother seemed to evaporate from our lives and we only ever heard her coming in late at night after playing bridge – a game she and Father used to enjoy together. I'd lie in bed listening to her humming a tune and kicking off her shoes thinking, *Keep quiet, Mother. Don't you know Papa is dying?* No one had said as much but I knew from the expression of Dr Klender each time he arrived with more morphia that my father's life was ebbing away.

It was the week before my tenth birthday when he finally succumbed to whatever was killing him. He was forty-four years old. 'Come pay your respects,' Mother told us, ushering us into his room, her mouth so pinched that face powder caked in the corners. As Paul started praying and swaying, she pushed me towards the bed.

My mouth agape, I stood staring at the waxy husk of the only parent who'd ever taken much interest in me. Fixated on his chest, I watched in vain for a flicker where his heart used to beat. There were coins laid on eyelids that would never again open and I wondered if he'd been afraid at the end.

Dressing for his funeral the following day, I put on the new grey suit that I now realised my uncle had made specially for the occasion. Although it was too roomy, I still wished Father could have seen me. As was the custom, our little family sat *shiva* for a week, receiving guests as my mother nodded her thanks through a black veil and my brother led the prayers. Taking the business of death extremely seriously, Paul considered it his dress rehearsal for becoming a rabbi.

Between visitors, I meandered to the parlour to pick at the food people had brought us, taking mouthfuls of *spaetzle* and *babka*, pickled cabbage rolls and *latkes*. Feeling a sudden constriction in my throat as I bit into a huge slice of my father's favourite seedcake, tears pricked my eyes and I cried, 'Look, Papa, I finally found my appetite.'

It was only when *shiva* was finally over that I realised my birthday had passed completely unnoticed. On that milestone *Geburtstag*, I'd missed out on the chance to celebrate 'from sun-up to sundown', avoiding chores and homework, as was the custom. There was no cake, no paper crown and not a single gift. Even *Onkel* Alfred forgot and, after helping my mother sell what remained of the meat business, he left us.

'Be a good boy, Fredy and don't forget the things I taught you,' he said, patting me like a dog before walking out of my life. His departure almost hurt me more than the loss of my papa. Only then did my tears fall. Clasping Emil to my chest, I wept bitter tears into my pillow on the wooden bed that had once been my father's.

No sooner had Alfred left than the furniture in our house was draped in white sheets and Paul and I were sent to be cared for by relatives while our mother went travelling. 'I'm going away,' was all she said by way of explanation. As I stared forlornly at the ghostly shapes of chairs, she told Paul, 'Look after your brother.'

Almost orphans, with those few slices of her tongue we were cut adrift from the life we'd always taken for granted.

'Don't worry, Fredy,' Paul tried to reassure me. 'Mother will be home soon and then everything will go back to normal.' He was wrong. She didn't come back for a year, by which time she had a new husband and a different surname. It was as if Father had never existed.

4

January 1942, Terezín,
Czechoslovakia

AND STILL THEY CAME. The sound of their feet marching in time reverberated around the buildings like ricochets. The hopeful, the resigned, the terrified and the innocent. Heads bowed, their faces expressionless as they trooped in from the station. More mouths to feed, more beds to find. More bodies to bury.

'The ghetto population has swelled seven-fold in a few weeks,' Leo Janowitz, the Secretary to the Elders, reported at a heated meeting. 'Conditions are becoming intolerable. People are dying needlessly.' There were numerous other complaints about everything from the queues for the latrines and food that was cold by the time it could be served, to the bribes charged by the Czech gendarmes who policed us.

Waiting until the end of the meeting, I followed Jakob out and began to shadow him on his rounds, starting with a visit to the kitchens to inspect the latest delivery of poor quality supplies. 'It's the children I'm worried about,' I told him, as he lifted the lid on a cauldron of soup and told the chef to add more vegetables. 'They've been wrenched from their homes, forced onto trains and brought to a place they can't begin to comprehend.'

Without saying a word, Jakob moved on to examine a flour shipment full of weevils.

'Crammed into crowded, unhygienic rooms, the only fresh air they get is standing for interminable hours for roll calls as the Nazis triple-check our numbers,' I added. 'We need to get them out.'

Leaving the kitchen and marching along a corridor, batting away complainants, Jakob told me 'You know very well that nobody is allowed out of the barracks so where do you suggest taking them?'

'Into special rooms where they'd be easier to manage. We could start giving lessons to those missing out on their schooling.'

Jakob turned with a glare. 'The last thing the SS want is more educated Jews, Fredy. They've warned of severe penalties for anyone caught teaching.'

'Whatever we do, getting them to a place where they can be children again would at least shield them just a little from despair.'

Ignoring the next crowd of petitioners waiting to ambush him outside his office, my mentor strode briskly inside. Undaunted, I followed him in, shutting the door firmly behind me as a dozen disappointed hands banged on the wood. 'The female barracks are completely overwhelmed and the hair of several women has turned white almost overnight,' I continued. 'They're at breaking point.'

Jakob ran his fingers through his own fine head of hair. 'I know all this, Fredy but we can't just find room for hundreds of children. Until more buildings are updated, every square centimetre of usable space is spoken for.'

Admitting defeat, I hung my head. I knew the Council had a mammoth task on its hands. For all of us, the sense of being trapped was suffocating as we began and ended each day hollowed out by hunger.

'This is our life now,' Jakob told me as he sat heavily in his seat, peeling off horn-rimmed glasses to rub tired eyes. A far cry from the ruddy-cheeked fellow I'd first encountered in Prague what felt like a lifetime earlier. 'Berlin gives the impression that the ghetto is governed by us, but all we do is carry out their orders. It's so cunningly thought out.'

'At least the SS are keeping away,' I remarked, grateful that they weren't patrolling daily.

'Only because they're terrified of disease. You heard that eight girls died of scarlet fever?' His expression darkening, he went on, 'We've decided to give the children under fourteen and people doing labour larger rations, but that can only be achieved if we reduce portions for the old and infirm.' Looking up at me with sorrowful eyes, he added, '*Ein Loch mit dem anderen zustopfen, Fredy.*'

We were simply plugging one hole with another.

*

Complaints to the Nazis about overcrowding went unheeded until the day Leo told me that the Council had finally received some good news. 'The SS agreed something needs to be done.'

Within hours an emergency meeting was convened to reveal the Nazi's solution. Once we'd all crowded into a hall, Jakob stood to speak. 'We have orders from Berlin to prepare and process a thousand prisoners for transportation to the Riga ghetto in Latvia.' There was a collective gasp. His features pinched, he added, 'They'll be leaving in forty-eight hours. We must decide who will stay and who will go. This will be a heavy responsibility.' As the room erupted and people started shouting, Jakob raised his hand. 'The Elders and their immediate families are excluded because of our vital work, as are those in the AK, foreigners, Jews married to Aryans and veterans of the Great War, but that won't make our job any easier.'

An uneasy silence fell as the news sank in. Much as we resented the overcrowding, none of us had expected this. We'd felt relatively safe in Czechoslovakia so the idea of being deported elsewhere horrified us.

'How can we dispatch people to an uncertain fate with rumours of forced labour camps?' Leo asked, voicing the concerns of many.

'Should we ask for volunteers from those desperate to leave or select only the able-bodied?' someone else enquired.

'If we send entire families, what will become of the young and old there?' I asked.

Jakob sighed. 'These are all questions we'll have to consider because if we pick only the healthy then their relatives will almost certainly elect to go with them.' The ensuing silence felt weighted with gloom.

'Whatever's decided, the children must be spared,' I insisted to murmurs of approval. Jakob nodded but refused to meet my gaze. As soon as the meeting disbanded, I sought out Gonda Redlich, head of Youth Welfare, a man I'd worked with in Prague.

'You have to help me save the children,' I pleaded. Agreeing to join forces, we stayed up for the next two days and nights removing as many as we could from the list of deportees. The pressure as the clock ticked felt immense. While Gonda remained at his desk checking names, I sped from barrack to barrack looking for anyone who would vouch for the most vulnerable children. When a motion was put to the Council that all orphans and unaccompanied children be sent first on the grounds that there were no family members to object,

Gonda and I vehemently opposed it. 'They're the weakest link in the chain with no one to speak for them,' I insisted. It took a few hours but we eventually secured an exemption for all those under fourteen.

Despite these small victories, compiling the list was still a sobering task. None of us slept. 'Before the war, our sole purpose was to send these children to a new life in a new land,' Gonda mused, his head slumped on his arms at his desk. 'Now, all we can do is try to save them from what is almost certainly a dreadful fate.' With every day a fight for survival, concepts of emigrating to a promised land seemed naive.

The question of who should be on the trains became a tactical minefield. The shame of sending friends was almost unbearable, with the sense of betrayal keenly felt on both sides. There were angry recriminations whenever someone lobbied to save members of their own family and guilt if they couldn't. 'You already reclaimed your cousin and his entire family from the list,' one Elder yelled at another. 'Now it's my turn.'

As the pages of names grew, along with a reserve list in case anyone died or was too sick to travel, the next task was informing each deportee in our rabbit-warren of a town. After a day's deliberation, the *ghettowache* police were sent out to deliver the dreaded pink slips of paper summoning those for the train, usually in the early hours of the morning. The head of each barrack then had to wake the recipients. 'From now on, everyone will fear a light being switched on in the dead of night,' Leo told me. 'And from the moment each hourglass is turned, they'll swarm to the administrative block to be saved from the list before the grains of sand run out.'

To add to the tension, the SS issued a declaration that prisoners should volunteer for future transports or submit reasons why they shouldn't be sent. Desperate for someone to blame, people asked why the Council was collaborating with the Nazis. Wild stories began to circulate that the Elders were making life or death decisions from the comfort of warm, carpeted rooms and had every luxury, which was far from the truth. In the room I shared, we had to chip ice from the windows and pray the temperature dropped below zero so we'd be permitted a little coal. Preferring to be on my own, I remained in my small office, working late into the night.

'You wouldn't believe the lengths people go to in order to avoid being put on that train,' Gonda confided, as we sifted through names to add to the roster of the condemned.

'It's soul-destroying,' Jakob concurred. 'The cooks offered me any meal I wanted if I'd save one of their own.'

'You think that's bad?' Gonda cried. 'Women are throwing themselves at me. Me, a soon-to-be married man. What would Gerta think if she heard?' As he thought of his fiancée, he peeled off his glasses and wiped them with a handkerchief.

'The doctors are being hounded, too,' I reported. 'I saw a man pleading with a medic for a pill to knock him out.' Scores more tried to get key jobs that would exempt them from being transported, such as working in the kitchens or becoming a member of the fire brigade. Bernd, a set designer I knew from Prague, signed up to the police for the privileges it would give him and his bride Anka. So did Zuzana's father, Jaroslav, a former toyshop owner who'd fought in the Great War and was happy to don the distinctive black cap with a yellow band if it meant saving his family.

It was he who'd told me something about Zuzana that I'd not suspected. 'She's a highly accomplished pianist, once destined to study in Paris until the Nazis invaded,' he said, his face falling at the thought of what she'd been denied. 'Now she can hardly bear to hear her beloved Bach.'

Nodding, I sighed at the thought of how many young lives had been interrupted and to what end.

*

Although I'd been able to 'de-list' children with Gonda, I wasn't nearly as important as people thought when they begged for my intervention. 'I'm sorry, but I cannot help you,' was a sentence I must have repeated a dozen times a day.

A woman named Ilse tried a different tack. After cornering me in a hallway one evening, the former showgirl with hair the colour of corn pushed me up against a wall with such force that it winded me. 'Oh, there you are, Fredy,' she purred, staring up into my eyes through the long, dark lashes that gave away her true colouring. 'The rumour in the ghetto is that you'll never find yourself a wife because you save your love for the children.' Walking her fingers up my shirt, she asked, 'Is that true, or is there more to that story?'

My flesh crawling with fear at what she was hinting, I gave her a nervous smile and reeled off an excuse I'd given for years. 'I'm flattered, but I'm not ready for a relationship yet.' I'd used the same line only that week when some teenage boys, troubled by the fact that I'd never had a girlfriend, tried to match me with a beautiful young woman who they said had a crush on me.

'Oh, Fredy,' Ilse whispered with a twisted smile, 'who said anything about a relationship?' Reaching up, she kissed me full on the mouth. Pushing her away, my lips throbbing, I fled.

When another woman grabbed hold of my arm in the line for the Distribution Centre the following morning, I thought it was going to happen again. It was a widow named Hana whose husband had died of the encephalitis that her baby then contracted. Binding the sick infant against her breast day and night even though she worked in the cleaning brigade, Hana's act of maternal love saved her child.

'Can you help us, Fredy?' she pleaded, her face streaked by tears as she told me her younger brother Pavel had received a pink slip. 'We won't make it without him.'

'I'll see what I can find out,' I said, although I suspected I could only delay the inevitable. Even if I could get him delisted, someone else would have to go in his place. After mulling it over, I came up with a solution.

'I'd like to volunteer for the transport list,' I told Jakob. 'I want to take the place of a young man whose sister relies on him.'

Jakob looked aghast. 'Absolutely not, Fredy! You're far too important to our work here to leave us. The children need you and there's much more to be done.'

'But I'm strong and single,' I argued. 'I have no dependants and there are others who can step into my shoes. Wherever these transports end up, I swear there'll be those who need me more.'

Jakob scowled. 'This discussion is over. Find another way to get that man reprieved but I forbid you from volunteering or even mentioning this again.'

Wondering what else I could do for Pavel, I discovered that if he complained of an illness convincingly enough to be admitted to hospital, he might be reprieved. When Hana told him, he refused to lie at the expense of another. 'He won't d-do it, Fredy!' she stammered, broken-hearted.

I found Pavel in the midst of the feverish preparations to provide those leaving with sleeping rolls, cooking utensils, handkerchiefs, clothing, food and a few basic medicines.

'It's not much but it's the least we can do,' I told him as I handed him his pack, secretly admiring his gallantry. Shaking his hand, I added, 'I'll watch over Hana and find her a position that allows her extra food. Our prayers go with you.'

*

My work with the transportees was interrupted by an urgent summons to a meeting in Jakob's office, which could only mean bad news. 'Nine young men from the AK have been arrested,' he announced.

'I thought they were safeguarded?' Leo asked.

'Only from the transport,' I replied. 'Nobody is exempt if they break the rules.'

Winded, none of us spoke until Gonda asked, 'What are the charges?'

Jakob sighed. 'Smuggling contraband and unlawfully purchasing gingerbread from one of the town's civilian stores. The most serious charge is attempting to send letters to relatives. The last thing they want is people back in Prague knowing how bad things are here.'

Gonda's face fell. 'Does this mean they could invent charges against us if they wanted?' Collapsing into a chair, he held his head in his hands. 'Don't you wish we could go to sleep and wake up when all this is over?' Looking at me through his fingers, he asked, 'Are we all just pawns in Hitler's demonic game?'

With news of the arrests adding to the shock of the first transport preparing for departure, it felt then as if no one dared breathe. Courtyards normally crowded during permitted hours remained half-empty as people melted back to their rooms to whisper in the greyness of the day. Few slept and the smell of fear filled the air.

The children picked up on the atmosphere and became fractious, something I noticed on my nightly tour of their rooms. By the weak illumination of a single lightbulb, I'd wander from room to room telling bedtime stories, reciting poetry, or singing a song. Sometimes I'd use a candle to create a shadow play on a wall with my hands or sing them a lullaby using a flute a gendarme had smuggled in for me.

That night, though, the children couldn't settle, so I simply sat with the youngest until lights out, hopeful that the dawn might bring better news for us all.

Wandering back through empty streets, I heard muffled voices and came across a group of teenage boys huddled on the floor of the stable where they slept. In the candlelight I spotted one of my helpers Anton, whose older brother was among those arrested.

'What's going to happen, Fredy?' he asked, his eyelids swollen from crying. 'Will they send my brother away simply for writing to our stepmother for food?'

'Try not to think about that now,' I told him, folding my legs beneath me to join them. 'We mustn't let our anxieties get the better of us, or the Nazis will have won.'

'But how can we not think about it when each day brings new hardship?' asked another.

'I know, Petr, but unless we find ways to take our minds off our concerns they can overwhelm us.' Afraid of their own shadows, the boys stared at me with doleful expressions. 'May we try something?' I asked. 'I want you to close your eyes and imagine that your fear is something in your mouth.'

After a few sideways glances, they nodded.

'Now let's pretend we're chewing on that fear. Move your jaws. Break down all that worry and dread.' I watched as their jawbones went to work. 'On the count of three, I want you to take a deep breath and swallow that fear. Ready? One, two, three.' I heard them all gulp.

After sitting in silence for a moment, I said, 'Now, let's recite some of our favourite poems.' When nobody spoke, I added, 'Very well then, I'll begin.' Taking a breath, my memory dredged up an image of a time long before. It was a moment packed away like treasure to be unwrapped whenever I needed it.

I was walking on the banks of a river with a man I'd once loved, who was reciting a poem. Rocking gently where I sat, I began to repeat it. *'Understand, I'll slip quietly away from the noisy crowd when I see the pale stars rising, blooming, over the oaks . . .'* Hesitating, I watched those around me allowing the words of Rilke to settle in their hearts. My eyes heavy with memory, I continued. *'I'll pursue solitary pathways through the pale twilit meadows with only this one dream – you come too.'*

By the time I reached the final word, tears were clouding my vision. Brushing them away I urged the others to share their favourite poems. From their lips flowed the words of Pablo Neruda and Vítězslav Nezval. A weeping Anton quoted prescient lines from François Villon that ended, *'In my country I am in a distant land . . . I am powerful but lack all force and strength.'*

Humbled, I left them and stumbled back outside. Those bright boys should have been enjoying the best years of their lives but instead they were chained to a world of hate.

*

Early the next morning I found myself in the carpentry shop where Bernd still volunteered before his shift as a policeman. Set up in the former riding school, there was row upon row of freshly made coffins. 'Do they really think we'll need all of these?' I asked, dismayed.

'They were the first things we were ordered to make,' Bernd replied, his expression sombre. We'd all witnessed columns of mourners in black armbands carrying flickering lamps as they followed funeral carts to the ghetto gates. That is where people had to bid farewell to their dead, as they were forbidden from attending the interment. Each body was taken to the mortuary to be ritually washed and interred by strangers in preparation for the next world. There'd be no sitting *shiva* with comforting victuals. Instead, the prisoners would have to go straight back to work, hollow with grief.

Silently, Bernd turned a new leg for a three-legged piano that had been discovered propped on bricks in a damp basement. The find caused great excitement as all we'd had until then was a wheezing harmonium to accompany the illicit musical events that had begun to be staged in attics and basements late at night. Looking up, he saw my expression and asked, 'What's wrong?'

'I can't stop thinking about what it must be like to come of age in this place,' I said. 'Within these walls our teenagers will have their first kiss, their first cigarette. What will being here do to them?'

'I'd like to think that they'll grow up more tender-hearted,' he said. After a small silence, he asked, 'Any news of the AK arrests?'

'I've heard nothing more. What do you think their punishment might be?'

He scratched his head. 'A public flogging, probably and they'll have to forfeit warm food for a while. They might be sent to the Small Fortress. I just hope the Gestapo doesn't ruin their hands. They're some of our best workers.'

'Let's also pray they're not put on the train tomorrow.'

Bernd shook his head. 'That won't happen. The AK are protected, remember?'

The next twenty-four hours proved that he was only partially right.

At dawn the transport left the ghetto. With no one allowed to leave their barracks and hardly any light, people were forced to say goodbyes at the courtyard gates.

I watched in silence as parents called out to sons and wives were wailed for menfolk as toddlers clung to their legs. Some wept wordlessly while others collapsed in on themselves, shivering with emotion and cold. The rest, determined to maintain their dignity, said goodbye only with their eyes.

Despite all our efforts, there were still a few children amongst those departing, travelling with mothers who'd insisted on accompanying their men. 'People are dropping like flies here so I can't believe things will be worse in Riga,' one mother told me, her eyes pleading with me to agree.

'I'm sure you're right,' I said, handing her toddler a piece of bread smeared with jam.

An older woman who was travelling with two teenage daughters insisted, 'My husband and I would rather stick together with our girls. Besides, if we let him go without us, we might never find each other again after the war.'

Once they'd melted into the fog and the sound of their feet shuffling through snow receded, I couldn't help fearing we'd never hear from any of them again. Turning away, I pretended to have something in my eye as I slipped quietly back to my room.

*

When the order came the following day for members of the Council to attend an extraordinary roll call, we had little resilience left to draw upon and gathered with fearful hearts. 'Are they going to announce more transports?' one man asked. 'How many will they send away this time?'

Jakob acted strangely that morning, claiming he couldn't attend because of pressing business. 'The SS know I can't be there,' he told me, as he hurried from my gaze. The minute I reached the designated courtyard, I realised why. Two gallows had been erected almost overnight. We'd been summoned to witness an execution. It was a perversely beautiful morning and, hearing the sound of aircraft, I looked up into the cloud-less sky to see three warplanes passing high above us, trailing ribbons of white vapour. Tipping back my head, I squinted in the hope that my will alone might make them change course and save us, but their vapour dispersed along with my hopes.

I closed my eyes, unable to watch as men I'd worked side by side with were led towards the wooden steps. Each carried a shovel over their shoulder like a rifle, with fresh mud on the blade. They'd been made to dig their own graves. All looked as startled as we felt, especially the youngest: a teenager I knew only as *Maus* who I couldn't imagine doing anything unlawful.

The leader of the stonemasons standing next to me growled, 'It's a bluff. They won't go ahead with this. They're only doing it to scare us. You'll see.' I wasn't so sure and neither was *Maus*, who looked frantically right and left as if waiting for someone to run up and save him. The sound of the steps beneath him being kicked away and the creaking of the rope as froth flecked his lips brought a bitter taste to my throat.

I couldn't take my eyes off the executioner after that, as one by one the men's lives were snuffed out. A primitive-looking creature with features like a fossil, his name was Ada Fisher. Word in the ghetto was that he'd been a butcher before getting a job dissecting corpses in a pathology department. An outsider, he'd been handpicked for the role of hangman.

As the noose was about to be placed around the neck of a law student I knew only as Bedrich, the doomed man charged at Ada Fisher with such a roar of indignation that he almost knocked him over. It was all we could do to stop ourselves from cheering. Bedrich was quickly surrounded by guards who held him tight as the rope was slipped over his head. Despite blows continuing to rain down on him, that brave young man cried out, 'May my mother be blessed,' seconds before the executioner kicked away his life.

*

The mood in the ghetto changed radically after the executions, especially when every prisoner in town, including the children, were filed past the gallows to see what happened to those who disobeyed orders.

Complaints about hunger, overcrowding and disease lost their importance once we knew people could be murdered for no reason. There was something else in the air too: a guilty sense of gratitude that we weren't the ones dangling. The hope that we might be saved soon was strengthened by the news reaching us that Axis forces were losing in North Africa and in the battle for Britain's skies and that Hitler had turned against his Russian allies. 1942 felt to mark the beginning of the end. After all, how much longer could the war go on?

Hoping to lift morale, the weekend after the hangings Jakob asked me to address a public meeting he'd arranged. 'You're so much better at talking to people than I am, Fredy,' he insisted. 'Your youthful enthusiasm raises spirits and is just what everyone needs right now.'

'But I don't speak Czech well enough,' I protested.

'We'll make it clear that this is for German speakers or those who can translate.'

Stepping up onto a table nervously that night, I cleared my throat and looked down on the crowd that was pressing in at the door of the hall. Blowing my whistle to attract their attention, I waited until they'd quietened down. 'Most of you know me,' I began, meeting their gaze. 'For those who don't, my name is Fredy Hirsch and I'm a youth leader and sports coach from Aachen, Germany. I was born in the middle of the last war and I pray that I'll survive this one. As you know, we have a lot of problems here and far too many are dying. But one thing these last few days have taught us is that we'd rather remain here than go elsewhere.' Despite a few disgruntled murmurs, I carried on.

'Within these walls, we've managed to set up a system of government that works. Every day – no matter how many thousands of us there are – we are all fed and given somewhere to sleep. The food may not amount to much and our beds may be on the floor, but this feat is still nothing short of a miracle.' Nobody spoke and everyone continued to stare at me blankly.

'Now is the time to give thanks,' I urged, 'because as difficult as it may be to believe, we're the lucky ones and we should be grateful for those working hard to keep everything running.' I started to clap, staring directly at Jakob, which triggered a slow but polite ripple of applause for the Elders. Once it died away, I carried on. 'Those of you who survived the previous war or studied history know that this, too, shall pass. Tyrants never win. Revolutions and conflicts end. This one will, soon and the light of justice will overcome this dark evil.'

To my surprise, people began to cheer as faces brightened with hope. Raising an arm and my voice, I cried, 'My father used to say, *He that cannot endure the bad will never live to see the good.* Those of us who live to see the good will one day tell the world of Terezín.'

5

October 1926, Aachen, Germany

'WHY DID MOTHER RUN AWAY, Paul? Was it something I did?' I asked him late one night in the small, cold room that we now shared in a strange house.

'No, Fredy,' he replied, his voice muffled from deep beneath his blanket. 'It has nothing to do with us. It's . . . well, it's just the way she is. Now try to get some sleep.'

I envied my brother's ability to fall asleep so quickly and remain oblivious to the world. My own head felt like a hive full of bees, buzzing around and bumping into each other. I had so many questions and no one to ask. *Why did Father die so young? What is Mother doing? Will we ever go home?*

The only thing that could distract me from what I called my *kopfgespräch* – or headtalk – was a good book and the one I most loved was called *Rabbit School*. Not only did it have beautiful illustrations but it told a story that felt very close to my own heart. Two young bunnies are sent to a school in the middle of a pine forest. Under the care of a long-eared teacher, they learn to write on slates and discover which plants are safe to eat. Their kind but strict tutor plays his violin, teaches them songs and supervises gymnastics and playtime. He also ensures they water and weed the vegetable garden.

I loved that wise teacher with his spectacles balanced on his nose, because he reminded me of *Herr* Steil. Watching over his infants with a kind of benevolent authority, he warned them about the evil hunter and his dogs and of the fox who crept through the countryside looking for dinner. '*On the way home, be silent and don't divert sideways off the path or go into dark bushes*,' the old rabbit cautioned. They must run like the wind to escape being eaten because, if the fox grabbed them, no amount of pleading would help.

If it hadn't been for the fellowship of the Jewish youth group that Paul and I joined I think I might have run away to the forest for good. Living with people we barely knew, I felt starved of affection and began to wonder if I even deserved love.

That unhappy period marked the end of my innocence as Paul sought solace in his rabbinical studies, leaving me to my loneliness and confusion. At such a tender age, I didn't know how to express my feelings so I turned in on myself and started reading everything I could.

Eager to belong, I became a human sponge soaking up everything the youth group taught us from nationalistic songs and marches to the value of discipline and patriotism. Learning more about Jewish history than I'd ever picked up in the synagogue, I saluted those whose commands were in the language of the so-called 'Promised Land' and joined in with their songs about going there to 'build and be rebuilt'.

'Only by demonstrating our strength in mind and body will we become the personification of the perfect Jew and regain the respect of the world,' our counsellors added. I still wasn't sure how we'd lost that respect in the first place but, with Paul's warnings of a lifetime of oppression engraved on my heart, I believed every word. My passion only deepened after our group was excluded from several sporting events that we'd been looking forward to.

Disappointed that our games had been cancelled, my brother and I jumped at the chance to help establish the Aachen branch of the much larger Jewish Scouting Association, which held its own events. In the scouts we were treated like little soldiers and practised roll calls, drills and field exercises to regain control of a Jewish flag. Everything was designed to build stamina, confidence and courage as we learned cross-country skiing, orienteering, first aid, self-defence and survival skills.

'The scout motto is *Allzeit Bereit*,' one of the most popular troop leaders told us proudly. 'We must be "Always Ready" to do a good turn every day, a maxim you should adhere to for life.' Listening hard, I loved the idea of waking up each morning with the intention to help someone and made a promise to stick to it.

Paul and I both enjoyed the scouts but travelling across the city to and from meetings in our uniforms became increasingly hazardous. Aggressive young Gentiles began to harass us, something that had never happened before.

One night a group of four followed us onto a tram and started to call us names. Looking us up and down in our distinctive uniforms, one of them shouted, 'Can anyone smell something nasty in here?'

'Yes, a *Judenschwein*,' another replied, sniffing the air and making the sound of a pig.

We were in charge of a group of young cubs who looked to us wide-eyed with fear, wondering how to react. Our leaders had taught us to turn the other cheek and only fight back if there was no other choice, but when one weasel-faced thug grabbed my cherished cap and threw it out of the window, I saw red. Using the left hook I'd recently been taught in boxing to spectacular effect, I thumped him so hard that he folded to the floor with a thud. Turning to my brother in triumph,

I was surprised to see anger in his eyes. 'No, Fredy!' he cried. 'You mustn't sink to their level.'

My eyes smarting, I went to offer my assailant a hand up but he spat in my face and scurried to the far end of the carriage. I vowed from then on to lead by example, escorting our troop off at the next stop even though it meant a longer walk home.

'We can play a word game on the way,' I told them. Before long, all memories of hostile youths were forgotten.

My diligence with them paid off because I was soon appointed the head of my own troop, having discovered an aptitude for leadership. Determined to maintain the sense of pride in my appearance that Alfred had drummed into me, I strove to become the best-dressed scout in Aachen with the most impeccably turned-out cubs.

Lining them up and inspecting their uniforms, necks, fingernails, even behind their ears, I'd tell them, 'Shoulders back. Heads up. Be proud to be German and smile, always smile, my *Kinder*. No one wants to see a grumpy, nervous lad with shoulders drooping. We must look as if we are happy to do anything for anyone.'

One ten-year-old named Wilhelm was so shy that he avoided eye contact with me whenever I gave orders or checked their uniforms. When I heard that he had a violent father at home, I realised he was afraid of men. Lifting his chin in my hand, I spoke gently, 'There's nothing to be frightened of here, Wilhelm, but I'll let you into a little secret. If you appear scared then people will treat you that way. Looking someone straight in the eye takes away their power. Do you understand?'

'Yes, Fredy,' he said, so softly that I had to bend my head to listen.

'And speak up, please, young man,' I added with a smile. 'Nobody likes a mumbler.'

'Yes, sir,' he shouted, saluting me before collapsing into giggles when I tickled him.

By my mid-teens I was so devoted to my charges that my own schooling started to take second place. My grades dropped in all subjects except physical education and my spare time was spent not on homework but on devising new ways of engaging the boys with games and handmade prizes.

Our happiest days were when I took them hiking. 'Name that bird,' I'd call as a woodcock flitted past as fast as an arrow. I'd show them how to safely forage mushrooms. Whenever a storm brewed, I'd lead them into a clearing and, shouting above the wind, cry, 'Don't cower from Nature under the trees. Marvel at her. You'll never feel more alive than when standing out in the rain.'

Instead of being proud of my scouting achievements, however, my family focused solely on my poor school results. 'If you want to be a teacher one day as you say, Alfred, then you'll have to apply yourself,' my stepfather declared after summoning me to his study one evening after scouts. 'It isn't enough simply to be popular among your friends or have children like you. Qualifications are the only way to prove that you're capable of imparting knowledge.'

Resentful of him sitting at my father's desk and calling me Alfred, I was too young and too blind to see that he probably had good intentions. It couldn't have been easy taking on a widow and two stepsons, but he'd made our mother happy and brought financial stability to our lives. Mother stood behind him, a hand on his shoulder and reiterated everything he'd said.

'I hope you're listening, Fredy,' she added, but I was no longer the toddler she'd dressed in a sailor suit to match my brother's and had little interest in her attempts at parenting.

Nor did I have much interest in anything else, least of all the girls who'd become the obsession of my schoolmates as we navigated puberty together. With hormones raging through my body and hair sprouting like weeds, I was teased for being frigid and aloof.

'You're too formal in the company of girls, Fredy,' one friend chastised. 'You need to relax more and not come across as quite so . . . well, stiff.' When they'd all stopped giggling at his double entendre, another accused me of behaving like an 'over-polite middle-aged man', which I took as a compliment. Not content with their lecturing, they attempted to pair me with girls on outings to the cinema or the park, but I'd give an excuse and flee to my scouts.

'I don't have the time or the money for messing about with girls,' I complained one day to Carl, a junior troop leader who'd taken to following me around. Short and stocky with a strawberry-shaped birthmark on his face, he was a physical and social misfit but patient with the younger boys. Living in my shadow, he secured my protection from the bullies who'd made his childhood hellish, beating him up and calling him *Fleck*, or Stain. I first came across him one day surrounded by a gang who were pushing and prodding him in the street, shouting, '*Fleck, Fleck, Fleck!* You're a stain on this neighbourhood!'

Pushing through the crowd, I grabbed Carl by the collar and dragged him out from their midst. We were almost clear of the bullies when one thumped me in the kidneys from behind and I doubled over. Carl ran off, too afraid to hang around as I pulled myself up slowly and turned to face the neighbourhood bully.

'What do you want, Walter?' I asked, keeping my expression blank.

He looked right and left to gauge the mood of his gang and then, prodding me in the chest with a finger, he said, 'I want you, *Fleck* and all your kind out of this town.'

'Really?' I replied, half-smiling. 'And tell me, what would your grandfather say?'

I watched his Adam's apple lodge halfway down his throat and get stuck, knowing that his grandfather had married my mother's cousin Ruth after his first wife died. Suddenly Walter didn't look quite so sure of himself but – not wanting to lose face – he wagged a finger at me and said, 'Just stay out of my way, Hirsch.'

Carl watched our encounter from behind a tree and couldn't believe that I'd faced down his tormentor. From then on, he was glued to my side knowing that they'd never dare bully him when I was around. Like me, he'd never dated anyone so we had that in common at least.

'Aside from the fact that I'm too busy for girls, they expect boys to pay for everything from cinema tickets to chocolates,' I complained, as he and I sat waiting for a tram one night. 'Personally, I'd rather have a pet rabbit.'

'Or a dog,' Carl suggested. 'Something you could take on a good long walk.'

'Exactly.'

Resting his hand on my forearm, Carl added, 'Girls don't understand us anyway, Fredy.'

There was something about the way he looked at me that made me jump up and stand by the kerb.

*

The lines went around the block for the grand opening of the new Ufa Palast cinema near Aachen railway station. With more than four hundred seats and a state-of-the-art sound system for the new talking pictures, it was one of the best things to ever happen in our town.

Mother, who devoured weekly magazines about movie stars and Hollywood, was more excited than I'd ever seen her as we sidestepped the queue and were allowed in before anyone else, thanks to her cousin Jan who was the new venue's manager.

Sitting in the plush red seats as the lights dimmed and first few notes of the overture struck up, I watched agog as the movie began and a stagecoach galloped into view. The storyline told of a matchmaker trying to persuade the town's mayor to marry off his daughter to the son of the region's wealthiest man. His plan is ruined when she falls for the stagecoach driver who rides into town.

'Who is that?' I whispered, staring at the actor playing the driver. Dashing in his uniform and hat, he had a strong jaw, kind eyes and a fine profile. Just looking at him gave me a strange feeling in my belly.

'Why, that's Willi Domgraf-Fassbaender. Born here in Aachen,' she told me with pride. 'He's a marvellous baritone as well as being an accomplished actor. I have some of his records at home. Handsome, too, isn't he?'

Mesmerised, I couldn't take my eyes off him and when he opened his mouth to sing and I heard his deep, rich voice, I almost wept at the beauty of it. Every scene without him felt like torture and I became so fixated on his face that I barely noticed the rest of the cast. The film ended far too soon and when the lights came back on I sat stock still in my seat, unable to move or speak.

'Oh, wasn't the leading lady beautiful?' my mother sighed. 'I just loved the way she did her hair.' Turning to look at me, still dazed, she nudged me knowingly. 'I thought you'd like her. One day you'll meet a girl like that, Fredy, and fall in love. Then she'll become my daughter-in-law and give us grandchildren.'

Reddening, I came to my senses. But as we crossed the Art Deco lobby, I froze again. On the wall was a giant poster in a glass-fronted case with a close-up of the leading lady and the actor who'd so moved me. Ignoring my mother thanking her cousin, I walked right up to it to gaze up in awe.

'That was so wonderful, Jan,' I heard Mother say. 'Fredy loved it too, didn't you? As you can see, he's quite smitten with the actress who played Marie. Well, you know what teenage boys are like.'

The pair of them laughed and then I felt Jan's hand on my shoulder. 'Would you like to take one of those posters home, Fredy?' he asked. 'I have a couple spare in my office. Then you can look at her as much as you like – in the privacy of your room.'

On our return, Mother found me some drawing pins so I could affix the poster to my bedroom wall. I then lay on my butterfly bed mouthing, 'Willi Domgraf-Fassbaender. Willi.'

Flicking through my mother's records later, I found one of him singing a song from the opera *Don Pasquale* and wore out three needles listening to it. What a man. What a look. What a voice. I had no idea what drew me to him so or why he gave me a strange feeling. I just knew that he was the most beautiful human being I had ever seen and that I wanted to look just like him.

My teenage crush occupied my mind for several months, leaving little time to be interested in anything else. I couldn't care less about the radical far-right extremists in the new National Socialist German Workers' Party. That is, until the day the 'Nazis' threatened to outlaw every Jewish youth group if they came to power. They might as well have said they'd cut off my legs. 'How can they even be allowed to say such a thing?' I asked one of our scout leaders. 'What would happen if we could no longer meet?'

'Don't worry, Fredy. The courts would never allow it,' I was assured. 'Our job is to keep trying to be the best we can be as we prepare for a better tomorrow.' He was right. Shaping the hearts and minds of the young had become my passion since Father died, as I strove to become somebody he'd have been proud of. I was Fredy Hirsch, the teenage son of master butcher Heinrich Hirsch and nephew of the successful entrepreneur Alfred Heinemann. I had standards to maintain.

With those mentors at the forefront of my mind, I began each day with the intention of making a favourable impression on everyone I met. Setting my alarm earlier than necessary, my routine began with a strenuous workout in my room followed by some stretching. Then it was time for my ablutions before a practice shave, even though I'd sprouted only a few patches of fluff.

Paying special attention to my crowning glory, I carefully tended to my hair, mimicking Uncle Alfred's swept back style and oiling it down with Brilliantine from my very own pot. Once I was dressed in neatly pressed clothes and polished shoes, I checked myself in the mirror and rehearsed my morning greeting – '*Guten Morgen*' – beaming at my reflection as I perfected a winning smile.

Not everyone at home appreciated my attention to detail, or the time it took, and some of my mother's rebukes really stung. 'Your father would have wholly disapproved of the way you preen yourself,' she complained. 'It isn't manly, Fredy. People are beginning to talk.'

'Then let them talk, Mother,' I snapped. 'I don't care what they think and neither should you.' She never seemed to appreciate that I was earning the respect and admiration of scores of scouts. My superiors thought so well of me that they'd dubbed me '*der Rattenfänger von Hameln*' – the Ratcatcher of Hamlin – after the legend of the Pied Piper who played his flute and was followed by adoring children. I took it as a compliment until I discovered how the story ended. When the Piper wasn't paid for ridding the town of its rats, he led all its infants away never to be seen again.

I was also no longer getting on so well with my brother Paul, who'd joined a seminary and began to challenge my enthusiasm for the Promised Land. 'To abandon our homeland and start a new life far away would only play into the hands of our critics now, Fredy,' he insisted. 'And what will happen to Jewish culture here in Germany if we run? We helped make this country successful and it's our duty to remain.'

'In a place where, according to you, we've "*always been oppressed and probably always will be*"?' I countered, throwing his words back at him. 'No, thank you.'

With Germany in political turmoil as the firebrand Adolf Hitler gained in popularity, I had even more reason to believe that we should leave. My stepfather disagreed. 'Don't be a *dummkopf*, Alfred,' he chastised. 'Hitler's merely a Charlie Chaplin lookalike. He and his party are a flash in the pan. They'll fall out of favour any day. You'll see.'

By the time I was sixteen, I was itching to get away from home. Taking matters into my own hands, I applied for a job with a youth group in Dusseldorf that I saw advertised in a Zionist newspaper. I was accepted on the basis of my application and references, but there was a problem. I needed parental consent.

'But where and how will you live, Fredy?' my mother asked when I told her I was leaving.

'I'll be given food and accommodation in return for teaching teenagers,' I replied. 'There's no salary but they'll cover my expenses and continue my education.'

'And who are these people?' asked my stepfather, who I suspected would be happy to get me out from under their feet.

'A branch of the Jewish Scouts that is planning to join forces with the Maccabis. That's a Zionist group from Czechoslovakia. They encourage young people to engage in physical activity, be good citizens and seek self-fulfilment.' Seeing them falter in the face of my determination, I added, 'This is all I've ever wanted.' With no prospects for me at home, they had little choice but to let me go.

I packed my rucksack and, sitting on the edge of my bed, I picked up my toy dog. 'Well, Emil, should I take you too?' I asked, brushing fluff off the balding patches where I'd cuddled him too much as a boy. One of his eyes was loose and his tail threadbare but all the same I kissed his nose and placed him inside my bag.

6

February 1942, Terezín Ghetto, Czechoslovakia

IT WASN'T NIGHTMARES THAT disturbed my sleep in the ghetto but dreams – especially those that took me back to the happiest days of my youth. The oblivion I sought at the end of each day was no longer a refuge. Lying on my thin mattress with hunger gnawing at my stomach like a rat, I resisted the urge to scratch my fleabites and tried to block out the snoring and coughing.

Skimming the surface of sleep, my dream transported me to a childhood morning lying in bed. I could smell the freshly ground coffee being brewed downstairs as our maid warmed the pumpernickel and prepared my breakfast eggs. Running my hands across my belly in happy anticipation, my dream ended the moment my fingers came into contact with the sharp ridges of my ribs.

Eyes snapping open, it took me a moment to focus on the peeling plasterwork and cobwebs before I remembered where I was. Waking cold and tired with a painful hunger, I felt my skin stretching ever tighter over my bones as I pulled my aching limbs out of bed with a groan.

After my morning wash and some time spent making myself presentable, I was waiting in line for breakfast when I was joined by Leo. He looked me up and down and asked, 'Where did you get that?'

Smoothing down the blue serge jacket I'd had a seamstress tailor to my liking, I smiled. 'The Distribution Centre. It took me several visits and a lot of rummaging before I found something I liked.'

Leo laughed. 'Only the best dressed man in Terezín could salvage a couture jacket from that crazy jumble. And don't tell me you found those Nazi boots there?'

Smiling enigmatically, I didn't confess that I'd had a gendarme smuggle them in for me. The price was heavy – a painting by an artist named Dinah I'd known since before the war. Desperate for decent boots, I offered my entire week's bread ration if she'd paint the gendarme's fiancée from a photograph he carried. Even though my belly growled with hunger for a week, whenever I admired the sheen on the black leather I was pleased with my trade. Paired with some taupe riding breeches, a white shirt and a tie I'd bartered for a hard-boiled egg, they set off my outfit perfectly. There were no mirrors in the ghetto but if I stood on the table in my office I could see enough of my reflection in the window glass to get an idea. Trying to ignore the fact that, at twenty-six, my hair appeared to be going grey, I hoped Uncle Alfred would have been proud.

Any pleasure was fleeting in Terezín, however. An announcement was made that the entire ghetto was to be confined to barracks and punished with a '*Lichtsperre*' or blackout for several days. When I hurried to Jakob's office to find out why, he told me, 'Three teenagers training to be locksmiths have escaped. Until they're caught, the electricity is to be switched off.'

'But why punish everyone?' I asked. 'It's bad enough that it gets dark early but candles are so few and far between that the nights will be interminable.'

The blackout was only lifted when the teenagers were caught hiding in a barn and sent to the Small Fortress pending a tribunal. 'Who'll represent them?' I asked.

Jakob looked up at me in a daze of exhaustion and shook his head. 'I'm not sure anyone will. Who'd dare pit themselves against the SS?'

Staring at the bags under his eyes and sensing that I was only adding to his burdens, I said, 'Very well. I'd like to speak up for them, if that's permitted.'

Jakob and his wife Miriam both tried to dissuade me but I was determined to help if I could. 'The one thing I've learned about the Nazis is that they respect *chutzpah*, so the best chance those boys have is if I can appeal to their mentality. Remember, I speak their language.'

The hearing was over almost before it began. Three Elders I didn't know well sat in silence behind a table, flanked by two members of the SS. Then the handcuffed escapees were brought in looking frightened and bruised but clearly relieved to see me. Giving them a small nod, I could tell that their spell in the Small Fortress had almost broken them. The prisoners who worked in the gardens there witnessed brutality daily, telling us of naked men and women hosed down with cold water until they died and others forced to run through courtyards pushing wheelbarrows full of rocks.

When a German clerk read out the charges and asked the teenagers how they pleaded, they glanced in my direction and then at the SS, hung their heads and murmured, '*Shuldig*'. Guilty. Within minutes the Elders sentenced them to deportation. The boys were too worn down to object.

Jumping up, I started to say something on their behalf but was told to sit by the SS. 'But they are only children,'

I protested. 'All they wanted was to go home to see their parents. Surely they have a right to a defence?'

An officer I knew only as Müller rose to his feet and took two steps towards me in that small, stuffy room. 'Those who plead guilty to a crime against the Reich have no defence.'

Straightening my spine, I took a step towards him and, checking his rank, I repeated, 'But they're only boys, *Herr Hauptsturmfürher*. Young men who found the courage to escape. Can you not show them some mercy?'

He turned to his fellow officer with a shrug. 'They're still alive, aren't they?' The man laughed. Turning back to me, Müller asked, 'What is your number?'

I gave it, before stating, 'And my name is Fredy Hirsch.'

I watched his jawline clench. 'I didn't ask for your name,' he told me with a glacial tone. 'And unless you'd care to discuss your family history with those on the next transport, this case is closed.'

Thinking of the children who depended on me, I stared into his merciless face and fought the urge to do or say more. Finally, I turned to the boys and said, 'Your bravery will never be forgotten.' With my inadequate words hanging in the air, I fled from the room.

*

Within days the SS made another announcement that sent shock waves around the ghetto. 'They're planning more transports,' Leo informed me and Gonda after another difficult meeting with the German High Command.

'Where to?' I asked, shuddering.

'They refer to them only as *Osttransports*. Trains of some ten thousand people each to camps in the East.'

'Ten thousand?' asked Gonda, aghast.

'And they'll pick the categories this time, making it harder for us to exempt people,' Leo added. 'But first, there'll be transports in from Pilsen, Brno and Prague.'

'Where on earth do they think we'll put them all?' I asked.

Leo shook his head. 'They ordered us to utilise all spaces: corridors, stairs, storerooms, even the catacombs. Or the Commandant said that they could always double the transports East if we'd prefer.'

Once the transports were announced it was all anyone could talk about. Morale plummeted and the latest batch of new arrivals seemed especially despondent as they heard they might be first on the list. One damp afternoon, I escorted a group of thirty middle-aged men upstairs to their third-floor billet, a mouldy space with windows almost to the floor. 'This was once an officers' mess, so it's bigger and brighter than most,' I told them.

Shuffling in, they stared at the peeling walls and the brick floor strewn with straw. Noses wrinkling, they inhaled musty air tinged with the distinctively pungent smell of rats.

'The carpenters are busy making bunks but, for now, I'm afraid you'll have to sleep on the straw,' I added. Throwing open the window, I said, 'With a bit of airing and a sweep out, though, this place will be as good as new.' Turning back to the room, I watched a well-groomed gentleman in a fur coat put down his leather suitcase with care before striding purposefully to the window. Before I could stop him, he stepped over the sill as casually as if he were stepping out to an evening concert. 'No!' I cried, rushing forward, but I was too late to grab him before he dropped onto the cobbled street below.

I stood staring down at his twisted body for several seconds, unable to take in what I'd witnessed. I watched people running over to him and heard someone shout for a doctor. It was only when I saw his leg twitch that I raced downstairs. Once he'd been carried to the infirmary I checked his ID papers and sought out his wife, billeted in the Dresden barracks. She showed only the slightest flicker of emotion when I told her. All she said was, 'My husband is a famous furrier, you know.'

Back in Leo's office afterwards, I told him, 'She was the kind of woman who, before the war, would have thought her cook being poached by a rival was the worst thing that could ever happen. Yet she sat like a statue beside her husband for the next three hours, watching him die.' Pausing, I shook off the memory. 'She was still wearing the clothes she'd travelled in: a fur coat with matching hat and gloves the colour of beetroot. I couldn't take my eyes off those beautiful gloves.'

Leo sighed. 'Several more men have chosen to kill themselves rather than remain here. Health Services have reported six suicides in the past week alone. Most are older, prominent Czechs who came here under false pretences. The Nazis led them to believe that Terezín would be an upmarket spa resort and a staging post for the Promised Land. They have given up their savings, homes and businesses in return for what they were assured would be the finest south-facing suites. The shame of their deception is too much to bear.'

*

A rare and welcome invitation the following day did much to lift my spirits. 'Come to my room to break bread with us tonight, Fredy. We have a wood burning stove so Miriam will heat us some soup. We'll make our own Friday night dinner.'

'Thank you, Jakob, I'd like that,' I said, realising I hadn't even registered which day of the week it was. 'I'll call by after my rounds.'

It would be a relief to sit quietly with like-minded adults after helping settle the children. Sitting beside a seven-year-old named Eva, with the girls around her also listening, I sang Brahms' *'Wiegenlied'* lullaby, sung to me at primary school. As Eva's eyes grew heavy, I kissed her forehead and adapted the final line to, *'Sleep blissfully and sweetly – dear Evička. See paradise in your dreams.'*

When I arrived at Jakob's door a few hours later, Miriam invited me into a room lit by candles and the glow from their stove. As the wife of the Council Elder, she was allowed to be with him but their Friday night suppers served on porcelain and silver were long gone as – like everyone else – the couple had been robbed of their family heirlooms. And instead of traditional roasted meats, our meal comprised of warmed-up soup and ghetto tea, with only the memories of Friday nights past to feast on.

Once I was seated on a wooden crate, I turned my gaze to the corner of the room where their son Arieh was sleeping. He was cradling Emil the toy dog, which I'd given him for his tenth birthday. Jakob handed me a bowl of Miriam's potato and pearl barley broth and a cube of black bread smeared with margarine. Cradling the morsel in cold hands, I pretended for a moment that it was warm Challah bread torn from a fresh loaf and dipped in salt.

In a hoarse voice, Jakob began the prayers. 'Blessed are you, Lord our God, ruler of the universe who brings forth bread from the earth.' Closing my eyes, I recalled how as a child Friday was the only day of the week when I felt more Jewish than German, embracing the ancient traditions. As delicious smells of roast duck with cherries wafted in from the kitchen, my mother would unlock the linen press and pull out the finest tableware and the best cloth, the huge silver candlesticks that her grandmother gave her on her wedding day and the best cut-glass.

With Miriam's simple fare devoured all too soon, Jakob stared into the fire in silence. I was beginning to sense a growing solemnity in him as the burden of his position took its toll. Nobody could have done it better but he only had to make one mistake and he'd end up in front of a firing squad. Trying to cheer him, I said, 'This has also been a week of good omens, hasn't it? Our first ghetto wedding, I hear. They tell me the two young lovers fell for each other across a crowded washroom.'

Miriam laughed. 'Yes and they cemented their union with a double portion of potatoes.'

'We had the first baby born in the ghetto, too! *Mazeltov.* Another Jew for Hitler, eh?'

Jakob half-smiled.

'I went to visit the mother with some milk and an extra loaf of bread I'd coaxed out of the cooks,' I continued. 'She plans to name him Zachary.'

'A strong name,' Miriam commented.

With a wry smile, I added, 'I told her that she'd have to forgive us but several of the men have been referring to him affectionately as "AK1": the first of the next generation.' My hosts gave me a look that said they shared my hope that baby Zachary would survive long enough to appreciate our humour.

*

Rising before dawn the following morning, I put on my gym kit and headed to the ramparts to do my exercises. It was misty out and the sharpness of the air after the staleness of the barracks spiked my lungs. Humming *'Alouette'*, the French song I was teaching the children, I stopped to inhale a gust of wind that blew a faint scent of pine trees from distant hills. My reverie was interrupted by the haunting whistle of a barge passing on the nearby river. Resisting the urge to blow my whistle and summon it back, I felt the stabbing pain of realising that ordinary life was continuing just beyond our fortress. What I wouldn't have given to leap over the walls and hide out on that solitary vessel as it melted away in billowing clouds of fog.

Hearing the familiar tramp of wooden clogs clattering on cobblestones, I turned to see the only other people awake at that hour: a ghostlike work party marching in regimented columns to the ghetto's makeshift armaments factories. Always leaving and returning in pitch darkness, they kept their heads down to form a trailing grey thread.

Ignoring them to return to my squats, lunges and push-ups, I heard the passing comments of the sentries. One called out that I was '*verrückt*' to go barefoot in shorts in winter. Another shouted, '*Der Athlet hat den Verstand verloren*': the athlete has lost his mind. Maybe I had but, as I stood there breathing heavily, the snow pressing up between my toes felt like the only thing anchoring me to the Earth.

'*Den Verstand zu verlieren ist besser als den Krieg zu verlieren*,' I yelled back as his comrades laughed. Losing one's mind is better than losing the war.

When I'd pushed myself to the point of near exhaustion, I hurried back to my barracks and a wash at an outside tap where the sting of the ice-cold water almost stopped the air in my throat. Dressing quickly, I smoothed down my hair and rubbed my boots before standing in line in the grey morning light with the rest of the inmates, all of us gripping our *Essen-Karte* food coupons. I was often one of the first in the queue. Not because

I enjoyed the tepid liquid ladled into my mess tin from the distribution window once my ticket had been torn, but because it gave me a better chance of surviving one more day.

Where has your appetite gone, Fredy? I could hear my father's voice echoing in my head as my stomach groaned. Oh, what I wouldn't have given for a single bite of the meat he'd put on my plate as a child.

Distracted by the sight of the SS patrol coming into view for roll call, I turned to those around me and started pulling faces. 'Oh dear. Here comes The Fool with his latest sidekick,' I muttered. 'His head is so bald under his cap that fleas hold skating competitions on it. Watch his lips moving as he counts out each step of his flat feet. Then wait for him to lose count, frown and start all over again.'

Those who could hear me collapsed into fits of giggles as they watched him do exactly that. Glaring across at them, the Nazi must have been wondering what on earth Jews in a ghetto had to laugh about.

I began to wonder too, as my stomach rumbled again and I began to fantasise about food. Seeing the sunken faces of those around me and suspecting they felt the same, I threw back my head and made an announcement. 'My name is Fredy Hirsch and this morning for breakfast I'm going to order two fried eggs on buttered ryebread toast. Then I want a side order of pancakes with honey and whipped cream. How about you?'

Amid groans, someone piped up, 'My name is Rudolf Limburg and I'm going to ask for smoked haddock with two poached eggs and a huge pot of fresh chicory coffee.'

Another cried, 'My name is Sabine Springer and I'm ordering an entire apple strudel all to myself. Oh and pastries and toast and a plate piled high with warm doughnuts filled with jam.'

A man who'd been given the nickname '*Sardinka*' because everyone knew how much he loved tinned fish, yelled, 'I'm going to eat a herring as fat as Hermann Goering!' We all laughed at the thought.

Before too long, others started calling out the names of dishes they ate only in their dreams and women took to reciting recipes in a ghetto game they'd devised called 'The Kitchen of Memories'. Just as they did in the barracks late at night, several began arguing over which sauce should go with what meat, with one crying, 'My mother never prepared goulash like that! It was always accompanied by a sweet tomato gravy,' while others debated how to make meatloaf or bread dumplings.

After a bowl of foul tea and a mouthful of mouldy chestnut bread, I did my best to convince myself I wasn't hungry anymore and tried not to think about red cabbage and creamy mashed potatoes. Even though such thoughts only made us hungrier, remembering it gave us a happy glimpse of what our lives used to be like.

'You were right, Fredy,' Jakob told me when I walked into his office after breakfast. 'What was it you said – we need to shield the children from despair? Quite so. If the Almighty is merciful, they are the only hope we have for the future.'

'They are,' I agreed, taking a few paces towards him. 'And if we can keep them from the horror, we can teach them the tools they need to survive. They'll learn German commands and how to stand to attention. We'll show them the importance of discipline, physical strength and how to do a good turn every day.'

Jakob nodded. 'The SS have informed us that all civilians in the town are to be moved out to make space for the thousands yet to arrive, so I'm transferring you to Youth Welfare with Gonda to find places suitable for the children.'

Grinning like an idiot, I cried, 'Thank you, Jakob, thank you. You won't regret this.'

With most of the civilian houses still occupied, I started by looking elsewhere and within days came across an empty attic. Exploring the upper floors of the barracks the Germans called Hamburg, I heard scratching and spotted a hatch in the ceiling. Grabbing a rickety chair and climbing up to crawl in, I turned up the wick on my oil lamp and found myself in an enormous slanting roof space under clay tiles supported by a heavy framework of beams.

The air up there was barely breathable and I pressed the collar of my jacket to my mouth as I ventured further in. The space was dominated by a brick chimney to carry the smoke of fires no longer lit. The floor was deep in dirt and when I took a few paces further in I disturbed a rats' nest, which explained the scratching. Scurrying in every direction, the creatures startled me and I stepped back into a skein of cobwebs. Brushing off the strands, I spotted a pile of rusty metal hinges, suggesting that the roof also leaked. Undaunted, I murmured, 'This is perfect!'

Within a few days, I'd persuaded a carpenter to fashion some steps and widen the hatch and I bribed another workman to patch the hole in the roof. He also cut a few slatted slits in the eaves to allow in a little air. After making some final adjustments, I sought out Zuzana who was teaching German to twelve young Czechs I'd placed in her care. 'I have a surprise,' I told them. '*Kommen, Kinder.*'

Grabbing my lantern and hurrying them to the attic, I helped them up the new steps to show them my discovery, holding the lamp high so they could see how much room there was. There was a bench made out of rough planks and a table from an old crate. On it were pages of SS forms the children could draw on, as well as old newspapers, some wrinkled wrapping paper, stubs of lead pencils, a handful of dolls and a single red crayon stolen or 'sluiced' from the hospital where it was used to mark temperature charts.

Registering their expressions of dismay, I laughed. 'Why the long faces? This is going to be so much fun. Once we clean the place and bring in some more light, we can read and sing with the little ones. We'll make papier-mâché puppets and put on a show, scavenging whatever we need.' I paused to allow Zuzi to translate before adding, 'Instead of being trapped in stuffy rooms, up here you can learn everything from history to Hebrew. When the weather improves we'll go outside but until then this will be our little piece of heaven.'

'But it's cold,' one girl complained.

'Not as cold as outside,' I countered.

'There are so many cobwebs, Fredy,' Zuzana said, grimacing.

'Cobwebs mean spiders,' added one of the smaller boys, peering into the gloom.

'Yes and rats too,' I replied, laughing as the children shuffled closer together. 'But tell me, what does this big old attic remind you of, huh?' The children looked from one to the other, confused. 'Think about it,' I prompted. 'Huge beams from which to suspend ropes and hammocks. Little light, as if we are below and listen how the timbers creak in the wind.'

The children shook their heads until a red-haired lad threw up his hand. 'Is it a ship?'

'Yes, Friedrich. Well done. It feels just like being inside a Spanish galleon, doesn't it? And who do you think might be living on such a ship?'

'Sailors?' offered two of the girls in unison, their eyes glinting in the lamplight.

'That's right. Sailors and who else?' Blank faces stared back at me as their minds searched for an answer.

'Noah?' asked an older boy.

'That's a really good answer, Hans. This is like an ark and we can create a play about Noah and his animals, but I was thinking of someone else.' Frowning, they watched as I reached behind the chimney and pulled out a piece of black cloth onto which I'd crudely painted a skull-and-crossbones. 'Pirates!' I declared, closing one eye and attempting a dastardly expression. The children doubled over with laughter as I hopped around the attic with my flag.

'My name is Captain Fredy Stinkalot and together we'll take to the high seas. We'll feel the wind in our sails and have treasure chests stuffed with gold. Every day we can embark on grand adventures to places far, far away from here. What do you say?' Looking at their faces stunned into amused silence, I prompted, 'Aye, aye, Captain!' Bouncing around, I stumbled into the rats' nest again as girls screamed. One skinny rodent ran out of the shadows, stopped, sniffed the air with whiskers twitching and scampered back.

Stamping my feet to scare him off, I cried, 'So what if we have a few stowaways, Shiverin' Zuzi? Doesn't every seafaring vessel, Handsome Herbert? We mustn't be afraid must we, Poopdeck Petr?' They laughed as I gave each of them names, adding, 'Now, let's find a broom and get this vessel ship-shape for our first great journey of discovery.'

'Aye, aye, Captain!' they clamoured.

Watching the children hurry back down the ladder, chattering with excitement, I told myself that my work with them was the Lord's will. I was raising their morale and readying them for a world in which they could hopefully live freely. No matter how much I convinced myself of my calling, however, I also knew it was my salvation. Each day that I awoke in mortal danger, it was the children who gave me a reason to go on.

7

July 1933, Frankfurt, Germany

'I WONDER WHAT THIS could be?' I teased, holding the brown paper parcel to my ear and shaking it. 'Could it be an exciting new board game or an American baseball hat? Oh, wait, I think I can hear something rattling.'

The children were wide-eyed with excitement at the arrival of a package all the way from New York, a delivery that caused quite a stir. I told the boys to guess what might be inside. 'Whoever's closest will get some *Schokolade* from the tin my brother sent me,' I promised.

'I think it's a clockwork car,' a boy named Karel suggested.

'Fredy's too old for toy cars,' another protested. 'I bet it's a fountain pen and some leather-bound notebooks for his articles and speeches.'

'Well, that would be useful,' I replied, with a smile. Others thought it might be books or clothing. Turning to the smallest and youngest boy known to all as 'Sparrow' I asked, 'What about you, Miloš?'

Bashful, the boy with the mop of red hair and freckles who'd been standing at the back replied, 'Something practical but lovely.'

Putting them out of their misery, I pulled a pocketknife from my shorts and sliced open the envelope attached to the box whereupon a postcard fell out. Turning it over in my hands, I gazed down at a photo of New York's Empire State Building. That's when I knew for certain that the parcel was from Uncle Alfred. On the back, in his spidery handwriting, he'd written, *Here's the latest contender for the title of tallest building in Manhattan, Fredy. Its antenna makes it sixty or so metres higher than the Chrysler Building I wrote to you about before, although I believe the latter is still aesthetically superior. We'll visit them both one day, my boy. Your loving Onkel.*

Thrilled by that idea, I cut the string and asked the boys to help me unwrap it. Inside a cardboard box were two packages: one small, one large. I handed the smallest to Miloš, saying, 'You open it for me.' His eyes like saucers, he carefully peeled back the wrapping to reveal another smaller oblong box. Nestling inside in green tissue paper was a shiny steel whistle attached to a braided cord. Engraved on it were the words *The Acme Boy Scouts.* A handwritten note from Alfred read, *Start each day with a new song.*

'Practical but lovely,' I declared, my voice cracking with gratitude. Grinning, I presented Miloš with his prize, placing two small cubes of chocolate into his hand. From the look on his face, he'd never won anything in his life before and he ran to a corner with a squeal of delight.

Asking the others to help me open the larger package, they gasped as I pulled out a buckskin case containing a pair of binoculars finished in leather and brass. Alfred had written an old Jewish proverb onto the attached note that read, *As you teach, you learn.* Blinking, I nodded.

'These will be perfect for our field trips,' I declared, as a dozen grubby hands reached out to hold them. 'No one touches them unless they have clean fingers and I mean not one speck of dirt beneath the nails. So, run along to the washroom and give your hands a good scrub. The boy with the cleanest fingers will hold these first.'

When they all ran out of the room, I read Alfred's note again. The proverb couldn't have been more appropriate now that my role had become part of something much bigger: preparing the children for a pioneering new life. The work that had started in Dusseldorf had brought me to Frankfurt where I found myself with even more responsibility. Placed in charge of group games, I was also expected to give lectures on the importance of physical fitness, something I'd never done before but which came naturally to me.

Determined to be the best mentor, I made a point of memorising the name of every child and taught them *jiu-jitsu*, a Japanese martial art I'd learned during my time in Dusseldorf. I also took the youngsters hiking, camping and swimming, regardless of the weather. It was so rewarding to see how they came alive in the wild, their eyes and spirits shining. 'That's it!' I'd encourage after another cold-water dip. 'Now let's run around in circles for five minutes to warm ourselves up.'

Sitting around a campfire afterwards eating goulash from mess tins like little soldiers, we discussed everything from Zionism to their favourite comic books. Whenever possible, I tried to instil in them the moral values I'd learned in the scouts. 'The Torah condemns those who say one thing with their mouth and another with their heart,' I reminded them. 'There can be no deceitful tongues amongst us.'

Although I missed the forests and hills of home, I'd never been happier than when I was with those boys. Back at my desk each night, I wrote to my brother to assure him all was well. In his replies, I'd learned that Uncle Alfred was still travelling back and forth to the United States on business.

He's considering moving there permanently because of the political situation, Paul wrote. *Even our stepfather is worried. The word 'Jude' was daubed on the window of the kosher butcher who'd been a rival of Father's. Maybe you were right to get away, Fredy.* I took no pleasure in that thought, especially not when – following three elections in a year – millions of Germans voted the Nazis into power less than two weeks before my seventeenth birthday. Not since I was ten years old had my *geburtstag* been so ruined.

*

'We need to get as many young people as possible to British Mandate Palestine, Fredy,' my team leader Mordechai told me. 'The election result has sparked even more attacks against Jews and people are starting to panic.'

'How hard will that be, though?' I asked, daunted by the task of sending children thousands of kilometres away to an unknown destination.

'There's a strict quota so if we can't get them there legally, we'll send them by any means available,' he replied. 'Even if they end up being held by the British until their applications are processed. That would be preferable to remaining here at the mercy of the Nazis.'

To help prepare for this exodus and in the hope that I might be selected to accompany some of the 'pioneers', I sat in on all kinds of lessons from Hebrew to the running the *kibbutzim*, the communal agricultural settlements. I also learned the Zionist anthem, '*Hatikvah*', written by a Jewish poet and set to the melody of a Romanian folk song. The Hebrew lyrics spoke of a longing in the Jewish soul, an ancient hope not yet lost '*to be a nation free*'.

I took Mordechai's words to heart when he assured me, 'This is the most exciting time in our history.' I was thrilled. It felt good to be part of a close-knit community with a common goal, living communally with fellow counsellors. With little or no money, we spent our spare time playing sport, reading battered second-hand books and discussing everything but politics. None of us could ignore a *Führer* who'd given himself dictatorial powers but we chose not to worry too much about a country we fully intended to leave.

I shared a small apartment with Heinz and Ernst, senior members of our group who spoke excellent German and seemed more interested in girls than forging a Jewish state. Living in such close proximity, we learned to tolerate each other's habits although it wasn't easy for me to overlook how messy they were. They, in turn, teased me about my obsessive routines and frequently protested, 'Stop hogging the bathroom, Fredy.'

One day when they were out and I was clearing up after them, I picked up Ernst's brown double-breasted jacket that had been casually discarded on the floor. I couldn't help but admire the quality. With leather buttons and a silk lining the colour of summer moss, it was good enough to have been stitched by my uncle. Slipping it on, I wandered into the bathroom and stood in front of the mirror turning this way and that, recalling the day Alfred fitted me for my first suit.

'Well, well, look at Fredy the Peacock!' Ernst catcalled from the open doorway.

Feeling a rush of blood to my head, I spun round to discover that he'd been watching me. Whipping off his jacket and throwing it at him, my face reddened further when I realised he was with his girlfriend Anna, someone who always left me tongue-tied.

'Who knew a peacock could be so shy in front of such a pretty hen?' Ernst joked, as I fled to my room. 'You should go after him, Anna,' he called, 'and show him a trick or two.'

Still a virgin, I'd never even kissed a girl and had no desire to try. My lack of interest puzzled my flatmates, who continually asked why I wasn't lusting after everything in a skirt. 'What's the matter with you? Is there something wrong with your equipment?'

'No!' I exclaimed, a little too quickly. Taking a breath, I added, 'I had my heart broken in the past, that's all.' It was only a little lie, I told myself and if it kept them off my case then it was worth the guilt.

Unconvinced, they teased me for keeping a toy dog on my pillow and then they asked their girlfriends what they thought of me. 'Oh, Fredy's just different,' was their reply.

'Different how?'

'You know, different . . . from *other* men,' the girls said as I listened from the next room, a pillow clutched to my chest.

Armed with that single response, Heinz and Ernst began to think things about me that I'd never even contemplated. One sweltering summer's afternoon when I was alone in the gym wearing only my shorts, my flatmates walked in unexpectedly. 'We know how much you think of your boys, Fredy,' Heinz began, twiddling his horn-rimmed glasses between his thumb and forefinger and staring at a space somewhere above my head. 'It's impressive how you remember all their names and they clearly adore you.'

Ernst nodded and added, 'Your devotion to them is unquestioned and you're getting excellent results in everything from fitness to practical skills.'

Lowering his gaze to make eye contact, Heinz cleared his throat and added, 'However, in light of how attached you've grown to some of the children . . .'

Ernst finished his sentence. '. . . and because of unwelcome gossip in some quarters, we – er, well, we fear that your position here may be in jeopardy.'

What felt like a shard of ice plummeted to my belly as I stood barefoot and half-naked a metre away from men I'd thought of as friends. Feeling utterly exposed as they built their indictment against me, my goosebumps rose like armour.

Heinz interjected. 'We've spoken to our superiors, Fredy and everyone agrees we need your cast-iron assurance that you'd never behave . . . inappropriately.'

The implication of what they were saying slammed into my solar plexus, robbing me of breath. Reaching behind me, I steadied myself against the parallel bars. How could they even think such a thing? Who could have spread this gossip? The children were my world and it made me sick to my stomach that anyone might think I'd harm them in any way.

My rage rising, I clenched my fists and stared at my accusers through narrowed eyes. Through gritted teeth, I said, 'You two know as well as I do that my behaviour with children has – and will always be – faultless. In light of your comments I will have to consider my position and will be seeking alternative accommodation. Now, get out.'

Their faces reddening, they fled from my fury and the matter was never raised again.

I don't know how I got through the next few weeks as I came to terms with what they'd suggested. Although I'd never been interested in girls, I'd not allowed myself to consider what that might mean. Was I really that different? My restless thoughts were interrupted by a childhood memory I'd long since pushed aside. Travelling home from the scouts with my brother one night in Aachen, an unusual-looking passenger had boarded our tram near the nightclub district and looked to be a little tipsy. He wore a velvet suit the colour of autumn plums paired with a jazzy orange cravat. Fascinated, I admired his courage until I noticed that he was wearing black eye-liner and staring back at me.

'Look away, Fredy,' Paul hissed under his breath. 'That man is not to be paid any attention. If he looks to be getting off at our stop, we'll travel to the next.'

Despite the warning, I was burning with curiosity and couldn't help but glance in the direction of the vision in plum. I noted the jaunty angle of his hat, the quality of his leather brogues and the silver tiger's head that topped his ebony walking cane. Long before our stop, he stood up to disembark. Before he stepped off the tram, though, he turned to me and – with a smile that wrinkled the powder around his lips – he blew me a kiss.

Not long after that encounter, I was sitting in my room planning an athletics meet with Carl, the boy with the birthmark who'd followed me to Frankfurt. Without any warning, he made a sudden lunge for me, grabbing my crotch with his hand as he thrust his tongue between my lips. In shock, I spat him out and pushed him away. 'What do you think you're doing, Carl? Get off me!'

After he vanished, the adrenalin pulsing through my body created a reaction in my pants that I had to clamp down on so hard it made me wince. Unbidden, a line from Leviticus 20:13 leapt into my head: *If a man lies with a man as one lies with a woman, both of them have committed an abomination; they shall surely be put to death.* My childhood rabbi had thundered those words across the synagogue until they stuck to the flypaper of my brain. The Hebrew word for abomination is *to'evah* and that's how I felt – an abomination of Nature because nothing seemed more unnatural to me than what I was feeling. Yet, no matter how much I tried, each time my mind flashed back to the moment Carl's lips touched mine, my body responded with the same physiological impulse.

After my flatmates' allegations, I found myself questioning everything I did and checking myself constantly in the presence of children. My flesh crawled at the thought that something as innocuous as a pat on the back or a hug of encouragement could be misconstrued.

Instead of supervising the boys in the showers as I'd always done to make sure they washed off the grime, I waited in the corridor until they came out fully clothed. I stopped giving massages to any injured during athletics and sent them to the nurse instead. On camping trips, after wishing them all '*Leila Tov*' last thing at night, I pitched my tent far from theirs and laced my door up tight.

'I want to be transferred,' I informed Heinz one morning. 'The organisation needs a physical education teacher in Dresden.'

He stared at me for a moment before nodding. 'Very well, Fredy,' he replied, adding, 'We'll be sorry to lose you.' Staring into my face, he added, 'May I ask why?'

Unable to tell him that I could no longer live and work alongside those who doubted me, I blustered something about wanting new challenges. His expression sorrowful, he looked as if he was going to say something but changed his mind.

Having moved five hundred kilometres to the Baroque capital of Saxony, I was put in charge of a much smaller group of teenage boys and girls, several of whom were awaiting their visas to the Holy Land. Longing to go with them and make a fresh start, I fell back into taking them on field trips and organising games to build up their mental and physical strength.

That was what I knew. That kept me going. As long as I could do my work then nothing else mattered, I told myself.

What I didn't factor in was the fluid nature of our organisation as people from one branch were frequently transferred to others. When boys I knew from Frankfurt arrived, unfounded rumours followed me. Summoned into the office of my supervisor, I stood facing him with a knot in the pit of my stomach as he told me, 'I don't believe for one minute that you pose a risk to children, Fredy, but it's my duty to make you aware of what's been said.'

I felt the pain of my continued persecution deeply. There were so many things I longed to say in retort, not least to question my superiors about why they'd never challenged some of the men in our group about their illicit liaisons with teenage girls. In my bruised emotional state, however, I offered the usual promises and brooded privately on the unfairness of their accusations. After confiding my innermost thoughts to a kind friend named Miroslav, I was shocked by his response.

'It's horrid, I know, Fredy, but I get why some people think that of you.'

'What?' I asked, dismayed. 'Why?'

'A lot of little things, I guess,' he replied, drawing on his cigarette as he shifted awkwardly in his chair. 'You hardly ever smoke. You don't drink and, forgive me for saying, you're a little vain. I've never met anyone as fit as you with better hair or whiter teeth, yet you've never had a girlfriend and you sleep with a childhood toy. Everything sets you apart.'

'But that's who I am, Miro!' I exclaimed. 'I can't pretend to be someone I'm not.'

My friend stared long and hard at me as he considered his response. Then he said, 'I understand, Fredy, but take some advice from a friend and get yourself a girlfriend.'

Mulling everything over later that night, a sudden realisation hit me. In emulating the style and conduct of my uncle Alfred, who was something of a dandy, I'd inadvertently revealed something that I hadn't yet accepted in myself. The truth was that I was more attracted to men than women and the idea of taking a girlfriend to hide my true feelings appalled me. Besides, it would hardly be fair to the girl as I'd be deceiving her and living a lie.

Broken once more by the fear that my innermost feelings might be a danger to my boys, I wasn't sure I'd be able to carry on teaching. It was Miroslav who convinced me otherwise.

'The children worship you, Fredy, and respond to you in a way none of us have ever seen. They don't care about your private life. They just trust you to encourage and support them and that's what matters. Let your results speak for themselves. No one can doubt you then.'

Bolstered, I resolved to continue my work while figuring out ways to be less conspicuous. I even went on a few dates with girls, behaving with the utmost courtesy and escorting them home. When a pretty teenager named Olga leaned in one night and said, 'You can kiss me if you like, Fredy,' I lifted her hand to my lips.

I also decided to become more militaristic and dignified in my bearing, modelling myself on a dashing soldier of the great Imperial Army from a time before I was born. Those brave officers stood ramrod straight in crisp blue uniforms with plumed helmets. In our broken Germany, they seemed to represent a glorious past.

I also decided that if I resumed my education and achieved all my qualifications as a teacher then people might respect me more. Getting qualified was an idea first sparked by a forty-year-old physical trainer who'd befriended me at the gym he ran. Admiring my dedication to my regime, Werner assisted me whenever I lifted heavier weights.

When he learned that I was a youth leader, he said, 'You need to become a fully trained athletics coach, Fredy, and learn the science behind fitness. It would help you enormously if you understood how muscles work and the ways in which psychology plays a part.' He added that the best sports science course in the country was the one he'd attended in Berlin. From the way he looked and the manner in which he carried himself, I had every reason to believe him.

'I'd never be accepted in a million years.' I gave a hollow laugh, knowing that as a Jewish minor without rights or qualifications I wouldn't stand a chance. 'Besides, going to Berlin right now would be tantamount to suicide.'

The way Werner looked at me made me realise that until that moment he hadn't fully appreciated that I was Jewish. Holding my breath, I feared how he might react.

'I can teach you the basics, if you like,' was all he said.

Exhaling, I smiled. 'Well, if you're sure?'

For the next few months I was his most devoted student, echoing his movements and reading his textbooks so diligently that *Herr* Steil wouldn't have believed it. Werner called me his '*kleiner Schützling*', or little protégé, and I was grateful to have a platonic friend in an Aryan. Werner paid no heed to popular propaganda that was fuelling the fires of hatred, as fierce as the flames in which the Nazis were burning Jewish books. All across Germany, citizens were ordered to prove their 'Aryan' ancestry. Organised groups carried out violent attacks on those seen as outsiders, some of whom were paraded on the streets with placards around their necks reading 'Jewish pig' or 'Race defiler'.

Hitler referred to us Jews as *untermenschen* – subhuman – but I doubt he had the vocabulary for a Jew who was also a frustrated homosexual.

*

Sitting in a café with Miroslav one morning in 1935, reading the daily newspapers, I felt a growing sense of dread. Scanning the reports with dismay, we read about another huge Nazi rally in a vast parade ground in Nuremberg attended by almost a million people. Behaving like a Roman emperor, Hitler introduced a swathe of anti-Jewish laws to 'protect German blood and honour'. The new rules stripped all rights from anyone perceived as 'non-German' or who opposed the regime.

'They're going to prohibit marriage or even sex between Jews and Gentiles, punishable with imprisonment and hard labour,' Miro read out loud, his face pale.

'It says here the same will apply to what they call "gypsies, negroes and their bastards",' I recited.

Swivelling his paper so I could read it, Miro pointed to a line that announced the banning of almost every youth organisation other than the paramilitary Hitler Youth and League of German Girls. 'What does this mean for us?' I asked him, feeling the colour drain from my face.

'It means it's over,' Miroslav replied, sliding back down in his seat with tears in his eyes.

I don't remember much about the rest of that day except that I found myself back in the gym that night slumped in a corner. When Werner came in to lock up, he discovered me in tears. 'Fredy, what's wrong?' he asked, hurrying over.

'My dream of becoming a teacher has been burned to ashes along with all those books,' I sobbed, waving the newspaper at him. 'Everything I've ever worked towards is gone. I don't know what I'm supposed to do now.'

'I do, Fredy,' he replied, holding out his hand to pull me to my feet. 'You're going to carry on improving your knowledge and techniques, because the things I'm teaching you will stand you in good stead your entire life.'

I took heart from his words until Hitler's *Reichstag* did something that made my blood freeze. In the Nazi bid to rid Germany of anyone 'impure' or weak, lists of suspected homosexuals were drawn up by the Gestapo in every major city. Some of the more subversive newspapers reported that almost all of the bars that men openly frequented for years – and which I'd never dared enter – had been raided and closed. There had been mass arrests. Men imprisoned on the flimsiest evidence were tortured or sent to camps as enemies of the Reich.

Afraid to step out onto the streets in case I, too, was apprehended, I was trapped in my room. Earlier that day I'd overheard a conversation outside that it was a crime even to have 'lustful intention', and that people were arrested for merely a glance. I could have been jailed for having a stranger on a tram blow me a kiss or even faced mandatory castration, which had now become a lawful punishment.

'These laws are an affront to civil liberty,' Werner declared, when he called by to see why I hadn't been to the gym. 'The Nazis think that because these people are a secret minority, no one else will dare to speak out, but they're wrong. Decent Germans won't stand for this.'

I wasn't the only one feeling the weight of oppression, according to the latest letter from my brother. *Our stepfather's mill has been seized and handed to an Aryan*, he wrote. *We've*

no income and have been ordered to list all savings and posses-
sions – right down to the silverware. In answer to a question
I'd asked him in my previous letter, he added, *Alfred has*
returned to Germany from America to be with his family. He's
determined to keep running his business for as long as he can.
Smiling, I gave a small cheer for my uncle.

Paul added that he, my mother and stepfather were seeking
permits to emigrate to South America. So much for standing
their ground. *We've added your name to our application,* he
wrote. *Please come home so that we can leave together.* Reading
his words triggered a pang of nostalgia for my brother, the
hills and forests of my youth and the friends I'd known there,
but I had no intention of joining them. If I was going anywhere
it was to the Promised Land.

Werner was the one who made up my mind for me. 'You
must get away, Fredy,' he told me late one night. 'I was wrong
and your family is right. It's too dangerous for you to stay in
Germany. You're not safe here. I can give you some money to
get you as far as the border where I have friends who'll help,
but you must leave now before it's too late.'

Fear clutched at my heart. 'All I know is here. This is where
I belong, with the children.'

My mentor took me firmly by the shoulders. 'Fredy, you've
been dreaming of a new life in a new land since long before
we met. You may not be able to get there immediately but
this is the first step. There are terrible things happening in this
country. Things you can't ignore anymore. You have to escape
while you can.'

'Where would I go?' I asked, my voice suddenly small. 'I
can't imagine France or Belgium welcoming a homeless
German after the war and I don't know any Polish or Dutch.
I can't go to Austria now it's been annexed by the Nazis.'

'What about Czechoslovakia?' Werner suggested. 'It used to be ruled by predominantly German speakers before it became a republic.'

'I suppose I do have an affiliation with the Czechs because of the Maccabis,' I reasoned. 'But Werner, the language! I don't have a natural ear, so how would I manage?'

'That will come in time,' he assured me. 'And remember: when you're teaching sport it's about movement and gestures, not words. Czechoslovakia is your best bet.'

I knew he was speaking the truth. If my work with children was to be taken from me then I'd have nowhere to live and even less protection. I wasn't alone. Thousands of other German Jews were abandoning their homeland and the streets were crowded with anxious refugees carrying suitcases, seeking transport out of the city.

The small room I'd been given by the Maccabis overlooked Dresden's main railway station and, hearing pitiful wailing one morning, I looked out to witness heartbreaking scenes of parents bidding farewell to their children. 'The British have organised a humanitarian scheme to get as many under the age of seventeen to safety,' Mordechai told me. 'It's a complicated process as each child has to be sponsored, have a visa and cover their costs, so it's only open to a few. We hope to find places for ten of our *Kinder* on the trains.'

I saw one distraught couple pressing the palms of their hands against the windows of a carriage as their two infants with cardboard labels hanging around their necks stared back at them in tearful bewilderment. 'We'll be joining you soon, my darlings,' the young mother cried, as she ran alongside the train when it started to move away. 'Be ever so brave and look after each other. We'll see you in England before you know it.' When she finally lost sight of her children in the departing clouds of steam, her mind shut down and she collapsed into her husband's arms.

Although there were times when I still felt like a boy, I was two years too old for the *Kindertransport*. With no other choices and time running out, in the winter of 1935 I packed Emil the dog, my whistle and my binoculars and set off for Prague.

8

March 1942, Terezín, Czechoslovakia

'RISE AND SHINE!' I CRIED, giving a short blow on my whistle before clapping my hands to wake the sleepy children. Every morning they were woken with my usual greeting and made to get out of their beds to strip-wash at basins of cold water. Others were led outside to the courtyard where they were lined up at a pump.

'Hurry now,' I called, as helpers handed out slivers of the horrid ghetto soap that never lathered. 'Tops off and be sure to clean all four corners – and all the funny, wobbly bits in between,' I instructed, making them laugh as I had the rest marching on the spot to keep warm. 'Remember, cheerful faces and happy hearts. No snivelling and no drinking from the tap, no matter how thirsty.' More often than not, the dribble of water from the pump ran out before the last in line could wash off any soap. Instead, they'd have to wipe themselves down with the only wet towel.

Once they'd finished washing, they made their beds and did some exercises before breakfast of bread, milk and fake tea or coffee. Daily orders were read out, giving them their chores, before they could peel off to secret lessons being held in the attics and basements of each barrack. 'You must be very careful,' I warned them before they set out. 'Schools aren't permitted here, so if the SS appear do exactly as your teachers tell you.' It was to the Council's credit that they chose to ignore the Nazi ban on education because, as Jakob put it, 'None of us are prepared to let the next generation fall even further behind with their schooling.'

People immediately offered their help. 'Materials will be a problem,' I pointed out. 'We'll need pens and any scraps of paper. And we need to find out of the way places for lessons that the guards don't know about.'

A former librarian suggested, 'We should collect up all the books and create a central lending library. Many volumes have been brought into the ghetto and they should be shared out.'

'I can help with that,' I volunteered. 'I'll send out the teenagers too young to work, who need a sense of purpose. They can gather them all up and start indexing them.' Having thought at first that people were foolish to carry something so impractical as a book, I now realised how important it was to provide nourishment for the mind.

Within weeks, thousands of volumes were amassed, stored in cupboards and empty rooms, even lining walls as extra insulation. A system was devised to send out mixed boxes to be exchanged for another at the end of the month. Each box could contain books from Dickens to Descartes, Wells to Wilde. I pulled out one well-thumbed book of poetry and exclaimed, 'These must have been read a thousand times.'

'And they'll be read a thousand times more,' Leo pointed out.

Armed with whatever tools might help them, everyone from Kindergarten supervisors to eminent professors held classes in literacy, arithmetic, the sciences, geography, art and history. They were paid for their services in bread, either by the Elders or by pupils desperate to learn. Even Zuzana paid her way in food, despite being constantly famished, as she couldn't bear to miss the Latin and Greek lessons of a professor from the University of Vienna.

'You're too skinny, Zuzi,' I scolded, giving her an extra portion of bread. 'Your health can't take all this learning.'

'I'm fine, thanks to those potatoes you brought me,' she replied, smiling.

The lessons did wonders for morale despite the enormous risks. For every class, a series of sentries had to be posted as lookouts. Each lookout was instructed to hiss a codeword or gave a low whistle if they spotted an approaching German or one of the unfriendlier gendarmes. 'If your teacher tells you to stop, you must busy yourself with singing, drawing, or playing until the danger has passed,' I warned the children almost daily. 'This isn't a game. Last week, a teacher and five students were caught mid-lesson because they forgot to post a sentry.'

'What happened to them, Fredy?' asked a girl named Magda.

'They were sent to the Small Fortress,' I replied and the children gasped. I didn't tell them the teacher was almost beaten to death for teaching political history. There were enough things to be frightened of in Terezín already.

After school, the children were permitted to play before having a free hour to visit parents and grandparents, if they had any. Then it was time for bed. 'Windows must be kept open at night, even in winter. It keeps fresh air flowing and deters bugs,' I instructed the oldest in each room. 'Make sure the blackout blinds are in place. Children may sleep in their clothes if it's cold but all bedding is to be shaken out and aired each morning.'

Draped from balconies and spilling out of windows, the colourful eiderdowns and bedrolls in every pattern painted a vibrant image of family life from a time before our monochrome existence. Several had been repurposed by seamstresses for those being transported; reducing the feathers so they could be rolled more tightly and carried on a deportee's back.

'The mattresses of bedwetters have to be scrubbed and put outside to dry,' I insisted. 'Set up a rota of people to wake the worst offenders in the night and escort them to the toilet.' Never letting up on my exacting hygiene standards, I carried out random inspections of everything from mess tins to fingernails. Suitcases and clothes had to be stowed away and floors cleaned. My inspections were the bane of the children's lives as it meant they had to get up extra early. A separate team of medical staff checked for the lice that carried typhus and for any small cuts or grazes that could become infected.

'You really are one of the worst torments of Terezín,' Zuzana complained to me one morning, her hair unruly as she struggled to comb it out. 'Everybody loves you like a father, except on the days when you try to catch us out. That's when they call you the *Zúchtmeister*.'

Studying her young face, I saw she wasn't yet mature enough to realise that being such a disciplinarian was saving them from dying of disease or drawing attention to themselves for transportation. Pushing away that thought, I started tickling her, saying, 'That's right, you dirty little urchin. Unless you obey *Zúchtmeister* Hirsch immediately, you'll be on bedwetting duty for a week.'

My vigilance didn't always work, however, and when I came across another empty bed or chair vacated by a child who'd died or been sent 'East', my spirits plummeted. After I'd lost three little girls from one family I'd been nurturing since they arrived, Jakob told me, 'You can't protect all of them forever, Fredy. We have so many diseases now – enteritis, tuberculosis, encephalitis and typhus – that are claiming lives daily. The

Germans have erected signs in every washroom featuring a skull and crossbones declaring *Achtung! Typhus! A Single Louse Means Death.*'

'What can we do about it, though? No matter how hard I try to keep the children clean, they are still plagued by bugs. Picking them off is an obsession. Almost every wall is speckled red with squashed bodies of critters.'

'I know and, now that winter is thawing, we'll be afflicted by even more bedbugs crawling out to feast on us every night, drawn by sweat. Scratching at the infernal bites is driving me – and Miriam – to distraction.'

'So what's the solution?'

Leo piped up. 'Total fumigation is the only answer to a bad infestation and the SS have supplied a new insecticide, Zyklon B, made of cyanide. The blue pellets apparently produce a lethal gas but can only be activated once a building is empty, which is almost impossible when we have nowhere else to put the occupants.'

'Is that the poison they used in the Hannover barracks?' I asked, dismayed.

'Yes, Fredy,' Leo replied, with a sigh. 'They didn't warn us that it was also lethal to humans, so when two old ladies went back to their room too soon they died a ghastly death. It still makes me shudder to think of it.'

Infestations were far easier to manage once we were allocated the first two *Kinderheims* Gonda and I had been campaigning for. In early March we relocated as many children aged between ten and seventeen as we could, taking them from overcrowded rooms to the dedicated buildings.

Grouped together by age and gender, each group had their own *zimmerälteste* or room leader, a young guardian who slept with them or close by. These were usually youth leaders

I'd previously worked with or those who'd excelled at managing children in the ghetto. Some were better than others but any found wanting were immediately dismissed. 'It's your job to supervise all your children,' I instructed. 'You must measure out every child's three-day portion of bread, including the extra we've negotiated for the youngest. Lying and stealing is forbidden and all property is to be shared.' Softening, I added, 'You must also offer a consoling word to those who are ill or wake crying in the night. Remember, we're not only their teachers but their surrogate parents, too.'

Hoping to instil pride in their new homes, I set a competition. 'I'll be handing out achievement badges for those who score highest in truthfulness, helpfulness and cleanliness. Everything must be spotless and I don't want to find a single blood-sucking creature.' The children groaned. 'And I'll be awarding points for the best hunters with the highest numbers of dead bugs. Prizes will include drawing paper, toys, food, crayons and ribbons.' The children cheered loudest at the mention of food, although toys and paper came a close second.

Trapped inside all day, they yearned for any kind of distraction. So when the Nazis agreed to permit cultural events and what they called our *Kameradschaftabenden* or 'companionship evenings' (that had been going on secretly for some time), the social life of Terezín exploded. Sensing the hunger for something new, I helped set up a Recreation department that encouraged musicians, actors, writers and directors to stage all kinds of performances. There was choral singing, lectures, jazz, the reading of satirical poems and – most popular of all – comedy, which mocked everything from the Nazis to the shortage of food. All of it a bittersweet reminder of the richness of our lives before Hitler.

Starved of mental stimulation, people lined up for the tickets that we distributed as fairly as we could. Those lucky enough to get one crowded into storage cellars, attics, stables and meeting rooms, sitting on the floor or on benches as the players took to temporary stages. Without any sheet music everything was played by heart or learned by rote, with instruments smuggled in piece by piece. Long after the SS had left the ghetto for the night, enrapt audiences listened in bliss as music restored their dignity. Every eye in the room glinted with memories until the final note.

'I'd like to let the children see some shows and stage their own,' I told Leo. 'It would be a huge boost.'

'I don't see why not. The SS are so afraid of disease that they rarely come into the ghetto and hardly ever at night,' Leo reminded me. 'The Elders have made sure the overnight gendarmes are friendly ones who want to watch the shows themselves.'

Reassured, I came up with a children's ballet for them to perform, about the resilience of the Jews. The children were so excited to take part that they rehearsed their dance moves and lines over and over long after lights out.

On the first night, it was such a thrill to stand in the wings, hissing stage directions as I watched them acting out my words, 'Keep in time. Boys left, girls right. Perfect! Keep moving . . . circles now, that's right . . . and smile.' Zuzana and another favourite of mine, a six-year-old-girl named Franka, were radiant as two of those dressed in orange paper who danced around like little flames.

Looking out into the crowd to gauge the reaction, I was stunned to see tears streaming down several faces. The play ended with a teenage boy, tall for his years, delivering the prescient line, '*A people can be put in chains, its spirit never.*'

*

Stepping out into the courtyard after I'd finished my inspections the morning after our triumphant first night, I was surprised to find it bathed in sunshine: the first true sign of spring. Stopping to enjoy the unexpected heat, I closed my eyes and tilted my face to the sun.

A Rilke poem that the man I'd once loved taught me appeared from nowhere on my lips and I found myself murmuring, '*The Earth is like a child that has learned to recite a poem.*' Opening my eyes, I shivered as a huge bird of prey swept silently overhead, casting a momentary shadow across my face.

I heard voices as others shuffled out of darkened corners to turn their faces skywards too. Peeling off outer clothing and swaying together, they reminded me of the sunflowers I'd grown from seed in the school vegetable garden.

Everyone in the ghetto had developed an unnaturally grey pallor after being penned up inside for three months. Even though I had much more freedom than most, I too noticed how papery my skin had become.

'It's malnutrition,' Dr Heller told me. 'We're inundated with cases of scurvy and leg ulcers, which only add to the misery of insect bites. Hair is thinning and turning grey and teeth are falling out. People need protein, vitamins and exercise – especially the youngest with undeveloped bones. Something has to be done.'

Deciding to address the Council of Elders, I asked Jakob to allow me to attend their next meeting. 'Prisoners must be allowed outside now, especially the sick and the smallest children,' I told them. 'It is vital for their physical well-being. I have enough helpers to supervise the children in groups on the ramparts for a few hours' fresh air and exercise.'

Jakob sighed. 'As you well know, Fredy, we've been pressing for this for a while but the SS keep turning us down. They don't want any risk of public disorder or cross-contamination.'

'Then let me try. They never stop warning us about the high mortality rate and object to how much wood we're using for coffins but I'm certain deaths would be reduced if they'd only let people get some sun on their bones.'

After pressing home my point, Jakob agreed to arrange a meeting the following day with one of the commandants who dealt with issues too trivial to trouble his superiors. It was the first time I'd been inside the German High Command and I could feel my skin prickling as he and I stepped over the threshold.

The *Untersturmführer* named Scholz wasn't much older than me but he'd grown so stout – no doubt on all the fine food and wine the SS enjoyed daily – that his chin spilled over his tunic collar. As I did with any officer, I strode into his office like an equal and, clicking my heels together, saluted him crisply. I gave my number but then extended my hand with a smile, saying, 'My name is Fredy Hirsch.'

Taken aback, he put out his hand but, realising his mistake, withdrew it quickly.

'Do you have children, *Herr Untersturmführer*?' I asked, as he stood wiping his fingers on a handkerchief to cleanse them of me.

'Er, no,' he replied with a vexed expression as he resumed his seat. Softening, he added, 'I do have two young nephews though.' I tried to banish a mental image of him bouncing the boys on his knees.

'Then I'm sure you can imagine how frustrated they – and their parents – would be if they'd been locked inside for months all winter and couldn't play outside.'

Arching his fingers into a triangle, he gestured for Jakob and me to take a seat. Staring me out, he replied, 'I imagine it would cause some distress.'

'You know what I'm going to ask,' I said, returning his stare. He shrugged. 'The answer remains the same. We can't have Jewish brats running all over the place like rodents. It would be the end of discipline and order.'

'What if they were marched out in small groups like little soldiers? And what if I trained them to perform military drills and field exercises to increase their understanding of German orders? I could build up the physical strength they'll need to be of use to the Reich later on.'

His eyes gleamed. 'Well, I suppose . . .'

'Fresh air and exercise would also eradicate the risk of contagious diseases and help protect the entire ghetto. The mortality rate would undoubtedly come down and the children's absence from the buildings for a few hours would give us the opportunity to delouse their quarters.'

As I waited for Scholz's response, I caught Jakob looking at me in open astonishment. Realising that he hadn't yet said a word, he pulled himself up in his chair to match my posture and said, 'Fredy's right, *Herr Untersturmführer.* We know that the death rate is of concern to Berlin and I can only endorse everything that has been said and assure you that the children will be closely supervised at all times.'

Scholz sent us away but eventually sent word that the children could venture out once a week – under strict supervision. He added that if the scheme proved effective in reducing the death rate then others could venture outside on Sundays too, in small groups and only for an hour at a time. 'If there are any attempted escapes or abuses of this privilege, it will be immediately rescinded,' Scholz warned.

The first day I was allowed to take them, I hurried to the rooms housing the youngest children and escorted thirty of them to a patch of grass close to the eastern ramparts. In case we were being watched, I made sure that they held hands and marched uniformly in pairs until we were out of sight. When we reached the spot, I was delighted to see rays of sunshine slanting down through the clouds. I don't think the grass had ever looked greener or the sky bluer in that moment. Vibrant purple leaves adorned a spindly plum tree that I'd never noticed before. The colour almost hurt my eyes.

I'd expected the children to be so euphoric at being anywhere but in their rooms or a colourless courtyard that they'd run headlong into the grass. To my surprise, they faltered. Huddled together in silence, they gazed in wonder at bees bouncing between the blades of grass looking for pollen. Other children stared up at the clouds making feathery patterns in the sky. Two boys climbed to the top of the rampart to see the distant mountains, still with a line of snow above a green smudge of forest. A few wandered across to a large, sweet chestnut tree in a far corner and placed starfish hands on its trunk, as if trying to connect to something.

Suddenly, I felt a hand slip into mine and grip tightly. It was Franka, her face wet. Bending to lift her into my arms, I asked, 'Oh now, why are you crying, *Liebling*?'

'It's . . . it's very p-pretty,' she replied, stuttering through her tears. 'It's l-like Mummy's garden.' Her heart-shaped face was twisted by longing for a mother who'd died in childbirth.

Softly, I told her, 'Well, that's a happy memory, isn't it? And one day soon, *mein kind*, you'll be back in that garden with your baby brother and can tell him all about your mummy.'

'I will?' she asked, wiping her nose on the back of her hand with a little sigh of hope before another cloud eclipsed her thoughts. 'But will it be safe, Fredy? Or will the nasty man next door bring the soldiers again?' Putting her down, wishing I could wipe her memory of what must have been a cruel betrayal, I gently nudged her towards those brave enough to venture further into the grass.

I was assisted that morning by two helpers I'd appointed, Andrej and Arno. Fine role models, they were scout leaders in their early twenties with plenty of experience between them. The Hebrew word for such assistants was *madrichim*, affectionately shortened to '*madri*', and those and others like them were invaluable to me. Together we stood and watched the children's shyness melt away as they began to play, even though they remained subdued.

A few of the older girls sat in a circle making daisy chains while Franka stood watching nearby, her thumb wedged firmly in her mouth. 'I thought they'd go crazy,' said Arno.

'They don't seem very happy at all,' Andrej remarked.

Watching twin boys falling back onto the rampart slopes with peals of laughter, I sighed. 'After all they've been through, this must be overwhelming. For some, it may be the first time they've been allowed to play freely.'

Andrej replied, 'When we play word games it's surprising what they don't understand – words like cow, horse or tractor. Some don't even know what we mean by cat because pets were euthanised by the Nazis before they were old enough to remember.'

'It's true,' Arno concurred. 'The words they're most familiar with are soldier, train, gun and a few German commands. They also have no concept of what money means because they've never experienced it. It's soul-destroying.'

Shaking my head, I said, 'Then let's teach them happy words. Pick a group and go through the names of everything here today – flowers, bees, birds – anything not war-related.'

The boys did as I asked while I established my own little cluster, picking a daisy and passing it around, saying the word *Gänseblümchen* repeatedly in German. Realising I didn't know its Czech name, I had to ask the boys who only laughed at my pronunciation. '*Sedmikráska*' was such a mouthful while the German name felt just right for the little *blümchen* that was as white as a goose or *gänse*.

Back in class afterwards, I encouraged the children to draw what they'd seen and write about how it felt. Their gratitude at being freed from imprisonment was heart-warming and they showered me with pictures, poems, even daisy chains. One day I returned to my room to find a small glass jar filled with wildflowers. Staring at the posy, my heart and eyes brimmed with memories of the flowers of my hikes in Aachen when my father was still alive.

Having been encouraged to express their feelings, a few of the older boys took it further, gathering their thoughts, poems and drawings into magazines they created, written in their best handwriting. Each new edition was handed around and read aloud on Friday nights, an event anticipated by all, especially those who'd never seen such a thing before.

I featured frequently in jokes about what a taskmaster I was. Aside from *Zúchtmeister*, I was also known as the 'Tsar' and 'Baron Münchausen'. The boys didn't stop there but made up songs mocking my poor grasp of Czech. There was even a cartoon of me marching children around a courtyard proclaiming, 'Clean minds, healthy bodies!' Not that I minded.

Anything that drummed my message home and made them laugh was fine by me.

My teenage reporters weren't the only ones secretly chronicling life in the ghetto and in my search for places for the children, I came across many a prisoner in dark corners, lifting floorboards, dropping packages into cisterns, digging holes or scraping out bricks.

If ever I discovered a hidden diary or letter, I'd put it back in the hope that someone else might discover it one day. I even hid a few of my own scraps that illustrated the absurdities of Terezín, including a timetable for those who policed toilets to make sure that they didn't overflow and that nobody stole the lightbulb. I also discovered that Gonda was writing a secret diary. I found it open on his desk, his neat handwriting in Hebrew and Czech.

'So what are you saying in that about me?' I asked him with a smile one day as I watched him silently writing.

Looking up, he snapped the diary shut and shoved it in a drawer. 'Nothing,' he replied, with such a guilty expression that I feared it must have been something bad. What if he knew about me? Was that the reason he and I had never seen eye to eye? Our most recent clash was when I'd argued that it was our moral duty to warn those coming to Terezín of the hardships they'd face. 'It's not fair to let people come here thinking they'll be sitting on sunny balconies waiting for a slow boat to Haifa. The chances are that half will die and the rest will be transported somewhere terrible. They deserve the chance to decide for themselves if they want to resist, escape or hide. Or at least pack what they'll really need.'

Gonda tutted. 'That could have devastating consequences for the entire community, especially if the SS found out the information came from here,' he argued. When others agreed with him, my temper got the better of me.

Jakob the peacemaker was the only one who could calm me down, telling me, 'Your desire to ease discomfort and save lives is to be admired, Fredy, but there are complex consequences that need to be considered. Not least what might happen if there was a mass rebellion once this information became known. Think what that might mean for the very children you hope to save.'

Despite my frustration, I trusted Jakob and had little choice but to back down. My suggestion was rejected and, once a dedicated rail spur was built into the ghetto that spring, trainloads of the tragically unaware were delivered even more efficiently to what my teenagers referred to as 'Hell's waiting room'.

When Jakob advised me to find ways to work more amicably with Gonda, I decided to forgive and forget. If Gonda believed his legacy would be his diary then so be it, even if he wrote bitter things in it about me. My legacy, I decided, would be the children for whom I cared so deeply.

From the moment I called out, 'Rise and shine!' I spent every day trying to teach them decency, honesty and courage. Whatever happened to me, I hoped they'd go on to lead full and happy lives armed with those qualities. That wasn't something to be hidden away in a drawer, behind a wall or under a floorboard but carried in the hearts of each and every one of them, for all time. This was my most fervent prayer.

9

October 1935, Germany to Czechoslovakia

IT BROKE MY HEART that I couldn't say goodbye to my Dresden children, such was the secrecy and urgency of my escape to Prague. My fears for those I was leaving behind robbed me of my sleep. I only wish I could have taken them with me – the Pied Piper leading them to a safe place where they'd never be threatened again.

Helpless, I penned them an open letter which Werner promised to deliver a week after I'd fled. It began: *My dearest ones. It was my privilege to know you all and to help prepare you for whatever lies ahead. Never forget how strong you are, in mind, spirit and body. Remember all that you have learned about solidarity, morality and fairness on the sports field and in life. With heartfelt good wishes, Fredy.*

Werner seemed as upset to see me go as I was to leave and pulled me into a bear hug at the station. 'Go well, my friend,' he said, forcing a smile. 'I will miss you.'

'I can't thank you enough,' I told him with feeling.

'And I want to thank you, Fredy, for all that you've taught me,' he replied, eyes glistening.

A laugh burst from my lips. 'What can I have taught you?'

Gripping me by the shoulders, he said, 'To hold on to my dreams, Fredy. You're just a kid without any support, yet you've stayed true to yourself and your *Kinder*. I so admire you for that.'

Afraid that my emotions might get the better of me, I mumbled thanks, picked up my rucksack and boarded the train.

Trading on my wits and with the help of Werner's friends along the way, I begged and borrowed food and shelter on my five hundred kilometre journey to Czechoslovakia. I covered the first seventy or so without incident but then secret police boarded at Erfurt and started patrolling the carriages.

'*ID papiry!*' a Gestapo officer barked as he slid open the door to the carriage I was sharing with three other men. In his trench coat and hat, he reminded me of a private investigator I'd seen in an American detective movie. My heart thumping, I showed him my papers. Seeing that I only had a tatty rucksack, he tossed them back and turned to the man sitting next to me, who'd paled visibly.

'*Was ist in deinem Koffer?*' he barked and I watched the man's hand trembling as he clicked open his suitcase to reveal neatly folded clothes. Rummaging through them roughly, the policeman's eyes lit up as he pulled out a small gilt carriage clock.

'It belongs to my grandmother,' the man said, his voice feeble. 'I'm taking it to her.'

'Not anymore,' the officer declared, smacking the man hard across the head. My fellow passenger fell against me before making his biggest mistake. Jumping up, he tried to grab the clock but the Gestapo officer drew his gun and pistol-whipped him with such brutality that the rest of us cowered in our seats. Only when the poor man's hair was matted with blood and he'd dropped to his knees with a groan did the beating stop. Pulling out a handkerchief and wiping flecks of blood from his own cheek, his assailant left with his prize.

Getting off at the next stop, still shaken, I decided to take the back roads to the border on foot. Wherever I bedded down for the night, even in a barn or a forest clearing, I made sure to strip-wash every morning with whatever water source I could find. I was determined not to look like the homeless refugee I'd become. Lying awake that first night, staring up at the stars as an owl hooted mournfully, my doubts began to crowd in. *You were a fool not to get out with your family. You could be living in a safe and distant land. Will you ever see your brother again?* As my vision began to blur, I curled up into a ball on the mossy floor and pressed my eyes shut against the flood.

Most of the walking was easy enough across flat ground but when I came to the foothills of the sandstone Elbe mountains the going was a lot tougher. Not that I minded being out in the open. It was good to be back in the wild and there were times when I considered hiding out there until the world came to its senses. Then I remembered the winters.

Reaching the isolated Czech border-crossing Werner had directed me to, I used my binoculars to check and noted that it was unmanned after dark. Waiting in the woods until night-fall, I crossed unchallenged, surprised that I didn't feel the elation I'd expected at being free. On the contrary, I felt as if I'd stepped over more than just a demarcation line and had somehow betrayed my country.

Ten kilometres south, tired, hungry and despondent with no food and one of my shoes falling apart, I stumbled into a Catholic church on the edge of a village and collapsed onto a pew. When a hand shook me awake a few hours later, I jumped up ready to flee only to see a moon-faced priest offering me coffee and a slice of seed cake. '*Tady jsi v bezpečí*,' he said repeatedly, before adding something else in Czech. When he realised I didn't understand, he gestured for me to sit and eat. Pressing my hand to my chest in thanks, I gobbled up the cake so quickly that he fetched me some more.

For the next two days and nights he let me stay under his sacred roof to regain my strength. A stranger in a strange country with the strangest of languages, I continued to doubt whether I'd made the right decision. Drawing on my memories of what else I'd written to the Dresden boys in my farewell letter, I recalled telling them, *No matter how bad things might become, you are Germans who happen to be Jews and you have rights like any other. Keep your dignity. Stand tall. Don't cower in the face of the enemy. Protect the weak. Do what you know to be right. Look bravely forward and start each new day with a song in your heart.*

'Bravely forward, Fredy,' I told myself, 'with a song in your heart.'

*

The morning I left for Prague, the priest handed me a black leather jacket, some boots to replace my worn-out shoes and folded a slip of paper and a five *koruna* note into my hand. An elderly nun who spoke German interpreted for him. 'This is the address of a church in the city,' she said. 'Find it and tell them Father Marek sent you. They'll look after you until you find your people.'

'Thank you, Sister. Thank you, Father,' I replied, taking the priest's hand in both of mine as my eyes welled with gratitude.

Prague was huge and its layout bewildering to a foreigner. Despite my hopes that German would be widely spoken, it wasn't and I couldn't make sense of the street signs or understand what people were saying. Luckily for me, Father Marek's directions were clear and I found the church in a cobbled side street in the Old Town.

Its priests were as generous as he'd been, welcoming me in without asking where I'd come from or what my religion was. I can't have been the first refugee sent their way. 'Děkuji' was the first meaningful word I learned in Czech and I said it over and over. Thank you. Thank you.

For my first few nights in the city, I slept on a pile of blankets on the tiled church floor that was so cold it took my stiff limbs thirty minutes to loosen each morning. Once the clergy realised I was trustworthy, they moved me to a day bed in a small back room. My first morning there I woke before the day had dawned and couldn't get back to sleep for worrying. Had I been right to abandon children like Miloš who'd latched onto me as a father figure? The only child of a German-Czech couple, how would 'Sparrow' fare in a world he'd never understand? And what about my athletes, those lithe teenagers who'd taken my Olympian dream and made it their own? I only hoped they were keeping up with their training.

Restless, I paced my room, playing my fingers across a carved oak coffer and feeling the weight of a silver candlestick. Lifting the lid on a slender wooden box, I inhaled the aroma of beeswax that took me back to Aachen and our neighbour who kept bees in wicker skeps. I turned the key to a large wardrobe and opened the door. Hanging inside were the exquisitely made vestments of Catholic tradition. Knowing I'd be undisturbed for at least another hour, I slipped off my nightshirt and pulled on one of the sumptuous robes. I could feel the heft of its gilded thread and the silkiness of the satin lining against my skin. I marvelled at embroidery Uncle Alfred would have approved of. Where was he now? Had he been able to get his family back to America or was he still at home on the Rhine? I prayed he was safe.

Opening the wardrobe door wider, I gasped at my own reflection in a full-length mirror. I hadn't seen myself for so long that I was taken aback by how thin I'd become and the grey that flecked my hair. Pressing my palms together, I mouthed 'Guten Morgen, Father Fredy.' Within seconds, I found myself doubled up with laughter, my first belly-laugh in years. 'What on earth would Paul say?' I asked out loud, tears streaming down my cheeks. It was only when I heard the church bell and caught a whiff of incense that I pulled myself together. Putting everything back exactly as it was, I locked the door on my fantasy.

*

'What did you teach back home?' The question I'd been expecting still took me by surprise, as no matter how much I'd prepared myself to lie it still felt wrong.

'Sport and sports science but also music, poetry and Zionism. I also play the flute.'

'Excellent. And how's your Czech?'

'Non-existent, I'm afraid, but I have some Hebrew.'

'Very well, I'm sure we can find you a position.' With the help of my hosts, I'd contacted a local branch of the Maccabis and was introduced to Franz, a German-Czech who'd fled from Hamburg and took me under his wing. My plan was to bluff my way into a teaching position, claiming I'd lost my certificates in my haste to escape. Thanks to Werner's tutoring, I pulled it off and settled into an airless dormitory with five other young men.

'You'll be teaching gymnastics to students who'll come in rotation from local schools,' Franz explained. 'They're young so language isn't as important at this stage.' Handing me a recorder, he wished me luck. Happier than I'd been in a while, I threw myself into my work. Gymnastics was my natural home and the children responded well but when it came to trying to teach them Jewish culture or poetry, I was stumped.

'I'd be better with German refugees,' I told Franz one day.

'But the children love you, Fredy. Is it the language?'

'That's part of it but I'd also prefer to work with children still traumatised after their perilous journeys. They'll need extra reassurance.' Once my request was granted and I began with a new group of children, one seven-year-old boy named Frank caught my eye as he was always on the periphery, especially during games in the park. Finding him alone under a tree one afternoon, I asked what was wrong.

'I can't do any of these stupid games,' he replied, his bottom lip wobbling.

'Yes, you can. It's not as hard as you think.'

Glaring at me, he snapped, 'Maybe not for someone who looks like a Roman god.'

'Now, now. You don't know how lucky you are.'

He looked up with a sniff. 'I am?'

'Of course. You have what's known as a low centre of gravity and you are strong. I'm going to teach you to hurl a heavy metal ball as far as you can. It's called shot putting and you're going to be brilliant at it.' I was right. Frank not only embraced the shot put but excelled at it. Games was no longer something to be dreaded and the better he was at his chosen sport, the more confident he became.

After that, I was invited to move into one of the larger apartments reserved for teachers and instructed to apply for a temporary residence permit. 'What would happen if I didn't?'

I asked Franz, nervous at the idea of alerting the authorities to my presence.

'They might deport you,' he warned. 'It's not worth the risk.' I wasn't so sure but Franz persuaded me to register as a political refugee and in November 1935 I was granted a temporary permit 'subject to renewal'. The ambiguous wording bothered me but I resolved to prove myself such an invaluable member of society that they'd let me stay.

Living communally, the fact that I was single and turned down romantic approaches by young women raised eyebrows again. Worried that people might start talking, I dated a couple of girls but never took it further. 'Why don't you like me, Fredy?' one nineteen-year-old sobbed when I said I couldn't take her to a dance. 'Is it because I wear a brace on my teeth?'

'Not at all, dear Berta,' I replied, patting her hand. 'I'm just too busy.' I never meant to hurt her or any of them but I couldn't stomach lying either. When I gave up dating altogether, I was dubbed 'Fredy the Heartbreaker'.

Not long afterwards a group of Maccabis from Germany arrived in Prague, reigniting old gossip. Franz saw how uncomfortable I was in their company and came to my rescue, asking, 'How would you like to help organise this year's winter games in the Tatra Mountains, Fredy? You'd be based in Brno.'

'Oh, I'd love that,' I replied. Not only did I want to get away but I'd heard Brno had a reputation as a modern, forward-thinking city. Packing my belongings, I raced around taking my leave before boarding a train for the two-hundred-kilometre journey east.

Forgetting to eat before I left, I arrived tired and hungry. With a similarly bewildering layout of streets as Prague, though, I was soon wandering around in a daze as I searched for the Maccabi branch Franz had recommended me to.

'Please, I look for Jo-sef-ska *Strasse*,' I asked in a cobbled mix of Czech and German, only to realise that fewer than I expected spoke my language. Weak from hunger, I ended up outside the vast, white-painted Brothers of Charity Hospital. After slaking my thirst at a water fountain, I sank back onto a low wall, closed my eyes and let my chin drop to my chest. With dusk looming and my belly groaning with hunger, I had no idea where I'd sleep.

'*Mohu ti pomoct bratre?*' The voice was as gentle as the hand that rested on my shoulder.

'*Sprechen Sie Deutsch?*' I asked in hope, looking up at the silhouette of a man.

'*Ja*,' he replied, sitting next to me without removing his hand. 'How can I help you, brother?' And with that simple question, I was saved. His name was Jan, known as 'Jenda', and he had the broad shoulders and taut physique of an athlete. Having just finished an eight-hour shift in the hospital where he was a medical student, he was probably as tired as I was but still walked me to Josefská. Once there, he made sure someone understood me. 'Take care of this young *poutnik*,' he told them with a smile before leaving.

'What's a *poutnik*?' I asked.

'A wanderer or – how do you say in German – or a stray. Like a cat,' he replied, laughing before walking away with a 'Meow!' I felt a small pang as I watched him go.

The Maccabis were expecting me, as promised, and a counsellor named Michal told me, 'Your reputation goes before you, Fredy Hirsch.' Gulping, I felt to have swallowed a stone but I needn't have worried. Franz had been true to his word and they'd only heard good things.

With his endorsement, I registered my arrival in the city as a political refugee but my temporary residency permit was denied until I could provide more information. 'What does that mean?' I asked with a rising sense of panic.

'You'll have to be interviewed as to your intentions and means,' Michal explained. 'The authorities are just trying to keep on top of the deluge of refugees.' Relieved, I threw myself into my mission and took on a large group of teenage boys and girls, training them for the Maccabiah Games. 'These Games were first held in Tel Aviv,' Michal explained. 'But the British cancelled this year's event, fearing a mass influx. So we're organising our own version before the Summer Olympics in Berlin, from which all Jews are banned.'

'So much for my childhood desire to become an Olympian,' I joked, secretly wondering if I'd ever have stood a chance if Hitler hadn't existed. The Maccabiah Games were a triumph and I'd rarely been prouder to be Jewish. Held in a pretty town surrounded by a chain of mountains, they were attended by almost two thousand athletes from seven different countries. My group won medals for cross-country skiing and gymnastics and I received a personal commendation for my 'inspirational leadership and outstanding team spirit'. International news organisations attended the event and images appeared in newspapers and newsreels around the world. 'All those opposed to Hitler are keen to show Jews fighting back,' one especially persistent photographer told me, as he took dozens of pictures. He even asked me to mimic the pose of the famous Greek statue Discobolus, the Discus Thrower, a marble masterpiece Hitler was reportedly obsessed with. Laughing out loud as I posed as what the Führer referred to as 'the perfect depiction of an Aryan', I couldn't help but imagine my mother and stepfather in a cinema somewhere spotting me on a newsreel.

*

'Could that be my *poutnik*?' The voice from behind caught me unawares as I was supervising a large group of children one glorious afternoon in one of Brno's parks. Spinning round, my heart stuttered when I saw Jenda with a bicycle, a broad grin across his face. Blowing my whistle to signal that the children could fall out, I told them, 'Let's take a short break before drill exercises.' Then I ran across to shake him by the hand.

'The stray cat has picked up more strays, I see,' he said, looking beyond me at the images of vitality and youth.

'Not strays but kittens ready to leave the litter and find their place in the sun.'

He tilted his head. 'So, you're a Zionist, too?'

I laughed. 'You mean as well as being Jewish and German?'

'No, stupid,' he said, grinning. 'I mean as well as me.'

The penny dropped. 'You're Jewish?'

'Of course.'

Feeling like a fool, I stammered, 'I-I didn't know.'

Jenda looked bemused. 'We have more in common than that, Fredy.' His words sent a tingle down my spine.

Clearing my throat, I replied, 'We do?' I couldn't take my eyes off his mouth, so I turned away to watch the children stretching. That's when I felt Jenda's hand on my arm. Facing him, I managed a nervous smile.

'May I buy you a beer later?' he said, his eyes luminous.

'Yes. If you like.'

'Actually, I have a better idea. Come to my apartment. I'll give you the address.' I watched as he scribbled something onto a piece of paper and handed it to me, his fingers lingering a second too long on mine.

'See you later, *poutnik*. I'll look forward to it.'

*

Everything happened so fast after that. In what felt like a parallel universe to my own, Jenda and I became a couple and it felt to me as if we had been kissed by the stars. I'd never really known true happiness until I met that man.

What surprised me most was how natural being with him felt, as if he was what I'd been waiting for my whole life. It was Jenda who finally helped me accept who I really was. He gave me the confidence – and the courage – to start again and once I was by his side I realised how lonely I'd been. Four years older than me with mousy hair and an aquiline nose, he had a ready smile and an easy way about him that I envied. He was very close to his family and we divided our time between their beautiful suburban home and his friend's apartment.

While I'd left school with poor grades and an even poorer grasp of languages, Jenda had been a star pupil with an encyclopaedic brain. 'I can read something once and recall it almost verbatim,' he told me. 'I'm lucky that way.' His parents and his sister Margarete, known as Grete, had the same mental agility and spoke several languages, making me feel like the school dunce. Luckily for me, they possessed an extensive library so I took it upon myself to fill in the gaps in my education.

Sitting in an easy chair across the parlour from Jenda, both of us reading in silence, gave me some of my most contented moments. 'Try this one next if you haven't already read it,' he suggested one day, handing me a Thomas Mann novel. 'It's about the decline of the German bourgeoisie over four generations.'

'Didn't Mann write *Death in Venice?*' I asked, recalling the impulses the novella had stirred in me as a teenager. The story tells of a widower who falls in love with a teenage boy on holiday in Venice yet despises his own feelings. He becomes so obsessed that he ignores warnings of a cholera epidemic and dies without having spoken a single word to the object of his desires.

'Yes, he did,' Jenda replied, giving me an inscrutable smile. 'Did you find it erotic?'

'You know I don't like to talk about those things,' I replied, lowering my head into my book. Still new to his world, I found it impossible to discuss my intimate feelings as my head wrestled with my heart. There was a part of me that feared being denounced, imprisoned or deported.

Hearing a chuckle, I sensed him moving about and suddenly he was standing behind me with both hands on my shoulders, kissing the crown of my head. Inhaling the unique scent of his sandalwood soap, I closed my eyes. 'Poor little *poutnik*,' he said, messing up my hair in a way he knew I hated. 'You'll get used to this soon.'

I couldn't tell him that getting used to us was what I was afraid of. I'd been on the run for years and not just from the Nazis. I feared I could fall for Jenda but wasn't certain that I even deserved love. And how would I cope if he abandoned me like everyone else? I was also unaccustomed to how fearless he was. Although he stopped short of holding my hand in public, he wouldn't think twice about draping an arm around my shoulders or leaning in to whisper something in my ear. My eyes darting at all angles, I'd shrug him off or push him away which he treated as if it were a game.

'Brno isn't Aachen, Fredy,' he told me as we sat in a darkened cinema, his hand on my thigh. 'You're living in a liberal society now. You won't be arrested, castrated or sent to a camp, as some in Germany are. People here don't care what others get up to. They just get on with their lives.'

'It'll take me time to adjust,' I whispered. 'And I have to think of the children. My work can't be jeopardised by rumours, as it almost has been in the past.'

He smiled and squeezed my leg. 'It's all right. Just know that – oh, how do you say it? – *Snesl bych ti modré z nebe.*' When I cocked my head quizzically, he added, 'I would bring you the blue from the sky, my sweet.' How could I not care deeply for this free spirit who was helping me create a new skin? But if this was what happiness tasted like then why was there still a void in my heart?

*

'Who allows them to publish this rubbish?' I exclaimed one morning, hurling Brno's German-speaking newspaper to the floor. Glaring at the caricatures of malicious-looking Jews with hooked noses on posters appearing across the Reich, I asked, 'And why doesn't the rest of the world do something?'

The Nazi propaganda machine had ramped up and was now comparing Jews to spiders, snakes and contagious rats running amok, consuming everything and spreading disease. Hitler positioned himself as Saviour, ridding the country of impurities. According to the latest reports, thousands of so-called 'undesirables' had been rounded up and sent to what they called '*Konzentrationslager*', because of the numbers concentrated there.

The irony wasn't lost on me that it was the Nazi's obsession with purity that had pushed me into the arms of the man I called *Sechs Käse* or Six Cheeses, because he stood as high as six wheels of cheese. Jenda thought the nickname hilarious, telling me, 'Poor Fredy, you grew up far too close to the Dutch border.' His easy-going manner was infectious, and I tried not to let myself be overwhelmed by my concerns, but I also found his lack of empathy difficult to understand. When pressed, he'd remind me, 'I grew up in an assimilated society and have never experienced any anti-Semitism or homophobia. I just don't understand it.'

Instead, he preferred to focus on his medical studies and fun with friends, accusing me of overreacting whenever I warned that Hitler was a serious threat to the wider world. 'You worry too much,' he'd tell me, pulling me into his arms. 'How many times have I told you that you're safe here?' Throwing another quote at me from his favourite poet, he added, 'Rilke was right, Fredy. We need to drink deep of Life's "mystic shining cup" to defy Death standing before us, our fate in his hands.' I longed to believe him but couldn't quite allow myself to and found a surprising ally in his mother, Jenni.

'You should listen to Fredy,' said the woman with the magnificent head of chestnut hair twisted into a bun. 'We can't afford to be so flippant about these things anymore. Fredy's family lost everything and were forced to flee their own country. He's homeless and virtually destitute because of the Nazis, so do him the courtesy of listening to what he has to say.'

I could have kissed her but Jenda's sister Grete did it for me, pecking her mother on the cheek as she looked across at me, her eyes full of pity for the impecunious refugee at the family table. I never knew if Jenda's mother suspected that we were lovers but I sometimes caught the way she watched her son's familiar way with me. Her husband Max, meanwhile, was so focused on his political career that I doubt he'd have noticed if his son had kissed me full on the mouth in the middle of Sabbath dinner.

With Jenda's family so accepting, I finally began to savour the sweet taste of happiness. Focusing on teaching – the one area of my life where I felt in control – I found peace in the rhythm of going to work and coming back to a place I could call home. I began to believe that Brno was somewhere I could remain – until I reached the Holy Land. 'We'll need fit, young doctors like you there too,' I encouraged Jenda, always including him in my plans. 'There'll be incredible opportunities to establish new hospitals, schools and houses.'

Even though Jenda had claimed to be a Zionist when we first met, his face took on an expression every time I brought up the subject. Then one afternoon, he blurted, 'I know that's your dream, Fredy, but it isn't mine. I don't need to travel halfway around the world to feel safe. For me and my family, this is our holy land, and I promise you, *poutnik*, the longer you stay here the less like a stray you'll feel.'

Determined to seduce me into his world, he persuaded me to meet some of his friends, taking me to a café frequented by medical students. As someone who'd never had time for a social life I found the experience unsettling, especially when everyone jabbered away in Czech. A few who spoke German tried to put me at ease but one named Bohdan did the opposite.

'So this is the German *Junge* we've been waiting to meet,' he announced. 'Jenda's latest toy.' Several friends laughed but he wasn't finished. Looking me over as if I were a side of beef, he added, 'Well, at least he's young and pretty like the rest. He could be a model in one of those toothpaste adverts you see on billboards – look at his teeth!'

I'd known people like Bohdan all my life. I'd even encountered a few Bohdans-in-waiting among the children I taught. Spiteful and jealous, they were the bullies in the playground who picked on the vulnerable. When he reached out to tousle my hair, I twisted his wrist with such force that he winced.

Just then, Jenda pushed through the crowd with fistfuls of beer. 'Pilsners!' he cried as his friends turned. Seeing my expression, he asked, 'What have you been saying, Bohdi? Fredy looks as if he's swallowed a bee.'

Rubbing his wrist, Bohdan glared at me and, taking a stein, replied, 'I'd watch him if I were you, Jenda. He's more spirited than your *usual* boys.'

'And considerably stronger,' I added, staring Bohdan out as another uneasy silence fell.

In normal circumstances, I'd have brushed off his comments but his barbs penetrated my tender new hide. Jenda's 'latest toy' he'd said. Young and pretty 'like the rest'. I wasn't stupid. I knew Jenda was an experienced lover and I was grateful. I just didn't want to think how he'd become so practiced in the art of love.

Jenda seemed riled by the awkward encounter too, although I wasn't sure why until a few days later. 'You let me down, Fredy,' he blurted. Drawing on his cigarette, he puffed smoke rings into the air. 'I wanted my friends to get to know the fun Fredy but you came across as a prude. You should start drinking more than just a sip of wine or take up smoking.'

'Smoking's bad for you,' I snapped. 'It affects the efficiency of the lungs. Besides, I can't adopt habits I warn the children against.'

Throwing his head back, Jenda gave a mirthless laugh and ground his cigarette into the ashtray. 'Oh, your *Kinder*. You care more about them than you do about me.'

'They fled a terrible evil, Jenda. Torn from all they've known, they've lost those they hold dear and I'm trying to keep them from despair. I have to care because nobody else does.'

'Listen to your ego,' he scoffed. 'You aren't the only one. You're part of a large organisation. You're not their god, Fredy

Hirsch, so stop acting like one.'

Sensing an incoming storm, I walked out. I didn't want to fight and I didn't care to think too deeply about what he said in case some of it was true. All I wanted was to keep doing my work. My residence permit was about to run out – something I hadn't yet told Jenda about.

*

Summer arrived to distract me: my favourite season as it meant being outdoors from early until late. Better still, I'd been invited to set up a programme for young men eager to be PE teachers and to help supervise them and a large group of boys and girls at a summer camp.

'The kids hike and play war games, swim in the river and learn about navigating by the stars,' my fellow counsellor Shragga told me. 'The accommodation is pretty basic and we cook on campfires. But it's great fun.'

'I can't wait,' I replied, delighted at the thought of getting away. Even Jenda seemed relieved that I was going.

There was a joyful spring in my step when I helped the children off their train in the small rural town before marching them up the hill to the neat row of wooden huts we'd be living in for the next few months. The following morning, I woke at dawn and stole outside in a rolling mist to inhale the heady scent of pine. It felt like I could breathe again. Setting off at a run, I hurtled headlong down the hill to the riverbank where I stripped off and plunged in.

Breaking through the surface of the water that had run straight off the mountains felt like shattering glass. Swimming along the bottom of the riverbed, worn smooth by the passage of time, my eyeballs burned as I blinked at silver-scaled fish scattering in my path. Coming up for air, my lungs fit to burst, I pushed up into a deep dark pool under some low-hanging trees and hollered, 'Yes!'

From that morning on, I became known as 'Fredy the Enforcer' as I woke the children with a 'Rise and shine!' and pushed them out to experience the same sensation. Once they'd emerged groaning and blotchy from their chilly baptism, I led them in thirty minutes of barefoot gymnastics before allowing them to return to the campfire for cocoa.

After breakfast, we played the 'wide game', a vigorous cross-country exercise in which Shragga and I were generals of opposing teams. The plan was to outwit the other and rescue a captured flag. Each player wore a paper ribbon on their arm. If it was ripped by a member of the opposing team it meant they were 'dead'. When I accidentally ripped the one on the arm of Misha, Shragga's six-year-old brother on our team, he lost all control, wailing, 'I don't want to die!' The game hadn't even started properly yet, so I tied some straw around his arm and said, 'There now. You're only injured.'

Once night fell, we gathered around the fire to tell each other stories and sing Hebrew and Czech songs. I couldn't help thinking about my childhood book *Rabbit School* with its teacher warning of the fox lurking in the woods. *Be silent and don't divert sideways off the path*, he'd advised. Echoing his message, I cautioned, 'The forest isn't a place for weakness. There are dangers here, including bears and wolves. Hunters too, so be sure not to stumble into their sights.' It was a metaphor for so much more.

Throughout that summer, I was so busy that I had no time to write letters but I sent Jenda postcards depicting the region's castles. I also let him know that I'd been invited to coach another camp in the mountains that winter. His letters back were sweet and, in one, he apologised for forcing his friends on me. *It was my sister who told me off. Grete reminded me how difficult it must be to be living in a foreign country surrounded by people speaking a language you haven't yet mastered. She said my friends were loud and obnoxious and that it was no wonder you didn't take to them.*

Then, one day, a curt telegram arrived from him which read, *Authorities looking for you. Residence permit expired. Serious trouble. Turn yourself in or risk expulsion and possible deportation. J.* My knee-jerk reaction was to run. If I hiked up into the Carpathian mountains near the Polish border, I could hide out until I'd decided what to do. But what of the children who were expecting me back in Brno and how would I survive when the snows came? Trying to stay calm, I kept my nerve and remained alone in the hills long after everyone else had left.

With winter approaching and food stocks low I returned to Brno on a warm September night. Fearing it too dangerous to go to Jenda's apartment in case the authorities were watching, I took a tram to the suburbs. It was only when I walked into his parents' house and smelled the Challah bread that I realised it was Friday night. 'Fredy!' Grete cried, jumping up to greet me after the maid showed me into the candlelit dining room.

Jenda looked up from his plate as his mother rose to welcome me. 'What a lovely surprise,' she exclaimed. 'Come, Fredy, sit with us. Eat.' Thanking her, I put down my rucksack and sat on one of their elegant chairs, painfully aware of my dirty, unshaven state and rough outdoor clothes. Nobody seemed to mind and the family kept the conversation light as my lover watched me in silence across the white linen tablecloth.

'Will you be staying in Brno for a while?' his father enquired. There was an uneasy silence before Jenda asked, 'Yes, Fredy, are you staying?'

Feeling my cheeks burn, I blustered, 'I may return to Prague.' I didn't explain that, as an illegal immigrant, I hoped I'd be harder to trace in the capital. Jenda got up from the table and I didn't see him again that night but Jenni insisted that I stay. Making up my bed in a box room, she clasped my arm and said, 'I hope everything is well with you and my son? Max and I consider you to be a steadying influence on his more – shall we say – impetuous ways.'

Forcing a smile, I told her. 'Jenda is the dearest of friends. You are all so dear to me. I don't know what I would have done here without you. Whatever happens, I hope that we can always keep in touch.'

Her eyes sad, she sighed as she leaned in to kiss me on the cheek. 'Sleep well, Fredy. Sweet dreams.'

10

June 1942, Terezín, Czechoslovakia

'WHAT DO YOU MAKE of the latest rumour, Fredy?' Leo asked me. 'Do you think it could be true?'

'It depends on which rumour you're referring to,' I replied. 'The one about Hitler being a Jew or the story about Germans melting dead Jews down to make soap?'

'No, the report about the trucks they load Jewish prisoners into before driving them around until they've choked to death on fumes.'

Smiling, I said, 'I think I prefer the one about Hitler being a Jew.'

'I'm serious, Fredy,' Leo persisted. 'Our engineers heard it on the BBC last night. They've made a secret radio hidden in an attic and picked up a broadcast that hundreds of thousand of Jews were murdered in Poland this way.'

Snorting my derision, I cut him short. 'If you start believing everything you hear, you might as well believe we Jews are only interested in money and sex. This latest propaganda is just another way to frighten us. I'm frankly surprised the BBC fell for it.' This wasn't the first time we'd heard about the mass murder of Jews. Only a few months before, other reports had come out of Poland that claimed those who were taken away for slave labour were shot or gassed.

In private, I'd asked Jakob if he believed such reports. 'No, Fredy, I don't,' he told me. 'Why would the Germans risk so much they've set up systems to help us emigrate?'

It was easy to believe him until we heard of events closer to home, in a town less than an hour from us.

A high-ranking German general and so-called 'Reich Protector' named Reinhard Heydrich was assassinated in Prague in June 1942 by members of the Czech resistance. Hitler demanded revenge.

'There's been a massacre in Lidice,' Leo told me. 'It's all over the radio. On the day of Heydrich's funeral, the town was razed to the ground and the SS murdered hundreds of men. Some women and children were also killed and the rest sent to camps.'

'Why?' I asked, aghast.

'Word is that the Gestapo came up with spurious evidence that his assassins had some connection with the place, just to appease Hitler.'

'My God.'

As was the way of the ghetto, news travelled fast. After the initial shock, the information became diluted, first by casual conversation and ultimately by comedy. Laughing in the face of adversity was a vital means of resistance. Our so-called 'gallows humour' was also a way of holding on to something good from our past.

Just as the children made up games like 'Roll Call' and 'Gestapo' in which the baddie always lost, so they drew on real life for entertainment. 'Hey, Fredy, did you hear about the prisoner up in front of a firing squad who refused a last cigarette?' a freckle-faced teenager named Aaron asked me one afternoon, his eyes twinkling with mischief. 'He told the Commandant, "No thanks. I'm trying to give up!"' Slapping his thighs, he bent double at his own joke.

Making fun of the situation allowed the children to let off steam and I was grateful for it, although it was easier to keep the younger ones amused than sulky teenagers. For them, life felt pointless and some even resorted to violence and wanton acts of vandalism. 'Three more windows were broken overnight,' Gonda reported to me one day, scowling. 'Blackout blinds have also been torn, food stolen and belongings destroyed. I suspect it's the same group of troublemakers.'

I wasn't surprised. 'Those boys are like flies trapped in a bottle and punishing them only seems to make them worse.' A serial offender named Erik earned the nickname 'Dachrinnen' or Guttersnipe. A deceptively sweet-looking lad of indeterminate age, he had earned pocket-money whistling like a nightingale in the coffee houses of Vienna. When he was caught trying to set fire to one of the ghetto stables not long after breaking into the potato store, we put him in a room for problem children.

Determined to keep the younger ones from lapsing into similar behaviour, I came up with a plan to keep them from becoming frustrated: one that would mean me begging a favour. Making my way to the carpentry shop, I found Bernd and his fellow workman and asked, 'Can anyone here make me some wooden dolls?'

'Dolls?' Bernd asked, wiping sweat from his brow. 'Are you mad? The men here can't keep up with the workload as it is. Aside from all the coffins, we now have to make bunks in kit form for the attics and smaller spaces.'

'I understand. I just thought someone might enjoy whittling a few dolls for the children.'

Disappointed, I wandered outside but was followed by an older man with a bald head and a pronounced limp. I heard him before I saw him as his footsteps made a strange, slapping sound. Turning, I noticed that his clothes were threadbare and the only thing that wasn't shabby was the yellow star stitched to the left breast of his jacket that we all now had to wear. His said *Jude* like mine but was accompanied by an inverted triangle with the letter T for *Tscheche*, Czech, where mine had D for *Deutsch* or German.

Looking down, I noticed that a toe was poking through the cap of one shoe and the other was held in place with twine, which explained the slapping. 'You can apply for shoes from the Distribution Centre,' I told him, thinking that was why he'd followed me.

Tutting, he reached into his pocket and pulled out a small peg-figure of a man. Patting his chest and grunting, he intimated that he had made it. Turning the carving in my hands, I admired its simple lines chiselled from an oblong of wood. 'This is good,' I told him, realising that he must have overheard my conversation. 'Can you make more?'

When he grunted again and nodded, I realised that he was a mute. Extending my hand, I said, 'My name is Fredy Hirsch. I'll take everything you make and pay you in bread.'

He shook his head and gestured smoking. Reaching for his imaginary cigarette, I pretended to drop it and grind it underfoot, saying, 'Smoking is bad for you.' When he frowned, I sighed and added, 'I'll do my best, but you know how dangerous the black market is. If not tobacco, I'll bring you some home-made beer. The cooks assure me it's drinkable.'

It was Leo that discovered that my saviour was a decorated German war veteran named Dirk who'd been injured on the Somme. 'He was awarded the Iron Cross but, as a Jew, his service to the Fatherland was all but forgotten, so he spent the years between the wars as a coffin-maker in Liberec.' Lucky to have found Dirk, I was delighted when he presented me with ten more dolls. Borrowing some paint from the decorators trying to breathe life into a derelict hospital, I sat by the light of a small candle at night to hand-paint each figure, styling one as a miller and the others as a king, a princess and a dairymaid.

The following morning, I rose early to hide six of the dolls in the new playroom I'd created in the attic. I packed the rest in my rucksack before retracing the route to the Kindergarten taken by the children of the town that I'd seen the day I arrived in Terezín. I hid them under bushes or left them peeping out from behind low walls.

Three days later, I found myself supervising a group of men digging a new well on a plot next to the Kindergarten. Hearing a bell, I turned to see children tumbling out of class in a noisy heap. Scarves flying, they ran full pelt into the yard. I couldn't help but smile when I spotted a group of girls settle in a circle with one of the dolls and a solitary boy, hunched against the cold, clutching a figure of a king.

As soon as I'd finished work, I sought out Dirk. 'You helped some Czech children forget about the war today, *mein Freund*,' I said, patting him on the shoulder. '*Dankeschön*.' Reaching into a sack, I pulled out a pair of sturdy work boots and handed them to him. 'I hope these fit.' The grin that transformed the veteran's wizened face gave me a glimpse of how handsome he must once have been. For a moment I thought he was going to embrace me but instead he shook my hand with a painfully firm grip.

'Can you make animals and other toys, too?' I asked. Dirk nodded with enthusiasm. Refusing further payment, he made it clear that the satisfaction of doing something good in a place like Terezín was enough.

*

'Somebody's been asking for you, Fredy,' Andrejz told me after he found me in an office salvaging used forms from the waste-paper bin.

Looking up, I asked, 'Who?'

'An elderly woman who arrived on the latest transport. She's accompanied by her husband. She says she knew you in Brno.'

I couldn't think of any elderly woman who fitted the description but said, 'Very well, I'm finished here. Where can I find her?'

'She volunteered to help with the orphans.'

Making my way to the orphans' block, I went from room to room looking for the mystery woman. I was also seeking out potential foster parents for the system Gonda and I had set up. In one room I found doctors carrying out lice inspections as the children lined up. A wall of suitcases had been erected to offer some privacy. As well as checking their bedding and clothing, the medics searched armpits, groins and hair – anywhere the pesky insects might hide. '*Raus Läuse!*' they chanted as they worked.

Another group shaved the heads of those infested before they, their mattresses, luggage and clothing were sent to the delousing station overnight. A teenage girl sat sobbing as an electric razor buzzed and her hair dropped to the floor in a carpet of curls. Crouching beside her, I ran my hand over her bald head. 'What is it, Ingrid? You should be happy. This means no more annoying little bugs. Besides, when was the last time you had a new hairdo for nothing?' Uncertain whether to laugh or carry on crying, she hesitated before accepting a potato from my rucksack in return for a smile.

Still looking for the lady who'd wanted me, I washed my hands with Lysol and wandered into the last room. Seeing no recognisable faces, I began to walk away when a voice cried,

'Fredy, it's me!' I turned to see a woman with hair as white as a swan's feather, twisted into a long braid. Stepping closer there was still no flicker of recognition until she smiled. Trying to hide my shock, I hurried over to embrace Jenda's sixty-year-old mother, who looked to have aged twenty years.

'Jenni! It's you.'

'Oh, Fredy, it's so good to see you,' she exclaimed, cradling my face in both hands.

'How are you, dear lady?'

'I can't complain,' she said, attempting a smile. More softly, she added, 'But it's been no vacation.' I laughed until I saw her eyes welling with tears as she added, 'I try to stay positive, Fredy, but things haven't been easy.'

'Jenda wrote and told me.'

'It's Max. He's not at all well and they say there's little they can do for him. He's a broken man. Being transported here was too much for him to bear.' My heart sinking, I knew that patriotic men like Max were often the first to lose the will to remain in a world they no longer recognised.

Wiping her eyes, Jenni tried to smooth down her stained dress. 'Listen to me, telling you all my problems before we've had a chance to catch up. Forgive me, Fredy, but as you can see,' she pointed to her hair with a grimace, 'life has rather taken its toll.'

'You look as elegant as ever, my dear,' I insisted. Pointing to my own greying hair, I added, 'And you're not the only one with a new look.' Walking her out into the courtyard, we linked arms and chatted like two old friends before making our way to the hospital.

Max was so unrecognisable that I would never have found him without Jenni. Lying on a mattress on the floor of an ante-room in the overcrowded outpatient clinic, the consummate politician who'd sat proudly at the head of his Sabbath table lay facing the wall, his hip and shoulder bones protruding like the folded wings of a bird.

'There you are,' I said, kneeling beside him despite the smell of decay. 'It's Fredy, Max. What's all this I hear about you lazing about all day and neglecting your chores? We can't have that now, can we? Why don't you sit up and I'll fetch you some soup?'

There was no response so I leaned over his prone body and rolled his head towards me. The skin on his cadaverous face was like parchment and when his mouth fell open to reveal bleeding gums and fetid breath, I almost gagged. With no light behind his eyes, he had the look of what ghetto slang called a '*Muselman*', a living skeleton without a spark of hope. As I rose slowly to my feet, Jenni registered my expression and let out a querulous cry. 'I'm so sorry,' was all I could say. Holding that frail woman in my arms, I thought back to all the happy times in their beautiful home and how cruel it was to see them so diminished. Within days, their names were added to the next transport.

When Jenni came to say goodbye, I pleaded with her to let Max be sent on alone. 'There's a chance I could reclaim you from the list to help with the orphans.'

With a sad smile, she patted my cheek. 'Thank you, my boy, but you're forgetting something. Many of those orphans arrived on the train with me and I won't abandon them now, nor Max.'

I gulped. 'What should I tell Jenda if I see him?'

Her face softened at the mention of her only son. 'Tell him . . .' pausing, she fought to compose herself. 'Tell him I'm sorry we were hard on him. Tell him that love is all that matters, in the end.'

I couldn't face watching the couple who'd been like parents to me being escorted out of the ghetto the following morning. Turning away, I ran into another crowd of deportees and spotted a familiar face in the crowd. Moaning inwardly, I hurried over, grabbed his arm and cried, 'Dirk, how come you're on the list?' Giving me a wry smile, he gestured smoking just as he had when we first met. 'You mean you were caught trading cigarettes?' He nodded and hung his head. 'But you're in the AK. You're meant to be exempt. Wait here. I'll see what I can do.'

Gripping my forearm, he wagged a finger and shook his head. We both knew it was too late and the old soldier seemed resigned to his fate. Reaching into his rucksack, he pulled out three wooden dolls and a painted train and handed them to me. Opening the bag wider, he showed me that instead of taking anything practical for himself, it was full of similar toys.

'That's kind of you,' I said, staring at the boots I'd given him as I struggled not to let my emotions get the better of me. Unable to find words, I pulled the man with the heart of a lion into a hug and hurried off.

Instead of watching them all leave, I ran fifty laps of the field, pushing myself so hard that I sprained my ankle on the uneven surface. There was nothing for it but to pick myself up and limp back to the work that gave me solace and strength.

*

'I should admit you to hospital, Fredy,' Dr Heller told me the day I collapsed with what turned out to be a horrid stomach bug. Unable to rise from my bed, I was shivering with a splitting headache and painful abdominal cramps.

'No,' I replied, knowing how bad conditions were in the medical blocks. 'Don't worry about me. Just tell me what I need to do to get better.' With instructions to drink only boiled water and eat a little white bread, I was nursed in my room by Ottla, a German-speaker in her late forties with piercing eyes. The younger sister of the Czech writer Frank Kafka, who died in 1924, Ottla had volunteered to look after those children who'd never known a mother's love. It was her way of working through her grief at being separated from her own family.

In her tender care, I gave in to the overpowering desire to sleep. Pressing a wet cloth to my brow, she nursed me through a fever until I gradually regained some strength. I was determined to resume my duties as soon as I could, despite Ottla's protests that I wasn't well enough. 'You need more rest,' she scolded when she found me sitting on the edge of the bed pulling on my shirt, my head filled with pain from the exertion. 'So many people have died of this infection that they've run out of coffins and are burying them on planks.'

'But the children,' I insisted. 'I have to see them.' Realising that I couldn't be dissuaded, Ottla helped me dress and then followed me on my rounds in case I had a relapse. There was no time for that, as I struggled to catch up with those who needed me the most.

The warmer weather may have heated chilly rooms and relieved aching bones but it also brought fresh misery, especially for the thousands living in the hell of the attics where rising heat and hardly a breath of air made the stench of human suffering suffocating. As Gonda put it so eloquently, 'Their very souls seem trapped up in those roofs.' Those who were able to descended to the courtyards with their bedding to sleep outside.

Flies then descended in a biblical plague, attracted by the reek of sweaty bodies and overflowing toilets. 'Winter was bad enough but this summer heat is making people even more intolerant,' I told Jakob in his airless office. 'Nerves are shredded.'

'I know,' he replied, fanning himself with a piece of cardboard. 'There's also been an explosion in the numbers of rats and mice. To add to the misery, the doctors tell me we have several new epidemics. Blood poisoning is a big problem too, triggered by an infection in the smallest blister. The old have been badly affected. For them, death comes far too easily.'

'And still more people come,' I commented, picking up the latest deportation order announcing new arrivals from Austria, Germany and every corner of the so-called Protectorate.

'It's never-ending, Fredy,' Jakob said, his voice still scratchy from another of the throat infections that plagued him. 'And there'll be hundreds more children too.'

Patting my exhausted friend on the shoulder, I told him, 'We'll manage. Remember, every transport brings helpers and teachers, artists and workers. I now have a cupboard full of wooden toys and papier-mâché puppets for the new arrivals to play with and I'm writing a comic musical about finding happiness even when we're sad.'

Jakob stared at me as if seeing me for the first time. 'How you manage to maintain that positive attitude of yours in this place is completely beyond me, Fredy.'

I shrugged. 'Humour and hope are all we have left, Jakob. They remind us that we're still human. Wasn't it the prophet Elijah who said he who brings laughter to others will be rewarded in the next life?'

'In that case, my boy, I will surely find you sitting at the right hand of the Lord.'

*

Scanning the crowded *Schleusse* one morning, I spotted a man stooping to give water to a woman who'd collapsed like a sack of potatoes. I would have recognised his back anywhere.

'Jenda!' I cried, pushing through the masses. 'I had no idea you were here.'

Grinning broadly, he placed a hand on my shoulder and shook mine warmly. 'Neither did I – until this morning. I was on a reserve list, all packed and ready, when my summons came at dawn. To be honest, I was bored in Prague without you and my parents and thought it was time I came and checked up on you all, especially as they're such lousy correspondents. Where can I find them?'

My throat closing, I stammered, 'O-oh, Jenda . . . I thought you knew . . .'

His hand slipped from my shoulder and he took a step back, shaking his head. 'No, no, Fredy. They're not . . . ?'

Reaching for him, I grabbed his arm. 'I don't know for sure, Jenda. Nobody does. They were sent east on a transport not long after they arrived. I was hoping you'd have heard something from them by now.' Quietly, I added, 'Your father was very sick, but your mother was in fighting spirit.'

Everything seemed to go into slow motion then as Jenda's legs folded beneath him and he fell to the floor. A piercing cry, almost animal, came from his lips. As people turned to stare, I helped him to a quieter corner. His public display of emotion made me realise that I hadn't cried like that in years, so inured to grief had I become. 'I'll get you something to eat,' I told him but he couldn't hear or see me, so blinded was he by loss.

It took him a full week to return to me and, even then, he was weighed down by grief. All he wanted was to be with me but I was too busy to visit him more than once or twice a week as there were important changes afoot.

Not long after Jenda arrived, the SS declared that everyone in the ghetto could move freely for the first time and visit one another without passes or a police escort. Almost immediately men, women and children flooded the open spaces to play, dance, breathe and sing. Such was the crush of people that the Germans erected signs warning *Stehenbleiben Verboten*, No Standing Still, and made thoroughfares two-way. With the streets so busy, artists and players began to give impromptu cabaret and theatrical performances, often playing the 'Terezín Anthem' which promised we'd be dancing on the ruins of the city one day.

'Free movement is a blessing and a curse,' Jakob stated glumly at the next Council meeting. 'We've had a thousand deaths this month alone.' It brought other problems too. Streets that once had us sinking ankle-deep in mud became dried and cracked in the heat. With so many feet tramping through the ghetto there was a new scourge of dust that found its way into every crack and crevice, covering surfaces like a shroud.

When the children complained of grit in their soup, I teased them. 'Nobody ever died from a bit of dust and, besides, you've been complaining for ages that your food has no bite.'

*

Summer turned to autumn and then the winter we all feared loomed. With even more people arriving from across Europe, there was open resentment that they weren't allowed to receive parcels when the Czechs were.

'Why don't you make them share everything out? I thought you Zionists believed in the common good?' asked a man from Cologne with six children. 'We have nothing but horrible soup while the Czechs feast on beans and sardines. They even get cakes and cookies and last week I watched someone unwrap a lemon. It's not fair.'

He had my sympathy but there was no logic to the edict and nothing I could do. 'Everyone in the ghetto is now eligible to receive Red Cross parcels, so let me make sure you're on the list.' To everyone's surprise, the SS allowed us to set up a Post Office for the delivery of parcels. I was able to get Jenda a valued position there, but he didn't stay long and volunteered to work in the infirmary instead.

The Post Office also handled the postcards we were permitted to send to friends and relatives every few months. Descriptions of Terezín were forbidden and each card was heavily censored for hidden meanings, although many people signed their names *Lechem*, the Hebrew for bread, in the hope of food. In my first postcard to Uncle Alfred, I wrote, *Dear Onkel, I'm starting each day with a song in Theresienstadt ghetto. Please send food if you can and an address for my family. Fredy.*

The sending of victuals and other necessities into the ghetto was helped enormously by a system established in Prague by a former assistant of mine, Heinzek, who hadn't yet been deported. With the help of friends and his father's contacts, the willowy seventeen-year-old did an incredible job raising money and gathering donations for those of us trapped. 'Even though I know you have so little, I still wish I could be with you all,' Heinzek wrote to me in one of his letters. 'I feel like the last Jewish boy left in Prague.'

Whenever packages arrived, there was great excitement as I'd gather each group of children in a circle and make a game of opening them. 'When I count to three you can start to open your parcels very slowly,' I told them. 'Remember to be careful not to rip the paper so that we can use it later for art.' All around me there were squeals of delight as people unwrapped items they hadn't seen in years.

'*Oma* sent me some of my favourite gingerbread cookies!' a girl called Klara cried. Then, her face fell as she added, 'Do I really have to share these with everyone, Fredy?'

'Let's have a look at what else she sent you. Maybe you could give up something that wasn't made specially for you.'

It never failed to astonish me that, despite so much hunger and want, there were still those whose selflessness shone like a beacon. When Klara saw how generous everyone else was being with their gifts, she decided they all should taste her grandmother's gingerbread. I rewarded her by returning my piece and adding an apple.

One of the most selfless among us was a recent arrival, an artist named Friedl Dicker-Brandeis who I first came across that winter teaching a group of young children in a bitterly cold attic. A tiny woman in her early forties, I found her sitting on a windowsill wrapped in all the clothing she possessed, the children gathered devotedly at her feet. 'Where do *regenbögens* come from?' she asked, translated by one of the teenagers for those who didn't speak German.

A mischievous boy with an infectious giggle named Bruno raised his hand. 'Rainbows are unicorn farts!' he declared, collapsing in on himself.

'We all look forward to seeing that drawing, Bruno,' Friedl replied. A student at the German Bauhaus School, she'd been deported to Terezín from the rural Czech town to which she and her husband had fled. Instead of packing things she'd need for her own comfort, she arrived with a suitcase full of brushes, paints, tissue paper and dyed bedsheets for costumes. Nor would she accept so much as a crumb in payment, although she must have been as hungry as the rest of us.

'Thanks to Bruno, I'm going to tell you a story about rainbows and unicorns that I think you might like but before we start I'd like you all to close your eyes and take some deep breaths,' Friedl told the children. I couldn't help but smile at the kindred spirit in our midst. Although she spoke hardly any Czech it didn't matter as the children understood her through instinct or translation. After she'd told them her story, she opened an art book and showed them a painting of waterlilies by Monet.

'Thinking of a rainbow, how many colours can you see in this picture?' she asked, as young eyes scanned the picture. The general consensus was three – blue, white and green. 'Look again,' she instructed and, to cries of surprise, they spotted several more.

After she set them drawing, I wandered around the room and was happy to see them so focused on their work, some with the tips of their tongues sticking out they were so engrossed. As I offered encouraging pats on shoulders, I was staggered by their pictures. Many were of Sabbath suppers with tables groaning with food but there were also birds and butterflies and I especially liked the joyful depictions of the Promised Land with palm trees and camels. Some were working on abstract collages with glue made from flour and water, paper flowers, or embroidering random patterns onto old SS forms.

'These are wonderful, children,' I declared.

'Thank you, Fredy,' they dutifully chimed.

Wandering over to where Friedl was stacking earlier works, I was dismayed to spot several graphic pictures of barbed wire fences, gallows, cattle wagons and soldiers with guns. 'These are chilling,' I commented.

Friedl sighed. 'I generally discourage images like these but in freestyle lessons this is what some of them come up with. One boy only ever draws a barren landscape with his village in the distance. When I try to get him to talk, he clams up. All he can do is draw it over and over.'

'You give him that outlet.'

'Yes but we need to give them more than art and drama, Fredy. These children need to be allowed to run and shout and vent their bottled-up emotions.'

'I couldn't agree more.'

Recognising the significance of the children's art, Friedl added that she was storing it in the two suitcases she and her husband had arrived with. 'These drawings may be their only legacy so the one thing I insist upon is that each child signs their work,' she added quietly, as we stood side by side gazing upon the children. 'I want them to remember that they aren't just numbers. If I get summoned for a transport I'll hide them somewhere or entrust them to a friend,' she promised. 'I'll let you know where, if I can.'

I stared into her benevolent eyes. 'Let's pray it doesn't come to that.'

*

Spurred on by her reminder of the children's needs, I asked for a meeting with *Untersturmführer* Scholz in the hope of persuading him that the rough field I ran around behind one of the barracks would make a perfect playground. 'We could hold track events and sporting tournaments there, including boxing matches,' I told him, unable to take my eyes off his nose which was getting redder each time I saw him. 'Everybody loves our football kickabouts in the courtyards but with more space we could set up proper matches for young and old with different houses pitched against each other. It would be quite the spectacle.'

Scholz's eyes lit up at that idea and before, I knew it, I was in charge of a committee to establish the 'Liga Terezín' ghetto football league. With no shortage of volunteers, we established three divisions of youth and adult teams, with promotions and relegations fiercely fought. The field proved too muddy and full of stones so matches continued to be played in the court-yards even though the goal was smaller and each side could only field seven players. 'We need a referee and a doctor on the side-lines,' I told Leo, 'and can you ask the seamstresses to make us football strips?'

'I'll ask but they're flat out making bespoke clothing for the SS and their wives.'

As I'd predicted, the matches were immediately popular and allowed men, women and children to holler for their teams as loudly as they liked. There were plenty of nail-biting games to keep everyone entertained and an All-Stars exhibition match planned at the end of the season. Youth Welfare and the Cooks produced some of the best men, most of whom were built up with extra food and privileges, but there were some valiant players from the Locksmiths and Joinery departments too. It was the team from Clothing Warehouse who called themselves 'SK Sparta' after a famous Czech team, however, that domi-nated the high-stakes matches.

'Aside from the children's homes and your comedy shows, this football idea is your greatest triumph, Fredy,' Jakob congratulated me one Sunday, as we settled to watch a match.

'It keeps the boys out of mischief at least,' I said, 'although I'm not sure about the adults.' Pointing to a noisy cluster of men buzzing around a bookmaker as they placed bets, I nudged him and the two of us chuckled like the old friends we were.

'You have given us a new problem, though,' Jakob added, with a wry expression. 'When the transports resume, we'll be inundated with petitions to reclaim the best players from the lists.'

Like everyone, I'd been grateful that there had been far fewer transports recently. A sense of dread returned when they were rumoured to be starting again. 'Do you know when and how many?'

He opened his mouth to speak but his words were drowned out by a roar from the crowd as the players emerged from a wood store that doubled as a locker room. Every arched opening in the arcades that surrounded the barracks court-yard on three floors was packed with people at fever pitch. Children perched on the ledges, their legs dangling, and they joined in with the cries of *'Tempo! Tempo!'* whenever play slowed, adding to the tumultuous noise whenever a goal was scored. There must have been over a thousand spectators desperate to be entertained until darkness or the curfew brought the match to an end. And they weren't the only ones.

'I see we have some dignitaries in the royal box today,' I pointed out, looking up at the opening in the middle of the upper arcade where senior SS officers had assembled to watch. 'They're like Romans watching gladiators in the Colosseum. I half-expect the Commandant to indicate life or death with his thumb.'

Above yet another round of bellowing from the crowd, Jakob shouted, 'I heard the SS ordered in a shipment of football shoes to distribute to their favourite players. Those boys have become ghetto heroes and are on triple rations as well as being swooned over by just about every female.'

'The SS are betting thousands of *Reichsmarks* on every match,' I yelled back. 'With money they stole from us.' We had to laugh, or we'd have cried.

Then the smile slid from Jakob's face. 'We did have other news this morning, Fredy,' he said during a lull. 'The next transports will be for as many as ten thousand old people.'

'Do we even have ten thousand old people left alive?'

'No and that's my point. It's a huge quota to fill, which means we'd have to pick the rest.' Looking at me, he paused. 'And Fredy, they say we can no longer exempt children. I'm sorry, my friend, but next time we won't have any choice.'

11

March 1939, Prague, Czechoslovakia

THE SNOWBALLS OF MY YOUTH were a far cry from the ice-hard, gritty missiles I launched in fury at the wave of Panzer tanks, motorcycles and soldiers that invaded Prague that bitter March morning in 1939.

Powerless against the might of the Reich and without any other means of protest, I stood on the streets with hundreds of Czechs shouting '*Raus, Raus!*' throwing lumps of snow, rocks, whatever I could find at Hitler's lumbering behemoths. People were weeping openly, especially when Wehrmacht soldiers returned the raised arm salute of ethnic Germans stepping out of the shadows with, '*Sieg Heil!*'

Carried along in a sea of shocked citizens to the city's central Wenceslas Square, I choked up as the swaying crowd began to sing the Czech national anthem '*Kde Domov Můj*' – 'Where My Home Is'. I only knew some of its lyrics about rustling pine trees and a paradise on earth, but I felt its passion deep in my heart. Now, with the turn of a calendar page, it was a paradise lost to us all.

Too despondent to protest further, I trudged back through the heavy snow to the room I shared with others and pulled out my rucksack from under my bed. Packing my binoculars and whistle, my clothes and other effects, I selected two books from the shelf above my bed – one of which was the Mann novel Jenda had lent me.

Dear Jenda, where was he now? And how were he and his family faring in Brno? For all the time I'd known him, he'd mocked my anxiety about the Nazis and promised I'd be safe in his country. What must he be thinking now after challenging my dream for a new life, especially as it very nearly came true. As part of my work with the Maccabis, we were preparing to send a group of boys to the Middle East: pioneers who'd been trained in Hebrew and learned how to grow their own food. They were equipped with money and papers sewn into the linings of their clothing but there was no guarantee they'd even make it.

'Their journey through Germany to Denmark will be long and perilous and they could be arrested at any moment,' a counsellor named Ari told me, his expression grave. 'Then they have to travel through Sweden, Finland, Russia and Istanbul before reaching Haifa – if they're lucky. They'll have no choice but to rely on guides who are often unscrupulous, taking their money before abandoning them. Even if they make it, the prices being charged for safe passage are outrageous and half of the promised ships aren't seaworthy enough to make the journey.'

Shaking my head, I tried not to imagine what might happen to such vulnerable teenagers. 'But this is their only hope of escape, isn't it?' I asked. 'And what if they're arrested by the British when they arrive? I've heard rumours of Jews being turned back.'

Ari sighed. 'They would be held on a British base but with everything that's going on here they're unlikely to be sent back to the Nazis.'

The money to pay for their passage had come from sponsors abroad and those sympathetic to the Zionist cause. There was enough to pay for a responsible adult to accompany the group, a once-in-a-lifetime opportunity. Late one afternoon, Ari told me, 'It's been decided that either you or Shragga will go with the children, Fredy. You'll draw matches tomorrow.' My joy at being considered was immediately tempered by the guilt of knowing I'd be pitted against my friend who'd recently become engaged.

The following day, Ari placed me shoulder to shoulder with Shragga before snapping the ends off two long matches. He then held them out to us. Knowing that the outcome could change the course of my life for ever, I took a deep breath and picked one. His jaw clenching and unclenching with nerves, Shragga selected his and it was immediately clear that it was longest.

'Congratulations, Shragga, you are going to the Holy Land,' I said, forcing a smile. Promising to keep watch over his mother and brother Misha, I managed to hide my disappointment right up to the day I waved their train off at the station, my eyes clouded by more than the coalsmoke.

Once the Nazi's distinctive red and black flags were draped over every major building in Prague, all hope of making it to safety dwindled. I couldn't even leave what the Nazis renamed the 'Protectorate of Bohemia and Moravia' without official papers. Sitting on my bed in my coat and boots with my ruck-sack on my lap, I lost track of time as the Occupation lengthened to days and then weeks. Fellow counsellors like Ze'ev, an eager young Czech, did their best to rally me but I hardly even heard.

'Don't give up hope, Fredy,' he told me. 'The Nazis won't last. The Czech government in exile is in London now so the British will come to our rescue, you'll see.' I was too numb to point out that the Allies had already betrayed us by ceding the Czech region of Sudetenland to Hitler. All my life people had been telling me not to worry, promising me that my father would get better, my mother would be back soon and that everything would be all right. It never was and, for those early days of Occupation, I no longer believed any of them.

At the end of that first blur of a month in which Germany's anti-Jewish rules began to exclude us from mainstream society, synagogues were burned and Jews openly attacked on the street. Thousands of ethnic Germans were granted Reich citizenship and promised riches if they informed on Jewish friends and neighbours. 'Every Czech citizen has been ordered to prove that we're not from Jewish or Roma stock,' Ze'ev told me, his optimism fading. 'We have to be registered and carry an ID card stamped "J" for *Jude*.' The Germans had me listed as 'stateless' but all I could focus on was the thought of that damning single letter, upon which my life or death could depend.

'We're to be issued with ration cards for far fewer items than Aryans and we can't buy them until later in the day after everything is sold out,' we were told by Ari. 'Jews are banned from all paid employment including teaching and only Aryan children can be educated. All cinemas, theatres, parks, restaurants and cafés are off limits, as is most public transport and we'll have to comply with a curfew.'

Jews also had to register all their property and hand over artworks, jewellery, furniture, stocks and shares. As I had nothing of value, I was able to bypass the lines of people queuing up outside Gestapo headquarters to turn in everything from radios to musical instruments. Putting my head down and crossing the road, I winced at the sight of the elderly being shoved or beaten by the SS if they attempted to sit down after standing for hours.

More pitiful still were the scenes outside vets and the offices of The Humane Society, where Jewish pets were being handed over to be euthanised. 'The system is overwhelmed,' Ze'ev told me, close to tears. 'Officials are setting up desks on the street to process all the animals. Those who can't face it are dumping cats in baskets and tying their dogs to railings, where they whine piteously. I can't bear to hear them.'

Walking past one such queue, I heard one little girl wail through her tears, 'Please *Maminko*, please!' She was cradling a large white cat in a black shawl. 'Can't we just give Miki to our neighbour?'

Seeing that her mother was too upset to respond, I turned back. Bending to the child's height, I said, 'My name is Fredy, so what's yours?'

Hiccupping through tears that fell like tiny pearls onto the shawl, she replied, 'Alice.'

'And how old are you, Alice?' I asked, tucking a curl of hair behind her ear. 'I think you must be at least twelve, you look so grown up.'

A crooked smile of pride tugged at the corner of her mouth. 'But I'm only ten.'

'Well then, ten-year-old Alice,' I said, brushing away her tears with my thumbs. 'You're not to worry, sweetheart. All the cats are going to a great big pen in the Zoological Gardens with dishes full of milk and kittens to play with. It'll be like a holiday for Miki and once everything gets back to normal you'll be able to bring him home.'

'Really?' Alice studied my face with suspicious eyes. 'There'll be milk and kittens?'

'That's right, darling,' her mother interjected, shooting me a grateful look. Leaning over her child, she stroked Miki's head and said, 'It'll be just like the nice young man said, so be a good girl now and dry your tears.'

There was worse to witness in the coming months as people were arrested and tortured to confess to crimes they didn't commit. Doctors, judges and lawyers were forced into humiliating labour, cleaning the streets or cutting public lawns with scissors as German guards brayed. Others were chained together or had offensive labels hung around their necks as people they'd once thought of as friends hurled insults. When people began whispering fearfully of deportations to labour camps as part of the Nazi plan of 'Judenrein' – Jewish cleansing – many chose suicide.

'One family was found gassed in their apartment last night,' Ari confided one morning, his face pale. 'The youngest was only two. The teenager who found them only went to deliver a food parcel. She discovered a note on the door telling her to summon the police but, smelling gas, she broke in to find them all dying.'

*

Helpless and afraid, my options were limited. I considered going back to Father Marek and hiding out in his church but I knew the risks would be too great for us both, especially as he was so close to the German border.

My only other thought was to try to make it back to Aachen and the forests I grew up in. 'I'd need false papers and it would be extremely dangerous to return but if I could get there I'd be safe – for a while at least,' I told Ze'ev and Ari. 'I know every trail and woodcutter's hut and could eke out an existence on fish, game and mushrooms, until winter. You could come with me.'

'But then what?' they asked, agog.

'Then we'd die of the cold, I suppose,' I replied. 'But even that would be preferable to dying at the hands of a Nazi.'

If it hadn't been for Jakob that might have been my end. As the newly appointed head of the *Judenrat* in Prague, he had an impossible task keeping up with the demands of the SS while managing the expectations of desperate thousands. Swamped by a flood of refugees, he and his staff ran from embassy to embassy seeking visas and safe passage for whoever they could.

'I've heard good things about you, Fredy Hirsch,' Jakob told me the day I was summoned to his office in the Jewish quarter. He was younger than I'd imagined, yet he already had the air of someone weary of the world. 'Everyone tells me that you are wonderful with children and especially at keeping them fit, healthy and optimistic.'

Shrugging, I told him, 'I've tried but to what purpose? None of that matters anymore.'

'Oh, but it does, Fredy. Now more than ever,' he declared. 'The situation hasn't changed. We need to keep hope alive, especially in the young and you're just the man to help us.'

It was only when I met his wife Miriam that I finally took what he said to heart, so impressed was I by her. 'People keep asking why Jakob spends what could be our final months of freedom together working all hours,' she told me. 'But he doesn't have to prove his love to me. I have that. I bore his child.'

'Aren't you afraid?' I asked. 'Don't you want to flee like everyone else?'

She laughed. 'Oh, we could have, Fredy. Jakob has been allowed to travel by the Gestapo and had papers for us to leave too, but when he feared another pogrom he chose to remain with his people. If he sacrificed that calling for us now, I couldn't live with myself.'

Faced with their mutual devotion, I reminded myself that as someone who was completely alone in the world I had more of a duty than most to do what I could, especially for the children. From that moment on, even though I was still flattened by events, I placed myself completely at Jakob's service.

My salvation came in the form of a muddy patch of ground five kilometres north of the *Stare Mesto* or Old Town. A sports field and running track named the *Hagibor*, which means 'hero' in Hebrew, it was part of a communal and cultural centre which had a Jewish orphanage and a care home for the elderly.

'The Nazis are squeezing us out of ordinary life, Fredy,' Jakob told me. 'They've now declared that there are only a few places in Prague where Jewish children may gather. One is the Old Jewish Cemetery, next to the fifteenth century Pinkas Synagogue.'

'But there's hardly a clear patch of grass there,' I protested, interrupting him at the thought of the thicket of lopsided headstones tumbling on top of the other.

'Indeed not,' he concurred. 'And one hundred thousand members of this city's once vibrant Jewish community are buried there, often twelve deep, so it would be sacrilege.'

'Where else can they go?'

'The other permitted playground is the *Hagibor*, which the Nazis think is too far out of town to be of any use.' Shrugging, he sighed.

'Nothing's too far if I could organise matches and races there,' I countered. 'Jakob, let me create an oasis of hope.'

Giving me a benevolent smile, he said, 'That would be wonderful, Fredy, but how will children get there now that they've been forced to give up their bicycles and are forbidden from riding on trams? For those living on the other side of town it would involve a five-mile round trip, especially when they have to avoid all public places.'

'We'll make the journey part of their exercise routine,' I replied, feeling alive again for the first time in months. 'I'll devise games they can play on their walk to keep them occupied. We'll just need to protect them from the fascist youth.' With Jakob's blessing, I was placed in charge of the *Hagibor* to which several hundred boys and girls flocked for athletics and football, to sing, study, take part in quizzes, eat together and learn military drills. Having rediscovered my purpose, I found myself in a completely different world.

All week, we lived in the city in fear of being arrested, deported, beaten or murdered by those who prowled the city streets looking for Jews to send to the Gestapo for no reason. At weekends, we could breathe freely and play without harassment in that unforgettable place.

'I hear some of the children are so bewitched by their time at the *Hagibor* that they are calling it Fredy-land,' Gonda commented one morning, his mouth pinched. As head of Youth Welfare in Prague, he seemed resentful of my role. 'It sounds to me like you're trying to create your own personal fiefdom, Fredy.'

'I'd prefer to think of it as a collective,' I responded. 'Everyone pulls together to make the most of our time there. I'm just relieved the children are prepared to travel all that way.' As more arrived each week, there were so many children that I had to stand on a table with my stopwatch and whistle so that everyone could see me.

'You girls to the right: I want you to line up in rows of ten and start doing star jumps,' I'd cry, giving them a shrill burst.

'Boys to the left do press-ups. Remember, together we are strong and while we're here nothing else matters.' Turning to a group who were less sporty, I told them, 'If you look inside the hut, you'll find some dominoes and chess sets. We'll be joined later by a magician named Borghini who's going to teach us a few tricks. There's music, too, because a composer Hans Krasa is rehearsing with children from the orphanage. Why don't you see if there's anything you can help with?'

Being at the *Hagibor* gave me a chance to reconnect with many of the children I'd taught before the Occupation, so I had Frank teaching shot putting and Misha, Shragga's brother, became my *Läufer* or messenger, running to and fro between groups. 'No ribbons on your arm this time,' I told him, ruffling his hair. 'Just lots of fun.'

And it was fun, except for those times when the sense of oppression returned to remind us that we were still living in the shadow of war. One sunny afternoon, a truckload of German soldiers screeched to a halt at the *Hagibor* gates and, as terrified children scattered, they flooded in, their weapons raised. Jumping down from my table, I quickly identified their leader and sprinted over to where he stood surveying the scene, legs apart. 'What are you doing here?' I demanded, my blood rising. 'This is the one place we are allowed to be without fear of harassment.'

The veteran soldier looked at me in astonishment: a young Jew standing before him barefoot in a singlet and shorts. 'We are checking on subversive behaviour,' he announced through thin lips.

'There's no such thing among children,' I snapped. 'This is privately owned land and we have every right to be here. If you and your men take one more step, you'll be creating a major diplomatic incident that will be reported to Berlin by the Council of Elders as a direct violation of our privileges.'

The officer frowned as he digested the import of my words. Looking over my shoulder at the sorry children clustered together on a muddy field, he hesitated.

'Get out!' I cried, pointing at the gate. 'Or do you want me to start making calls?'

Faltering as his men stood around him awaiting orders, he stepped back from my fury and nodded, a smile tugging at the corner of his mouth. 'You do realise that all this is only temporary?' he sneered. When I didn't respond, he yelled, 'Let's go!' and waved an arm in the air as his bewildered men retreated to their truck.

Everyone held their breath until the noise of the engine faded. It was only when I turned around that they started running towards me, hollering with glee. Misha shouted, 'Three cheers for Fredy! *Hip, hip, hurá!*'

We were never intimidated at the *Hagibor* again and our time there allowed us to forget that we were living in mortal danger. It was only on a Sunday evening, when I blew my final whistle to mark the end of activities in time for curfew, that the children remembered. The looks on their faces as they began the long walk home were painful to see. It was as if a curtain had fallen on their happiness – and on mine.

*

'Can you please do something with my boy?' the well-dressed man pleaded, as he presented his son to me at the *Hagibor*. 'He has more energy than he knows what to do with and now that he's banned from school my wife and I are at our wits' end.'

Laughing, I looked down on the thirteen-year-old boy named Heinzek who reminded me of a baby giraffe I'd seen in the

Prague Zoological Garden. Puny, he was all legs and freckles with red hair corralled under a cap that was too big for him. A scrap of a boy physically, he was bright-eyed and full of enthusiasm.

Warming to father and son immediately, I gladly took Heinzek under my wing and not only taught him how to box but to put his boundless energy to good use, sending him all over the city. A fast learner, he hung on my every word and became adept at avoiding the Hitler Youth and the Gestapo, hopping on and off the permitted rear carriages of trams and ducking down side streets as he looked for things I needed for the *Hagibor*.

'Do you think you could try to find me some plimsolls, running shoes and football boots?' I asked, thinking of the children who turned up in their best – and only – shoes. Making them run around barefoot was acceptable in the summer but winter was coming.

'I can try,' Heinzek replied and within a week he presented me with a box of mixed shoes in every size.

'How much?' I asked, nervously, knowing money was tight.

'Nothing,' Heinzek replied, as my mouth fell open. 'They were donated by people who approve of what you're doing.' Next he secured me some shorts, singlets, even gymslips for the girls. Without asking, the box that arrived after that was full of toys.

'I need to meet these kind people and thank them,' I told Heinzek, gazing in wonder at items that would make perfect prizes and Yom Kippur gifts. 'Can you take me to them?'

The boy shuffled awkwardly on his feet. 'Er, no, I don't think so, Fredy,' he said, his face reddening. 'I've been warned that we'll be tortured to death by the Gestapo if they find out.'

I frowned. 'Then how did you meet them?'

He hung his head. 'I-I can't say.'

'Heinzek?' I lifted his chin with my hand.

Wincing, he said, 'They are . . . well, acquaintances of my father.'

*

'Fredy! We can't thank you enough for taking Heinzek off our hands,' his father told me as he welcomed me to his home.

'It is I who should be thanking you,' I replied. 'He's a remarkable boy. There seems to be nothing he can't do and he does it all one hundred per cent.'

'And at one hundred kilometres an hour!' Fritz joked.

Walking into their candlelit dining room took me straight back to nights spent with Max and Jenni in Brno and I felt immediately at home. Just like Jenda's parents, Fritz and his wife Marie welcomed me warmly. I was immediately struck by how beautiful she was, with pale grey eyes and porcelain skin. After she'd served stuffed cabbage and mashed potatoes, the best meal I'd had in months, Fritz invited me into his office where he worked privately as a banker for Jews. 'So, Fredy, Heinzek mentioned that you wanted to talk?' he asked, settling into a chair. 'I hope he's not in trouble.'

'Far from it,' I replied, looking him directly in the eye. 'I'm actually here to talk about your acquaintances who've been so generous to my organisation.'

Showing no sign of surprise, Fritz carried on lighting his pipe as he watched me over the flame. After sucking in a mouthful of smoke, he asked, 'What makes you think that's anything to do with me?'

'Your clever son,' I replied. 'Unless I'm mistaken, it's thanks to you that he's been able to get me things that none but the

Resistance could source. Don't worry, I'm not interested in details. I just want to be introduced.'

'To what purpose?'

'So that I can stop putting Heinzek in any more danger. It would be better – and safer – if I dealt with them directly.'

To my surprise, within days Fritz gave me an address of an apartment south of the city. 'Be there at 6 a.m. Tuesday and say simply "*Motyl*" to whoever opens the door.'

Having discovered that *Motyl* meant butterfly, I was let in by a frail old woman who showed me to a room where a man was waiting. Not only was he younger than I'd imagined but I recognised him immediately as Kurt Novak, a popular journalist on a Czech newspaper who wrote under the pseudonym *Pepík*. Since the Occupation, his newspaper had been forced to publish Nazi propaganda or face closure. What the Germans didn't know, but which was common knowledge among the Czechs and Jews, was that he and his colleagues inserted coded messages into the text, relaying vital information to those who knew where to look. Kurt was their cuckoo in the nest.

'I wanted to thank you for the things you sent,' I told him as I shook his hand and stared into eyes of rich hazel-green. With a chiselled jawline and an unruly mop of brown hair, he reminded me of Willi Domgraf-Fassbaender, the handsome movie star I'd lusted over as a teenager.

'No thanks required,' he replied, his manner guarded. 'Our work isn't just about propaganda and sabotage. It's about maintaining a sense of normality for ordinary citizens, especially for those who'll help shape the future.'

'Exactly. And that's what we're trying to do. But one thing puzzles me. Why risk your lives to help Jews, many of whom are refugees from Germany – like me?'

He let out a short laugh and wandered to the window. Pulling back a corner of curtain to check that I wasn't followed, he kept his back to me when he said, 'You think you're different from anyone else? Like the diabetic old lady who owns this flat and would die without her insulin or the priest who stores weapons for us in his crypt? The Gestapo wouldn't think twice about putting a bullet in my brain for helping any one of you, so what difference does it make which Bible you read?'

It was my turn to laugh, which made him twist his head. 'What's so funny?'

'I can't remember the last time I spoke to anyone who saw me as a human being and not just a Jew.' With that first exchange, Kurt and I came to an understanding. Although I wouldn't do anything to risk the children, I'd act as his eyes and ears in the city and at the *Hagibor*, reporting back on anything useful that I heard. In return, he'd continue to use his contacts in the black market to get me what I needed. 'How about a thousand visas?' I asked, with a wink.

'It would be easier to get you into the SS,' he replied, his face cracking into a grin.

*

'So, we are at war,' the opening sentence of the announcement on Polish radio on the afternoon of 1st September, 1939, sent yet another shock wave rippling across Europe.

Huddled around the wireless at the Maccabi headquarters that night, my colleagues and I listened in stunned silence as the newscaster reported that Germany had invaded Poland at dawn, marching across the border and bombing many towns and cities in a full-scale invasion. In a statement Adolf Hitler declared, '*We will fight the battle for the honour and vital rights of reborn Germany.*'

'Armed forces have been mobilized in Britain and France,' the broadcast continued, 'but after the Soviets signed a non-aggression pact with Germany last week, they are committed to not providing any assistance.' Completely surrounded, we were trapped in the eye of a cyclone.

'That's our last escape route cut off, too,' Ze'ev pointed out, as we sat in a daze once the broadcast ended.

'But surely this will mean Britain and France will come to our rescue now?' someone asked, their eyes hopeful.

'Why? They haven't helped Poland,' Gonda pointed out, bitterly.

In the coming days and weeks, we remained glued to the radio listening to news of Poland's brave attempts at resistance, especially in Warsaw. 'Should we have taken up arms here and done more?' I asked Jakob after hearing the latest reports. 'I know Czechoslovakia is tiny compared to Germany but was it naïve to assume the Allies would come to our aid?'

'Probably, but it's too late,' he said. 'All we can hope for is that they'll intervene on behalf of us all now.' When that didn't happen and the Red Army invaded Poland from the east, our collective spirits slumped. The future seemed bleaker than ever.

Aside from my work at the *Hagibor*, there were few distractions from the suffocating sense of oppression crushing my chest. At night, I lay in my bed wondering what disaster would befall us next and how we could possibly save the children from it. If it hadn't been for the welcome invitations to dinner with Fritz and Marie, I'm not sure I would have coped. To my surprise they also invited Kurt, who proved to be a welcome distraction and a lively and amusing guest, telling us some hair-raising stories about his youth.

'You were fostered?' I asked, surprised. 'Why, what happened to your parents?'

He sighed. 'I never knew my father and my mother was – how should I say – "busy" elsewhere. None of my fosterers could handle me, so I did as I pleased. By the time I was thirteen, I pretty much ran the street life of the neighbourhood where I grew up in Karlsbad. Everything I needed I stole, but never once got caught. The only guidance I had was from an old librarian who taught me to read after the library was closed.' Looking at him with fresh eyes, I realised that he'd never quite lost the look of a wily street kid, which was one of the things that made him so attractive.

I continued my work at the *Hagibor* throughout the winter, trying to come up with games that would be unaffected by snow. Kurt came to report on a few of our football matches, standing on the side-lines in a raincoat watching me with an intensity I found strangely reassuring.

Thanks to him, I took delivery of some warmer coats and boots for the children who skated with me on the Vltava River. He also delivered footballs, hoops and stopwatches for my helpers. Each time he came, he'd impart some new information about the Nazis. 'We hear that they're looking to set up a large Jewish ghetto somewhere outside Prague,' he told me. 'Several places have been considered and Eichmann himself is involved in finding the perfect place.'

I passed his worrying news to the Elders, who were immediately suspicious. 'Where are you getting this from, Fredy?' Jakob asked. 'We've heard nothing of this.'

'I can't say,' I replied. 'Trust me, it's better this way.' He believed me but not everyone did and I began to hear whispers of a rumour that I was collaborating with the Nazis.

'Which Germans are you talking to and why?' Gonda demanded, his expression full of suspicion and, even though I felt the familiar clench of persecution in my guts, I refused to answer.

World events took turn after disastrous turn. On one terrible day—10ᵗʰ May, 1940 – the Nazis invaded France, Belgium, Luxembourg and the Netherlands. Soon after, I received a letter. *You were right to be nervous, Fredy*, Jenda wrote. *I hope you're keeping safe and are able to safeguard your children. They're lucky to have you.*

He and I had kept in touch in the eighteen months since I'd moved back to the capital, although he was a far more diligent correspondent than I was. His letters detailed how difficult things were in Brno, especially for his parents whose house and belongings had been confiscated. *My father is broken. He can't forgive himself for refusing to believe that this could happen in a civilised country.* Then, one day, he wrote to tell me he was coming to Prague. *With nothing to do but reflect on my mistakes, I feel the need to be with you. I'll offer my services to your organisation if they'll have me – if you will.*

I was looking forward to seeing him, although my feelings for him had changed. There would always be a place in my heart for Jenda but I was mistaken when I'd imagined being in love. Mine had been the infatuation of a naïve young man in desperate need of affection. Jenda and his family had given me that, for which I'd always be grateful, but he and I were too different and, in our final months in Brno, we felt to be doing a dance I didn't know the steps to.

I met him at Wilson Station and was surprised to see how much thinner and less sure of himself he was. After I found us a quiet corner in which to talk, he began to apologise again but I pressed a finger to my lips. 'There's no need. Everything's changed. We have to look forward now, not back.'

'Yes, Fredy,' he replied, unusually docile. 'You're right. I'm just so happy to see you.' Reaching for my hand, he squeezed it before I pulled away.

'When I said everything's changed, Jenda, I meant everything. Including us.'

I watched him scan my face before a cloud crossed his eyes. 'You've met someone,' he said, so softly that I almost didn't hear him over the noise of the trains.

'No.'

'You have. I can tell.'

I shrugged. 'If you're asking if I've become friendly with someone then the answer is yes, but not in the way you think.'

His brow wrinkled into a frown. 'A stranger or someone you know?'

I sighed. 'Don't do this, Jenda. I've never asked about your private life.'

'Well?' He was like a dog with a bone.

'There is a man I've met in the course of my work but there's nothing going on.'

My words were met with a suspicious sneer and his comment, 'Yet.'

Sighing, I said, 'You told me once that I thought of myself as a god, Jenda, but the sad truth is I'm only human and I missed having a friend to talk to.'

'So I gather.'

Leaning forward, I whispered, 'We live in dangerous times. I'm certain you've sought friendship where you could.' He blinked. 'Well then.'

Eyes glimmering, he said, 'I thought what we had was special. It was for me, anyway.'

I sat back in my chair. 'You'll always be special to me but I must focus on those who need me now. There's no room in my heart for anyone else. When this war is over and I've done what I believe I was put on this earth to do, then I may think differently. Until then I remain wholly in their service.'

Jenda attempted a smile. 'I applaud your devotion, as always.' Rising to his feet, he gave a hollow laugh. 'Rest assured I'll be looking forward to the day this damn war ends with even more enthusiasm.' Through friends in Prague, he found himself a small room to rent and, after hearing my poor attempts at Czech, he volunteered to interpret for me. He also helped translate some of my articles as, with Kurt's encouragement, I'd found an outlet in writing about the importance of mind-body strength for youth in our newsletter and in Prague's Jewish newspaper.

It was good to spend time with Jenda again, although I don't think he ever lost hope that we'd get back together. And while my friendship with Kurt was entirely platonic, I still didn't want Jenda getting in the way. All he knew was that I had a contact on the black market and the need for secrecy was vital. 'Meeting this man sounds dangerous,' he commented, his gaze unwavering. 'Or is that the thrill?'

12

October 1942, Terezín, Czechoslovakia

A MIRACLE OCCURRED on a beautiful autumn day in 1942, something so extraordinary that it almost felt like a dream. The cutest puppy anyone had ever seen came bowling into the ghetto like a furry cannonball and ran dementedly from person to person, wagging its stubby tail.

No one knew where he came from and nobody knew his name but everybody fell in love with that little golden mutt instantly. 'Can we keep him, Fredy? Can we?' the children clamoured, crowding me as I cradled the fluffy creature on my lap.

'I don't know,' I answered. 'He might belong to someone. Besides, how would we feed him?' What felt like a hundred children piped up that nobody lived near the ghetto, so he must be a stray, and offered ways of sharing our food with him and asking the cooks for scraps.

Laughing, I said, 'Well, let's see if he wants to stay first, shall we? He ran in here from somewhere and one day he may run back.'

Little Franka squeezed in between the legs of some of the older children to stroke the puppy's velvet-soft belly. 'What's his name?' she asked, her eyes brighter than I'd ever seen them.

'We'll have to give him one, dear Franka,' I told her, smiling, as a cacophony of suggestions flew at me. Raising my hand,

I said, 'Quiet now or you'll frighten the poor mite. How about Budulínku, after one of your favourite bedtime stories?' 'Yes, yes,' they cried and the name stuck.

The Czech folk tale of *Budulínek* was one I'd never heard of as a child but it had a message that I liked. A little boy whose more familiar name is Budulínku is left home alone by his grandmother who warns him not to let anyone into their cottage. But a sly fox persuades him to by offering him a ride on her tail. Once inside, she eats his only meal and runs off. Despite his grandmother's warnings, he is similarly tricked on two more occasions, losing his lunch each time. When the fox finally gives him a ride, she carries him deep into the forest where she holds him captive to care for her cubs. After he's saved by a passing organ grinder, the boy promises never to disobey his grandmother again.

I quickly realised that our very own Budulínku had a message of his own – to remind us of the importance of play. That little dog brought so much joy to the ghetto I couldn't have wished for a better gift. Running from room to room, he begged for food or to play and was happy to sleep with any child, despite my concerns about fleas. The children washed and groomed him, playing games with him all day until he fell asleep, his little legs twitching in his dreams.

Whenever I was teaching gymnastics on the ramparts or supervising the dance class for girls learning the *Hora*, Budulínku would come barrelling into what was an exhilarating sight. Arms linked, the girls would go faster and faster in a circle as they sang *Hava Nagila* at the top of their voices. That was, until that naughty puppy began to run in circles around them, yapping madly and nipping at bare ankles in his enthusiasm to join in.

Even the ghetto guards and some of the SS were enchanted by our furry interloper. And when he ran into the middle of a tense football match one Sunday afternoon, everyone cheered as the players ran around trying to catch him before he bolted through the courtyard gates.

Then one day in November, our precious pet vanished. No one knew where he had gone and I feared the worst, as I knew a stray cat had been killed and eaten by some teenagers. I was relieved when someone said they'd spotted Budulínku running out of the main gate after it was opened for a truck, even though I wasn't sure whether to believe it. His loss affected the children more deeply than losing members of their own family in some cases and I spent weeks consoling them.

'Won't he be cold and hungry?' they'd cry, tears wetting their cheeks. 'Who's going to feed him and brush out his coat?' others asked. One girl had knitted him a red coat for winter and was distraught that he'd never get to wear it, so I pretended that I'd heard that he'd run back to his original family in town.

'As soon as I have the address, we can send it to him,' I told her, forgiving myself for the lie.

*

'Alfred? Alfred Hirsch?' I heard a voice call as I stepped out of my barracks into the busy street, my mind on rumours that Jakob was soon to be replaced as the Head of the Elders.

Distracted, I turned to see a straggly line of exhausted deportees being led to their accommodation on the opposite side of the street. I could tell straight away that they were German from their clothes and the names painted in white lettering on their suitcases. One old man had stepped out of line and was standing staring at me as if he'd seen a spectre. Painfully thin, he hadn't shaved in days and his coat was threadbare. 'Alfred, is that you?' he called, as I tried to place him. Then the *pfennig* finally dropped.

'*Herr* Steil! Yes, yes, it's me.' Hurrying over to where he stood, I grabbed his hand and shook it vigorously. 'I'm so glad you're here, Sir. I am at your service.'

My childhood teacher's pale eyes filled with tears and for a moment he couldn't speak. His skin was a strange, unhealthy hue and he looked even frailer close-up. 'Thank you, Alfred,' he whispered. 'I'm very happy to see you again, my boy.'

Taking his suitcase, I linked my arm through his and led him back to my barracks where I sat him in a corner of my office and went to find him some bread and soup. He ate slowly and with great care, his expression one of embarrassment. When his bowl was empty, he put down the spoon, reached into a pocket and pulled out a soiled blue handkerchief with which he dabbed his lips. He looked like a tramp but his manners imbued him with such dignity that I was almost moved to tears.

As he leaned forward to replace the handkerchief, his overcoat fell open to reveal something I'd only seen a few times in the ghetto. It was an inverted pink triangle mounted on a yellow triangle to make a Star of David. This rare badge signified that the wearer had been identified by the Nazis as Jewish and homosexual. Catching my eye, he quickly drew his coat across his chest with skeletal fingers.

'Well, now that you've dined in our finest eating establishment, *Herr* Steil, let's book you into the Presidential Suite,' I told him brightly. 'I trust that it will meet all your requirements. It has silk sheets, a rolltop bath and twenty-four-hour room service.' Helping him to his feet, I added, 'Kindly walk this way.'

Standing unsteadily, he squeezed my hand and, looking me directly in the eye, said, '*Vielen Dank, mein Junge.*'

After calling in a few favours, I managed to find him a lower bunk in a room of six men of a similar age, all of whom spoke German. One was a professor of philosophy and another a poet, so I hoped he'd fit in. Checking on him every few days, I was glad to see him gaining strength even though he was still painfully thin.

'I've heard all about your work here from my roommates, Fredy,' he told me one day, as he sat propped up in bed, his voice weak. 'Nobody has a bad word to say about you. Quite the contrary. I always knew you'd make something of your life.'

It was pitiful to see so many once-proud men like *Herr* Steil reduced to husks, physically and mentally. Among the teeming mass of humanity crammed within our walls, the old were at the bottom of the pile. Shoved into bare rooms or lofts far from any facilities with no privacy, many suffered from chronic diarrhoea caused by poor diet. Too weak to make it to the toilet, they lay in their own dirt, stinking of ammonia and excrement, waiting for death. The rest roamed the streets looking for food.

'At the kitchen where I work, it's the elderly who beg the most for a few vegetables and always want thicker soup from the bottom of the cauldron,' Miriam told me one Friday night. 'They prowl around the garbage bins like feral cats in search of anything from discarded onion skins to potato peelings. The Germans give those scraps to the pig farmers who supply them with pork, yet these poor wretches fight for them in the gutter.'

Jakob drew his breath across his teeth. 'I've seen similar hordes descend on the tables where they serve the soup, desperate to lick off any that was spilled. They also scrape out the blackened rind from inside the soup kettles, despite our warnings that it's rotten and will make them ill.'

'Can nothing more be done for them?' I asked.

Jakob sighed. 'No matter how many times we ask for extra food to increase their rations, our requests are dismissed. The SS act as if there's no point feeding those who'll die anyway and the sooner they do the more there'll be for everyone else.'

Every day we saw disabled war veterans and elite members of society standing in line for soup or the latrines. As one of my coarser co-workers put it, 'Those folks with their noses in the air may have been rich and famous once, but their *Scheisse* stinks just the same.'

Leo explained why so many so-called *Prominente* had been sent to Terezín. 'The Nazis are worried there'll be questions in the West about what happened to those who are famous. They want them here so they can be inspected if necessary but until that happens their status offers them little protection.'

Wanting to do more for the elderly, I organised a group of teenagers to visit them on Sundays. Mostly girls who volunteered, they braved the sights, sounds and smells of those terrible rooms to read aloud or sing songs. I was so proud of them.

'We must never forget that the older generation are our sacred oracles,' I told them. 'They have lived through wars and have wisdom and advice to impart, if only we listen.' My words took my mind back to Aachen when *Herr* Steil had saved me from childhood despair.

I'd been working in the abattoir's cold store, as I often did after school, alongside a veteran named Wolfgang who'd lost a leg in the Belgian trenches. One day he broke down as he was cutting up a lamb's carcass. Pushing away the meat, he turned to me with wild eyes and started speaking about the war. '*I never wanted to kill people, Fredy, I just wanted to fight for my country*,' he said. '*Things were so bad when we got there, though, that men ran away.*'

His face corkscrewed in pain, he added, '*I too decided to run as far away as I could. I crept from our trench in the dead of night but then it happened. We took a direct hit and everyone in the dugout disappeared under that vile, sticky mud. I was the sole survivor, minus my leg . . .*' Staring at the side of lamb, he added, '*. . . lying next to me, it looked like that.*'

Pulling me to him until my face was squashed against his stained apron, he wept inconsolably as I fought for breath. When he finally let go, I gazed up into eyes seared by the memory of his unit drowning in blood and clay. Gulping, I fled and ran to the hills, not stopping until I was deep in the calm of the forest. Later that evening, as friends and neighbours searched for me, Wolfgang – exhausted by the images in his mind – slit his own throat.

All I could think about afterwards was that, for him, death was preferable to life and that troubled me. I'd learned in the synagogue that suicide was a punishable offence under Jewish law and I feared for his soul. My father was too upset to talk and it wasn't something I could speak to my mother or brother about, so I approached *Herr* Steil one day after class. '*I'm sorry to trouble you, Sir,*' I began as he wiped the chalk from the blackboard.

Turning, he studied my frown and put down the duster. '*What is it, Alfred?*'

Hesitating, I shifted on my feet. '*It's about death, Sir.*'

'*Go on.*'

'*The Bible says that if we keep our covenant with God we'll be promised a good life.*'

'*That's right.*'

'*But it also speaks of a dark world beneath the earth that we go to when we die, even if we've been righteous. Gentiles are there too.*'

'*It's called* Sheol, *the grave of all humanity.*'

'*And we're punished there if we've offended?*'

Herr Steil offered me a seat and sat beside me. '*What's brought this on, Alfred? Have you done something you think you might be punished for?*'

'*No. I mean, I don't think so, Sir. Someone I knew died and I'm afraid he'll suffer.*'

'*Why? What did he do?*'

I hung my head. Saying it loud would make it real. '*He took his own life.*'

Herr Steil sat silently for a while before speaking. '*I know of whom you speak, but you needn't worry. There is compassion for those under mental strain, so rites will be observed.*'

'*They will?*' I asked. I couldn't bear the thought of Wolfgang being in eternal torment.

'*Is there anything else?*'

I frowned. '*If Gentiles go to* Sheol *too, then what's the difference between us? Doesn't that mean we're all the same in the end?*'

Herr Steil seemed taken aback. Rubbing his chin, he said, '*That's a big question, Alfred, and one I'm not sure I'm qualified to answer. But yes, we are all just human. Your rabbi would be the best person to ask.*' Our rabbi terrified me with his talk of abomination so I never asked him, but even after all those years the question never left me.

Having never forgotten his kindness, it was a privilege to help him in the ghetto. 'Would you consider teaching some of the little ones, Sir?' I asked him one afternoon. 'We have very few textbooks but plenty of other volumes and, unless I'm mistaken, you taught from memory anyway.'

His watery eyes lit up. 'It would be my honour.'

Seeking out the relevant clerk in the Education Department, I was directed to a converted broom cupboard at the back of a near-derelict barracks. The space was just large enough for a chair and a small desk, piled high with paperwork. 'Ah, there you are,' I said to the stranger, giving him my warmest smile. My breath came out in clouds as I spoke and I noticed that the hapless clerk had stuffed his clothes with old newspapers to ward off the cold.

'My name is Fredy Hirsch from Youth Welfare and I'd like to register a new teacher for children aged six to twelve,' I announced, happy with my task. 'He's a multi-lingual German teacher with excellent credentials. His name is Leopold Steil.'

'Papers?' the man responded impatiently, extending his hand in fingerless gloves without looking up. Clearing a small space on his desk, he opened *Herr* Steil's identity card and began to write his name in a ledger. Hesitating, he ran a blackened fingernail along a line of ink and adjusted his glasses. Looking up at me, he said, 'He wears a pink triangle.'

My skin prickled. 'That's right.'

'And you want him to teach children?'

'We'd be fortunate to have such an experienced tutor.'

The clerk fixed me with a stare. 'But he was arrested under Paragraph 175. He's a homosexual.' The word curled his top lip. Staring at him properly for the first time, I noticed the inverted purple triangle stitched over a yellow one signifying that he was a Jehovah's Witness: a religious organisation that considered homosexuality a mortal sin. 'Well?' he queried. 'You surely don't want to take the risk?'

Shuddering, I told him, 'There'll be no risk. This gentleman was the best teacher in my school. I can vouch for him personally.'

The clerk sighed. 'The decision is out of my hands. It will have to go to committee.'

Knowing how long that could take and how embarrassing it would be for *Herr* Steil, I thumped my fist on the table, almost toppling one of his paperwork stacks. 'No! This man is frail and will die here unless he has a reason to get up each morning. Teaching may save him and the children will benefit enormously. I shan't leave this office until you approve him.' Seeing the fear in his eyes, I softened. 'Please. Let this old man be judged in *Sheol*, not on this earth.'

The man smirked. 'There is no Hell,' he told me as one hand reached instinctively for the triangle that defined his belief and the other shoved the ID papers back across the desk.

'Oh, yes there is,' I snapped. 'And we're both in it.' Grabbing the documents, I hurried from the room.

It took me weeks of lobbying to get *Herr* Steil approved by the authorities but he was admitted to hospital with pneumonia before I had an answer. Even Jakob and Gonda had seemed reluctant to support my quest and their hesitation troubled me. At one of our Friday night suppers Miriam picked up on my mood and, when Jakob stepped out to deal with a problem, she asked me if everything was all right.

'Yes,' I replied, but when she gave me a look, I shrugged. 'I've been trying to get something done but it feels like I'm riding a dead horse.'

'Is this about your schoolteacher? Jakob mentioned it.' When I nodded, she said, 'Maybe you're too close to the problem, Fredy.'

I felt a sudden chill. 'How do you mean?'

She took my hand. 'I mean that the resistance you've been facing shouldn't come as a surprise to you . . . after your own experiences in the Maccabis.'

My heart leapt like a deer as blood rushed to my head. Pulling away, I said, 'You know about that?'

'Of course, Fredy dear. We've always known.'

Stunned, I took a few moments to let that sink in. I'd been so careful to keep my reputation intact. To discover that people knew all along shattered that illusion. 'Does anyone else know?' I asked, fearing her answer.

Miriam's expression looked horribly like pity. 'Yes, Fredy. Even some of the children do, but nobody cares because we love and trust you. You mustn't worry.'

Jumping up, I fled the place that had felt like a sanctuary to me, bumping into Jakob as I hurried away. 'What's wrong?' he asked but I could only mumble something and stumble past.

Going straight to the hospital, I sought out *Herr* Steil whose counsel I felt in desperate need of. Pulling my collar over my nose to stifle the smell as I picked my way across the crowded sickroom, I eventually spotted him lying on the floor in a cone of yellow light. All around him wheezing old men in various states of undress lay on similar filthy mattresses, their pitiful cries for deliverance going unheard.

Kneeling by my schoolteacher's side, I took the cluster of bones that passed for his hand and scolded myself for not visiting him sooner. '*Herr* Steil, it's me, Alfred,' I said, trying to hide my reaction. 'How are you feeling?'

Rolling his head towards me on a neck that was all sinew, he attempted a smile. 'A little better, I think,' he lied. Looking into his sallow face and yellow eyes, I knew then that his only exit from that building would be on the funeral cart.

Blinking and clearing my throat, my voice cracked as I told him, 'Well, I have some good news. You've been approved to teach and your pupils can't wait to attend your classes. I've told them all about you.'

He stared at me through rheumy eyes. 'You were always a terrible liar, Fredy.'

My mind flashed back to a day in class when a boy who'd never liked me spotted me sketching birds instead of writing out stanzas of a poem.

'*Herr* Steil, Alfred Hirsch is drawing again, not writing,' the boy piped up, his fat fingers waving in the air. The son of a Jesuit priest whose Jewish grandfather had insisted he attend a Jewish school, he'd taken against me from my first day there, barging into me at every opportunity and stealing my lunch. I never understood why. The day he snitched on me, I slipped my picture half under the lid of my desk and returned to the poem I was supposed to be studying. I heard *Herr* Steil's footsteps approaching from behind and froze when his shadow fell over my desk.

'Is this true, Alfred?' he asked.

Turning, I looked up at the man who seemed ten feet tall and said, 'No, Sir.' As I uttered the lie, I felt my skin redden under my collar as *Herr* Steil's eyes burned into me. My head pulsing, I feared I might burst into flames.

'Very well, get on with your work,' he said, taking a step away. Relaxing the pressure on the desk, my sheet of wild birds fluttered out from under me and landed at his feet. Holding my breath, I watched him bend to pick it up. When he turned back, I stared intently at my inkwell, waiting for the inevitable. Instead, he placed the page carefully in front of me.

'Good work, Alfred,' he said. 'Only I think the owl might be improved if his face was more heart-shaped.' I never dared lie to him again.

Kneeling by that kind man's side all those years later and fighting against a choking sensation, I leaned in. 'I once asked you a question you never answered, Sir.'

'I remember.'

I was astonished. 'You do?'

'You wanted to know the difference between Gentiles and Jews if we all go to *Sheol*.'

I nodded. 'I still want to know. Are we all the same in the end, no matter what?'

With enormous effort, *Herr* Steil pulled himself up on his elbows so that he could better see his dying bedfellows. 'Look around you,' he rasped, as I took in the dystopian scene. 'There are forty-two men in this room and we'll all soon be in *Sheol*.'

I held my breath as he fought to catch his. 'Some are Jewish, some Catholic, a few are political prisoners and there are Communists, Protestants – and at least one homosexual.' He gazed at me then with knowing eyes.

I stared at all those grey men in grey pyjamas under soiled grey blankets in that grey room and my eyes filled with tears. Inside each husk was a human being who'd had a life and a family, who'd known love and fear, the joy of art, sex and beauty. In the space of a few years, the Nazis had reduced them to pale phantoms before hastening them to a miserable, premature end.

'Looking around, can you tell which of us is which, my boy?' *Herr* Steil asked, his eyelids growing heavy. When I shook my head, he told me, 'If this war has taught us anything, it is that we are the same, all of us, no matter how we once defined ourselves. We will all descend to the underworld and we will all be judged.'

'And how will you and I be judged?' I stared at him intently as I waited for his answer. He was the only person in the world I could have asked.

The old man nodded. 'We will be judged for our hearts, Alfred,' he replied, his breathing shallower. 'For the love we gave and the love we received.'

His voice growing hoarse, he began to cough; a hacking, terrible spasm that shook his entire body. Fetching him a little water, I cupped the back of his sweaty head in my hand as he sipped through cracked lips. Flopping back down onto the straw, he closed his eyes and, for a moment, I feared he'd never open them again. Looking up in hope at a passing doctor, I shuddered as the medic in a dirty white coat gave me a small shake of his head.

When *Herr* Steil spoke again his voice was so soft that I had to inch even closer. 'For you and me, Fredy, that love has been for the children; those young minds we've strived to improve.' Opening his eyes once more, he clung to my sleeve and turned his face to me with sudden urgency. 'Only the strongest will survive, Alfred . . . your work is just beginning . . . as you teach, you learn. As you learn, you teach – remember that.'

His use of the very proverb my uncle had sent me years earlier shook me. I had a hundred more questions but fatigue overtook him and I could tell he needed sleep. 'Goodnight, *Herr* Steil,' I said, squeezing his arm and feeling only bone.

'*Auf Wiedersehen, mein Junge*,' he whispered. I knew then that by morning he'd have parted from this life, crossing the gossamer veil.

Hurrying blindly from the room, I staggered out into the street. It was past curfew but the night sky sparkled with stars and there was a soft yellow moon that made the god-forsaken town look suddenly very beautiful. Unable to keep up my facade, I sank to the hospital steps as tears burst from my eyes. Cradling my head in my hands, I sobbed like a baby, wishing I'd had more time with that remarkable soul. There was so much he could have taught me and so much I still needed to know but it was too late.

If only I'd understood his heart when I was younger I could have turned to him for guidance, especially after my father died. Jenda had been the first person to open the world up to me but that hadn't worked out in the end. As I had been for most of my life, I found myself completely alone.

Hearing footsteps, I saw the figure of a gendarme walking my way but didn't expect him to bother me. I was well enough known and my status allowed me to be out after hours. Wiping my eyes on my sleeve, I lowered my head and pretended to tie my shoelaces as the footsteps drew closer. Hoping they'd pass, I sighed as they kept coming until I found myself staring at a pair of grubby black boots.

Looking up at the silhouette of a man, I was unable to make out any features but when he spoke my name I jumped to my feet.

'Kurt! What are you doing here?' Staring into his face with disbelief, it was as if I'd summoned his cheerful presence by thought alone.

'Well, I figured you could do with some help,' he jested, returning my embrace with a slight wince.

'When did you get here?'

'Three days ago. I finally ran out of luck. The Gestapo arrested me not for my black market activities but for a coded message in the newspaper.'

'The Gestapo arrested you?' I stepped back to take a better look. 'Did they hurt you?'

Kurt laughed. 'When they threatened to send me to a concentration camp, I told them that I'd prefer to come to Terezín as I had friends there.' I could just imagine him saying that to the humourless henchman of the Reich and was amazed he was still breathing.

'And?'

'They broke my nose and fractured my cheekbone for my trouble,' he said, 'but here I am, a cuckoo in your nest.' He turned his face so that I could see the bump on the bridge of his nose and the ugly bruising that ran from his temple to his throat.

'Oh, Kurt,' I said, reaching out to touch his cheek but he grabbed my hand and didn't let go.

Shivering, I felt a rush of something I hadn't felt in a long time. Silently we stared into each other's eyes as my heart thumped against bone. Then, without warning, he pushed me into a doorway out of the long reaches of the moonlight. As our lips met, his hands felt cold against my skin and something metallic was pressing into my back but when we fell together all rational thought slipped away.

With my tears still salty on my lips, the words of my teacher resounded in my ears: *We will be judged for our hearts, Alfred. For the love we gave and the love we received.* There in that pitiful place, in the arms of that beautiful surprise of a man, I finally believed him. At one of the lowest points of my life Kurt had arrived to save me from despair and that moment of salvation was all I cared about as the stars and moon set on my ghetto celibacy.

13

December 1941, Prague, Czechoslovakia

'ALFRED HIRSCH?' THE SKINNY teenager with pale brown eyes stared up at me with a strangely blank expression.

'Yes,' I replied, gazing at the boy standing on my doorstep next to another about the same age. He had a large satchel slung over his shoulder and was holding out a white postcard.

'Here is your transport summons,' he said, thrusting the card stamped with numbers into my hand as my knees almost buckled. 'Report to the Exhibition Hall in thirty-six hours.' Turning away before I even had a chance to close my mouth, he was gone.

Blinking at the card I'd been warned was coming, I still wasn't prepared for the shock of knowing that deportation was now a reality for me. Only the day before, Jakob hadn't been certain. 'You're on the list of people to come with us to help set up the new ghetto at Terezín, Fredy, but because you're German and classified as stateless we don't yet know if you'll be approved by the SS.'

Not knowing whether to be happy or sad at the news, I felt forlorn either way. A big part of me wanted to go with those I'd been working alongside for almost three years but there was another, smaller voice in my head that told me that to become a prisoner of the Nazis was suicide, especially when the tide of war felt to be turning in our favour.

'In the last few months, Hitler has attacked Russia, which will tie him and his men in knots for months and the Americans have entered the war,' Jenda had reported after speaking to a friend with a hidden radio. 'It can only be a matter of time before we are liberated.'

It was Jakob who convinced me otherwise. 'Whatever the outcome, the rise in anti-Semitism across Europe isn't going to stop overnight, so this could be a unique opportunity for us Jews,' he told us at a public meeting to discuss the so-called 'resettlement' of thousands. 'The Germans wish to relocate us to a ghetto where we can live out the war without persecution. They are calling it a model camp and we'll be able to establish our own government and protect thousands. Once the war is over, as it surely must be soon, the Germans have vowed to help us get to the Promised Land.'

We all knew how tirelessly Jakob had worked to achieve this deal, travelling to Berlin and Palestine, researching ways to speed up the mass emigration of Europe's Jews. Anything that might save them from a worse fate. 'The hope is that, once the ghetto is established, key members of the administration will return to Prague and continue to negotiate on behalf of other countries similarly.' The pride in what he'd achieved was written all over his face and, despite my reservations, I was willing and ready to help him fulfil his dream.

Kurt was more sceptical, as was Fritz who invited me for what he jokingly called my Last Supper on the eve of my departure from the city. Marie prepared a veritable feast, determined to fatten me up, she said, as we tucked into a delicious goulash and *knedlíky* bread dumplings. After dinner, we men retired to Fritz's study where they both tried to persuade me not to go. 'We've been talking, Fredy and if you stay in Prague we can keep you safe and put you to work with the Resistance,' Kurt insisted.

Fritz added, 'We know you won't want to abandon your children or the *Hagibor*, but there'll be other ways you can help them. Heinzek can act as your go-between and you can still send instructions to the ghetto to continue your work. You'd just have to stay hidden for a while until we get you new papers.'

I sat very still as they continued to list all the reasons why I shouldn't board the train to Terezín. 'The Nazis can't be trusted, Fredy,' Kurt reiterated. 'You, of all people, know that. Once you're behind those gates you may never see freedom again.'

'But what about the children?' I asked. 'The whole point of me being there is to safeguard them. I can't hide away in some attic while they're sent to a ghetto without me. I'm touched by your concern but I have made my decision and I shall go where I'm most needed.'

Surprisingly, Jenda seemed to understand and came to see me early on the morning of my departure, sitting on the edge of my bed watching as I packed my whistle, binoculars and a few clothes into a rucksack. 'I know I can't dissuade you, so I came to say good luck,' he said with a sad smile before handing me his leather-bound copy of Rilke's poems.

'Oh, Jenda, I can't take that,' I said, trying to give it back. 'It's your favourite and one of the few things you have from home.'

'I want you to have it,' he said, placing it in my rucksack, as his bottom lip wobbled. 'It is the nearest I can give you that's a little piece of me.'

'Thank you,' I said, my voice soft as I laid a hand on his arm.

Standing, Jenda folded me into his arms. 'Take good care of yourself, Fredy,' he said in my ear. 'I hope to see you again someday but, whatever happens, I will never forget you – or what we had.' Then he turned quickly and left.

Blinking back tears, I stood staring into the empty space he'd occupied and was filled with regret. I hadn't been as kind to him as I should have been. It was he who'd rescued me five years earlier in Brno. I owed him so much and yet I'd wounded him so badly. I only hoped he'd forgive me.

A tap on my door made me look up. Miriam stood in the doorway with a bundle in her hands. 'All set?' she asked as she walked in. 'I've brought you a few things that you won't have thought to pack yourself.' Opening the bundle, she pointed out a jar of caramel she'd made. 'It's sweet and full of butter, so if there isn't much food it will keep you going for a bit.'

'But this must have used up your entire week's sugar ration!'

'Don't worry about that. I have plenty of soup.'

There was also a bag of flour, some salt, cheese, beef dripping and a loaf of bread. 'These are for Jakob,' she added, pointing to a letter and his prayer shawl that he left behind in his haste to leave for the ghetto a few days earlier. 'And I've put in a small saucepan for you to heat food with. I imagine conditions will be basic to begin with.'

'Thank you, dear Miriam,' I said, taking the bundle and spreading it flat so that I could carry it in my bedroll.

'I have something else, Fredy,' she said, reaching into her coat pocket. 'It's a letter from Germany. I'm afraid it's several months old because it was sent to Prague, then Brno and has only just been brought back here by one of the Maccabis.'

Staring down at the tattered envelope with my name and address in handwritten black ink, I took a deep breath. 'It's from Uncle Alfred.' Looking up in a daze, I watched as Miriam nodded silently before drawing me into a warm embrace.

'I'll leave you then, my boy,' she said. 'God speed. Send my good wishes to Jakob and tell him that Arieh and I will join him as soon as he summons us.'

Sitting down, legs shaking, I stared at the envelope for several minutes before running my fingernail along the edge and opening it with care. With trembling hands, I pulled out the single page of blue writing paper and took a deep breath. *My dearest nephew*, it began. Three simple words, powerful enough to open the floodgates. *I hope this finds you safe and well. I am writing to you on the eve of our deportation to Łodz in Poland. Life has been very difficult here in Germany, so we are relieved to be leaving for what we hope will be a safer place . . .*

Swallowing, I stared up at the sky through my small window and noticed the sun rising above the wintry pink clouds. All that I'd heard about the Łodz ghetto was that it was a harsh, overcrowded place where inmates were forced into doing labour for food.

Turning back to the letter, I read on. *I don't know if you have had any contact with your family but the last message I had from your mother was a while back to let me know that they and your brother Paul had arrived safely in Bolivia and were settling into their new lives. Although grateful to be away from Europe and in an enclave with other German Jews, living conditions there were challenging and they were struggling with the climate and altitude. I wrote back straight away but the letter was later returned, so I assume they'd moved on.*

Relieved at the news, I took some solace from the fact that my family had managed to escape after all. So often I'd wondered where they were and how they were faring. I'd felt for Paul especially as, in the space of a few years, he'd been forced to give up his rabbinical studies just as he was about to be ordained and all his beliefs about assimilation and standing our ground had been shattered. One thing was certain, my brother would throw himself into good works abroad and do all he could to offer spiritual succour to those who most needed it. A pioneer in his own right, albeit in a different land to the one we'd once envisaged, his congregation would be lucky to have him.

Alfred's elegant handwriting began to falter in his final paragraph and, as a lump rose in my throat, I imagined him sitting at a desk late into the night penning what he knew could be his last letter. *As I sit here writing this, I am wracked with guilt for not being a better uncle to you, Fredy. I know how hard it was to lose your father at such a tender age and then your mother too, for a while. Paul was older and had found his path but I should have done more for you, my beautiful boy.* A tear splashed the page, blotting the word 'boy' but I quickly dabbed at it with my sleeve. It was all I could do to get through the last paragraph.

I sensed a vulnerability in you, Fredy, that I pray you have learned to master. Now it is too late to show you all that I hoped to or to teach you what I have learned. Although from what I've heard of your marvellous work with children, it is perhaps you who should have been teaching me. Be strong and blessed, Fredy. With God's help and your own resilience, you will survive this nightmare and have a sweet life. Your loving Onkel Alfred.

*

Closing the door on my life in Prague was one of the hardest things I ever had to do. After I'd said goodbyes to those in our group who were remaining behind for now, I picked up my belongings and walked away from them, the children, the *Hagibor* and the city that had given me sanctuary.

Accompanied by Leo, Gonda and around forty other administrative staff, I walked the mile through the snow and ice to the vast Exhibition Hall where we were to be registered for transport. As we stood in line waiting to be admitted, ordinary citizens passed us on the street with mixed expressions on their faces: some of pity and a few of open contempt. One woman with a daughter of around ten years old hurried up to me and pressed a green apple into my hand.

'Good luck, Fredy,' she said, as she kissed my cheek, her eyes moist. 'May God go with you.' To the best of my knowledge, I'd never met her or her child before and had no idea how she knew who I was. It was Leo who put me straight. 'Your photograph appeared everywhere after the Maccabiah Games and then again because of your work at the *Hagibor*,' he said. 'Any Jewish parent worth their salt in this city knows exactly who Fredy Hirsch is.'

Hearing a low whistle, I turned and was surprised to see Kurt standing across the street, leaning against a doorway with a cigarette in his hand. He was watching me with the same intensity as when he'd stood on the side-lines at the *Hagibor*. With our eyes locked and no need for words, I found his presence comforting. When I was the next in line for admission to the Hall, Kurt drew on his cigarette and then dropped it to the ground, grinding it into the snow with his heel. Thrusting both hands deep into the pocket of his overcoat, he gave me an almost imperceptible nod of his head and turned away.

Two steps away from becoming a prisoner, I watched his broad shoulders disappearing into the crowd. '*Lebewohl, mein Freund*,' I whispered. Farewell.

*

Once inside the Hall, we were treated largely with respect as representatives of the Council, but – as always – there were a few rogue Nazis whose deep-seated hatred for all Jews compelled them to act with brutality. When one of them shoved Leo hard in the ribs for dawdling in the line for registration, making him double up in pain, I didn't stop to think and quickly stepped between them with my hand raised, barking a sharp, 'Nein!'

'Nein?' the thug queried, squaring up to me with a snarl. 'You dare speak the language of the Master Race?'

'I am a son of Aachen in Westphalia, so that makes me one of your so-called master race,' I replied, eye to eye with him, my shoulders pressed back as Leo watched. The brute's eyes gave a momentary flicker of doubt. Before he could make his next move, I grabbed Leo by the arm and moved him forward in the line, turning my back on his assailant for good.

'You idiot!' Gonda hissed, glaring at me. 'You could have got us killed.'

'But Gonda,' Leo cried, 'he was only trying to protect me!'

'That's as maybe but he was also showing off and that kind of behaviour can only lead to trouble.' Turning to me, he added, 'Things are very different now. You're not in charge of Fredy-land anymore. We are all working together and everything we do impacts on the rest. Guard your tongue and your temper or things will go badly for you.'

I was so shaken by Gonda's outburst that I remained subdued for the rest of that long afternoon. Questioning my response to the unprovoked violence against Leo, I wondered if Gonda had a point.

Jakob had been kind to me in Prague and had allowed me to do as I pleased but as a close collective under SS supervision in Terezín we'd have to pull together much more. The idea that there could be consequences for the Council if I over-stepped the line was a salutary thought.

After hours in the unheated Exhibition Hall without any food or water, I shared out Miriam's caramel and longed for a hot drink as I shivered, fearing that I hadn't packed enough warm clothing. Wearing two pairs of socks, two vests, a thick pair of trousers, a jacket, shirt, sweater and winter coat, I was still chilled to the marrow and no amount of running on the spot could warm me up. It was the same for everyone around me, and the elderly and the young felt the cold most keenly.

'*Achtung!*' the call finally came. Formed into pairs, I stuck with Leo as we were marched in time to the nearby railway station. A passenger train with shabby third-class carriages awaited us. Filed inside the frozen compartments, we huddled together billowing steam as we were counted and recounted by guards. It seemed to take another hour before there was a sudden lurch and the train slowly began to move. Sitting by a grubby window, I scraped away the ice and peered out at the grey city whose only splashes of colour were the ubiquitous Swastika flags.

Thinking back to the day I'd first arrived with Father Marek's scrap of paper in my hand, I reflected on how much had changed. Back then I'd been a naïve nineteen-year-old with no real sense of the world. Damaged, apologetic and afraid, I was like a fawn alone in the forest, the buildings of Prague towering over me like beech trees as I took my first faltering steps.

Six years later, I was fully grown with a clear idea of who – and what – I was. I'd found my calling in teaching, my strength in physical exercise and myself in the arms of another. I'd gained in courage and confidence to become Fredy Hirsch, a stag in his prime, honed and muscular, leaping effortlessly over every hurdle.

In leaving the sanctuary of Prague, though, I was stepping beyond the protection of my herd and heading for an unknown wilderness. All manner of dangers lay waiting for me if I strayed from the path. And like the teacher in *Rabbit School* had warned so prophetically, if the wily fox grabbed me, then no amount of pleading would help.

14

August 1943, Terezín, Czechoslovakia

'A NEW TRANSPORT ARRIVED this afternoon but there's something strange, Fredy.' When Gonda clenched his jaw, it lifted his spectacles a centimetre. The pale grey eyes behind them gave me a haunted look. 'The SS have commanded everyone overlooking the new railway spur to remain inside and not even look out the windows,' he added. 'We've been told to send water to the train, which means they're not unloading them yet despite the heat.'

I could only imagine the suffering. In the height of summer, the wagons would have been unbearably hot and by the time they reached us the occupants would be in a desperate state. 'Where have they come from?' I asked.

'That's the other strange thing. The log says it's a "special" transport comprising twelve hundred orphans from Bialystok. We've never had trains from Poland before as the traffic's always been in the opposite direction. The rumour is that they're headed for Switzerland as part of a trade for German prisoners-of-war but if that's the case why bring them here?'

'Why wasn't I told about this sooner? I should have been told, Gonda.'

'We had very little warning. They're being taken to that new barracks beyond the ghetto walls. There's something fishy going on.'

Frowning, I couldn't help but agree. The Nazi transportation system ran like a well-oiled machine and rarely varied from schedule. The usual routine with each new 'consignment' was that stunned occupants were forced out of their wagons and marched to the *Schleusse*. Nor had there previously been a transport comprising only children. 'Let me be among those taking them water so I can find out what's going on,' I pleaded.

Gonda shook his head. 'No, Fredy, you can't. There's a ban on communicating with them on pain of death and anyone sent will be closely supervised.'

'Even if I can't talk to them, I could at least see what state they're in.'

'No, Fredy. I forbid it.'

After searching the ghetto for Kurt, I found him in his room taking delivery of smuggled goods from a friendly gendarme. Pulling him into the corridor, I asked what he'd heard about the new transport.

'They say the children are feral and won't let anyone near them. Why, Fredy?'

'I have to see them.'

Gripping my arm, he hissed, 'Don't be an idiot! You can't risk it.'

'Says the man who risks his life every day to get things people need – or sometimes simply to surprise me with something,' I replied.

My lover squirmed at the comparison. 'This is different, Fredy. The SS are all over this. There's something special about that transport and if you get caught I . . . well, I might never see you again.' I watched him swallow the thought before adding, 'I couldn't bear that.'

Squeezing his hand, I stared into the eyes of the man who made me feel complete for the first time in my life. After checking that no one was around, I quickly pressed my mouth to his. 'Fear not, *mein Prinz*. I promise I'll return to claim you as my prize.'

*

Making my way to one of the *Kinderheims*, I sought out Ottla who'd nursed me when I was ill. 'An unusual situation has arisen,' I explained. 'A trainload of children aren't being allowed off their train. Annoyingly, I'm not allowed to take them water but if you volunteered you could report back to me.'

She readily agreed and was among twenty or so personnel taken to the station early that evening. When she returned a few hours later, I could tell that she'd been crying. 'Oh, Fredy,' she wailed. 'They were the most pitiful I've ever seen: dirty, covered in sores and infested with lice. Even though they're severely malnourished and in need of hydration, they were too afraid to accept water. We weren't allowed near and only the sickest were taken off and driven to the quarantine block. The volunteers have been told they'll have to remain with them throughout, which will leave us terribly short-staffed.'

'What about the rest?'

'It was only as night began to fall that they were forced out of the wagons and marched away, flanked by an unusually large number of SS.'

'And those nearby? Were they still not to look?'

She nodded. 'Every building had closed windows.'

As word started to circulate about the unusual transport, the Elders were instructed to nominate further volunteers to care for the traumatised children. When Ottla offered her services, she slipped out of my reach.

Seeking Gonda early the next morning I demanded, 'I must be permitted to make a formal assessment of the Bialystok orphans. I hear they're in a dreadful state.' The twenty-seven-year-old – the same age as me – who'd always behaved as if he were a decade older, shook his head. Although we frequently clashed, I was usually able to persuade him. This time there was no shifting him.

'You can't fix this problem, Fredy. We've been told the children are riddled with disease and we have quite enough of that here already. You're on strict orders to remain in the ghetto so do not disobey them again.'

In my hurry to ignore every word he'd said, I ran straight into Jenda on my way out of the barracks, almost tripping him up. 'Sorry,' I said, before I realised who I'd barged into. 'Oh Jenda, it's you.'

Hearing his familiar chuckle, I felt a small pang of something for the man I'd once cared for. 'You're always in a hurry, *poutnik*,' he told me, his eyes smiling. 'Who are you rushing to save now? Or are you running towards a certain someone's arms?'

Swallowing my guilt, I said, 'I hoped you'd be happy for me.'

'I am,' he said in a way that felt genuine. Then, staring at the floor, he added more sombrely, 'I'm just sorry I wasn't enough for you.'

'Oh, you were more than enough, Jenda,' I whispered, squeezing his arm. 'And I will be forever in your debt.'

'But I suppose now you've found true love . . .' he said, half in jest.

I looked him straight in the eye. 'We fell into each other's hearts.'

The smile slid from his face but he nodded. 'I'm glad, Fredy. Truly.' Placing a hand on my shoulder, he added, 'Take good care of yourself, my stray.' As I watched him walk away,

I thought back to the evening I'd first met him in Brno when he saved me and not just from a night on the streets. I was about to leave too when I heard him call my name and turned to see him watching me. His brow furrowed, eyes glinting, he recited, '*I'll slip quietly away from the noisy crowd . . . I'll pursue solitary pathways through the pale twilit meadows with only this one dream – you come too.*' Then he turned and kept walking.

*

Still worrying about the Polish orphans, I realised I could do nothing until I learned more so I grabbed the wooden train Dirk had given me, the last of his toys, and began my rounds. I started in the infirmary where I'd heard that little Franka was poorly with an infection. Arriving at the children's ward, I was shocked by the number of infants lying on the floor, many of them coughing violently or shivering with fever.

'I'm looking for little girl named Franka,' I asked a nurse who shook her head and directed me upstairs. I did as she suggested and asked again there.

'You're too late,' I heard a man's voice behind me say. Turning slowly, I saw Franka's father kneeling beside a tiny, shrouded figure, his face drowned in sorrow.

'Oh no,' I cried, stepping closer and laying a hand on his shoulder, partly to steady myself. 'I'm so sorry. When did this happen, Hans?'

'Last night,' he replied, his voice hoarse from crying. 'She's with her beloved Mama now.'

There was little I could do or say so, after promising to call on him later, I fled back to my office cradling the toy I'd earmarked for sweet Franka. Only then did I allow my tears to fall.

After pulling myself together, I made my way to the vegetable garden to check on the children working there. The irony wasn't lost on us that, as we starved, Terezín had a large, well-stocked vegetable garden within the fortress walls where fresh produce was grown but only to feed the SS. The prisoners who worked there and in the fields beyond were all subject to random searches by guards who had orders to shoot anyone caught stealing. One poor man was beaten to death for hiding a cabbage under his jacket. Hungry and surrounded by food, many still took the risk.

One of these was Zuzana, who once boasted that she'd smuggled fifty spinach leaves in the lining of her sleeves. When I pleaded with her to be careful, she laughed. 'Don't worry. The head gardener is helped by a Jewish boy who distracts the old man in return for a potato.'

Walking up behind her as she hoed between rows of leeks that morning, I smiled when I heard her humming quietly to herself. 'Starting each new day with a song?' I asked.

She turned to greet me with a grin and cried, 'Oh, Fredy, I'm so happy to see you.'

It had been a while since I'd visited the garden and, as I looked around, I noticed that there had been a few changes. Beyond where she was toiling, there was a new log store and a row of wooden cold frames built against the base of one wall. A small hut had been erected for the head gardener. Despite the heat, its fire was lit and its little chimney trailed woodsmoke, the smell of which took me straight back to the charcoal makers of my homeland. 'When was that built?' I asked Zuzana.

'Last month. We pray we'll be allowed inside in winter to warm ourselves by the stove.'

'Is this man bothering you?' I heard the jovial voice from behind me and turned to see Aleš, a Czech gendarme we all knew and liked. When Zuzi returned to her hoeing, I studied the new log store and then the sun's position in the sky and, with a small gasp, suddenly realised that on the other side of the wall lay the Kreta barracks where the Bialystok children were being held.

Staring up at the rough-hewn wall, I figured that although I'd lost muscle strength and agility, I could still scale it with the help of the log store. If I hit it at the right angle, I could use my momentum to scrabble up and pull myself over the top. I had no idea how big the drop was on the other side but I hoped to find something to break my fall.

Sidling closer to Aleš, I reached into my pocket for a packet of cigarettes and offered them to him. Alarmed, he pushed my hand away, saying, 'This can only mean you're up to something, Fredy. I won't go to the Small Fortress for you.'

'You won't have to,' I replied. 'I'm just going to nip over that wall for a few hours and then I'll be back.'

'Are you insane?'

'Almost certainly but this is something I need to do. What time does your shift end?'

'Four o'clock. But this is madness, you idiot. What if you're caught? And how will you get back?'

'I won't be caught and I'll find a way back. Don't worry,' I told him, slipping the cigarettes into his pocket. 'Just create a distraction in a few minutes.'

Aleš shook his head. 'For God's sake, be careful,' he warned. 'And you'd better be back here before my shift ends or we'll both be on the next train east.'

When I gave him a nod, he started yelling at a group of teenagers, accusing them of being lazy and ordering them to dig over a bed at the far end of the garden. As everyone turned to see what the fuss was about, I threw myself at the wall.

Luckily for me, there was a block of sheds on the other side, so I dropped onto them and then the ground. I was in.

Running towards the new barracks, I waited behind a stack of wood for a passing patrol to turn the corner before walking briskly to the door. A few steps inside I was surprised to find Ottla weeping into the arms of a fellow nurse.

Gasping, she grabbed my arm and pushed me into an empty office. 'Fredy!' she cried, wide-eyed. 'You shouldn't be here. You'll be done for if you're caught.'

'I have to see those children,' I insisted. 'Please, Ottla, take me to them.'

'I can't, Fredy. Besides, they're in a wretched way. The last batch that arrived here late last night fled to a storeroom at the back of the building and are refusing to come out. We're trying to get the rest out of their clothing so we can delouse them but each time we try they become hysterical.'

'Then let me help.'

Sighing, she stared into my eyes and shook her head in exasperation. Reaching into her pocket, she handed me a kerchief to use as a face mask before pulling her own up over her nose. She then marched me along a corridor as if I had every right to be there. Whenever we passed anyone, I kept my head down and stayed close behind her.

We heard the children's screams before I'd even put a foot inside the huge hall where most were being held. I wondered if Kurt was right. Maybe they were feral. When Ottla opened the door, I was presented with the sight of several hundred children huddled together in a colony, their backs against the walls. In the foreground stood an exasperated Dr Koči, a man I knew from my visits to the hospital. He had one boy by the arm and was trying to pull off his clothes as the child fought, scratched and attempted to bite him. Hurrying forward, I grabbed the boy's other arm and pulled him away from the medic whose coat was ripped, his mask dangling off one ear. Pulling down mine, I gripped the lad firmly by both shoulders, crouched to his level and locked eyes with him. '*Nie!*' I said forcefully. '*Nie!*'

The boy stopped squirming and stared at me, panting with rank breath. 'You must strip,' I insisted, but he shook his head vehemently. Turning to the others, I pointed to the washroom visible through an open door at the far end of the block. 'You . . . shower: *Waschraum.*'

At mention of the showers, hysteria broke out. Scattering in every direction like rats, a few of the children made it through the door and outside where they ran straight to the barbed wire fence, tearing skin and clothing as they scrambled skywards in their urgency to escape. I'd rarely seen such panic. Ottla, the doctor and I stood helpless with the rest of the staff, not sure which way to turn.

It was past noon by the time we'd corralled them back inside, several of them bleeding from the barbs and it was only when they were settled into a whimpering heap, still in their filthy rags, that I turned to Ottla and said, 'Now take me to the others.'

Silently, she led me to a storeroom at the back of the hall where the remaining children from the train were hiding in darkness. Pointing to the door which was slightly ajar, she lit an oil lamp by the door and handed it to me saying, 'The bulb's been stolen. We've tried and tried to coax them out, to no avail. If you can't then the SS will.'

Stepping forward, I could smell them before I saw them. A pungent odour of sweat, excrement and decay rose from their clothing as they shifted position nervously. Raising my lamp as the light pushed back the darkness, I blinked into the gloom to see forty or so faces blinking back at me.

It was their eyes that betrayed them. Pupils black as death, sunken into hollows like deer prints in the snow. Eyes that had seen things. Terrible things. The light of their innocence extinguished by dread. In those windows to the soul glinting back at me I saw what they knew about war and my heart cracked.

Theirs were the faces of minds bent double by cruelty, witnesses to the worst of humankind. Yet not one of these orphans of Bialystok had walked on this earth more than fourteen years and they likely wouldn't survive one more.

Holding my lamp a little higher, I picked out the sharp edges of each cadaverous face. Spindle arms and legs covered in sores poked out from ragged clothing like twigs in sacking. Many were shoeless or had feet wrapped in rags. Huddled together on a floor covered in plaster dust, their bodies rigid, they formed a single bundle of misery. Under the intensity of my gaze, the littlest ones began to tremble and the shivering quickly spread.

'*Nie boj sie,*' I told them with a smile, speaking what little I knew of their native tongue. Don't be afraid.

It was too late for that. The terror in their eyes was almost as old as they were.

'*Jestes tutaj bezpieczny.*' You are safe here.

Memories of that promise made to me in the past flashed into my brain but I quickly banished them. These boys and girls had a million reasons not to believe me either and I wasn't sure if they even understood, as many probably only spoke Yiddish.

Careful not to make any sudden movements, I reached into my jacket pocket and pulled out a hunk of ghetto bread. Gingerly, I held it out to them but still they didn't stir. Bringing the food to my mouth, I gestured eating and pointed to the hall behind me where the rest of the orphans were finally settling. '*Woda*,' I said. Water.

I watched lips, split by thirst and sores, open and close unbidden.

Taking a few steps back, I reached for a wooden pail that had been left near the door and, using the ladle, sloshed water into three tin cups that I slid closer to them. Wiping a patch of floor with a rag, I laid down the bread before stepping back and returning them to near darkness.

It must have been a full ten minutes before an emaciated boy with mud-caked hair who could only have been nine crept forwards on scabbed knees, as timid as a mouse. Constantly glancing back over his shoulder at the others, he froze when he spotted those waiting to help them in the hall. Like a deer catching sight of a hunter through the trees, he remained still for longer than seemed humanly possible.

Eventually one of his matchstick arms emerged as he reached for the bread, stuffing it inside his sweat-stained shirt. Still kneeling he grabbed a cup and, hooking the pail with his fingers, dragged it back into the corner, scraping a trail in the dust.

Glancing up at a small high window that cast a little light, I noted the shadows creeping across the wall and knew that time was running out. The children had to be processed before the SS came and I needed to get back for roll call. Edging forward once more, I said in my poor Polish, 'You come now – guards soon back.'

There was whispering before the boy came into view, standing this time and as insubstantial as a reed. Pointing at me with a filthy finger, he said, 'You, German,' his voice scratchy through lack of use.

Patting my chest with the flat of my hand, I said, 'My name Fredy Hirsch. Prisoner here.' Pointing to him, I asked, 'What your name?'

'You German.'

We stared at each other in silence before I added, 'We not have long. Please into hall. Food medicine.'

The boy shrank back into the gloom to whisper to the others. After what felt like an age, there were sounds of movement and, one by one, the children shuffled squinting into the light. Their sallow skin was stretched across cheekbones discoloured by fading bruises and dried blood. Squashed together, the last survivors of the Bialystok ghetto moved as one – a sorry procession of bones.

Once I'd coaxed them to join the rest, we did our best to calm them. 'Let's try feeding them before we attempt anything else,' I suggested, so someone sent word to the kitchen.

'Be careful not to give them too much,' Ottla warned the volunteers. 'Stomachs starved of food for long periods won't be able to handle it. We've lost hundreds that way.'

When the twenty-five litre soup kettles arrived we ladled out what smelled like caraway broth into twenty tin bowls at a time, making sure to scoop around the bottom for any pieces of vegetables.

'*Zupa*,' I announced, holding out a bowl but not one of the children came forward. Taking a mouthful to show them that it wasn't poisoned, I left the kettle and retreated.

It was only later when we adults were sitting in the opposite corner eating from our own bowls that a few of the older boys stumbled forward, dizzy with hunger and started handing out tepid soup. Watching carefully, I was touched by their self-styled hierarchy: the taller children feeding the smallest and youngest first. No one fought. None argued. They simply sat together cross-legged on the floor awaiting their turn. These children were far from feral. They were a collective.

Watching closely, I realised that one teenager with a long face and two oversized front teeth appeared to be their unofficial leader. There was something hard and desperate about him. His red hair reminded me of a fox and his eyes glowed like coals. Wary, he watched me constantly as he slunk between his charges, distributing bowls and pulling the rough blankets we'd given them around sleepy shoulders.

I moved closer and leaned against a wall. *Very well, Mr Fox. I'll wait.*

Settling next to his pack, he positioned himself between them and me, his head resting on bony knees. For more than an hour, he maintained eye contact with me, hardly even blinking. Squatting so that we were at the same level, I gave him a smile and held out my hand in a gesture of friendship. He didn't move a muscle but kept watch so I sat as he did and waited some more.

When the children finally succumbed to sleep and he could no longer fight his own exhaustion, I inched forward on my hands and knees. One metre away from the Fox, I sat back again. Suddenly, his eyes snapped open and his entire body jolted as if charged with electricity. Swivelling his head, he checked his pack with a practised sweep of the room then turned to me with a slight snarl, as if daring me to come closer.

Stock still, I spoke softly. 'My name is Fredy Hirsch. I help you.' His eyes flickered as if with recognition of some long-forgotten compassion but then his jawline tightened again.

'They keep you here – *Quarantäne*,' I said, hoping my mix of German and Polish was good enough for him to understand. 'Once clear infection – you come ghetto.'

I suspected he understood some German after four years of Nazi occupation but I didn't want to scare him off. There was so much that I wanted to ask about what had happened to frighten them all so, but I knew I had to tread carefully.

Before I could strangle any more of his language, he said, '*Ich verstehe.*' I understand.

'*Gut*,' I replied, gratefully. 'What is your name?'

Silence.

'You have to trust me and these people,' I told him, speaking softly. 'We only want to help you.'

Still, he said nothing, but his eyes read my lips.

'The first task of the doctors and nurses is to get everyone undressed and washed,' I continued. 'They'll burn your clothes, delouse you and give you fresh clothing. Disease has already claimed thousands and may kill you all too unless you let us take care of you.'

He blinked for the first time, as if weighing up what I was telling him.

'Please, what is your name?'

Silence, then: 'Łukasz.'

'*Danke.* Tell me, Łukasz, what are you afraid of?'

His gaze darted to the washroom and back again. I watched his Adam's apple bob between the cartilage in his throat before lodging halfway like a stuck lift.

'The showers?' I asked.

With a stare that could pierce my soul, he gave a furtive nod.

Confused, I twisted my head to stare at the washroom with its new chrome showerheads and white tiled walls. For those of us with such limited facilities, the thought of a hot shower with proper soap felt like a luxury. I didn't understand.

When I turned back to face the Fox, I was shocked to see a single tear carving a clean white track down his cheek.

Fighting the urge to cradle that brave young kid in my arms, I found my own eyes misting over and dropped my gaze to the floor in the hope that he hadn't seen. When I looked up again, he was staring at me with a changed expression and then he shuffled closer.

Gripping both my hands with bony fingers, he peered into my face and hissed, '*Smierc!*'

My Polish failed me and I shook my head.

'*Tod! Tod!*' he said, more urgently in German.

Death.

'*Tod?*' I repeated, shaking my head. '*Nie*. Here? *Nie*. In the washroom? *Nie*.'

Sinking back into himself, his face suddenly that of a terrified little boy, he rocked back on his haunches and clasped at his throat with both hands. Imitating the sound of someone choking to death, he pointed a bony finger upwards as if at the showerheads and rasped, '*Gaz! Gaz!*'

15

August 1943, Small Fortress, Terezín, Czechoslovakia

'*HALT!*' A VOICE BARKED then, '*Stuj!*' Turning with the smile I reserved for friends fixed to my face, I strode purposefully towards the Czech gendarme I'd been too preoccupied to check for when I slipped back out of the Kreta barracks. With the Fox's words burning a hole in my brain, all I could hear over and over were his cries of '*Gaz! Gaz!*' and all I could see was his expression.

As I faced up to the guard pointing a gun at me, I was disappointed to discover that I'd never seen him before and – worse – he showed no signs of knowing who I was. 'Fear not, my friend,' I told him in German. 'My name is Fredy Hirsch and I'm here legitimately as head of Youth Welfare. What is your name?'

'*Co?*' he replied. '*Neumim nemecky.*' I don't speak German. The one Czech phrase I knew best.

'*Muj pritel,*' I replied. Me friend.

Jerking his gun to so that I would raise my arms, he gestured towards the guardhouse I'd spotted beyond the new barracks. Standing my ground, I said, '*Ne, ne. Muj pritel. Fredy Hirsch.*'

When I went to lower my arms, he yelled, '*Prochazka!*' Walk.

Turning away from the wall as he fell into step behind me, I gave it a last lingering glance. In ten leaps, I could have sprung up onto the sheds and over the wall to sanctuary – if he didn't shoot me first. When he jabbed me in the back with the barrel of his gun, I knew I'd missed my chance. My luck didn't improve as none of the men in the guardhouse knew me either. They only knew that I was expressly forbidden from being there. After they telephoned their superiors in the German High Command, a burly SS officer appeared: his face red with fury that I'd defied orders to keep away.

'Do you think you can do what you like here?' he screamed with breath that smelled strongly of meat. 'Well, do you?'

'No, sir,' I replied, with a martial click of my heels.

Like a sudden storm that arrives without warning, he closed the gap between us with surprising speed and punched me hard in the belly, shoving me off balance. I fell to the floor winded but, before I could spring back up, his steel-capped boot connected with my ribs with such force that I heard bones crack. The pain was a fresh surprise and I suddenly found it hard to breathe. I rolled on to my side to protect myself as his other boot landed in my kidney and then fists started raining down on me.

My mind flew back to my boxing lessons in the scouts. 'You must only hit back in self-defence and only if there is no other choice,' I was instructed in a far gentler time. The rules had changed since then and I knew that retaliating to an SS officer – even in self-defence – would be tantamount to suicide. Curling into myself, I used the fists that could have felled him to protect my face, as waves of pain rose and fell with every beat of my heart.

I think he might have kicked me to death had there not been a sudden cry of, '*Halt!*' before a second pair of boots came into blurred vision. Hauling myself upright to a sitting position with a groan, I found myself staring up into the eyes of Scholz, the Nazi who'd granted most of my requests in the ghetto. He was looking down at me with a fathomless expression. The blood from a cut on my forehead half-blinded me and my bottom lip was so swollen I could barely open my mouth but I attempted a twisted smile of gratitude.

Hoping for some mercy, I rose to my feet unsteadily only to hear him say through the ringing in my ears, 'You've gone too far this time, Hirsch. I can't help you anymore.' Turning to my sweaty assailant who was wiping my blood from his knuckles, Scholz snapped, 'Take him to the Fortress. He can keep his clothes. He won't be there long enough for it to matter.'

Before I could respond, I was dragged from the guardhouse and tossed into the back of a truck like a sack of rubbish, cracking another rib. In a choking cloud of exhaust fumes, the vehicle lumbered off, taking me out of the ghetto for the first time in almost two years.

*

The brooding hulk of the infamous Gestapo prison loomed before me in the late afternoon sun like a sleeping giant. Passing under its black and white stone archway and into a processing area, I looked in vain for a friendly face.

I'd heard so many stories about the Small Fortress that it had become an almost mythical, redbrick *Sheol* in my mind; a place where people were cruelly judged. Prisoners who survived the experience spoke of tiny punishment cells where they were kept sixty at a time and ordered to remain standing. Others told of men and women in solitary confinement, sometimes for years. In the execution courtyard reached by a long tunnel, prisoners were hanged or peppered with bullets. Now I was one of those trapped within its forbidding walls with no idea what my punishment might be.

Knowing that Aleš would be waiting for me on the other side of the garden wall, I prayed he'd get word to Jakob so that he could start negotiating my release. With little time to consider the alternative, I was marched down one of the dark, subterranean corridors and stopped outside the door of a cell, which one of my guards unlocked. The stench of putrefaction was immediately overpowering as I was propelled inside with a boot in the small of my back. But what affected me more was the haunted expressions of the sixty or so men and teenage boys crammed onto wooden bunks. Faces like skulls staring back at me, many with shaved heads, but several with hair and a few old timers with matted curls and straggly beards. Almost all had been issued with old Czech uniforms, no doubt taken from the defeated army.

Holding onto my ribs as I recoiled from the sourness pervading the room, I opened my mouth to speak but found that I could make only a stammering announcement through my pain. 'My name is . . . Fredy Hirsch. Youth Welfare.' Hundreds of exhausted eyes blinked back at me unimpressed. Nobody spoke. Then a small voice in a corner broke the silence, asking, 'Fredy, is that really you?'

Peering out of my one good eye I watched an emaciated, red-headed boy climb down from a top bunk and take a few steps towards me, stirring dust motes that danced in the light from a small window. Squinting at him in the gloom, I realised it was Miloš: the little 'Sparrow' I'd taught in Frankfurt.

'Miloš . . . what are you doing here?' I cried, limping over to greet him with slow, careful steps. Ever since I'd fled Germany I'd thought of him often and always fondly. The timid boy who'd won chocolate for guessing the contents of my gift box from Uncle Alfred.

'I'm so pleased to see you, Fredy,' he told me, his eyes glistening. Reaching for the whistle around my neck, he held it with a wistful expression. 'You still have this.'

'I do. As you . . . predicted it is practical . . . but lovely.'

'I never forgot your kindness,' he told me, his eyes glistening. 'We were bereft when you left. It felt like we'd been beheaded. Nothing was ever the same again.' Seeing the regret on my face, he asked, 'Do you still have your binoculars?'

I nodded, adding, 'Well, I did.' Searching his face, I asked, 'Did your parents survive too?' His contorted expression was enough for me to bow my head.

It must have been seven years since I'd last seen Miloš, which would have made him fourteen. Still physically slight, he looked older. His hair was matted with dirt and the vermin that had made it their home. 'How long have you been here?'

'A few months, I think.' When I asked how I'd missed him in the ghetto, he replied, 'We were only there for a day. Mother and I were arrested soon afterwards.'

'Why? What did you do?'

'Nothing. It was Father. He was Czech, remember? A tailor from Lidice.'

Closing my eyes and recalling how almost everyone from that town was murdered and how anyone with a connection to it was punished, I whispered, 'I'm sorry.'

'Father was brought here six months ago. We found out later that he'd been tortured to death even though he'd not been to Lidice in decades. When Mother and I arrived in Terezín, a Nazi officer made the connection from our names and sent us here too. Separating us broke my mother's heart and she was dead within a week.' His chin dropped to his chest. A broken bird.

Gripping his arm, I rasped, 'Look at me . . . Sparrow. We'll get through this. I hope to be released, but . . . I won't go unless I can . . . take you with me.'

His eyes filled with tears. 'Do you mean that, Fredy?'

'I won't leave you . . . I swear.' The irony wasn't lost on me in the coming days that determined as I was to protect that orphan, he ended up saving me. As he bound my ribs and tended to my cuts and bruises with a damp rag, he explained when food was delivered – what little there was of it – and how to avoid being selected for hard labour.

'Some are forced to move one pile of rocks from the corner of a yard to the other until they collapse,' Miloš told me. 'Others have to dig a swimming pool using only spoons or their bare hands.'

Living, sleeping and eating with so many, sharing a single toilet and sink, I learned much about humanity and about myself. There were those who stole, cheated and lied and others who gave up and died. Hoping to appeal to the rest, once I was feeling stronger I made an announcement. 'I'm going to start giving lessons to the teenagers and any of you who are interested,' I told them. 'If there are any teachers here or those who can help, please let me know. I'll start by teaching German and poetry but would welcome other suggestions.'

There were the inevitable grumbles and moans but by the end of that week, I'd managed to enlist ten children and three teachers. There was a historian from Pilsen who taught them about the Trojan Wars and a music master from Brno who hummed pieces by Dvořák and Bach. A former industrialist from Ostrava gave maths lessons and I made a friend in a man mountain named Ladislav who gave me a bloody, toothless grin and told me, 'I can't teach but I would like to listen.' Barrel-chested, the former farmer stood over two metres tall and had been tortured by an SS dentist for hiding a Jewish family in his barn. The guards came for him whenever they needed some muscle and, incredibly, he'd often return with a little food or random luxuries such as soap, a candle or a comb.

'They'll kill you if they catch you,' I warned him one day, after he handed me a pencil and a pack of cigarette papers.

'They'll have to catch me first.'

Staying up late, I sat in the circle of light cast by a stub of candle and wrote a note about Łukas and the Bialystok children to Jakob on individual cigarette papers. *What if the rumours are true and we've sent thousands to their deaths?* I wrote in my smallest handwriting. *Informed decisions must now be made.* Running out of paper I concluded, *Save a boy named Miloš Abramowicz before me. I shan't leave without him.*

I then rolled each wafer-thin sheet, one inside the other, with the utmost care and wrapped the note tightly into the barrel of a broken fountain pen Ladislav found in a bin. 'There are friendly Czechs in the kitchens who'll find a way to get this to the ghetto,' he promised.

Three days later when he handed the pen back to me I was crestfallen until I saw a smile on his lips. 'It's a reply, Fredy.' Unfurling the single sheet of paper inside, I read Jakob's note: *You're on next transport. 5,000 including Leo, many AK and hundreds of children. Miloš too. I reported on what you told me but I've lost all authority. May God go with us all.*

Even though I'd volunteered for transports in the past, the news that I was being sent to what I suspected was my likely death felt like a stab to my heart. After all those years on the run, Fredy the white hart was finally in the huntsman's sights.

None of the Nazis who'd come to use the familiar '*du*' with me instead of '*sie*' in the ghetto had lifted a finger to save me.

Not even Scholz, who used to smile and say, '*Was möchtest du wissen?*' – What do you want now? – whenever I walked into his office. With that simple switch of pronoun, he and others had lulled me into a false sense of security that I'd be safe on their watch. How foolish of me not to have noticed that when Scholz stopped me being murdered in the guardhouse he'd used *sie*. My fate – once determined by the single letter J – was now sealed by those three letters.

Sent east, I'd be following in the footsteps of the nameless thousands I'd watched tramp out of the ghetto, their backpacks rolled tight. With the arrogance Jenda once accused me of, I'd made a promise to Miloš that I'd save him too. Now the boy would probably die in a gas chamber, gasping his final breath. I alone would bear the responsibility for his death and for all those I might have been able to save had I not jumped over that wall.

Pushing aside my fears, I sat quietly by myself for a few minutes before calmly informing Miloš that we'd be leaving on the next train. Seeing the terror in his eyes, I did my best to calm him. 'Aren't you afraid, Fredy?' he asked finally.

'I don't know what there is to be afraid of yet,' I replied, as lightly as I could. 'If we stay here, we'd probably starve or die of disease. There's a chance now that we might be sent to a place where we can work and create another community. That's all we can hope for.'

Within days, Miloš and I were roughly woken by armed guards who grabbed us by our collars and marched us outside to a truck of fifty or so other male prisoners in a far poorer state. There was no time to say goodbye to Ladislav and our cellmates, although I'd already wished him good luck and urged the others to carry on with their lessons. Driven back to the ghetto and delivered to the railway spur, all I had on me were the clothes on my back and my whistle tucked inside my jacket.

In the chaos and confusion of the loading point, I took a few deep draughts of the last breath of summer and watched thousands being pushed into box cars and cattle wagons by the SS. They were assisted by Jewish and Czech police, many of whom seemed as reluctant as their unhappy cargo. Scanning the crowd, I couldn't see Kurt or Jenda among them and prayed they weren't squashed like sardines into carriages further down the train. Either way, my heart clenched at the thought that I might never see either of them again.

Locking arms with Miloš so we wouldn't be separated, I helped him up into our designated wagon and then climbed up after him, pressing my back against the wall closest to the doorway. 'We don't want to be pushed to the middle,' I told him. 'There will be less air there.' Fighting not to lose my footing, I grabbed any children being helped up and pulled them to where we stood. 'Over here,' I cried. 'You'll be safer here.'

Looking out, I suddenly spotted Bernd in the crowd, expressionless as he helped elderly prisoners up wooden steps and into the wagon next to ours. 'Bernd!' I cried, 'Bernd!'

Lifting his head, he grimaced. He abandoned his post and hurried over, pushing his way through the tumult. 'Fredy, you're here. We didn't know if you were alive or dead. Are you all right?'

Bending down so he could hear me, I yelled, 'You must convince the Elders to stop the transports. The Bialystok children saw their people gassed. That's why they've been kept separate. It's imperative that no more are sent east.' I never had the chance to hear his response because those around me started surging towards the door in their desperation to escape.

Knocked off my feet, I was almost trampled underfoot as the swell pressed forward only to be beaten back in an unholy clamour of screams.

'Fredy!' Miloš cried, pulling me to my feet and clinging to me as the heavy wagon door slammed shut with an almighty clang and the giant bolts were drawn across. There was a terrible silence in the darkness. The only air seeped in through a small, high window in one corner, its barbed wire silhouetted in the early morning light. Gasping for oxygen, we all leaned instinctively towards that tiny opening like saplings in the wind.

None of us knew how long our journey would take but we already dreaded its murderous progress. We'd had nothing to eat since the previous night and all that was on board was a single bucket for a toilet and a pail half-full of water. When the wagon made a convulsive lurch everyone fell against each other with anguished cries as we began to slowly roll away from the life we'd managed to create in Terezín.

Closing my eyes and gripping my whistle as a talisman, I murmured a prayer for those I'd known and loved within our red-brick Star of David. I pleaded for the strength to face what lay ahead. With no space to sit or lie and people wailing for food, water and loved ones, I called out, 'My name is Fredy Hirsch and I am from Youth Welfare. Are there any children here travelling alone?'

A few timid voices replied and, at my request, they were pushed through the crowd to where I stood with the rest. One little girl was hoisted aloft by a man and moved, on arms and hands, from the far end of the wagon. Patting each of them on the head, I squeezed their arms to reassure them of my presence in the gloom.

As our eyes slowly grew accustomed to the dark, I watched a man my age clasping a woman in his arms as he kissed her hair and forehead repeatedly and murmured something.

'What's he saying?' I asked Miloš, who was standing closer.

'He's telling his wife that everything will be all right and she must only think beautiful things.'

Moved by his courage, I watched the woman cradle the man's face in her hands as she said something back to him through her tears. Miloš gulped before he translated. 'She's asking what name they should give their unborn child.'

Pinching the bridge of my nose to stop my tears, I heard her husband's response: 'Mishka for a boy, Hana for a girl.'

'May God go with you all,' I murmured, bowing my head.

Auschwitz II-Birkenau

1

September 1943

'ALLE RAUS! RAUS!' The first words we heard when the wagon doors slid open chilled my soul. The Nazi aggression was snarling, as were their dogs. Our miserable three-day journey from Terezín to Poland had only been the beginning of our torment.

Having been pulled from the train, stripped, showered and tattooed – although I was spared that – we finally learned the name of the place where we'd been told we would all die: Auschwitz.

Barely given time to think, we were herded into another large building after the *Sauna*. Kept waiting for hours without anything to eat or drink, fear clawed at my gut but the children were even more frightened so I did my best to distract them. Standing amidst a huddle seated on the concrete floor, I cried, 'Who remembers Budulínku?' I was met with blank faces by minds too stunned to process words.

'Budulínku,' I reminded them. 'The little dog who ran into our hearts.' When several weary hands shot up and a few faces broke into a wary smile, I added, 'Well then, who'd like me to retell the story from a dog's point of view?'

Even those slumped over with exhaustion lifted their red-rimmed eyes towards me. 'Very well, then, I'll begin. Once upon a time there was a dog called Budulínku, who was left alone in his kennel by his mother when she went for a walk with their master ...' I spun the story out for as long as I could and I was just beginning another when the doors burst open and the guards marched in. Driven outside into a shower of autumn rain, we stopped to turn our faces to the heavens and capture whatever moisture we could before being shunted to another section of the camp or *lager*.

Marching mechanically in rows of five, we passed large wooden buildings housing hundreds of skinny, shaven-headed inmates who stared at us in wonder. I thought they were men at first but I realised they were women when several ran to the wire to cry, '*Gyermekek! Kinder!*' holding out their arms pleadingly.

'Why are they looking at us like that?' Miloš asked. 'It's as if they've never seen people before.' I couldn't speak, so unnerved was I by the sight of grieving mothers who hadn't seen children in a very long time.

After passing through a heavily guarded gate, we saw laid out before us thirty or so identical black wooden blocks resembling barracks. Beyond our compound all that could be seen were row upon row of similar buildings disappearing into the distance in all directions, as far as the eye could see. The scale of the camp shook me as did the fact that there wasn't a blade of grass, a tree or even a bird to be seen. This was a place of such windswept desolation that even Nature had shunned it.

Around the camp's vast perimeter stood a double row of high barbed wire fences supported by concrete posts curved over at the top, as if bowing their heads in shame. The sinister humming and signs reading *Vorsicht! Hochspannung Lebensgefahr* told us that the wire was electrified.

'How am I going to keep little ones away from that?' I asked in dismay.

Moments later, a white-haired man who'd been flung a bathrobe and slippers in the *Sauna* broke away from our ranks and started to march steadily towards the wire.

'*Halt! Halt!*' guards cried but the gentleman only quickened his pace, almost tripping over the shallow ditch at the foot of the fence before clambering doggedly on. Clamping my hand over the eyes of Tomáš, one of the orphans, I spun him away as the old man flung himself at the wire with a piercing cry.

Ordered away from the scene and the stink of singed hair, we were led to the muddy main street of our camp, where women and girls were placed to one side of the sticky divide and men with boys on the other. 'This way for the waiting room,' roared one of the SS, laughing as we were pushed three hundred at a time into the airless blocks that had dirt floors and no windows. Outside a sign read *Pferdestall* and I realised the buildings had once been stables for horses. Inside, the high ceiling had slits that ran along its length to allowed in a little light and air. With only a few three-tier plank beds completed, the space was vast but there were so many of us that most had to lie side by side and almost on top of each other on the floor.

Having organised everyone so that children could lie on the stained straw mattresses that lined the bunks and the sick and elderly on the floor nearest the door, I gave out instructions. 'Bigger boys at the top,' I said, making the teenagers take the uppermost bunks they could more easily negotiate. 'Little ones side by side at the bottom and adults in the middle.' Squeezing in, they lay alongside each other, stacked like logs. Our only covers were a few thin blankets disinfected with the distinctive-smelling Zyklon B.

*

Despite our pleas for food and water, we were given nothing until a few hours later when giant soup barrels were carried in by more prisoners in zebra stripes. Each of us were then issued with what would become our most prized possession: an aluminium bowl with a handle. We ran to the line, desperate for something to wet our lips. 'Children first,' I pleaded, pushing them to the front despite complaints. All we were given was a little black bread and some abominable liquid they called soup. We'd considered the *Suppe* in Terezín to be inedible but what we wouldn't have given for it then. The Auschwitz soup was made of rotten potatoes, turnips and *rutabaga* or swedes. Depending on which end of the barrel it came from, its consistency was either warm, salty water with a few chunks of something rotten and unidentifiable, or cold and congealed like runny porridge. It tasted so foul that many spat it out even though they knew this was all they'd be given.

'This smells like boiled socks!' a woman complained. 'I can't eat this, it has too much salt!' another cried, tipping the gelatinous contents of her plate on the ground. Two emaciated men, eyes shiny with hunger, fell upon it, scraping up the mess along with spoonfuls of mud.

Fighting the urge to gag, I downed my own vile broth and wiped the bowl clean with my finger, before encouraging Miloš and the children to do the same. 'Save your bread for later,' I advised but they couldn't wait. Nibbling at mine, which tasted like a mix of chestnut flour and sawdust, I said, 'It's not so bad once you get used to it.' With a wink, I added, 'Don't worry, there's a nice big slice of fresh air for dessert.'

Hearing loud clanging, we saw a man in stripes banging a rail with a metal rod. This 'gong' heralded the start of our first inspection and gave the men in charge of each block the signal to blow their whistles and wield their weapons of preference.

Still plagued by thirst, we were pushed into serried rows as SS officers stood waiting to take stock of us.

'Come, *Kinder*, quickly,' I said, grabbing hands and lining up the boys nearest to me. 'Stand tall, heads up, eyes straight ahead.' Hurrying along the line, I pulled the children into groups and put Miloš and some other teenagers in charge, hissing, 'You boys, make sure the younger ones stay put.' Then I took my place at the other end, next to Tomáš and the smaller ones who were snivelling and restless.

Once we were standing to weary attention, the SS began to patrol our ranks. They were accompanied by the shaven-headed *Lagerälteste* or camp elder, an unattractive German wearing an inverted green triangle that marked him as a criminal. His mouth was twisted into an ugly smile as he wandered up and down the rows carrying a bullwhip, paying special attention to pretty women and young boys. My guts churning, I prayed he'd leave them alone, especially the children, whose number I estimated at around three hundred.

When a striking-looking *Obersturmführer* stopped in front of me with the thug – who I later discovered was called Böhm – I lifted my chin and attempted to look my best, despite my strange, mismatched clothes. Arching an eyebrow above piercing blue-grey pupils, the SS officer stared at my triangle with its identifying letter and asked, '*Sie sind ein Deutscher?*' You are German?

'*Jawohl, Herr SS Obersturmführer,*' I replied, clicking my heels and saluting.

Another curve of his brows told me he was impressed. Looking around at the children swaying with exhaustion next to me, their eyes glued to my face for guidance, he muttered something to Böhm, whereupon the brute saluted him before the officer moved on. Turning to me, Böhm declared, 'You're the *kapo* of your block. Discipline them well and things will go better for you.'

I soon discovered that being block supervisor was an influential but bittersweet role. After roll call, one of the prisoners in stripes hurriedly took me to one side to explain my duties and show me the groom's room at the entrance to our block that was to be my new home. In it was a wooden pallet bed and a fireplace without any wood or coal. 'You'll be entitled to larger rations and freer movement,' he told me, his face expressionless as he affixed my *kapo* armband. I couldn't help but wonder if the privilege came with a price.

*

'Rise and shine!' I cried after a few short blasts of my whistle, on my first official duty the following morning. I had to wake inmates from the brief respite of slumber the minute the gong sounded. As shouts of '*Aufstehen!*' echoed across the plain, five thousand sleepy people told to 'Get up!' yawned and stretched aching bones before rising to their feet or climbing from bunks.

'Come now, quickly,' I pleaded. 'Everyone in line for the latrines. Adults, please make sure all children stay with our column and don't do anything to attract attention.' As people started squabbling and children wailed, I blew my whistle again. 'If you don't quieten down and do as you're told, they'll replace me with someone else. Is that what you want?' A sudden silence fell.

Reluctant to leave the warmth for outdoors, we awaited our turn to run to the communal latrines at the far end of the camp. 'I need four volunteers to carry the night pails to be emptied,' I called. Only one hand went up so I selected three more who reluctantly lifted the overflowing buckets.

Arriving at the latrines at the same time as women from another block, we were immediately stunned to silence. Not only did the pungent stink of excrement and disinfectant hang over us like a cloud, making eyes water, but the toilets comprised two hundred or so open holes cut into three parallel rows of concrete slabs, positioned above deep trenches. There was no screening, no water, no privacy and no paper.

'*Schnell! Schnell!*' guards screamed, hurrying men and boys to the right, women and girls to the left. 'We only have a few minutes each,' I warned, translating the guards' instructions as everyone dropped trousers or hoisted dresses to sit back-to-back with strangers to do their business. The guards bellowed and leered, urging people to hurry and whipping those suffering from diarrhoea or constipation who lingered too long.

Staggering out into the dawn as the mist stretched gnarled fingers into the camp, we ran to the nearby washrooms where the cloudy well water trickled pathetically into metal troughs. 'Wash whatever you can and hurry,' I called.

'But there's no soap!' someone cried.

'Or towels.'

'I know,' I said, wiping what little I could wet of myself with my dirty shirt. 'Use your clothes.' Checking on the children, I saw Erik, the troublemaker from the ghetto, stick his tongue out at a guard who looked at him murderously. Quickly stepping between them, I turned Erik away with a sharp rebuke. 'Don't you realise that insolence here will get you killed?'

Once everyone was back in the block still shaken, my next task was to record how many people were too sick to move or had died overnight. Going from bunk to bunk, searching for a flicker of life in the waxen-faced, I recalled the prisoner-functionary warning me, 'Death is the only excuse for anyone avoiding roll call, so drag out the corpses and stack them behind your block.'

'What happens to them then?'

He shrugged. 'They'll be counted and collected for the crematorium.'

There was no time for relatives to grieve for those whose hearts were not yet cold. I had to hurry everyone outside to stand in line for a portion of indigestible bread and a ladle of the tepid black liquid they called coffee.

'This tastes like dishwater!' Miloš exclaimed, his nose wrinkling. The name soon stuck, even though the dishwater was our only means of quenching our thirst. As other prisoners clustered around me – to ask questions, break down, or beg for more food – I fended them off to focus on my next and most important task: morning roll call.

Horrified, I watched veteran *kapos* intimidating their charges, cursing and whipping the weakest. 'Get moving, you scum!' I heard one holler. 'You're not in Terezín anymore.' From the colour of the green triangles sewn onto their clothing, I could tell that many were longstanding prisoners and career criminals like Böhm. There were also men – and women – classed 'asocial' wearing black badges. These were the preferred enforcers of Nazi rule.

Refusing to wield the stick I'd found waiting for me in my room, I decided to use persuasion rather than violence. 'I know you're tired and hungry,' I told them, 'but we must obey orders until we figure out how the camp operates. I need your help. I can't do this alone.'

Gathering the children, I asked, 'Do you remember the game we played in Terezín, where the person who stood still the longest won a prize?' A few nodded. 'Well, we have to do that again now, standing together and keeping very still. Do you understand?'

'Is there a prize?' a few asked.

'Is it something to eat?' others clamoured.

'Maybe,' I lied, 'or perhaps the winner will get to wear something special for the rest of the day.' Their groans of disappointment gave me little hope of success and I was right to be anxious, as morning roll call proved to be my toughest test. Trying to keep everyone together and upright as we stood miserably for hours while the Germans counted us, lost count and started all over again proved impossible. The old and sick collapsed, children got bored and sat down and several wandered off, thumbs in their mouths.

'I'm hungry, Fredy,' they'd cry, or 'I want to go back to bed.' I had to run after one toddler who'd ambled up behind an SS guard and was about to reach into his pocket with grubby little fingers.

'I know this isn't fun,' I'd soothe, scooping up others before the officers returned to redo the count. 'But it won't be long now. While we're waiting, let's play a game. How many animals can you name that start with the letter B?' It took a while but after I started them off, others piped up as we worked our way through the alphabet. Unable to step out of line too often, I enlisted adults and teenagers to shuffle those most at risk to the back while offering an encouraging word.

Looking around at the other columns run by the 'greens' or 'blacks' though, I realised that ours was a shambles and I was the worst *kapo* in the camp. Fearing the consequences, I was wracked by anxiety: knowing that we'd be put through the same ordeal at sunset and every day for as long as we were there.

*

'Please, tell me what you can about this place?' I asked one of the prisoners in stripes who distributed our food, having watched him for a day or two and noticed that he seemed more human than the rest.

'Meet me behind your block when we come for the bodies later,' he hissed. True to his word, he arrived with a wheelbarrow into which to toss that day's tally – an old man who weighed so little that I could carry him under one arm. 'What do you know?' the functionary asked, as I laid the corpse in the barrow.

'Very little.'

He sighed the sigh of a man about to impart terrible news. 'This is BIIb, the so-called Family Camp in Auschwitz-II Birkenau.' I almost laughed. The word *Birkenau* means birch trees, a lyrical phrase that brought to mind the happy forests of my youth. Yet here, there were only a few clumps dotting the horizon and the rest was a marshy wasteland.

'This *Familienlager* is linked to the main camp known as Auschwitz I, a cavalry barracks two kilometres south-east,' he continued. 'There is also Auschwitz III, a chemical plant manned by several thousand slave labourers taken from the ghettos.'

Under constant supervision from the watchtowers and with never enough time to linger, my informant drip-fed me information whenever he could. I named him The Bookseller after learning he'd once owned a bookstore in Leipzig. A few mornings later, he came for four bodies I'd asked Miloš to help me with. 'What was that music we heard last night?' I asked, as we threw the first onto the back of a low wooden cart.

'That's the *Zigeunerlager* gypsy camp next door,' The Bookseller informed us, as we returned for the next corpse. 'It was the first in which families were allowed to remain together, wear civilian clothes, keep their belongings and their hair. Nobody knows why. Yours is the second camp afforded such singular privileges but it's still highly unusual.'

'Why, what happens to the rest?' Miloš asked, as I flinched. I suspected the answer but didn't want him to hear it.

'Everyone here who isn't worked or starved to death goes straight up the chimney,' The Bookseller replied, so casually that I almost gasped. As Miloš shrank away, our informant laughed, 'Did you think getting a tattoo meant you'd be saved? That isn't roast beef you can smell, sonny.'

Sparrow's brow furrowed as he struggled to take in something so unimaginable. Looking at The Bookseller and back again at me, he stammered, 'What, wait . . . you mean – that horrible smell . . . is people b-being burnt?'

The man's mirthless laugh revealed several missing teeth. 'Oh, they die all right,' he chuckled. 'Choking their last breaths on Zyklon B as they claw at the walls of the gas chambers. Just as you shall one day, my lad. As we all will.'

Seeing the blood drain from Miloš' face, I reached for him but he broke away and ran off. Turning back to The Bookseller, I lowered my voice. 'They'll learn the truth soon enough but, please, let me tell them in my own way. This is impossible for young minds to comprehend. For any mind . . .'

The man shrugged and studied me through wide-set eyes. 'No one wants to believe it at first but, trust me, you'll get used to it.'

'Never,' I replied. Reeling from the thought and knowing then what Łukas and the Bialystok children had witnessed, I ran my hands through my hair and groaned. 'My God when I think of all those souls we delivered up for destruction, deciding who should be on the list. We even helped them pack! The Nazis made us complicit in their diabolical plan.'

'We all are,' he replied. 'They tricked us into believing we had some control over our fate, yet they refer to their mass extermination programme as "*Ausrottung*". Eradicating vermin. That's how they think of us.'

I shook my head. 'All those brilliant minds lost. An entire generation wiped out – and for what? What the hell happened to humanity?' Pressing my fingers against a sudden pain in my temple, I could have wept.

2

October 1943

IN THE SHADOW OF those infernal chimneys, it took all my mental strength to remain upbeat with the children but I was determined to try to save them from the horror, starting with Miloš. Pulling him aside, I told him, 'Don't take too much notice of what that man said. We don't know that's true. People like him may have been sent here to torment us.'

Shaking his head, the fourteen-year-old had a look in his eyes I'd hoped never to see. 'You believe him, though, don't you, Fredy? You didn't dismiss what he said.' Dropping his head into his hands, he cried, 'I don't want to die! Not after all I've survived.'

Placing an arm around his shoulders, I told him, 'Try not think like that. Remember, we're being treated differently here for a reason. We just don't know what it is yet.'

Staring at the chimneys stabbing the sky, Miloš whispered, 'I'd go to the wire rather than there.'

Withdrawing my arm, I snapped, 'I forbid that kind of talk. We've survived years of the Nazis and now they're losing the war. Every day Allied planes fly over us on their way to the front. We just have to hang on a little longer.' One by one, as the older children discovered the true purpose of the camp I did my best to console them. I also gave them strict instructions never to mention the chimney or gas chambers to the little ones. 'We must keep their spirits up and help them to hold on until the war's over,' I insisted. 'It can't be long now.'

As was the way of camp life, a few resorted to humour to get them through, grading the colour of the smoke from the chimneys to guess who was being burned. 'There goes another trainload,' the teenagers would cry, pointing at the thick white clouds rising to the heavens. 'They must have had plenty of fat on them. The smoke's black if they're thin.' Their joking eventually lost its appeal when they realised how little there was to laugh about.

Every morning after roll call, I led all the children under fourteen into a corner of our block where they could be distracted and entertained. It wasn't easy. The youngest didn't understand about order and discipline. All they knew was that they were cold, hungry and tired. Restless, they continued to run amok through the block and around the legs of those of us standing like statues during the daily count. Terrified of catching diseases, the SS shooed them off every time, batting them away like flies.

With Miloš and another young man named Seppl acting as my *Läufer*, I sent them to every bunk to see if they could find teachers, artists or singers who could help me with the children. Their first sweep of the building was disappointing. 'People are too depressed, Fredy,' Seppl told me in my room. 'They just want to stay in their bunks.' Pulling out a square of bread, he started chewing at a corner.

'Where did you get that?' I asked suspiciously, as I'd banned all theft and dishonesty in our block.

'A man from my hometown gave it to me,' he replied, his right cheek bulging.

'Why?'

'He said he was going to die tomorrow.'

Fearing another suicide, I frowned. 'What did he say exactly?'

'He showed me a phial that contained his last dose of insulin,' Seppl replied. 'He said he'd soon be joining his wife in eternal rest.' Shaking my head, I asked him to point the man out. I resolved to sit with him in his final hours.

'He's not the only one who's planning to die,' Seppl added, equally casually, swallowing the last of his bread. 'Some teenagers are talking about forming a group to go to the wire together.' Closing my eyes, I gathered my thoughts for a moment before asking him to bring them to my room.

'Fear is like a contagious disease,' I told them as they stood shame-faced before me. 'It spreads very quickly and can take us prisoner. The only way to be free of it is by using our minds. I know it's hard but we must find a purpose and remain positive. Your work here with me is of vital importance. You are beacons of light in the darkness, helping me to push away the shadows.'

When no one said anything and many stood staring at their feet, I added, 'I will soon have an even more important job for you. I've come up with a plan to recreate a little piece of Terezín in Auschwitz and you're a big part of it. I won't be able to do it without you. Do you understand?'

'Yes, Fredy,' they chimed, lifting their heads. I didn't know how I was going to manage it but I knew that I had to find a way to get as many children as I could out of the blocks and into a place where they felt safe, like at the *Hagibor*: a little piece of heaven in hell. But I couldn't do it alone.

*

'We need to do something about youth welfare,' was one of the first things Leo Janowitz said to me when we were finally able to speak in the washrooms one dawn. 'There's nothing for the children to do.' Still dressed in his long brown robe, the man I'd once jokingly dubbed 'The Monk' was preaching to the converted.

'I have an idea,' I told him. 'But before we talk about that, tell me what happened to Jakob in the ghetto. Is he all right? His note to me in the Small Fortress said he'd lost all authority.'

Leo nodded. 'He was replaced by a German Elder and the anti-Zionists were squeezing him and other Czechs out of the Council.'

'Did they respond to what I told him about the Bialystok children?'

The Monk hung his head. 'The new leadership dismissed it as a fantasy: the product of a child's overactive imagination.'

I could hardly believe what I was hearing. Determined to look forward not back, I told him that I planned to approach the SS officer who'd first appointed me as a *kapo* and ask him a favour. Leo was appalled. 'A favour, Fredy? Are you insane? This isn't Terezín. People like us don't ask favours of the SS here and, if we dare, we end up dead.'

'That's a risk I must take. We have to be allowed to establish a separate children's block like we did in the ghetto. It's not as crazy as it sounds because the precedent has already been set. I'm told that the gypsy camp has a *Kindergarten* and a playground. They even get to cook their own food.'

Leo looked surprised. 'But what makes you think you can get us the same privileges?'

'I don't, but I have to try. If anything happens to me, I'm counting on you to take care of the children.'

The following day I got up well before roll call and ran ten times round our block, allowing my mind to settle to my task. With the searchlights sweeping back and forth across the camp and the last few stars scattered palely in the sky, the slumbering blocks looked almost bucolic. I imagined myself back in the Slovak summer camp where I'd risen with the dawn chorus to swim in the river. There was no dawn chorus here and my reverie was broken by the unwelcome sound of a shot ringing out. Another prisoner who lost all hope had stumbled slowly towards the singing wire, knowing that a bullet would bring deliverance even if the current didn't.

Dropping to the ground to do a few press-ups as I heard more shots parting people from their lives, I ran to the wash-room. Stripping off, I broke the ice in the trough and cleaned myself as best I could in cold water before rubbing my teeth vigorously with my finger. No matter how much I scrubbed, though, my skin felt tight with grime. Each morning, I grieved for every sliver of soap I'd ever casually discarded and every tap I'd carelessly left running before the war.

I pulled on the clothes I'd been able to procure as a *kapo* from the *Kleiderkammer* clothing warehouse. In amongst piles of random, musty garments taken from those about to be gassed, I'd found a warm, blue military-style jacket similar to the one I'd had in the ghetto but a size smaller. It was only when I slipped it on that I realised how much weight I'd lost: it fitted perfectly. I also came across a pair of black leather riding boots that were a size too big, some dark breeches and a white shirt with a deep collar. I even found a tie to match and a ribbon from which to suspend my whistle. I was deter-mined that the children saw me as the same Fredy they'd known in Terezín, not someone who looked dirty or defeated. Wetting my hands with spittle, I slicked down my hair.

After roll call, the SS officer I'd dubbed Eyebrows went to take my report on the numbers of dead but I held onto the form that Nazi efficiency demanded. 'I can be of some assistance to you, *Herr Obersturmführer*,' I told him, locking eyes across the sheet of paper. 'I have a solution to the problem of traumatised children disrupting the camp and spreading disease. It will simultaneously raise morale and improve discipline.'

The man, who frequently expressed exasperation every time toddlers wandered from the ranks to jump in muddy puddles or tug at SS breeches, glared at me murderously. After looking as if he were deciding whether to shoot me on the spot or send me to be gassed, he said, 'You have five minutes.' Summoning Böhm to join us, he led the way to the guardhouse by the gate.

My explanation took twice as long but I launched straight in. 'We need to set up a dedicated block for mothers and infants under eight and for children aged eight to sixteen, *Herr Obersturmführer*. Block 31 at the far end of the camp is available, I believe, and once it's established we can conduct all their roll calls inside and teach them German so that they'll understand orders. I'd also teach them German poems and songs to give them a greater appreciation of the glorious Reich.'

Eyebrows said nothing.

'We achieved this goal very successfully in Theresienstadt,' I continued, being careful to use the German name for the ghetto. '*Obersturmbannführer* Eichmann himself congratulated us on the activities we staged there. I believe he attended one of the children's concerts and was seen to applaud enthusiastically at the end.' The mention of Hitler's deputy was enough to make Eyebrows pull himself upright in his seat, especially when I added, 'I'm sure *Obersturmbannführer* Eichmann would be even more impressed if similar success was achieved here in Birkenau.'

Eyebrows remained perfectly still as his mind whirred. The temptation to bring the Family Camp to the attention of such a powerful Nazi made him clear his throat. 'I will raise it with the Commandant,' he said, nodding at Böhm whose gimlet gaze bore into me. 'We will shortly be receiving more *Stücke*, including several hundred children, so I'll be relying on you to help maintain order.'

Wincing inwardly at his use of the word *Stücke* – 'pieces' – I tasted bile in the back of my throat and realised that The Bookseller was right. That was how the Nazis thought of us. Inanimate. Worthless.

I emerged from the building somewhat surprised that my heart was still pumping. All that mattered, though, was that – subject to permission from Birkenau's senior SS officer, *Unterscharführer* Fritz Buntrock, known to all as 'Bulldog' – I'd secured the use of Block 31.

With an earth floor and no bunks, it was next to the washroom and delousing station and far enough away from the rest of the camp to afford the children a little peace. It also looked out on to a narrow open space that could make an ideal playground in better weather – a privilege I hoped to bargain for in time after I'd cleaned it of the toxic bleaching powder the Nazis sprinkled liberally everywhere.

The major disadvantage of the block was that it was closer to the crematoria and gas chambers. Although we had no direct view of the buildings, anyone playing outside couldn't help but see the lines of prisoners appearing almost daily, trudging to an inevitable end. With nowhere else suitable, I decided I'd just have to find a way of keeping the children inside whenever another transport arrived.

Having been relieved of my duties as *kapo* at my request, I donned an armband that read *Jugende Älteste* and moved into the narrow groom's room at the rear of Block 31. Helped by Leo and a growing team of staff led by a woman the children called 'Auntie' Hanka, who'd run an orphanage in

Prague, I set about trying to achieve the impossible. Everyone I spoke to was staggered that I'd been able to secure permission for the block but it was the response of the men in stripes that surprised me the most.

'For years our only encounters with children have been pulling them off the trucks and pointing them towards the gas,' The Bookseller told me. 'To see healthy boys and girls playing or going to school would be a welcome – if bittersweet – reminder of life before. Tell us what you need and we'll get it from *Kanada*.'

'What is that?' I asked.

'It's the nickname for the *Effektenlager* where the personal effects of the murdered are processed. They called it that because Canada is a land of plenty many once dreamed of escaping to,' he added with wistful eyes. 'Everything from gold teeth to spectacles, jewellery and false legs is sorted and valued for sale with the SS taking what they want and creaming off the profits. With the help of my friend Willi, I can get you almost anything you need.'

He was true to his word and Willi, a forty-year-old criminal and *kapo* from the nearby men's camp, first brought me wooden crates from which I fashioned simple stools and benches. Placed in charge of the prisoners making bunks and updating the camp's water supplies, Willi was a benevolent Gentile who helped when he could. Unbidden, he smuggled in a handful of books including a Mark Twain novel, a Russian textbook, an atlas, a book on psychoanalysis by Sigmund Freud and a volume of poetry that was falling apart.

Later we were given a book by H.G. Wells, a French almanac, a Bible and some science textbooks, all of which were hidden under the floorboards in my room. Looked after during the day by one of the boys and a girl named Dita who had a beautiful singing voice, those precious books became our own little library.

A nurse from the camp's infirmary donated some medical forms for the children to draw on as well as two crayons. In a bin behind the guardhouse someone found a pile of discarded files. A woman who made military caps in a camp factory sent strips of fabric for crafting and Dinah the artist sneaked us some paints and brushes from the shed where she made signs warning of the importance of hygiene.

'Let me know what else I can do, Fredy,' she told me and I smiled, remembering the day I first spotted her sketching the children doing athletics in a Brno park. Wandering over to where she sat under a tree, I asked if I could see her drawings and laughed at her cartoon of us stretching in formation.

'*This is very good*,' I said, genuinely impressed and she told me how she'd won a scholarship to the prestigious School of Applied Arts.

'*I first fell in love with animation when I was fifteen and saw the Walt Disney movie* Snow White and the Seven Dwarfs. *It's my dream to help create something like that*,' she'd added.

'*And one day you will, Dinah, I feel sure*,' I'd replied.

*

When everything was in place and Block 31 was ready, my teenage helpers began to bring the three hundred or so children to me before roll call. Holding hands, the snaking lines of youngsters – some as young as four – came willingly, although they weren't so keen when I made them strip-wash first.

'I know it's cold,' I told them as they bellowed their complaints, 'but I wouldn't make you do it unless it was really important. We must keep the block vermin-free. The sooner you do this, the sooner it will be over. No one gets any breakfast until everyone has washed.' I hated to see how bony they were under their ragged clothing.

'Now let's all run around the block three times to dry off,' I instructed. Ignoring their moans, I told them, 'This isn't a competition to see who's the fastest. It's about being the best you can be. Once you get moving, I promise you that your aches and pains will melt away. So, come on now, follow me.'

After they'd warmed up, the rosy-cheeked children filed into the block for a head count, grateful to be out of the bitter wind. Thanks to Willi, they each received a breakfast of a piece of softer white bread and a cup of sweet lukewarm tea diluted with a little milk. In time, I intended to ask for better rations so that we could make our own soup and break up the monotony of the diet, as Willi had given me another valuable tip.

'Hundreds of packages arrive for those long dead and are sent to *Kanada*,' he'd told me. 'You could ask for those parcels, too, as most contain perishable goods that have to be thrown away.'

'I shall. Thank you for letting me know.'

The children adapted quickly to days spent in the block and enjoyed the athletics I taught them between singing and storytelling, but I longed to brighten up the drab interior that had very little light. Knowing that Dinah had access to paints, I asked if she could decorate the walls.

The girl with beautiful eyes studied me for a moment before asking, 'What do you think the children would like?'

I smiled. 'Something cheerful and fun.'

Posting Miloš as a sentry to warn if any guards approached, Dinah set to work. She began by sketching out a pretty Alpine scene viewed from the deck of a Swiss chalet before filling in the cartoon-style outlines with colour. There was a little wooden balustrade with flowerpots in the foreground, a mountain peak covered in snow and a bright blue sky dotted with clouds. She added a few sheep and cows with birds wheeling overhead. Halfway through, she turned to reach for a new brush and realised that she was surrounded by children watching her in silent appreciation, as was I. Smiling, she asked, 'What else would you like?'

Their eyes bright, as one they pleaded, '*Snow White and the Seven Dwarfs*!'

She looked at me in open surprise before throwing her head back to laugh. 'Did you put them up to this?'

'No,' I replied, truthfully.

'Really? But that's the film I'd loved so much that I unpinned my star and crept into a cinema to watch it seven times in a row so that I could memorise every detail.'

Returning her smile, I said, 'Sometimes fate makes us travel a road for a reason.'

Closing her eyes, she summoned those happy memories before resuming painting. First, she drew Snow White dancing in the flower-filled meadow. Then she added Dopey as her dance companion, balanced on the shoulders of another dwarf under a long coat to bring him up to her height. 'This one in glasses is my favourite,' she said. 'His name is Doc and he plays an accordion. Others play instruments too but never Grumpy. I'm going to put him over there with his arms folded and a scowl on his face.'

Her transformation of that drab old wall was so astonishing that I welled up and whispered, 'It's perfect.'

The children were thrilled, too, treating the artwork with enormous reverence. 'It's their very own *Mona Lisa*,' I exclaimed, as I watched them step up to it gingerly, hands outstretched in wonder.

With some paint left over, I asked Dinah to decorate the door and outer wall of my room. 'I want it to look like the witch's house from *Hänsel und Gretel*. It was said to be made of gingerbread, if I recall, and on my door you can draw the wicked witch with an evil face and a big wart on her nose.'

Dinah was surprised. 'Why something so scary?'

'I want the children to fear me a little and, most importantly, to respect me,' I said. 'They'll need moral, physical and psychological strength to survive this, so discipline could mean the difference between life and death.'

When Dinah finished painting, I had to laugh out loud. 'That's even better than I hoped,' I cried, studying the gnarled witch who looked uncannily like me.

3

November 1943

'ALOUETTE, GENTILE ALOUETTE,' a young man named Avi sang out in fine voice as he stood in the middle of the children's block conducting the children. 'Alouette je te plumerai.'

Singing along, children of all ages gazed at one of our most popular teachers with beaming smiles. The song I'd first taught them in Terezín was a favourite, especially when a teenager named Helga sang a verse solo. Sadly, the girl with the voice of an angel was in the infirmary with tuberculosis. Many had died of it but Helga was strong and the doctors told me she'd recover.

'Je te plumerai la tête,' the children chanted as they pulled on their hair. I chuckled. Dinah laughed too, so I wandered to where she was standing and asked, 'Do you know what the words mean, apart from being a pretty song about a bird?'

'You may not want to know, Fredy,' she replied, grimacing. 'The lyrics are pretty grisly.'

'They are?'

'Yes, it's about French-Canadian trappers plucking a dead lark.'

A sudden memory of lying in long grass on the hills above Aachen, watching the fluttering wings of skylarks hovering above me as they sang, flooded my brain.

A better song was called 'The Laughing Optimist' from a famous Czech tune, which the children had adapted especially for me. The words included the line, '*Fredy keeps us smiling,*

Fredy keeps us clean, Fredy never stops laughing, although Fredy's sometimes mean.' Mean or not, I could never have achieved what I did in Block 31 without teenage volunteers like Avi, Dinah, Hanka and the others.

'The aim is to keep them too busy to think about where they are or what might happen to them,' I told my new recruits, inventing jobs for them so that they too could escape being selected for slave labour. 'The children's block must be a sanctuary; a place for them to feel safe. If they ask where departed loved ones are, tell them they've gone to Camp H.'

'What does the H stand for?' someone asked.

'*Himmel,*' I replied. Heaven. 'We'll divide them into groups of twenty according to age and sit them in circles. Those without a seat can sit on the chimney.' The word chimney, so dreaded in the camp, meant something very different in the Children's Block – a brick flue running horizontally between two chimney stacks that could provide a little warmth if Willi could get wood to light them.

'We don't have any blackboards or chalk and we only have a little paper and a few crayons,' I continued, 'so you will have to become walking, talking books and give improvised lessons from memory. I'm looking for natural storytellers or those with a dramatic flair.'

'What kinds of subjects do you want us to teach?' one matronly woman asked.

'Everything and anything that keeps them distracted or gives them hope,' I replied. 'We also want to plug the gaps in their education as much as we can, so maths, literature, science, art – the standard curriculum. And no subjects that might be considered controversial.'

'What's in it for us?' a man growled. Taking a mental note of his face, I resolved not to avail myself of his services.

'Nothing at all, apart from the pleasure of doing something good.'

'No extra food?'

'Absolutely not. The food is for the children only. None of the helpers or teachers will receive as much as a mouthful and anyone caught stealing will be dismissed. That is my strictest rule.'

Inviting a few to see how we operated, I had them watch me give a lesson on the Canadian boy scout pioneer Ernest Thompson Seton. 'Seton was a British citizen who went to live in America at the end of the last century,' I told a huddle of children sitting on the floor. 'Who knows where America is?'

A few hands flew up and one girl said, 'The other side of the Atlantic Ocean.'

'That's right, Hella. Well done. Mr Seton lived alongside wild animals and came to respect them, giving several of them names like Lobo and Raggylug.' The children chuckled. 'Later, he set up an organisation called the Woodcraft Indians to teach children how to have purposeful lives and enjoy being outdoors.'

'What does "purposeful" mean, Fredy?' a boy asked, his hand raised.

'Good question, Frederick. It means having a reason to get up every morning excited about the day. That's how I feel every morning when the gong sounds. I can't wait to see you all and help you find a purpose.'

*

'Fredy, you're needed in one of the women's blocks,' Seppl told me one day after running in breathlessly.

'Why? What's happened?' I asked, reluctant to leave my charges.

'Another fight's broken out. It's the usual trouble but the *kapo* has called for you.'

Asking Hanka to carry on talking about the Greek myths, I went to my room to fetch my rucksack before heading out with Seppl. I could hear the shrieking before I was even close. Looking around anxiously for Böhm or the SS guards, I hurried inside to find nine women brawling like cats on the floor. Their *kapo*, a twenty-year-old named Tilla with a reputation for cruelty, was beating any she could reach with her stick, splitting lips already bleeding and almost taking one woman's eye out.

'*Halt!*' I bellowed, but I might as well have whispered it. 'Halt, I say! Stop this immediately, or the SS will.' A few of them stopped scrapping and peered up at me, panting through matted hair. One woman's dress had been ripped open to reveal her breasts. 'Cover yourself up,' I told her. Trying not to breathe too deeply because of the general smell, I asked, 'Who started this?'

Tilla marched over to me, her face red and sweaty with exertion. 'These bitches are out of control,' she hissed. 'They steal and lie. I swear they're one step away from killing each other.'

'Unless you do it first,' I commented coldly, without even looking at her.

Ordering the women to get to their feet and straighten themselves out, I made them line up in a row before I stood before them, stony-faced. 'You're worse than the naughtiest children,' I scolded. 'This isn't the first time I've had to arbitrate.'

'She stole my bread!' shrieked a middle-aged woman, pointing at a slender woman further along the line. 'That was the second time this week.'

Turning to the alleged thief, whose left eyelid was swelling, I asked, 'Is this true?'

The woman shrugged.

'It is true, Fredy,' a small voice piped up from one of the bunks. Looking up, I saw a stick-thin teenager peering out from under a blanket, her skin yellow. 'She took it for me.'

The accused woman spun round and hissed, 'Don't, Jana!'

'What are you to each other?' I asked.

The thief said, 'She's my sister. She's sick.' Pointing at the complainant, she sneered. 'She can afford to lose some blubber. Jana can't.' Another fight would have broken out then if I hadn't kept them apart so I banished the matron to the far end of the block and told all but the sisters to go back to their bunks. Stepping closer to Jana, I said, 'Why haven't you been taken to the infirmary?'

Her eyes grew even larger in her cadaverous face. 'Because I'll never come out.'

Bowing my head, I nodded. Turning to Seppl, I said, 'Find Dr Heller and tell him I sent you. Ask for some white bread and a little milk. I'll wait here until you bring it.'

Clambering up the bunks to take a closer look at the sick girl, I asked, 'Do I know you?'

She gave me a thin smile. 'Not really. I was only in the *Kinderheim* for a few days before you were arrested in Terezín and then I was put in a transport.'

'She was ill when we arrived,' her sister said, 'but now she's worse. I just wanted to give her something that might help.'

I climbed back down. 'What is your name?'

'Martina.'

'Very well, Martina. I will arrange with Dr Heller for you to get special rations for Jana until she's better. Seppl will bring them each afternoon. But there is one condition. You must promise you won't steal from anyone again. Understood?' She stared at me for several second before nodding. I hoped she meant it.

Wishing Jana well, I walked to the far end of the block where the complainant stood, trying to make herself more presentable. Reaching into my rucksack, I turned my back on the block before handing her a half loaf of bread. Her eyes lit up and she snatched it from me, immediately tearing off a chunk to eat. Watching her, I said, 'Did you know that our faith is said to be based on three things – the Torah, the service of God and acts of loving kindness.'

She swallowed so abruptly that I thought for a moment she might choke.

'In the ghetto, much kindness was shown to the less fortunate,' I reminded her. 'Every day, people risked infection to sit with someone until their breath ran out. Others saved their rations to make cakes of sorts for special occasions. Mothers with extra breastmilk donated it to those with none.'

With a shameful expression, she hung her head, the remainder of her bread held limply in her hand. Lifting her chin, I said more softly, 'A woman stole a piece of bread to save her dying sister. She'd have given up her own ration first.'

Her eyes filled with tears.

'We have all been thrown together in an impossible place with unthinkable consequences,' I added. 'It will go better for us all if we show loving kindness to those going through the same hell.'

*

The excitement of the children was palpable, especially among the boys. Holding up a tatty tennis ball Willi found, along with some wood for our fires, I told them, 'You can play with this ball at the far end of the block before curfew. When the weather gets better we'll take it outside but if anyone kicks it near the wire I'll take it away.'

It was getting harder and harder to think of ways to keep them from the horrors of the camp. Although the children no longer endured roll calls outside, they could still hear shouting and screams. One afternoon when winter was its harshest and the days felt threadbare, those cries were so desperate that I went to the doorway to see what was happening. Rows of people stood like statues, hardly daring to breathe as they leaned against the wind. The camp commandant Buntrock was whipping two old men who were on their knees attempting to do press-ups on hands red-raw with cold.

'*Mehr!*' he bellowed, as he rained more blows on their bloodied backs. '*Tu mehr!*' Do more.

Bulldog was dressed in a greatcoat and a fur cap and appeared to be drunk, which was when he was at his most sadistic. Swaggering around wielding blows whenever the mood took him, he was merciless as he forced the frail prisoners to keep going. When one collapsed again into the frozen mud, Bulldog kicked him so hard in the face that teeth and blood went flying.

'Oh!' I heard a small voice behind me.

Spinning round, I came face to face with an eight-year-old boy who'd followed me outside. 'Why does that man want to hurt them?' he asked, his eyes clouded with fear.

Taking him inside, I sat on the chimney and pulled him onto my knee. 'It's all right to feel scared or upset, Daniel,' I told him. 'Sometimes I get scared and upset too.'

'You do?'

'Yes, because hurting someone is bad, isn't it?' He nodded. 'People shouldn't hurt each other, should they?' He shook his head. 'But sometimes it can't be prevented. All we can do is keep ourselves safe and talk to people we trust about how it makes us feel.'

He stared at me so intently that I couldn't think what else to say. Giving him a quick hug, I set him down saying, 'You know you can talk to me anytime, but let's think about something else now.' Standing up and taking his hand, I led him back to his group.

Every day, seven days a week, we provided hours of education and entertainment with a break for lunch, inventing memory games and encouraging the children to use their imaginations. Watching them play Cowboys and Indians one day, I was saddened to hear a boy tell a so-called baddie: 'I'm the sheriff around here and soon you'll be taking the only road out of here: up the chimney.' In other games, the camp's vocabulary crept in, even though few understood the true meaning. One little girl setting up an imaginary kitchen told her friend, 'If we keep baking enough bread the Bad Men will run out of gas.'

Determined to divert their minds from the truth, I devised competitions for everything from cleanliness to singing, sporting prowess to poetry. An old man made them some dolls out of wire and rags that were nothing like the wooden figures Dirk once made, but the children didn't seem to notice. He also fashioned pencils from splinters of wood picked from the edges of rough bunks, sharpening them with a filed-down spoon. Our fingertips were blackened each time we rolled them in the charcoal paste that was a poor substitute for lead, but it worked.

Another game I made up was called 'Fall Down, Stay Down' in which I hoped to teach the children never to react if they were struck by a Nazi or a *kapo*. They took turns to bash each other over the head with a stick made of rolled cardboard.

Giggling hysterically, the one who was hit had to drop to the ground and stay there, even if they were tickled, hit again or prodded. 'Stay down! Stay down!' the others would cry until laughter got the better of them.

In the game they loved the most, the children had to run around madly but then stop dead whenever I called out 'Freeze!'

'Clever, Fredy,' Dinah said as she watched us play one afternoon. 'I presume that's meant to stop them in their tracks if a Nazi approaches?'

'It may also save them from the wire,' I replied. 'It's one of the reasons there are so few birds here, you know,' I said, walking to the open doorway. 'The minute we hear the tell-tale popping sound one of my helpers runs out to pick up the corpse of whichever bird accidentally touched the fence. I keep the singed bodies in a sack and pluck the feathers for crafts.'

'*Alouette, gentile alouette*,' Dinah sang softly with a wry expression.

Hearing the rumble of trucks, she and I turned to see the latest transport of hapless souls arriving. Turning back, I made sure that there were no children watching. First, the deportees were unloaded from overcrowded trucks onto a new ramp that was being built, we presumed for a rail spur to come directly into the camp. Separated by gender, the prisoners were pulled wailing from their vehicles amid shouting and barking.

A team of SS doctors stood waiting to preside over them like judge and jury. All those deemed unfit for labour were sent left, while those who looked healthy went right, headed for labour camps. Those too weak to move were thrown to one side like sacks of wheat and shot.

Frozen to the spot, Dinah and I watched as a young mother who'd been sent left with her toddler crouched to smooth her daughter's clothes and tie a red scarf around her head, before resuming their place in line. Standing close by, an SS guard yawned before reaching into his pocket to retrieve his cigarettes. Casually, he lit one before taking a slug from a half-bottle of vodka. His unseeing eyes followed the unsuspecting mother and child as they skipped hand in hand towards death.

'Fredy, Fredy, you forgot to say Freeze!' one of the children cried immediately behind me, tugging on my jacket as I turned away from the horror.

Seeing the tears in Dinah's eyes, I quickly squeezed her hand.

'Apologies, my dears,' I replied, fixing a smile. 'Now, who'd like another turn? On the blow of my whistle, off you go!'

The piercing sound of a different whistle at the door made us all jump. Turning quickly, I saw Seppl gesturing wildly and, clapping my hands together, I cried, 'SS patrol, everybody! You know the drill. Books away. German lessons only.' As they sprang into action, I made sure my hair was slicked down and polished my boots on the back of my breeches.

SS patrols often drove into the camp, if the main *lagerstrasse* wasn't so muddy that their vehicles would sink, but they usually went straight to the infirmary blocks opposite. This morning was different and, as Seppl sprinted back inside giving me a warning look, I picked up the recorder The Bookseller had brought me from *Kanada* and began to play.

A handsome young guard with the rank of *Rottenführer* cried, '*Achtung!*' before stepping aside. Eyebrows strolled in, hands clasped behind his back. After I saluted and clicked my heels, the two men did a slow sweep of the room, stopping to listen to a lesson or admire the naïve paintings hanging from a discarded strand of barbed wire. They then moved to Dinah's artwork, nodding their appreciation, before stepping to a corner where an old man was folding the pages of a newspaper into birds. Close by, a pretty young woman named Renée was teaching girls how to make beads out of splinters from broken wooden spoons. She then threaded them onto strands of cotton from an old cloth, showing them different knots.

Bewitched by Renée, the *Rottenführer* froze in his tracks. He couldn't take his eyes off the twenty-year-old with raven black hair and green eyes who kept glancing nervously at me.

'Impressive,' Eyebrows commented as he came round to where I was still standing to attention. Stopping in front of the fireplace, he stared at the six little girls huddled under a single blanket in front of it, cupping their hands around bowls of soup.

Frowning at the flames licking at the puny splinters in the grate, Eyebrows looked up and snapped, 'I don't recall permitting this chimney to be used.'

Without missing a beat, I quipped, 'Well, what's another chimney around here between friends?'

Instantly regretting my words, I watched his jaw flex as his hands dropped to his sides. To my astonishment, instead of pulling out his service pistol, his face cracked into a broad grin. When he began to laugh the *Rottenführer* began to laugh too, their shoulders rising and falling with mirth.

'*Sehr gut,*' Eyebrows cried, slapping me on the back, as his deputy threw me a look of open appreciation. 'Very good. Between friends. That's very funny.'

Still chuckling as his underling gave Renée one last lingering look, Eyebrows wandered away from our oasis and I let out a long sigh of relief. Watching him go, I saw him automatically press a handkerchief to his nose and brush flecks of human ash from his shoulders before setting off.

4

December 1943

'I HAVE A SURPRISE for you, children,' I announced, as hundreds of faces tilted expectantly towards me as I stood on the chimney, hands on my hips. 'How would you like to put on a play to thank all those who've helped us?'

I could hardly hear myself think for their approving cries. Thrilled by the idea, young and old threw themselves into the production, coming up with a dozen different ideas for the performance until they finally settled on one of their favourite books: *The Wonderful Adventures of Nils* by the Swedish author Selma Lagerlöf.

This story was recited to them from memory at least once a week by a white-haired old lady the children affectionately called *Babička* or Grandma. Sitting by the fire to warm her old bones, that seventy-five-year-old widow who'd lost her son, daughter-in-law and both grandchildren, recited the story in gripping instalments that had them all agog.

'Who wants to hear again about Nils, the naughty boy shrunk by a magic gnome?' she'd ask, as devoted pupils flocked to her. 'And who can tell me what happens next?'

'He flies around Sweden on the back of a goose and learns how to be good,' cried Daniel.

'That's right,' she said, giving him a benevolent, if sad, smile.

Playing the different characters the boy meets along the way, the children rehearsed their lines diligently, turning everything into a game that ended in fits of giggles. 'Clap, clap, clap your hands,' the girls chanted as they clapped. 'Nils, Nils, drop your pants!' the boys called, before they all squealed. One group sat in a corner making goose puppets from scraps of white fabric smuggled in by slave labourers making machine gun belts. In another corner, Avi led a group in choir practice for the singing parts.

I chose a Friday night for our first performance of *Nils*, to which I invited as many of our helpers and teachers as I could. 'Can we bring families and friends?' they asked.

'On a first-come, first-served basis and only if there is room on the night,' I replied, still worrying that they'd be bringing vermin into our clean block. The subsequent lines of people waiting outside in hope was gratifying to see, if a little daunting.

'These people are starving,' I commented wryly to Dinah as we peered out at them from the doorway, 'and I'm not just talking about food.' Those lucky enough to squeeze inside sat enrapt as the children paraded up and down, dressed in innovative costumes made from rags. The chimney was their stage and the production was a shambles as they forgot or stumbled over their lines but it didn't matter.

'Nobody will mind if you make a mistake,' I'd assured them before the show began. 'Just keep going and enjoy yourself.' From the looks on their faces and the glint in eyes lit by candlelight they were doing just that.

Deciding to make it a weekly event with audiences coming on rotation, we went on to adapt many of the children's favourite stories. We created a musical loosely based on *Gulliver's Travels* in which I played Gulliver. Another on the story of Noah and the Flood as first suggested by Hans in a ghetto, who I cast as Noah much to his delight.

'Can we do *Robinson Crusoe*, Fredy?' several asked after that but I told them, 'We could but that story only really has two main characters.' Seeing their disappointment, I smiled. 'Although I suppose we could include a pack of mischievous monkeys and a shipload of Spanish sailors?' Their cries deafened me.

*

One word sent a shiver down all our spines whenever it reverberated around the block: *Achtung!* Once during rehearsals it came unexpectedly and, turning, I saw a group of five SS officers led by Eyebrows shuffling in after throwing open the door.

Where was our lookout?

'Carry on!' Eyebrows barked, as they looked upon us frozen to the spot. Clustering to one side to keep away from anyone infested, the men stood awkwardly at first in their immaculate uniforms and shiny, polished boots until they relaxed a little and began to enjoy watching the children prancing about on the stage. In their eyes, I saw something I hadn't expected. Their features softened as they listened to the songs and chuckled at the mistakes. Mostly young, these were men who would have had wives and children of their own back in Germany.

It was Willi who gave me an insight into the lives of some of the senior officers stationed at the camp. 'In a far corner of Auschwitz I, the Camp Commandant Hoess lives in a luxurious villa with fruit trees and a walled garden,' he told me. 'His wife and children are with him, along with servants and gardeners. The family frequently hosts children's parties and dinners, despite the background roar of the crematorium furnaces.'

Dinah informed me that the SS had their own canteen, cinema, sports club and theatre and were given paid leave as in a regular job. 'Several told me how much they'd enjoyed their holiday skiing in Austria while others went hiking in the Black Forest. Having kissed goodbye to their loved ones after their break, they come back here to supervise the murder of hundreds of thousands.' It was beyond comprehension.

One of our most frequent visitors to the block was the young *Rottenführer* I'd first seen with Eyebrows. His name was Viktor Pestek and he started bringing sweets and other treats for the children, even though I told the little ones not to accept them. To my horror, some of the teenage girls developed a crush on him: calling him '*Milacek*' or sweetheart behind his back before collapsing into hysterical giggles. I even caught a few of them pinching their cheeks to make them rosier whenever he strolled in. As I told Dinah, 'It disturbs me how differently they behave around him. I see now how easily they could be manipulated or misled.'

Dinah smiled. 'Oh, Fredy, they're just being girls,' she told me. 'Let them have their fun. There's no harm in it, is there?'

'Just like there's no harm in you secretly dating Willi?' I asked, as she blushed. 'You know he's completely smitten and calls you Greta Garbo?' Dinah's colour deepened and she gave me a shy smile before walking away.

It was soon apparent that Pestek had also developed a crush: on my prettiest teacher, Renée. Intrigued and scared by his attention in equal measure, she came to ask my advice. 'I don't know what to do, Fredy,' she said. 'He seems nice but he can't be, can he, if he's in the SS?' Her cheeks flushed, she went on to breathlessly inform me that he was nineteen, a Catholic who grew up in an ethnic German family in Romania where his father was a blacksmith. 'He claims his mother persuaded him to join what she called the elite branch of the Germany army but that once he was ordered to murder people he was shocked.'

'So why didn't he just leave?'

'He says it's not that simple. He'd have been shot for desertion.'

'How did he end up here?'

'He was declared unfit for frontline duty after being wounded but says he's so appalled by everything here that he works with the Resistance.'

Listening as she talked, I realised that for her to know so much they must have already met privately. Taking her hand, I told her, 'Renée, you must be careful. The consequences of striking a friendship with this man could be deadly and I can only imagine what his punishment might be if he was caught fraternising with a Jew. You are playing a very dangerous game.'

Heedless of my warnings she continued to see Pestek, claiming that she did so for the extra food he provided for her and her mother. I was wary of any contact with a Nazi but in time I grew to relax more in his company as he proved to be useful. It was Pestek who introduced me to Rudi, a young Slovak *Blockschreiber* or registrar who had contact with a large network of spies and Resistance members throughout the entire compound. Luckily for us, Rudi operated out of the adjacent quarantine camp BIIa, separated from us by an electrified fence over which packages and messages were frequently thrown.

Thanks to Rudi and people like him who risked their lives to help us, my *Kinder* fared far better than the rest of the camp where dysentery, scabies, meningitis typhus and constant starvation continued to claim lives. I only hoped that I could keep that up until the day war ended. I prayed that was soon.

*

'Remember: whatever toughens us, strengthens us,' I told the children as I made them march around the block to dry off after their morning wash. Even as the temperatures plummeted, I never let up on my regimes. 'Shoulders back. Heads up. Be sure to keep a cheerful heart.'

Like them, I felt the cold creeping into my very marrow and worried that some might catch pneumonia from the exposure but that was a risk I had to take. I hadn't yet lost one of my charges to disease and was determined to keep it that way. If I could keep them fit, I knew they'd stand a better chance of making it.

There was one thing I couldn't do much about, however, and that was hunger. This was our greatest torment and felt sometimes all consuming, even for me. Seeing people scratching around in the mud for a blade of grass, a dandelion or even a worm, I no longer flinched. There were moments when I, too, longed for something, anything, to fill the void. For growing children, these cravings were often overwhelming and could – if not managed – lead to theft or worse. The women in the barracks were still creating imaginary feasts every night, as they'd done in the ghetto, but this only made the hunger worse for the little ones so I decided to try some self-hypnosis.

Sitting them cross-legged on the floor with their eyes closed, I urged them to take a few deep breaths. 'As your body relaxes, focus your attention on your stomach,' I instructed. 'Place your hands on your belly and rub it in little circles to warm it up. Can you feel that?' Spotting a boy peeping at me out of one eye, I reminded them, 'Eyes closed and that means you too, Felix.'

Guiding their visualisation, I told them to imagine their stomachs were full after a hot and hearty meal. 'Feel how tight the skin stretches over your fat bellies,' I said. 'You're warm and sleepy from all that food. Tell yourself quietly in your head, *I'm not hungry. I'm not hungry. I am full.* Now slide down onto the floor and take a little nap.' Watching them curling into contented little balls, I silently thanked Werner for lending me his textbooks what seemed like a lifetime earlier.

Self-hypnosis could only stave off hunger, pain or fear for short periods, however, and I knew that I needed to pluck up the courage to ask Böhm for more food. Dealing with him was a scarier prospect than negotiating with the SS.

The man – who I discovered was a convicted murderer and pimp – was an enigma no one could figure out. One minute he'd appear at our door with a pocket full of sweets, inviting the children to sit on his lap as he beamed with joy. The next he'd be in a red mist of rage, tearing through the blocks beating anyone in his path and handing out random punishments that sometimes resulted in death. Then one day Leo told me something about him that chilled my blood. 'Böhm has chosen a new *Piepel*.'

Piepel was a word I'd first learned in the ghetto but which was much more commonly used in the Family Camp. It was given to a teenage boy employed as a runner and messenger by privileged prisoners in return for double rations and the opportunity to live separately. In return the boys were often subjected to systematic sexual abuse. 'Oh,' I replied, not sure I wanted to hear more.

'It's Erik,' he said. 'The guttersnipe you attempted to discipline in Terezín.'

Groaning, I held my head in my hands. The fact that Böhm had a *Piepel* didn't surprise me, but the fact that it was Erik made me sad. It suddenly made sense of seeing him running across the camp dressed as a bell boy, which I'd thought strange.

Leo told me that *piepels* were frequently dressed in uniforms like hotel staff.

'For a boy like Erik this could mean the difference between life and death, but he will live with the constant threat of being disposed of as soon a prettier replacement is chosen. And the sad truth is that *piepels* often become as violent and arrogant as their masters - if they survive.'

'What can we do?' I asked with a sigh.

'Nothing, unless you want to incur the wrath of Böhm,' Leo said. 'I just thought you should know.'

'If only I'd offered Erik work in the block,' I berated myself. 'But I feared he'd be too disruptive. Maybe I could have a word with him?' Leo gave me a sceptical look.

Spotting Erik hastening across the camp the following day, I stepped out to intercept his path. 'I've never seen you looking so tip-top, my boy,' I told him with a smile, pretending to admire his epaulettes and gold braided cap, no doubt stitched by one of the seamstresses Böhm paid in vodka. 'I never doubted that you'd find a way to survive here.'

Staring at me with deadened eyes, the boy with the beautiful face said nothing as I noticed that his hair was an untidy flop and his fingernails bitten to the quick. Looking past me as if in a hurry to be elsewhere, he shifted from foot to foot.

'I just wanted to let you know, Erik, that if you ever need to talk to anyone, or if you need sanctuary, you'd be welcome at the children's block,' I added. 'We'd be happy to include your whistling in one of our shows and I'm always in need of an extra pair of hands.'

Locking eyes with me, Erik's mouth twisted into a sardonic smile. 'I bet you are, Fredy Hirsch.'

Shuddering at the implication, I began to object but he cut across me. 'Thanks but I'm spoken for. Find your own *piepel*.'

Speechless, I watched him hurry off on some heinous errand. Bumping into Willi soon afterwards, he asked me what was wrong and I told him.

'Well, you know why he agreed to do it?' he asked. When I shook my head, he explained. 'Erik's parents were transported here soon after arriving in Terezín and Erik is using his position to help them. Thanks to Böhm they have a bunk to themselves and receive extra food. Despite appearances, it seems that he's a devoted son.'

Walking to Böhm's block the following morning, I knew there was no point in raising the subject of Erik no matter how much the arrangement disgusted me. Dreading my meeting, I found the camp elder sitting at his desk.

'I have come to ask for some cauldrons so we can prepare soup in the children's block, *Herr Lagerälteste*,' I began. 'And the children would benefit enormously if some of the perishable packages sent to *Kanada* could be diverted to them.'

Böhm said nothing as he sat watching me over fingers pressed together to form an arch.

'It would also be helpful if we could apply to the International Red Cross to ask for parcels of food, soap, pharmaceuticals and toiletries. We had them in Theresienstadt and they provided much relief.'

There was a short silence and then he said, 'Is that all?'

'Yes, *Herr Lagerälteste*,' I replied, still standing to attention.

'The Nazi High Command has already approved communication with the Red Cross,' he told me, his voice unusually calm. 'You will be allowed to write letters to families and friends periodically and can ask for necessities to be sent via the Reich Association of Jews.'

Delighted at the news, I felt a smile tug at the corner of my mouth.

'Whatever you write will be strictly censored and must include references to the excellent conditions here,' Böhm added. Seeing my expression, he said, 'I'll also see that you get some fresh milk and marmalade. I know the children love sweet things.'

Wary of his motives, I thanked him and made as if to go but he stopped me. 'You know, I was certain you'd be sent to the gas for your impudence in asking for a children's block,' he added, eyeing me with curiosity. 'Instead, it appears that you have the SS eating out of your hands. I'm told several senior officers plan to attend your next play, which must – of course – be entirely in German.'

My heart sank as we'd previously performed in a light-hearted blend of Czech with a smattering of German and I knew how hard it would be for the children to relearn their lines.

Böhm wasn't finished. His eyes glinting, he rose from his chair and came to stand two steps away from me, his breath smelling unpleasantly of sardines. 'You're probably pleased with yourself but do you realise that all you've done is play straight into their hands?'

I felt my Adam's apple bob uncomfortably in my throat.

'The Nazis are making a film of Theresienstadt soon to show the world how well Jews are looked after there. When they do the same here in Birkenau, you can be assured that Block 31 will feature prominently. It is perfect for propaganda. They couldn't have planned it better themselves.'

Looking into eyes blackened by hate and trying not to let his words hit home, I took a breath and tried to persuade myself that the benefits to the children outweighed any advantage I'd unwittingly handed to the Nazis. *But was he right? How long would this dastardly game last? And what would happen after the films were made?*

Desperate to escape his gloating and my own dark thoughts, I almost made it to the door when he lobbed his parting shot in a voice drenched in hatred.

'You know, Hirsch, if you hadn't been born a Jew you'd have made an excellent member of the Waffen-SS.'

5

January 1944

'*Achtung!*'

The command from behind was accompanied by a sudden blast of cold air before a softer voice said, '*Guten Morgen, Kinder.*' Turning quickly, I clicked my heels together and gave a sharp salute to the man in the immaculate grey-green uniform silhouetted in the doorway. Beyond him I could see a gleaming Mercedes-Benz. I hadn't heard it pull up because of the children's laughter.

With his Iron Cross prominently displayed on his left pocket along with a War Merit Cross and several military ribbons, our visitor was the image of an exemplary soldier who'd seen front-line action even though he didn't look much older than me. Although senior SS frequently visited the Family Camp, this was the first time the officer I recognised as Birkenau's First Physician had come to the children's block. He usually only visited the infirmary opposite.

Ignoring me and brushing off fresh snow as he stepped inside, the man bent at the waist to pat the heads of two small children who ran up to him with innocent curiosity. Winking at the four-year-olds, our visitor reached into the pocket of his belted tunic to retrieve sugar cubes normally only fed to SS horses.

Open-mouthed, the children stared in wonder after he placed them into their palms. Having never seen anything like that before, they turned to me for guidance.

Resisting the urge to swat the cubes off their hands as if they were poison, I gestured that they were edible so they put them in their mouths with caution. Tasting sweetness, their faces wrinkled with delight and they ran to their friends to stick out their tongues and show off the melting white squares.

'*Danke, Herr Hauptsturmführer,*' I said quietly, as my visitor turned to me with a smile revealing a gap between his two front teeth. It might have been attractive on anyone else.

'You may call me *Herr Doktor,*' he replied. His thick head of brown hair was slicked back stylishly and his olive skin was as unblemished as his uniform. He had the look of a thirties movie star with keen, intelligent eyes the colour of moss.

Stepping further into the room, he scanned the faces with an expert eye as the children sat huddled in every item of clothing they possessed. I prayed that Dita and the other teenagers I'd put in charge of our illegal library had already hidden the books under sweaters or beneath crates.

On a short blast of my whistle, the youngest children began to recite a poem they'd been taught specially for moments like this. As our visitor stood, legs apart in his jodhpur-style breeches, a pair of white kid gloves in one hand and a riding crop in the other, their sing-song voices rang out with Heinrich Heine's 'There Lies The Heat of Summer'. Mouths billowing vapour, they looked relieved as they made it to the final line, '*Der Winter wird auf den Wangen, Der Sommer im Herzen sein.*' Winter on your cheek but summer in your heart.

Beaming, the officer tapped his thigh with his crop by way of applause. Turning to me with unexpected warmth, he said, 'My men keep telling me how much they enjoy visiting this refuge in our midst, so I had to come and see it for myself.'

'You will always be welcome, *Hauptsturm*–apologies, *Herr Doktor.*'

Strutting around the room, he patted the head of a blonde girl and smiled benignly at several of the boys. 'The work that you've done here has attracted the attention of Berlin,' he informed me, studying the little stools made from offcuts and the drawings on the walls. 'They're thinking of replicating the system in other camps and want a detailed report about your methods and thinking.'

My stomach did a backflip at the thought of bringing myself to the attention of anyone in Berlin. What did that mean? What would they do with such a report? My mind racing in time with my heart, I felt to have lost all saliva but forced my mouth into what I hoped was an expression of gratitude. 'Yes, of course, *Herr Doktor.*'

Staring me out for a moment as if he was reading my mind, he added, 'You must let me know if there's anything you need.'

Wondering where to start, I was about to ask for some coal and the use of a separate barracks for the infants when a cluster of skinny children stepped forward. Eyes sunken into hollowed cheeks, they made no sound as they peered up at our visitor sheepishly, hands outstretched.

'Now, now, little mice,' I said, quickly stepping between them and the man who could decide whether they lived or died. 'What have I taught you about manners? We never beg. Hurry now and return to your studies.'

Renée crept forward to take them back but the First Physician barked, '*Halt!*' and she froze. We all did. Reaching into his pocket once more, he retrieved a handful of cubes and cast them to the floor as if throwing scraps to dogs. 'Here, a gift from your Uncle Pepi,' he cried. Dozens of children dropped to their knees and scrambled for their prize as he laughed.

Swallowing, I waited until the feeding frenzy was over before shooing them back to their places. Turning to the doctor, I said, 'As you can see, they are ravenous, *Herr Doktor*. Hunger distracts them from learning German. If we were allowed more Red Cross parcels we could give them a thicker soup, so that they'd be better able to–'

'Yes, yes,' he interrupted, waving me away as he stepped past to better examine the mural of *Snow White and the Seven Dwarfs*. 'Who is responsible for this artwork? It is quite accomplished. I may have a use for them.'

Studying my blurred reflection in the sheen of his black leather boots, I ran my hands through my hair and shrugged, trying not to catch the eyes of those around me holding their breath. 'A woman from one of the blocks. I don't recall her number . . .'

'Then you must.' His tone forced me to look up into eyes that had taken on a steely glint.

Dropping his gaze to my tailored jacket buttoned to the neck, my breeches and boots, he pursed his distinctively M-shaped lips. 'You are in a privileged position here: working with children. It would be unfortunate if you were unable to continue your project.'

'*Yawol, Herr Doktor*,' I replied, pulling myself to my full height to return his glare.

As he turned to go, I spotted something that almost threw me off balance. In the fold of his left ear was a small circular birthmark that looked exactly like the metal button in the ear of Emil, my childhood Steiff dog. The similarity was so unnerving that I lost myself for a moment until I realised that he was studying me with equal intensity.

Blowing my whistle twice, I gave the children the cue to jump to their feet and stand to attention. 'Say goodbye and thank you to *Doktor* Mengele.'

As one, their voices trilled, '*Dankeschön, Doktor* Mengele.'

Smiling, he pulled on one of his white kid gauntlets before extending a hand. Caught off guard, I reached out to feel the grip of the man who could have us all killed by a single flick of his glove. I returned his handshake just as firmly before he gave a cursory nod and left.

Waiting until the door closed behind him with a fresh blast of wind, I finally let out a breath I hadn't realised I'd been holding. I reached into my back pocket to pull out my recorder and asked, 'Now, who'd like a song?' before striking up the quivering first notes of Beethoven's 'Ode to Joy'.

*

As alarming as Mengele's visit had been, there was little time to dwell on it because a week later the extra '*Stücke*' I'd been told about arrived in a blizzard on Christmas Eve. Two trains carrying another five thousand or so prisoners from Terezín disgorged friends and family members who were forced to march in close formation towards the empty blocks, just as we had been.

By chance that bitter night I was among a group of men, including Leo, who'd been summoned to the infirmary for a briefing on more stringent procedures for delousing after yet another epidemic of typhus. As we were being escorted back across the bleak plain by guards, leaning into the wind, I heard the rhythmic crunching of feet on snow and looked up from under my cap to see a bedraggled line of new arrivals staggering into view. Quickly sweeping my eyes over them for children and any recognisable faces, I couldn't help but smile at the sight of Zuzana and her mother marching side by side.

'Zuzi,' I called out. 'You're here!' When none of our guards reacted, I pretended to drop something to get a little closer as she passed and hissed, 'Tell them you're a year younger. Say you're fifteen.' Unless I warned her, I feared she might be selected for forced labour.

Pale and dazed after arriving in that hellish place, she half-stumbled at the sight of me so I could only hope she heard what I said and picked up the urgency in my voice.

The shock of seeing familiar faces in our midst was always tempered with an overriding sense of anxiety. 'We barely have enough to eat or drink as it is,' Leo protested. 'And most people are still sleeping four to a bunk. Can you imagine how much of a torment daily roll-calls will become with an extra five thousand? Where on earth will we put them all?' The one thing he hadn't mentioned lay like a dead weight on my shoulders. Overnight, I'd be responsible for potentially hundreds more children.

The new arrivals were ordered to remain in their crowded blocks for a period of quarantine but once Zuzana heard about the children's block she defied orders and made her way to me. When our door opened and she stepped inside, skinnier than ever, I looked up and frowned. 'Oh, Zuzi, what am I going to do with you? You shouldn't be here.'

She stared at me as if she had seen a ghost and almost ran to where I sat on the floor with a group of eight-year-olds. Placing a hand on each of my shoulders, she peered into my face and cried, 'It *was* you I saw out there in the snow, Fredy! I hardly recognised you. You're so thin – and so grey.'

Suddenly self-conscious, I ran my fingers through ungroomed hair and wondered if that was true. I hadn't seen my own reflection for some time but had I changed that much in the three months since I'd seen her? Gazing at my fellow prisoners, I saw how much weight we'd all lost and how haggard many had become. Those in their twenties and thirties looked much older and a few appeared quite deranged with mad hair and faces hollowed by war.

Frowning, I reminded Zuzana that she was still in quarantine and would only be allowed to leave her barrack once the allotted period was over. 'But Fredy–' she protested.

'No buts,' I insisted. 'You can't bend the rules. Not here.' I was about to send her away when Pestek walked in to announce brusquely, 'The children need to be counted.' Knowing that this was only a ruse and that he had secret pockets full of tinned fish for them, I stood up, saluted him as required and asked, 'So who have you robbed and murdered today?'

Zuzana, who'd taken a step back in terror the minute she saw his uniform, nearly passed out. Seeing me openly insult an SS officer in public was beyond her experience and she expected me to be shot on the spot.

Pestek laughed and replied, 'If you weren't so damn charismatic, Hirsch, I'd have you sent straight up the chimney,' and I laughed in his face. He then offered me a cigarette from a silver case but I refused, by which time Zuzana believed she was hallucinating as a cigarette in Auschwitz was worth an entire loaf of bread.

Her face pale, she stood like a block of marble in a corner, watching aghast as I led Pestek to my room to take delivery of his goods. We chatted for a while and it was only when he left that I rounded on her. 'Next time, wait until you're summoned,' I scolded. 'Having you in here against the rules could have had consequences for us all.' Worried that she might also have brought disease into the block, I sent her packing, saying, 'This isn't a game.'

Once she was allowed to move freely around the camp having been declared lice-free, Zuzana returned. Looking sheepish, she walked in but I stood up, gave her a broad smile and cried, 'There you are. I have the perfect job for you.' I immediately assigned her as a teaching assistant to a group aged between four and twelve, some of the three hundred and fifty children that arrived on her transport. We couldn't cope with them all at first, so we took the most vulnerable and promised the rest could join us soon.

Just as she'd done in Terezín, Zuzana helped supervise classes in art and poetry and was as good as ever at making up fairy tales and rhymes. Every week, she helped me teach the children a different song, a treat they looked forward to with great excitement. She even introduced a few English tunes that her late father Jaroslav had taught her as a child. 'Today we're going to learn a new song called "London's Burning",' she announced. 'It's very easy as there are only four lines but we get to sing them as a round, with one group starting two bars after the other. Don't worry, Fredy and I will show you and then it'll come easily.'

Even if they didn't understand the words, the children adored that number and sang their hearts out. '*London's burning, London's burning. Fetch the engines, fetch the engines. Fire Fire! Fire Fire!*' I couldn't help pondering that so many of these charming songs had such dark origins.

*

As the days passed, many others who'd arrived on the December transport made themselves known to me, including a teenager named Marie. 'I don't belong here,' she insisted, showing me the gold cross suspended on a chain around her neck. Staring at it, I wondered how she'd been able to keep that for so long and knew that she'd soon be compelled to trade it for a piece of bread. 'I'm Catholic,' she wailed. 'I want to be a nun. The Germans are saying that my dead grandmother was Jewish which means my mother and I are too, but I never even knew her. Can't you help us?'

I also spotted Misha, the younger brother of Shragga who I prayed had made it safely to the Promised Land. Remembering the vow I'd made to him to watch out for his mother and brother I told Shragga's mother to bring Misha to the block the following day and I would find him work. 'Oh, thank you, Fredy,' she replied, clasping my hand. The pure-hearted woman added, 'But there's someone else you should attend to first. She's in an extremely distressed state.'

Hurrying through dirty snow to the block she directed me to, I was shocked to find Jakob's wife Miriam almost unrec-ognisable from the indefatigable matriarch I'd known in the ghetto. Inconsolable, she sat wrapped in a shawl letting out cry after keening cry as her bewildered son Arieh sat beside her in silence, tightly squeezing my childhood toy Emil.

'Miriam,' I cried, grabbing hold of her arms to stop her from rocking herself back and forth. 'It's me, Fredy. Come now, what's the matter?' Looking into her eyes, I realised that her mind had failed her and she was too distraught to speak.

Misha and his mother were watching. Waving the boy over, I forced a smile. 'Quickly now, Misha, take Arieh to Block 31 and stay with him there until I come.' To his mother, I whis-pered, 'Bring me something, anything, for her to drink.'

Kneeling at Miriam's feet, I pressed her hands into mine and made soothing noises until her tears were spent. With ragged sobs, she eventually made eye contact and cried, 'Oh, Fredy!' It took me over an hour to calm her and find out what had happened. 'It's Jakob,' she told me eventually, her voice so quiet I had to lean in. 'The Gestapo arrested him and sent him to the Small Fortress.'

'On what charge?'

'They claimed he'd falsified transport numbers to aid and abet the escape of prisoners.' Pausing, she dabbed at her eyes with a sodden handkerchief. 'They wouldn't let me see him and then Arieh, my mother and I were put on the December transport after being told that he'd be on the same train.' Rocking again, she wailed, 'I watched them load the prisoners from the Fortress onto a separate wagon, Fredy. I would never have recognised Jakob but for his coat. His face was caked in blood and he could barely walk.'

By the time their train finally arrived in Birkenau, Miriam had been taken unwell. 'I never saw what happened to him,' she cried. 'All I knew was that he wasn't with us, as I'd been promised. Oh, Fredy, what have they done to him?'

'Leave it with me,' I said, patting her hand. 'I'll find out where he is and if you can see him or at least send him a note to let him know you are safe.'

Miriam's beautiful brown eyes widened with hope. 'Really, Fredy? Could you?'

It took two days of digging but with the help of Pestek and Rudi, who acted as a courier between the secretaries, *Kanada* and the rest of the camp, I discovered that Jakob had been taken to what was known as 'the Bunker' in Auschwitz I, the most feared Gestapo prison of them all. Few came out alive.

Knowing that such information would cause her complete collapse, I reassured Miriam that he was in good health and suggested she help me out in the children's block as deputy house mother to Hanka, 'Until you're reunited with your beloved.' I also took on Arieh to support Misha in preparing, lighting and manning the fires on which we boiled the foul water and cooked our daily soup. 'Report to my office every morning and I'll give you some boxes to chop up,' I told the pair. 'The chimney must be kept hot enough at all times or we'll freeze.'

Turning to Misha, who was eleven, I asked, 'Do you know how to make soup?' When he nodded, I asked sceptically, 'You know how to make a roux?'

'With flour and fat,' he told me, confidently. 'I used to help *Maminka*.'

'Very well. I may be able to get some semolina from the gypsy camp so make the soup very thick but not too salty, as that will only make the children thirstier. And keep the potato peelings for roasting.' Placed in charge of two giant cauldrons, one at each end of the block, each morning he'd cook the root vegetables Böhm had an underling deliver and keep stirring so that the soup didn't go lumpy. He had his work cut out as Arieh didn't know a thing about fires and his often fizzled out. Seeing how busy Misha was, running from one end to the other to keep both going, I rewarded him with the privilege he'd probably hoped for all along.

'When the soup's ready, Misha, you may taste it to check the seasoning and the thickness,' I told him. 'Only a small taste, mind you, not a bowlful. If I find out you've been taking more, I'll give the task to someone else.' Having a thicker and more nourishing soup would make all the difference to the children during that desperate first winter in Birkenau. As would the food we discovered in the pitiful packages sent by relatives of those who'd perished. In amongst cakes, noodles and rice were heartbreaking notes urging prisoners to 'stay strong' or giving instructions where to meet after the war. *Go back to the summer house in Dobruška when it's over*, one sender wrote to her brother. *The key is under the pot. I'll meet you there as soon as I can and we'll swim together in the lake once more.*

A man urged his son, *Don't lose faith. God is with you and will watch over us all. Look after your little sister and be a good boy for your mother. I'll see you all soon.*

Welcome as the parcels were, not only for their contents but for the wrapping paper we could use for lessons, I knew they'd be too much of a temptation for many so I made one thing absolutely clear to the children and my helpers. 'Remember, we do not steal and we do not lie. Anyone found thieving food will be banished from the block, with no right of appeal. Deceit will not be tolerated.' I knew that unless I was rigorous then those starving beyond our walls would think nothing of bribing children to steal them some food and our hard-won supplies would be swallowed up by the camp's black market.

Emerging from my room one morning, I spotted Misha huddled by the fire at my end of the block with a bowl on his lap. Looking furtively right and left and checking that everyone else was busy, he picked up the bowl with both hands and downed it in one, dripping some of the contents onto his shirt. 'Misha!' I cried and he dropped his bowl with a clatter of surprise. 'Come here.'

Wiping his mouth on the back of his hand, he sidled over to me with such a look of guilt that I almost forgave him. Pulling myself together, I laid a hand heavily on his shoulder and told him, 'You know the rules, I couldn't have been clearer. I'm afraid I'm going to have to let you go.' Crestfallen, he nodded, accepting his fate. Dragging his feet, he allowed me to escort him to the door where I made an announcement. 'Misha is leaving us today. He stole some soup and knows the punishment. Say goodbye, everybody.'

His mother looked up at me, horrified, but I shook my head. Discipline was everything.

*

'The war could be over very soon,' Rudi told me, his eyes shining with hope. I scoffed. I'd heard it all before. Almost every week for five years people had been telling me that any day we'd be free. 'Berlin's been heavily bombed, the Russians have entered Poland and the siege of Leningrad has ended with a German retreat,' he added. Seeing my expression, he insisted, 'This time it's for real, Fredy, but when the Russians arrive things could get crazy here so you must prepare the children.'

'Prepare them how?' I asked. 'What can I do or say that will ready them for a bloodbath?'

'As soon as we know the Red Army is near, the Resistance has agreed that we'll disable the wire to let you and the children escape first,' he went on. 'Throwing a wet blanket or a metal chair at the fence should short-circuit the system. We'll cut an opening and someone will deal with the watchtowers so you can get them out and hide in the woods until it's over.'

I didn't sleep for days thinking about what he'd said and then I dared let myself believe it might be true. Stockpiling food in my rucksack and under the floorboards, I tried to think of ways I could steady the children for what they might have to face. Gathering them together one morning, I blew my whistle and clapped my hands to make an announcement. 'Today we're going to play a game that's all about self-control. The boy or girl who can stay silent the longest will win extra soup and bread and get to wear this for an entire week.' Pulling out a cap of blue cloth made specially for me by one of the camp's seamstresses, I turned it slowly so that they could see the words 'Block 31' embroidered on the front.

'Ooh,' several of them cried, their eyes bright, but I knew I had them at the soup.

'And I mean totally silent,' I reiterated. 'No whispering or giggling. No pinching of arms or legs to make someone squeal.'

A hand shot up. 'What if we need to go to the toilet?' a girl asked.

'That's fine, Olga. You just put up your hand and we'll take you.' Quieting the hubbub, I went on, 'Now, everyone sit cross-legged on the floor not too close to the person next to you. Close your eyes, take a deep breath and focus on being a big round boulder in a fast-flowing stream . . .'

Another hand shot up and one of the girls cried, 'I need to go to the toilet.'

'Me too!' said another. Laughing, I wondered if it was my mention of a stream.

When everyone had been, we started again. Looking into their trusting faces, I told them, 'Close your eyes and think about being a tree.'

'Can I be a cedar tree?' asked one girl who was taller than her peers.

'Yes, Klara. You'd make a wonderful cedar. Whatever tree you are, I want you to feel your roots reaching deep into the ground, deeper and deeper, anchoring you to the earth. Now remember, trees don't speak. Trees don't giggle. Trees stand tall and silent and when anyone walks through the woods they can't tell one tree from another. That's how I need you to be.'

In my mind's eye, I saw myself hiding them in the forest. I could almost hear soldiers shouting and dogs barking as the children cowered in a hollow under a clump of trees bathed in a green light. '*Be silent and don't divert sideways off the path*,' the old rabbit had advised in my childhood book. As our imagined hunters drew closer, I pressed my finger to my lips and gave the children the stare that meant, 'Disobey me at your peril.'

6

January 1944

'A MAN HERE HAS been calling your name,' Dr Heller told me, two weeks after the December transport arrived. 'He was badly beaten soon after he arrived and was unconscious for a while but he keeps asking for you now.'

Wondering who that might be, I wandered to a corner of the infirmary filled with scores of crumpled humans lying half-dead on mattresses to find Kurt propped up on a pillow with two black eyes and his arm in a sling. Hurrying to his side, I cried, 'Kurt, you're here! Are you all right?'

Opening his one good eye, he turned his head to peer at me through purple bruising. 'I've been better.'

'What happened?'

His attempt at a shrug only made him wince. 'The *kapo* on my block took umbrage when I wrestled him to the ground for beating a defenceless old woman.'

'You fool,' I replied, shaking my head. 'You're lucky he didn't kill you.'

'That would have been inconvenient, especially after I'd volunteered to follow you.'

My jaw dropped. 'You volunteered? Why?'

'Why do you think, Fredy?' he said, with sudden softness, gazing at me with such affection that I felt a lump in my throat. Seeing my reaction, he attempted a smile. 'Besides, I knew you couldn't manage without me. Unless you have contacts in a place like this, you'll end up dead. I wasn't going to let that happen.'

I was very glad to see him, even though I thought him crazy for following me. For the next few days I visited him daily. I couldn't wait to get Kurt out of that infernal pit: those who didn't get better after a week were examined by Mengele before being sent to the gas chambers.

When he was finally strong enough to leave, he was sent to a different block and appointed *kapo* to replace one who'd been beaten to death by Bulldog. Wasting no time, he joined the small group who comprised what little resistance was possible in Birkenau, making it his job to find out whatever he could. 'The men who run the gas chambers and the crematoria are at the heart of everything, Fredy,' he told me one night when we were alone in my gingerbread room. 'They're called the *Sonderkommando* and they can barely speak of the things they're forced to do. They just block their minds and get on with it, knowing that the clock is ticking. Every six months, a new commando is selected from healthy prisoners and the previous lot are gassed. By then, they almost welcome it.'

'That's terrible,' I said, appalled. 'And they can't refuse the job?'

'No, it's that or straight to the gas. This way, they hope to last until the war ends. They live in a special barracks with everything they want, even though there's no pleasure in it for them.'

'Is there nothing they can do?'

Kurt sighed. 'All they dream of is the destruction of the machinery of extermination, even if it costs them their lives. Anything to stop the genocide.'

'That's something we all want,' I replied, 'but without weapons or explosives, what could we do against hundreds of SS with machine guns? It would be a massacre and there'd be reprisals. Think of Lidice.'

'They're aware of that, Fredy, but like me they're of the opinion that if we're going to die anyway it would be better to die fighting. I don't know details yet but they're putting a plan together so we must be ready.' Shivering, I said nothing but in my mind's eye I saw how that might play out. No matter how well planned a rebellion might be, it would have unthinkable consequences for children caught in the crossfire. I knew it was in Kurt's nature to defy authority, something he'd been doing since he was a child, but his talk of an uprising filled me with dread. Then he added something that chilled me further.

'I've told them we will help in any way we can, so don't be surprised if they ask you to start something. Everybody knows you're the most important prisoner in the Family Camp.' Holding my tongue, I pretended I had something urgent to do and walked back to the block where the children were just leaving.

'Gute Nacht,' I called. 'Schlaf gut.' My wish that they sleep well was genuine, even though I knew it unlikely. Having been warmed by the fire all day, the moment they returned to their unheated barracks to lie fully clothed alongside their mothers, fathers or foster carers was the worst part of the day. Squashed into their bunks, longing to be warm and dry, they were jerked back to the reality of Birkenau with its injustice and bickering, coughing, cheating and dying.

They weren't the only ones who dreaded their leaving. After I watched them trail away in the twilight, I turned back to the block to face its unaccustomed silence. Tasting bitter solitude,

I lay alone in my bed as the fingers of light began to sweep back and forth across the room, their rhythm as familiar to me as the ticking of our family clock. The doubts I'd been able to push away during the busy daylight hours crept out of the shadows like feral cats to paw and scratch at my mind. Fretting about what Kurt had said, I went over and over it in my mind. *'Don't be surprised if they ask you to start something . . . you're the most important prisoner in the Family Camp.'*

As much as I detested the Nazis and all they represented, I realised that we'd settled into an uneasy kind of status quo and I was terrified of losing the privileges for the children that I'd fought so hard for. Yet the thought continually ambushed me that the entire endeavour was pointless if we were all going to perish anyway. In saving the children temporarily for what we hoped was a better tomorrow was I merely prolonging their agony until they suffered a far more violent end?

No matter how hard I tried to banish such thoughts I kept hearing Jenda's voice in my head, the day he told me, 'You're not their god, Fredy Hirsch, so stop acting like one.' Had my arrogance clouded my judgement to the point that I could no longer see what was best for my *Kinder?* Denied the release of sleep, every night in that god-forsaken place I began to imagine myself as the witch in *Hänsel und Gretel*, fattening the lost children to feed my own gnawing hunger. Or was I the Pied Piper of Auschwitz, using my whistle to lure children away from all they knew and loved, never to be seen again? Only time would tell.

*

'Some day my prince will come . . .' Helga's voice rose like a bird to the rafters of Block 31 and took flight in my heart.

Standing on the chimney dressed as Snow White with a strip of red cloth in her hair and a cardboard collar stitched to a belted shirt, the willowy teenager transported us to another world.

Accompanying her on my recorder as she sang of dreams coming true, I played the Handsome Prince, dressed in a sacking cape and paper crown made by Dinah. All around me stood the 'dwarfs', their eyes sparkling in the light of oil lamps placed at the front of our 'stage'. Reciting their lines with enthusiasm, they looked as if they didn't have a care in the world. A true collective, just as I had taught them, they'd step in and improvise if anyone faltered or forgot their words.

Closing my eyes to focus on Helga's beautiful voice, I imagined lying in my childhood forest listening to songbirds. Gone was the stench of burning human flesh, replaced by the sweet scent of pine: the defining aroma of my youth. Feeling knots unravelling in my gut, I could almost see the clear waters of the lake fringed with wildflowers as colourful butterflies danced all around. Nature in all its glory.

Opening my eyes again, my heart was filled with love for Helga who was giving her all to her performance under a sheen of make-up applied to mask the effects of the tuberculosis. All through rehearsals she had coughed and coughed but somehow, tonight, she wasn't and I gave her an encouraging smile.

Turning to our audience, I studied those in the front row: SS officers sat in tight-fitting uniforms and white gloves, smiling up at those they intended to murder. Among them sat Mengele who'd recently assumed control of the children's block after arguing that it fell under his jurisdiction as Head of Health. No doubt he wanted to take the credit for our success. Alongside him were officials from other camps, openly astounded to be watching a musical staged by children in the middle of Auschwitz.

To the left sat more SS including Bulldog, Eyebrows and Mengele's creepy sidekick Dr Klein. A man with an impressive head of thick brown hair, Klein often brought chocolates into the block but when those who accepted them vanished, never to be seen again, we urged the children to refuse them no matter how tempting.

It was Kurt who later informed me of Klein's role in the infirmary he and Mengele set up in the gypsy camp. 'He is in charge of pseudo-medical experiments on racial differences between Aryans and those considered inferior,' he said. 'There's a lot of secrecy surrounding what they're up to and I don't believe half the stories. But then I remember that we never believed the Nazis could gas people, either.'

A few rows back sat the *kapos* like Böhm and there was another face I recognised: Ada Fisher, the executioner of Terezín who now brutalised the men in his block yet came to smile at the children. Fixing an expression on my face that I hoped looked civil but distant, I watched them all like a hawk.

Beyond our enforcers huddled emaciated prisoners relegated to the back of the block by the SS, for fear of infection. It gladdened my heart to see the wonder in their eyes as our amateur production transported them to a time before the Earth cracked. Helga's voice always touched hearts and many were weeping at the beauty of it. Even those of the self-styled 'master race' in the front row were visibly moved, dabbing at their eyes with neatly pressed monogrammed handkerchiefs. Several looked openly surprised and I imagined them at the Commandant's villa afterwards sipping cocktails and exclaiming, 'We never knew a Jew could be so talented!'

Turning back to the stage, I sought the familiar comfort of the children, all wreathed in smiles. Wearing costumes fashioned from cardboard, rags, webbing and paper, there had never been a cast more committed to their roles or more excited to step out from behind the holey blanket that served as a curtain. In our version of 'Snow White' there were more than twenty dwarfs representing virtue, cleanliness and discipline. They had names like Spick and Span, Rinsey and Spotless, Trusty and Kindly. 'But I thought there were only seven in the Brothers Grimm fairy tale, Fredy?' Hanka had pointed out when I first drew up the cast list.

'There were but how can I leave any children out? I chose it because Mengele liked what Dinah painted on the wall, although now she's having to paint gypsies for him because of it.'

Hanka frowned. 'I know we never talk about what happens here in front of the children but do you think they'll appreciate the symbolism?'

I gave a hollow laugh. 'You mean will they get a morality tale about the perception of beauty and an evil protagonist wanting to destroy something pure? A few of the older ones might but the more important message is that bad things don't last and Snow White lives happily ever after. That will give the children hope and hope is all we have left.'

I didn't tell her that my greater concern was that the SS would get the symbolism too and realise that they were represented by a corrupt and wicked Queen.

Hanka had offered to take that role but she was too well-loved to be convincing, so instead I cast her as the Magic Mirror who declares Snow White the fairest in the land. She was ingenious with her costume, pushing her face through an oval of grey paper and surrounding it with a decorated cardboard frame.

I made loyal Miloš my page, a boy named Yehuda the compassionate Huntsman and a raven-haired teenager named Ille played the Queen in a black sheet with a chalked face and lips tinted with beet juice. Dinah made the Queen's crown and mine and had the children paint them gold with coloured paper triangles as jewels. Ille had cut her hair short to deter lice so Dinah painted strips of paper black to match her hair before gluing them to her crown.

Once the show began, Dinah sidled up to me and whispered, 'Why are there so many SS here tonight?'

'For the same reason I suspect we've been saved from the gas. They want to show other camp leaders how to create a semblance of normality in case the Red Cross make a surprise inspection.'

Dinah frowned. 'But surely any inspectors would see the smoking chimneys and all the half-starved prisoners and realise that there's nothing normal here at all?'

I shook my head. 'The Nazis would shut down the furnaces, clean the place up and gas anyone who looked unwell before bringing in healthier replacements. Anything to quash rumours that they're annihilating hundreds of thousands of people.'

*

Of all the Germans watching the performance that night, it was Mengele who perplexed me the most. He was impossible to fathom. A seemingly intelligent man with a fine physique, military deportment and a keen, inquiring mind, we could almost have been related. Several people had commented on the physical similarities between us as we stood side by side discussing the children's needs whenever he visited the block. 'You could be brothers, Fredy,' one teenager told me and I shuddered.

Yet, every time a new transport arrived, we saw the same supposedly civilised man standing at the head of the lines of dispossessed to coldly separate mothers from their children, young from old, the fit from the unhealthy. Day after day he sent thousands to be gassed as if doing nothing more than directing traffic. And from what Kurt told me, the physician who told the children to call him 'Uncle Pepi' and who'd taken an oath to heal the sick was doing unspeakable things to prisoners including children who'd slipped through my grasp. That was surely the worst kind of evil.

Trying not to think about that, I smiled at Zuzana standing the other side of the stage holding the hand of one of the more bashful girls. I'd enlisted her to supervise the younger children and she'd been tireless in fixing costumes and getting them to rehearse their lines. She had the most trouble with Bruno, the boy who'd made us laugh about unicorn farts in the ghetto. To keep him out of mischief, I'd made him our new stoker for the fires and cast him as a comic dwarf named Cheeky. I brought Misha back to play a part, too, and gave peripheral roles to several other orphans.

When Zuzi returned my smile and gave me a little wave, I was relieved, hoping she'd forgiven me for snapping at her a few days earlier. The poor girl wasn't to know what pressure I was under. After another poor night's sleep, I walked into the block to find her reading Sigmund Freud's book on psychoanalysis. It was bad enough that girls like her were missing out on the pleasure and pain of being teenagers but to see her engrossed in such a serious book in a place like ours pushed me over the edge. Furious, I'd snatched it from her, crying, 'That's not suitable reading for a young girl! Go outside and be a child.' Her shock at my tone as she fled in tears filled me with guilt for so long.

I was happy to make it up to her a day later when she owned up to accidentally receiving an extra portion of bread. 'Telling me was the decent thing to do, Zuzana,' I told her, as she beamed at me devotedly. 'You may keep the extra bread for your honesty. Good girl.'

Focusing on the sweet, unformed faces of my cast, I hoped I'd been able to instil that same sense of decency in them all and protected them from the worst of camp life. Brick by brick, I'd try to build a wall in their hearts against the suffering.

If I'd done one thing for them, I had given them their moment in the limelight. In a different life they'd have starred in school productions, taking their bows in front of proud parents before returning home for hot chocolate and a slice of poppy seed cake. Instead, they were in a place their worst nightmares could never have conjured.

Helga's heavenly voice lifted us above all that. Mesmerised, I drew strength from the purity of the song and especially the thought that when the birds sing again in springtime then love will blossom and dreams come true.

A short distance beyond our lamplit walls thousands more parched and broken prisoners were being marched in tattered lines towards the gas chambers. Even above the music, we'd heard the dreaded rumble of the trucks. As they battled through the snow to what they'd been promised were hot showers, some may even have heard Helga's sweet, sentimental song in the distance. I only hope it gave them some solace before they were turned to ash.

7

February 1944

WINTER BROUGHT DEEPER, HEAVIER snow which covered the camp in a thick white cloak that made everything look dazzlingly clean. In the chill grip of an easterly wind, inmates fell upon the pristine drifts to scoop snow into their bowls for fresh water when melted.

Children had snowball fights and, as I watched them running around and squealing with delight, it didn't seem possible to me that we'd soon be marking five years since I threw snowballs at the German tanks rolling into Prague. 'Come now,' I called, summoning them from the open doorway. 'We can come back out once I've done the count and build a snowman.'

I was never more grateful for our roll calls inside the block. Countless adults lost all their body heat, collapsed and died during those interminable hours. There was another problem too. The camp's limited water supply froze in its pipes, preventing us from washing. Our skin already grimy and sore from scratching, we lived in overripe clothes that stank. With the water supply so inconsistent, cleanliness was impossible to achieve but I was determined to maintain hygiene even if it meant living up to my name of 'Fredy the Enforcer'.

'Listen up. I know how much you want to play but first we're going to try a different kind of game. You are going to file outside in groups of twenty, one group at a time, strip off your clothes and roll naked in the snow.' There were cries of disbelief but I held up my hand. 'The good news is this is also a treasure hunt because hidden in the new snow are scraps of cloth, thread, paper, pebbles for marbles and lumps of clay. Who wants to play?'

As the children ran outside, I told my helpers, 'While they're doing that, we must quickly rub their clothes with snow to get rid of any lice or fleas they might have picked up. Then they can put them back on, run inside and sit by the fire to dry off.'

My game didn't come as a complete surprise to them as once a week I made them wash their clothes before putting them back on wet. Even if it was raining or sleeting, I stood them outside, saying, 'Don't cower from Nature. Marvel at her,' just as I used to tell the scouts in Aachen. The children's howls of indignation as we peeled off their tatty garments in minus ten, however, could have woken the entire camp. Puffing billowing clouds of vapour as they pressed handfuls of snow against their bony little bodies, they cried, 'But, Fredy, it's too cold!'

'This won't take long,' I soothed even as their skin started to turn blue. 'Chip-chop and remember to rub all four corners and all the funny, wobbly bits in between.' We also wiped them down with a rag drenched in the last of the Lysol.

While my helpers took over, I wandered to the back of an adjacent block to scoop snow into a wooden crate but stopped in my tracks. Up against the back wall were six bodies stacked like wood, stripped of all usable clothing. Their skin stretched tightly over bone had an ethereal look and their lank hair was adorned with a blossom of frost. Those whose faces were turned to the sky looked almost angelic as snowflakes clung to frozen eyelashes and frosted their lips, softening deathly grimaces.

*

While I fought to keep the children alive, Kurt continued to communicate with Rudi, Willi and the others. Fragment by fragment he brought me news, including the information that the Germans were being pushed back on all fronts, something we'd suspected by the increased numbers of Allied planes flying overhead. 'We just have to hang on a little longer,' he told me. 'It's almost over, Fredy.'

'Any news of Jakob?'

'He's still clinging to life in the Bunker, we're told, but thousands more have died in the gas chamber this week alone.' Not that I needed telling. 'The worst days are when the Nazis run out of gas,' Kurt added, his face sombre. 'The *Sonderkommando* said last week the SS burned an entire transport in fire pits beyond the *Sauna*.'

'We saw the clouds of black smoke and then fat flakes of ash rained on us. I mouthed silent prayers for them all.'

Kurt's next piece of news sickened me even more. 'Mengele's going to be a father,' he told me. 'They say the baby was conceived when his wife came here for her summer holiday. Apparently he's very excited.'

The idea of that man having a child when he sent thousands of children to their deaths was too much. Kurt added, 'There's also a rumour that Eichmann's coming to visit the camp.'

'What for?' I asked, taking a breath.

'Nobody knows but perhaps to meet the man who set up a children's block in the middle of the Kingdom of Death. You'd better practise your salute.'

The idea of saluting someone so closely allied to Hitler appalled me but then I began to think about how I might turn such an encounter to the children's advantage. I'd do a deal with the Devil if it meant saving them.

*

Two nights later Kurt crept across the camp for another of our secret *rendezvous*, running from block to block to avoid the searchlights. Only this time he arrived with a strange expression on his face and seemed weighted by the burden of the news he carried. When he told me to sit down, I did as he asked and stared up at him in tense silence.

'You remember I told you that the orphans from Bialystok left Terezín a month after you, as part of a prisoner swap?' When I nodded, he sighed. 'I'm afraid that didn't happen the way we thought, Fredy. I only just found out. They were sent here. The *Sonderkommando* said the children had to be forced at gunpoint into the gas chamber. One teenager attacked an SS officer with a knife and several others were shot trying to resist.'

Doubling over, I groaned as their final moments played out graphically in my head. Convinced that the boy with the knife was Łukas the Fox, who'd shown such courage and devotion to those he cared for, I wept. 'Those poor children,' I cried. 'Their short lives had been filled with so much horror.' Looking up, I asked, 'And what of their carers? What happened to Ottla?'

One look at his face told me the answer before he replied, 'I'm afraid they perished too. All fifty-three of them.' I let out such a howl then that the searchlight that swept over my block shuddered to a halt before sweeping back and forth to identify the source. For several days all I could see in my mind's eye were the pitiful, haunted faces of the Bialystok orphans.

With little enthusiasm for anything, I delegated to my assistants and remained in my room, claiming I had a cold. The children must have picked up on my mood because, in the hope of cheering me up, a teenager named Jirí surprised me with a present. 'It's a book of poems,' he told me. 'We know how much you love poetry, Fredy.'

Turning the handcrafted gift in my hands, I saw that it had been made out of wrapping paper threaded together with twine and held in place with a painted cardboard cover. It was an astonishing feat.

'I remembered several of the poems myself and asked others to recite their favourites and then I wrote them all out by hand. There are more than forty,' he told me. Flicking through the pages, I saw the names Rilke and Bezruc, Heine and Dyk, and smiled. Although I thanked him for it as warmly as I could, I knew he could tell that my mind was elsewhere.

Nor was I in the mood for any interference. Returning to the block after a meeting with Willi one day, I was appalled to discover two men and a woman in white coats examining some of the youngest children. After lining them up in their underwear, they were taking measurements of their heads, noses, legs and torsos using callipers and rulers.

'Stop that right now!' I yelled, stepping between them and forcing them away from the children. 'What do you think you're doing?'

'Dr Klein sent us,' one replied. 'He wants us to make comparative studies of Jewish children.'

I almost punched him. 'Don't be an idiot!' I cried, staring accusingly at his own yellow star. 'Are you so brainwashed that you believe that nonsense? You should be ashamed of yourselves. Now get out!' The incident angered and frightened me in equal measure. If Klein started to take a medical interest in my children then what was to stop him doing experiments on them too?

*

'There are some new rumours I need to tell you about, Fredy,' Kurt told me one afternoon in my room, his eyes wary. Sensing my fragile emotional state, he'd been treading carefully with me for some time. He waited for the right moment to disclose what else he'd discovered from his contacts in the Resistance. 'The clerks who work in the *Kommandatur* say more people are to be transported here from Terezín and that your group will have to go to make room.'

'Go where?' I asked, feeling a sudden chill.

'Nobody knows. A labour camp maybe.'

Sensing from his use of 'maybe' that there was another possibility, I asked, 'What aren't you saying?'

Kurt studied his fingernails. Without looking up he said, 'It's the papers we all had to sign when we arrived. They carried the coded note: *SB6 Quarantäne*. The clerks say SB stands for *sonderbehandlung* or 'special treatment', which usually means gassing. They think the six refers to six months but nobody can understand why the Nazis would keep us here if they plan to kill us six months later. It isn't logical.'

'Perhaps SB refers to the special treatment we've been given?' I asked. 'Everyone admits it's unusual.'

'Maybe,' he repeated, sending a shiver down my spine. 'But what of the number six, Fredy? That can only mean six months, which would mean your time here in the Family Camp would elapse in less than a month.'

Shaking my head, I jumped up. 'No, no. That won't happen. The SS come to the block. They watch their performances. They know the children by name. They wouldn't murder them now. It doesn't make any sense.'

Kurt reached for my hand and pulled me next to him on the edge of my bed. 'The belief is that this camp only exists in case of a Red Cross inspection but that hasn't happened. With new children arriving, the Nazis can simply replace you.'

Suddenly angry, I snatched my hand away and asked him to leave.

'Fredy—' he began but I turned my back. When I refused to listen to anything else he had to say, he reluctantly crept out.

I didn't sleep at all that night or the next. Instead, I lay awake boiling with resentment at the unwelcome reminder that we were still at the mercy of sadists. From the day the Nazis came to power, they'd systematically stripped us of our rights and tried to crush our self-respect. Refusing to give up hope, we'd obeyed their commands and relinquished our identities, believing, always believing, that their reign of terror was temporary and that rescue was imminent. But what if it wasn't? What if this was how the world order remained? Did Mengele and the others know all along that we were merely in a waiting room for death?

I didn't care what happened to me but I feared for my *Kinder* with every breath in my body. Still refusing to believe that the SS officers who knew me and the children would send them to be gassed, I also knew the little ones wouldn't survive a labour camp. Especially if I wasn't there to protect them. With questions crowding my head until I felt like it would explode, I needed answers.

*

Three days later, as I stood in the doorway watching and waiting, I saw Mengele's staff car pull up outside the infirmary, as it did every week. Smoothing down my hair and straightening my now oversized jacket, I hurried out as he stepped carefully from the car to avoid spoiling his riding boots in the half-frozen puddles.

'*Läufer!*' he bellowed and Misha darted out to salute, just as I'd taught him, in keeping with his new position. Blind obedience was what the Nazis demanded. After despatching the boy on some errand or other, Mengele brushed a speck of dirt from his sleeve and pulled on his white kid gloves. Whistling an operatic tune, he was about to head into the infirmary when I intercepted his path, stepping directly in front of him. Eye to eye, I saluted and, although visibly taken aback by my impudence, he nodded and waited for me to speak.

'I need Block 29 allocated as a second place for the children, *Herr Doktor*,' I told him crisply. 'Block 31 is too overcrowded. I plan to separate boys from girls and infants from the older ones but must have them in adjacent buildings.' Before he could object, I added, 'Block 29 is currently the *Kleiderkammer* but the clothing could easily be transferred to one of the blocks that haven't been converted yet.'

Tilting his head as if examining my face anew for Aryan features, Mengele paused before saying, 'You must speak to the camp elder who will direct your request to the Commandant but I won't object.' When I didn't move or respond, he asked, 'Is that all?'

'No, *Herr Doktor*,' I replied, fighting the urge to blink. Clearing my throat, I added, 'I need your assurances that the children will be protected from all future transports.'

A few paces behind Mengele, Dr Heller had stepped outside to see where he was. As the blood drained from his face, the camp's second-most senior doctor gave me a warning shake of his head. Ignoring him and locking eyes with one of the most feared men in Auschwitz, I prompted, '*Herr Doktor?*'

If Mengele was shocked by my directness he did well to hide it. 'Of course the children will be protected from future transports,' he replied with a smile. 'You have my word on that. And I'll be sure to put you on my list of *Prominente* to make sure that you, too, are safeguarded on account of your work here.'

'*Herr Doktor*,' I replied, snapping my hand to my temple.

When I told Kurt what I'd been promised, I was unprepared for his response. 'You think having Mengele's word makes a *Pfennig*'s worth of difference?' he said, almost laughing in my face. 'Haven't you learned anything about the Nazis? They're as slippery as eels and twice as slimy. Even if he wasn't lying, he only promised they'd not be sent away. Nothing was said about not gassing you all to death.'

'But . . .' I began.

'No buts. Eichmann is coming and that's making everyone nervous. Nothing good ever comes of a visit by the man appointed by Hitler to oversee our extermination.'

'But he came to Terezín and saw the children perform there,' I countered, my heart lifting. 'And the report I've completed about the children's block is marked for his attention. If I could speak with Eichmann directly, I could get an assurance from him that the children will be saved.'

Kurt said nothing but the look on his face told me that he thought I'd gone mad.

*

'Should I make the calendar for a full year until December '44 or beyond, Fredy?' Renée asked. It was almost impossible to remember which day it was in Birkenau until she had the children help her create a calendar out of cardboard and wrapping paper.

Every morning, a different child was allowed to cross off the day with one of our precious crayons. All around the margins were the birthdays of the children and teachers, including mine on 11th February. She'd also marked the High Holidays like Purim, Passover, Rosh Hashanah, Yom Kippur and Hanukkah to remind us to celebrate them in some small way with an extra titbit or a Hebrew song.

'Let's take it one year at a time,' I told her. In truth, time was irrelevant in a place where every day carried the weight of a month and survival was often minute to minute. As the date of my twenty-eighth birthday approached, however, I became aware of a flurry of activity in one corner of the block and suspected that Zuzana and her group were up to something. Teasing them, I'd start walking towards them as I watched them panic and try to hide whatever they were making. Then I'd stop, scratch my head as if I'd forgotten something and walk away. On the morning of my birthday, Zuzana asked, 'Will you be in the block later this afternoon, Fredy? We have something we want to show you.'

'Yes, of course. I'll come and find you after I've been to see Böhm.'

I walked to his block and knocked on the door. Hearing activity inside, I hesitated and stepped back before the door flew open and out rushed Erik, flushed of face, adjusting his clothing. I heard a grunt from within so I waited a few moments and knocked again.

'What do you want?' a voice growled. Stepping inside, I found Böhm half-reclined on his bed and presented myself with a salute. 'Oh, it's you. What now?'

'I need to talk to you about Block 29, *Lagerälteste*,' I said. '*Hauptsturmführer* Mengele told me that, subject to your approval and that of the Commandant, I can use it as a second children's block.'

Böhm moved with surprising swiftness and, before I knew it, he'd spun me around and had me in a painful armlock, his breath hot on my ear. 'You spoke to Mengele? You didn't come to me first? Who do you think you are, you preening fucking ponce? Block 29 is under my control. It's the clothing warehouse where I do a lot of good business and that is what it shall remain.'

'But *Lagerälteste*,' I began to protest, 'the *Hauptsturmführer*–' Pushing me face-down onto his bed, Böhm reached for his bullwhip and, with a knee in the small of my back, he began lashing at me from behind, paying special attention to my head and face. Feeling the sting of his whip and tasting blood, I struggled to break free but the man who was built like a battleship had me firmly in his grip. It was only when I realised he was unbuttoning his trousers as he hissed, 'Or is this what you really came for?' that I found the strength to twist away and run for the door. One mighty punch to the head almost felled me again but – with my ears ringing – I fled.

Limping back to the children's block, several people stopped to stare as blood dripped down my shirt. Behind me, I heard Böhm roar, '*Piepel!*' and Erik hurried back to his master. I was still shaking when I reached the door and, anxious that the children shouldn't see me, I hid my face in my hands and ran straight to my room. Zuzana, who'd been watching and waiting, followed to tap urgently on my door. 'Fredy? Fredy, are you all right?'

Spitting out a bloody fragment of tooth, I called, 'I'll be right with you.' Dabbing at my face with a rag, I quickly changed my shirt and smoothed down my hair before emerging to a gasp from my most diligent assistant.

'What happened?' she cried.

I waved her away and with a painful smile, saying, 'I was cheeky, asking for something, that's all. I'll be fine. Now, what did you want to show me?'

The children had organised a surprise party, making me a birthday card and little handmade gifts. There was a washing line of sorts made out of string and two rusty nails, a small figure made out of wood and rags with a blue jacket and embroidered grey hair and a tiny 'cake' of compressed white bread and jam. '*Všechno nejlepši k narozeninám!*' they sang in unison. Happy Birthday, Fredy. I couldn't help but think: how many more birthdays would I get to celebrate?

*

It took me a week to recover from my beating and I kept out of Böhm's way but when Mengele visited the block a few days later he immediately realised that I'd been attacked and refused to believe me when I told him I'd tripped. Summoning Böhm, who looked scared for the first time, he demanded, 'Who did this?'

My assailant leaned in to look closely at my injuries as if he knew nothing at all about them before shrugging. Then Mengele did the same, examining my face with the expertise of a medical man. Identifying two long red scars on my right cheek, he declared, 'This is from a whip.' Seeing me drop my gaze as Böhm's fell too, he immediately assessed the situation and told the *Lagerälteste*, 'Block 29 will be assigned to Hirsch for the *Kinder*. See that it is done.'

Böhm saluted and waited to be dismissed but Mengele gave him a steely glare. 'We've been informed that the Wehrmacht requires violent criminals for the Polish front to help deal with partisans and troublemakers. I'm thinking of recommending you.' The *Lagerälteste* paled visibly at his words and, before Mengele even left the camp that day, Block 29 was emptied and mine.

The first thing I did was ask one of our new helpers, a girl known as Mausi, if she'd paint a mural on the walls. Another young artist in her twenties, she'd come to the block after arriving in the December transport and offered to help teach the children art. 'What would you like me to paint?' she asked.

'Anything you like.'

'How about children from around the world?' she suggested. 'I could do smiling Eskimos in front of igloos, Indians by their tepees and children in Chinese and African dress, all in bright settings.' She also painted Bambi and Mickey Mouse from memory. Chatting to her while she worked, I discovered that her talents had already been noticed by the SS who'd set her to work for them. 'I paint gypsies with Dinah,' she said, 'but I hate the work. I have to report to Dr Mengele and I've even been invited to his private quarters. He has a huge Persian rug on the floor and paintings on the walls. It gives me the creeps. Next, he wants me to work on the family tree of some Hungarian dwarfs. I'd much rather work for Eyebrows.'

'Why, what do you do for him?'

Mausi smiled. 'He saw me drawing fairy tales for the little ones and liked them so much he asked me to make some hand-painted books for his own children. He even took one of my gypsy paintings home to give to his wife for Christmas.' Shaking my head, I wondered once more how men so complicit in such brutality could sleep at night.

*

'We need to find the best singers in the camp for a recital. Adults too,' I told my staff. 'We'll dress the children as if they were in a church choir and place the cutest at the front.' Once I knew that Eichmann would be coming to Birkenau, I set about staging a performance that the SS would bring him to see.

Everyone loved the idea and, once I'd selected the music, we immediately began rehearsals as it had to be ready for whenever the delegation from Berlin arrived. We were just about ready the day Eichmann and his cronies swept into the camp in a convoy of vehicles.

The German top brass filed in and took their seats, smiling up at the children standing patiently in rows on the stage wearing sheets of paper coloured white with chalk and red cardboard ruffs. Each child's face had been thoroughly scrubbed and their hair washed and combed.

'Place those with paler features at the front,' I instructed. 'Their Aryan looks might remind our visitors of their own children. Put the teenagers and young adults behind to provide the harmonies.' Standing in front of my ragtag choir in a jacket and trousers I'd washed specially, I gave them my most encouraging smile. After playing the key of D on my recorder, I raised it as a baton.

The piece I had chosen specially for the occasion was '*Dona Nobis Pacem*', the canon taken from the prayer for peace in the '*Agnus Dei*' of the Latin Catholic mass. They performed it so beautifully that by the end I could hardly see them for tears of pride. When the last note faded, however, our performance was met with such stony silence that I hardly dared turn around. Once I did, still blinking, I saw that everyone including Eichmann was dumbstruck. As soon as he saw me turn, he stood and started clapping. Then everyone else did too and as the children took their bows I stepped aside to allow them to bask in their glory.

With the stealthy movement of a cat, Mengele rose from his seat to stand beside me in the shadows. 'What made you choose that piece?' he asked, his eyes still fixed on the stage. '"Grant Us Peace"? You are at peace here. It is we soldiers who have to fight at the front.'

'Precisely, *Herr Doktor*,' I replied, thinking quickly. 'And the children were expressing their heartfelt gratitude that it is you who allow us that peace here.'

The muscles in his jaw hardening, his eyes bored into me in search of sarcasm but when I held his gaze unflinchingly he could do nothing but look away.

When our little show ended, I was presented to Eichmann along with Leo, Miriam and a few key members of my staff. After saluting, I handed him the report on the children's block that had been asked for. He stood well back for fear of infection but congratulated me on what he referred to as my 'cultural experiment'.

Only then was I was permitted to address him. Staring into his almost colourless eyes, I said, 'I have been promised, *Herr SS Obersturmbannführer*, that the children will be allowed to remain here for the duration of the war. I trust that I also have your assurance?'

Glancing right and left at those who'd dare allow a Jewish prisoner to address him in such a manner, he bobbed his head without altering his expression. Feeling an icy stab to my heart, I stared at him intently: willing him to give me a direct answer and prove Kurt wrong. But he remained resolutely silent. Sensing the awkwardness and knowing that my time with him was running out, I beckoned Miriam over.

'This is Jakob Edelstein's wife, *Herr Obersturmbannführer*. She's extremely concerned about her husband, the first Elder of Theresienstadt and a prominent member of the Jewish

Council. As I'm sure you know, he has been imprisoned without charge in the main camp for several months.' Eichmann, who'd met Jakob on several occasions in Prague and in Terezín, turned to her then and exchanged a few words out of earshot before he swept back out of the camp like a sudden squall.

Miriam hurried over to me afterwards, her eyes beaming. 'He said Jakob and I would be reunited soon, Fredy!' Her smile was reward enough for me but over her shoulder I spotted something new and hard in the face of Eyebrows that made me shudder. It was an open expression of pity as he watched Miriam clinging to me in gratitude.

His eyes said: *You're all doomed. You poor, deluded fools.*

8

March 1944

Zuzana found me one morning before roll call, sitting on the chimney, a blank postcard in my hand. Picking up on my mood, she settled quietly beside me and asked, 'What is it, Fredy? What's wrong?'

Wrenching my gaze from the floor, I looked into the smoky grey eyes I'd first seen after she'd fainted in the ghetto years earlier.

I murmured, 'I don't know who to send this to, or what to say.'

'Few do. It's not easy to communicate with friends or family in less than thirty words. And why have they told you all to postdate them March 25?'

'They claim they won't reach the recipients before then because they'll have to be censored in Berlin first.'

'Do you believe them?'

'I don't know what to believe anymore.' I didn't have an address for my brother or Uncle Alfred. Jenda was beyond my reach somewhere and his family were lost to me, so I decided to write instead to Heinzek and his parents. Unbelievably, the enterprising teenager was still in Prague. He had never stopped sending parcels of food, clothing and sustenance, each delivery a bundle of hope.

Painfully aware that time was ticking inexorably towards six months after our arrival and wondering if this would be my last message to him, I filled in my name and obeyed the instructions to write my address. We were forbidden from citing the name Auschwitz and ordered to write it as *Birkenau, Neu-Berun, Upper Silesia* even though, as far as anyone knew, Neu-Berun didn't exist.

Still uncertain what to say but hoping to warn Heinzek of what awaited people sent east, I wrote *Mavet grüsst euch*, which translated to Mavet greets you. *Mavet* means death in Hebrew. I signed off with the name Fredy Hirsch *Hoffnung*. *Hoffnung* means hope.

*

Not long after we sent the cards, word flew around the camp that the entire September transport was to be sent to work in a chemical plant at a place called Heydebreck.

'The Germans have told professionals to register for work assignments there, listing any skills,' Miriam reported. 'People seem happy at the news, saying Heydebreck has to be better than here. Someone told me they'd rather work for food than starve to death in Auschwitz.'

I shook my head. 'But a chemical factory is no place for children, Miriam. And none of this makes sense as only a handful of us are fit for labour. Most are walking skeletons, so weak that they can barely make it to the latrines.'

Within days, a stony-faced Kurt came to give me an update. 'A secretary who works for the SS told us that an order has arrived from Berlin to start giving your transport "special treatment" on 7th March, exactly six months after your arrival.'

'That's the birthday of Masaryk,' I told him, my knees buckling.

Kurt sat next to me. 'It would also be the eve of Purim, commemorating the deliverance of Jews from annihilation.' We looked at each other in silence.

'Does anyone know yet what "special treatment" means?' I asked.

Kurt hesitated. 'They're still convinced it can only mean one thing.'

Feeling as if I'd been kicked in the guts, I fought to remain calm as I bent double and held my head in my hands.

'Fredy,' Kurt said, shaking me. 'You must save yourself. Mengele said he'd protect you, so you must keep him to his promise.'

Looking up, I whispered, 'But I have to save the children.'

Dropping to the floor to kneel before me, he took both my hands in his. 'You can't save them, Fredy,' he said, his eyes filling with tears. 'In your heart you must have always known that. But if you save yourself, at least you'll be able to protect those left behind.' Shaking my head, I pushed him away. 'If you live, we can stay together,' he added, so quietly I almost didn't hear him. He eventually stopped talking when he realised I wasn't listening. A few minutes later I heard the door close.

Alone at last, I sank to my knees and prayed for a sign that this torment was somehow part of the Almighty's plan. Was being tested to the limits of endurance the sacrifice we had to make for our future? Curling into a ball, I rocked myself gently back and forth until sleep somehow found me.

*

When I woke with a start an hour or so later, the news of the previous night slammed into me again like a locomotive. What if it was true? How could I save the children or at least shield them? My mind spinning in its own hell, I couldn't bear to think of them enduring what the Bialystok children had gone through.

I was under no illusions about what happened in the gas chambers. The *Sonderkommando* had explained the mechanics of mass murder in graphic detail in the hope that someone might be able to escape and tell the world. Kurt relayed to me what happens in the belly of the beast. First, the unsuspecting are led into an undressing room. 'It's lined with hooks and polite signs instructing people to fold their clothes to be collected after their shower,' he read. 'It's all so pre-meditated.' Once naked, the heavy metal door to the gas chamber is pulled open and people are coaxed – then forced – inside by SS officers with guns and batons.

'The men who work there say the worst part comes when the door slams shut behind them. There's piteous wailing and desperate banging. An SS officer armed with a canister of Zyklon B crystals will be on the roof ready to pour them down a metal tube that leads into the chamber. As soon as the crystals come into contact with air, deadly gas starts streaming from fake shower heads in the ceiling. Then the screaming begins.'

Covering my ears, I wanted to block out the last part of the story but, panting, I dropped my hands to listen, realising that if I knew I could maybe do something to help the children if our turn came.

'Desperate for the only sliver of air that seeps in through the small opening in the ceiling, the strongest trample the weak in their futile attempts to survive.'

'That's enough!' I'd cried. 'I can't hear any more.'

Thinking back to all he'd told me, I began to wonder if our only option was to fight back after all. Then I began to question how many members of the Resistance there were and how effective they might be. I knew of several who'd been stockpiling matches, bottles and flammable liquids to set fire to their mattresses if the war looked like it was coming to an end but they were all so young and inexperienced in the business of death. My thoughts then turned to Łukas, who'd been brave enough to resist even though his struggle had an inevitable end. Maybe I could summon some of his courage in his memory.

The camp gong jerked me from my inner vortex and I jumped up, wild with despair. Dizzy from lack of sleep and numb with foreboding, I staggered out to gaze at the date on the calendar – 6th March – before hurrying out to supervise lines of children headed to the latrines.

'*Guten Morgen, Kinder*,' I chanted with a rictus smile.

'*Guten Morgen*, Fredy,' they replied in sleepy unison and my heart almost shattered. How many more days did we have left to exchange greetings before the gas chamber door slammed shut on us with an ominous clang? Desperate for more information as rumours flew around the camp like a flock of wild birds, I searched in vain for Pestek and Eyebrows, but they were nowhere to be seen. Even Dinah didn't have any news.

'All I know is that Mengele assured me that my mother and I wouldn't be sent away because of my artistry,' she said. 'Dr Heller and his family, plus two other doctors, a pharmacist and some nurses have been promised the same thing. Their patients and any twins in the infirmary will also remain. You must surely be on that list for the same reason?'

On that strangest of strange days, I felt to be floating above the camp watching myself go through the motions. The smallest things almost undid me. After Miriam heard that children in the infirmary might be saved, she checked the temperatures of some of the six-year-olds with a hand to their foreheads, asking if they felt unwell.

When it was the turn of a favourite boy the others called 'Embryo,' she said, 'Are you sick?' but he shook his head. 'Could you say that you are?' she asked, hopeful of saving him.

'No!' he exclaimed. 'I'm not a liar. Fredy would be cross.' Blinking, I had to turn away.

After lunch, Yehuda approached me. 'Please come to our block tonight, Fredy. A few of us have a surprise for you,' he said with a smile.

He was visibly taken aback when I snapped, 'I can't. I'm too busy.' I felt terrible when I learned that they'd been holding back some of their precious rations for weeks to throw me a party to mark two years since the opening of the first *Kinderheim* in Terezín. It was an anniversary I'd insisted we should celebrate each year but which I'd barely registered now.

The following morning, just after the children arrived in the block and I could see Kurt hurrying to see me, all prisoners were ordered to remain inside as truckloads of SS soldiers were driven into view. Soldiers we didn't recognise stood on the periphery, gripping their MP40 submachine guns with a purposeful stance, safety catches off.

'What's this?' Miriam wailed, clinging to my arm. 'Is it happening now, Fredy?'

Then an order was issued: 'The September transport are to be separated from the December intake and moved into camp BIIa for quarantine. Take all your belongings with you.' Terrified by the first part, people squeezed what encouragement they could from the second. 'That's good, isn't it?' Grandma asked. 'They wouldn't want us to take our things if we were going up the chimney.'

Fleeing from them all, I ran to my room to quickly sort out the pages of a fresh report I was writing for Eichmann. I planned to leave it for Miriam to send on. That's where Kurt found me. His face distraught, he gave a small sob when our eyes met.

'Now, now,' I scolded. 'No tears. If the children and I do have to leave, I'll meet you in Prague after the war, like we planned. Just imagine it, Kurt. We'll sit at a street café drinking real coffee, eating strudel with whipped cream, as we reflect on the madness of these years.'

Kurt's attempt at a smile failed but he played along with me. 'You can open the orphanage you've dreamed of running, Fredy, and I'll get a proper job. At night we'll sit by the fire in our parlour drinking *slivovice*.'

'And reading each other poetry.'

'We could get a dog.'

'And call him Budulínku.'

'Yes, Fredy.' Kurt nodded, his expression clenched. 'Yes, please, to all of it.'

A knock on the door was enough to separate us. I opened it to see Miriam and Hanka standing before me, their faces pale. Sniffing, Hanka said, 'It's time to go.'

'Very well, Auntie,' I said and picked up the clothes I'd rolled around my recorder. Lifting a floorboard, I pointed to the food supplies telling Miriam, 'All we have is here. There are some packets of German custard powder that only need a little milk, so make some up as a treat later for any children who are especially distressed.'

'Don't you want to take something with you?'

'I have some tea, tinned sardines and a little bread. That should be enough until we get to Heydebreck.' Replacing the floorboard, I turned to Kurt and squeezed his hand before stepping out into the block, leaving him alone with his tears.

*

The three hundred children of the September transport and their families started gathering their few belongings. Dov, who was in the infirmary, was exempt on health grounds and a few others were saved by virtue of being *piepels* or *Läufers*. Miloš, looking like a whipped puppy, stood stupefied in the middle of the block so I slapped him on the back and instructed him to help the little ones.

Bruno, who'd played 'Cheeky', was running around saying goodbye to everyone as if he was about to go on his holidays. 'Don't you worry about me,' he told a group of girls huddled around him in sympathy. 'I'll be the best stoker in Heaven, where it's always warm. I'll send some heat down to you.'

I watched another group joking that they'd soon be hearing 'the gong of St Peter', and I saw a fourteen-year-old hand her woollen gloves to a friend, saying, 'I won't need these where I'm going.' As I listened to their attempts to keep the mood light, I realised that they were a collective to the end, finding ways to share the burden and get through even this, the most difficult of days.

My remaining staff had been tasked to do their best to distract the December children from what was about to happen but nothing could shield them from the atmosphere. A boy I'd named '*Kanínchen*' because he reminded me of a pet rabbit, ran full pelt into me with tears streaming down his cheeks. 'Fredy, Fredy, why are you leaving us?' he sobbed, rubbing his eyes with tiny fists. Smiling, I hoisted him into my arms and balanced him on one hip.

'I'm going to go somewhere new and start another school, *Kanínchen*,' I told him, swallowing my emotion. 'You should be happy for me and for those coming with me.'

'Can I come, too?'

'No, *mein Junge*. You have to stay here with your friends and get big and strong so that you can grow up and help everyone else.'

'But who's going to teach us a new song every day?' he asked, his face crumpling.

Fighting the urge to break down, I told him brightly, 'Well, there's Seppl and Hugo, Zuzana, Arieh, Miriam, Kurt and Jan. They're staying, so you needn't worry.'

Another boy clinging to my thigh looked up at me with big green eyes and asked, 'But can they play the recorder as well as you?'

'I don't know but that's a good question. I'll be sure to check. And they can ask Willi to find another to replace mine, as I'll need it where I'm going.' Looking up, I saw Zuzana standing like a statue, fists clenched, knuckles white, as her eyes burning holes into my soul. Leo was standing close by, his own face stricken, and looped a comforting arm around her shoulders. Unable to face her yet, I carried *Kanínchen* over to a circle of tiny chairs and sat down on one of them, looking like Gulliver in Lilliput.

'I'm going to draw you all a picture,' I told the children who'd shadowed me across the room. Taking a sheet of wrapping paper and a piece of charcoal, I quickly sketched a train standing in a station, billowing steam. Beside it, I drew a tall, thin man in a hat, suit and tie with a big smile on his face. It was my smile: the smile of defiance that had been fixed to my face since 1939. He was waving.

Taking one of the little wooden pegs we'd made from splinters, I clipped my drawing to the barbed wire line so that everyone could see it. 'If ever you feel sad or miss me,' I told the children. 'Just look at this picture of me and wave at it, all right? Wherever I am, whatever I'm doing, I promise you that I'll feel your love and be waving back.'

Standing quickly, I strode directly over to Zuzana and pulled her into my arms. With her head pressed flat against my chest, I could feel her sobs heaving her rake-thin body. Handing her over to Miriam with a quick nod, I walked to the door with a smile glued to my lips and gave two short bursts of my whistle. Like clockwork soldiers, the children jumped up and stood to attention.

'It's farewell, not goodbye, my precious ones. Be kind. Stay strong. Take care of each other and I'll see you soon.'

9

March 1944

IT WAS ALL I could do to put one foot in front of the other and walk away from the sanctuary we'd created: an island of humanity in a raging sea. Steadying my breathing with rhythmic gulps, I joined the evacuation queue and tried to focus on the people around me. To my surprise, I spotted some of the doctors and Dinah, her mother and the nurses who'd all been told they could stay. Poor Dinah was shaking violently as she shuffled forward with the rest.

She only stopped shivering when a woman with a beautiful voice began to sing a tune that reared up from my past and almost undid me. '*Wenn der Herrgott net will, nutzt es gar nix.*' If the Lord doesn't want us, it's no use at all. Concentrating on Miloš, Bruno and the boys around me that I'd managed to keep alive, I held my head high and marched ahead of them like a soldier, my whistle swinging like an amulet.

It was hard to ignore the pitiful calls of those watching us from the doorways of their blocks, where they'd been ordered to remain. Outside his block, a stony-faced Böhm watched, too, alongside Willi whose face was crumpled with grief.

After a quick sweep of the roll call area, I spotted Eyebrows staring at me with such a forlorn expression that I almost felt sorry for him. Giving him a quick nod, I gasped when he not only returned it but clicked his heels together and raised his hand in a salute.

Once we passed into BIIa and found our way into the different blocks I made sure the boys were all together before double rations of bread and soup were carried in.

'This is a good sign,' a man cried, as people cheered. 'The Nazis wouldn't feed people they intended to kill.'

Nor would they provide them with hooks and tell them to fold their clothes, I thought.

Unable to swallow, I gave my portion of soup to a teenager who was the sole surviving relative of his three younger siblings, after his parents had died of suicide and disease. 'It may be a day or two before our next meal, Frederik,' I told him. 'Be sure to eat every drop.'

*

A messenger arrived soon afterwards to tell me that Rudi the registrar wanted me to go to him. I was about to leave the block when Leo jumped up from where he was comforting a boy and intercepted me. 'Be careful, Fredy,' he warned. 'If the Resistance has a plan to get us out of this, it'll be a crazy one. Rudi may be an old hand here but, remember, he's only nineteen and doesn't know everything.'

Grateful as always for his counsel, I squeezed his arm and murmured, 'Thank you, my friend.'

Rudi's *Läufer* directed me to a small, whitewashed room next to the camp's administration office but before I knocked on the door I took several deep breaths. Inside Rudi was pacing the room, his face so careworn that he looked far older than his years. When he offered me a seat on his bed I refused so he squared up to me to blurt his news. 'It really looks like this is the end for you, Fredy,' he said, breathlessly. 'The consensus is that you're going to be gassed.'

My heartrate slowed almost to a halt as my brain tried to absorb what he was saying.

Hesitating, he peered into my face. Continuing more slowly, he added, 'Aside from the Bialystok children, this will be the first time that so many of you being pushed into that gas chambers will know exactly what's going to happen. If you resist, the SS will open fire. But if you don't, all of you will die and the killings will go on and on.'

Silently, I watched a pool of sweat gather in the dimple above Rudi's top lip. Standing before me was someone with direct contact to the Resistance. Doubt began to creep into my heart. When he offered me a cigarette, I noticed for the first time that my hand was shaking as he lit it for me. Coughing violently, I picked a strand of tobacco from my bottom lip and continued to stare at him silently.

'What are you going to do?' he asked.

'What can I do?' I replied finally, my hand clamped around my whistle.

'You're the spiritual heart of this camp, Fredy. If there is to be a revolt, everyone agrees you'd be the best person to lead it.'

Everyone agrees.

Feeling suddenly cold, I stared into his doe-brown eyes as I considered the options. Something small and bitter gathered in my throat as I stubbed out my half-smoked cigarette and ground it into the floor with my heel. 'You can't be certain about this,' I said, pressing back my shoulders. 'It doesn't make sense that the Nazis would keep us all this time to kill us now.'

Rudi nodded. 'I can't deny that it seems completely illogical. But it's the code, Fredy. SB6. The code is indisputable.'

'I disagree. If it's never been used before then none of you can really know what it means. I'm not prepared to risk the children's lives by starting a rebellion against something that may not even happen.'

He examined my face for a moment before nodding. 'Let me see what else I can find out.'

I doubt anyone in the quarantine camp had any rest that night. I know I didn't. Sleep was impossible as my head thumped and my bones pressed painfully against wooden planks. My mind swirling with fears of what the dawn would bring, I was swamped by a sense of powerlessness. In the early hours, I climbed silently from my bunk and wandered out into the mud. Staring up at the night sky, my view of the heavens was thwarted each time the infernal searchlights swept back and forth.

Across the wire still humming its deadly song, Camp BIIb lay slumbering under a yellow crescent moon. Blocks 29 and 31 stood empty now but in my head I could hear the faint voices of the children laughing and chanting the songs we'd taught them. The previous six months had felt like an eternity. Every day had been a battle for survival.

Looking across the dark plain in the general direction of the officers' quarters, I closed my eyes and sent a silent plea to the men who would decide our fate. Many of them were the same men who came to our block seeking solace from the horrors beyond. Men I'd entered into an unholy alliance with because I knew it was the only way to barter for the lives of children.

Sinking to my knees, I closed my eyes and pressed my hands together. 'These days and nights of suffering are hard to bear, Lord. Fill me with strength that I may fight for what's right.' Gazing up at the stars, the words of 'Ode to Joy' came to my lips. '*Above the starry canopy, There must dwell a loving Father.*'

'Father, if you are there,' I whispered as a single tear rolled down my cheek. 'Please, I beg you, guide me now.'

*

Roll call almost came as a relief. I hadn't stood outside like that for months yet the act of being shoulder to shoulder with my fellow prisoners, slowly sinking into the cold, wet clay as the hours passed, brought me back to myself. Across the wire, I could see the inmates of the December transport doing the same, each of us searching hopefully for the faces of those we knew and loved.

As soon as it was over, prisoners from both sides ran to the wire to shout messages and throw over food and other items. I was about to do the same and ask for news from the blocks when Rudi summoned me again. Walking to his room as if to the gallows, I passed a few of my helpers leading a group of the smallest children to the latrines. I was so absorbed in my thoughts that I didn't even respond when they called, '*Guten Morgen*, Fredy.'

Rudi wasn't alone this time. He was accompanied by members of Birkenau's Resistance groups, all of them steely-eyed. No one spoke at first but then Rudi stood up. 'It's bad news, I'm afraid, Fredy. The *Sonderkommando* has received its orders. The furnaces are being stoked. They've been warned to process four thousand bodies. If there's one thing consistent about the Nazis it is that they don't waste fuel unnecessarily.'

Don't waste fuel unnecessarily.

Rudi had the kind of face that looked as if it was smiling even when it wasn't. At any other time it might have been endearing but on that bitter morning I found it unsettling. His eyes twinkling despite himself, when he saw the colour drain from my face he suggested that I sit. Feeling suddenly faint as my headache worsened, I dropped my head and stared at his mud-caked boots, noticing for the first time that the laces were mismatched. My breath came in long, deep draughts, expanding and contracting my ribcage like an accordion.

Rudi waited for a moment before continuing. 'I was instructed to pass this information on to the Resistance in your transport this morning. After a vote, we all agree that you're the most dependable person to lead the uprising before you are sent to the gas.'

We all agree. There it was again. Only I was the one person who hadn't been asked.

'You're the only one who can do this, Fredy,' Rudi insisted. 'It has to be someone everyone respects and will obey, regardless of their politics. The minute you blow your whistle, the *Sonderkommando* will make their move to destroy the crematoria and then everyone else will join in. There's hope that some of the other camps will mobilise too once they hear shooting and explosions.'

Shooting and explosions.

Feeling as if the walls were closing in on me, I shook my head before finding my voice. Looking up, I asked, 'What if you're proved wrong? What if we really are going to Heydebreck and the furnaces are being stoked for an incoming transport?'

'Don't you understand, Fredy? Heydebreck's not happening,' Rudi snapped. 'It's all part of their charade. No orders have been drawn up to provide trucks to transport you anywhere.'

'Perhaps they're doing things differently this time,' I countered, desperately rooting around in my mind for something to cling to.

Ignoring me, Rudi added, 'There'll be no selections and only a handful on a reserve list are to be saved. The *Sonderkommando* run an extremely efficient slaughterhouse and are forced to calculate everything down to the last piece of wood. Four thousand *Stücke*, the order said. That's you.'

The last piece of wood.

Losing courage and feeling pain in my chest, I whispered, 'But what about the children?'

The smile dropped from his face completely then, as if that was the one question he'd been dreading. Stepping closer, he laid a hand on my shoulder and said, 'They're going to die, Fredy, just like the tens of thousands before them. They murder children every day. What would be the difference to them?'

'But they *know* mine.'

'Now's the time to smash the heart of the factory,' he insisted. 'The hope is that a handful of prisoners – maybe one or two per cent – will escape to tell the world what's happening here. This is your opportunity to save all those thousands of kids who are safely at home now but will soon be sent here unless we do something. Only you can decide if their deaths will be for nothing or a sacrifice worth paying.'

My mind writhed as it tried to wriggle free from the grip of his words. I fought to focus on the questions I should ask and the arguments I needed to come up with to stall for time. Eventually, I stammered, 'W-what weapons do you have?'

Rudi couldn't disguise his embarrassment as he mumbled something about petrol bombs, a hand grenade, some metal tools, plus a little gunpowder and the means to light it.

'But that wouldn't be nearly enough against a hundred machine guns!'

He hung his head. Like me, he'd run out of answers.

'How long have we got?'

'The *Aktion* will almost certainly start tonight.'

322

'Give me an hour or so to consider this,' I said, rising unsteadily. 'I need time to think.'

'Of course, Fredy. Please, use this room. I'll leave my *Läufer* at the door for anything you need. I'll be back before curfew.' Before he left he said, 'You are already the hero of Birkenau, Fredy, but with this final act of courage you could end this for good.'

*

Time seemed to stand still even as I heard Hell's stopwatch ticking. My head was pounding painfully. Shaking, I realised I hadn't eaten a thing for over thirty-six hours and I hadn't slept in days. 'Can you fetch me a doctor?' I asked the skinny *Läufer*, who sped off with a swift nod of his head.

Two medics I knew arrived surprisingly quickly, standing before me in their grubby white coats. 'What's wrong, Fredy?'

'I have a horrible headache and I need something to calm my nerves,' I said before muttering something about an important decision. Seeing their expressions, I realised that they were anxious about their own situation, so I asked, 'Have you heard anything?'

'Mengele's on vacation but someone's trying to reach him. We were promised we'd be escorted back to BIIa before nightfall with our staff, our families, the auxiliaries and patients,' one replied.

'What about Dinah and her mother?'

'They're on the list too.' Seeing my expression, they paused. 'Sorry, Fredy. The messenger said nothing about you or the children but then we haven't seen the list.' When they saw I was no longer able to speak, they told me they only had a few medicines with them and handed me a large white pill. 'This will help you relax,' the first doctor promised.

Lying back on Rudi's bed after they'd gone, it occurred to me that in a few hours' time he would likely be the only living being left in this part of the camp. There wasn't any water to drink but I put the pill I'd been given in my mouth and threw my head back, swallowing it whole.

Closing my eyes, I tried to focus on my breathing, just as I had taught the children to do. The children. I should be with them now, holding their hands, not feeling sorry for myself. But with my head hurting so much and exhaustion creeping in, I knew that I needed to stay for a while and think.

For the first time I finally understood what it was like to feel as hopeless as a *Muselman*. The hope that had sustained me ever since the Nazis came to power had not only deserted me but I now blamed it for deluding me for so long. Eleven years earlier, I'd hoped that Hitler would be defeated in an election but he won. I'd hoped his anti-Semitic talk was just rhetoric but it wasn't. Fleeing to Czechoslovakia was, I hoped, enough to save me from Hitler's clutches but being there made me too complacent to escape further.

My hopes for a life in a new land were doomed long before I drew that short match. Pinning all my hopes on a future for the children kept me fighting for survival in Terezín and Auschwitz in the hope that we'd be liberated. It was that same naïve sense of hope that had allowed the Nazis to push millions of us into cattle wagons with hardly a murmur before we formed orderly lines for the gas chambers.

Paralysed by hope, our fighting spirit diminished by it, we kept holding on to one more day of life, as if someone would save us. Until the day our time ran out. Even as we appeared to be hours from annihilation, I still hoped Rudi was wrong and that a last-minute message would spare us.

My breathing slowing, I finally began to feel calmer as I continued to wrestle with my conscience. Rudi was right. No matter how desperate, a rebellion was the only chance of saving the hopeful of the future. If I refused to lead it, an uprising would probably happen anyway as I was sure they'd find someone else to take up the cry.

At least if I was the one blowing the whistle, I could choose my moment and maybe keep the children in the middle where they'd be better shielded from gunfire.

Gunfire.

The longer-term consequences were unthinkable, though, as there was no way I could escape with so many children in tow. And the reprisals would be brutal if any SS died and the crematoria were destroyed. Every Nazi officer in Birkenau would be held responsible and the hunger for revenge would be all-consuming. What if they decided to punish the December transport too? Our actions could inadvertently lead to the liquidation of the entire Family Camp. Zuzana, Miriam, the remaining children, their teachers and helpers: these people had a far better chance of survival if the war ended before their turn came in three months. Without weapons, they'd all be mown down in a hail of bullets from the watchtowers. Tens of thousands could die.

The responsibility lay on my shoulders like a layer of Auschwitz clay and I could still hear the stopwatch ticking in my brain. Feeling nauseous, I was tired, so tired, of thinking. Suddenly thirsty, I went to lick my lips but my tongue felt numb and heavy in my mouth. The urge to sleep was overwhelming. My mind dimming, I pictured myself on the banks of a freshwater lake I'd known so well as a boy.

Stripping off, I plunged in and dived to the bottom, swimming alongside silvery fish as together we skimmed over boulders smoothed by time. I gulped and I found to my astonishment that I could breathe underwater. Floating halfway to the surface, I gazed up through the lake at the blue sky and the green pine trees and spotted a huge hawk circling lazily overhead.

I rose further and saw my father and Uncle Alfred standing on the shore with my brother Paul. All three were smiling and waving so I waved back. My father was wearing his bloodied apron, a knife still in his hand. Alfred looked as dapper as ever in a three-piece tweed suit and Paul had a striped prayer shawl draped over his shoulders as he beckoned me to surface.

I tried to swim higher so I could show Alfred my whistle but my limbs no longer obeyed me. My arms felt to have lost all strength. Making a supreme effort, I managed to kick my legs and rise to the surface only for froth to start gurgling from my lips. Attempting to wipe it away, my arm flapped around helplessly and kept missing my face.

My mind foggy, I sank back under, shivering violently. I looked up and saw a beautiful white hart step gracefully to the water's edge. I'd never been so close to one before and its fur seemed to sparkle in the sunlight. Looking directly at me as its long, pink tongue lapped thirstily, its perceptive brown eyes fringed with pale eyelashes never once blinked as they gazed into my soul.

A sudden noise startled it and the hart sprang away in four elegant bounds as I reached out to it in vain. Then Rudi appeared on the shore, splashing into the lake. Grabbing hold of me, he lifted me under my arms and slapped my face. 'Fredy! Wake up! Fredy!' he shouted but I could only hear him distantly and my body was too waterlogged to be raised.

When he dragged me half onto the shore and ran off, all I could hear was my own breath gurgling in my lungs. The next thing I knew there were more voices and someone shaking me violently. Moments of lucidity were intermittent as the lake drew me back under. I think I heard Rudi again, then a blurred white coat appeared through the ripples as another voice said, 'Drugged . . . suicide.'

Restless, my legs flailing, I tried to swim up again but my body resisted even as Rudi became hysterical, sobbing, 'They'll all die now . . .'

'It would be kinder to leave him then,' the muffled voice said.

Kinder.

Kinder.

That's when I felt myself slipping under and sinking slowly to the bottom of the lake. I sank deeper and deeper, my arms and legs weightless before coming to a gentle rest on the soft sand. At one with the lake as air from my lips rose in a stream of silver bubbles, I had never felt so completely at peace.

*

Somewhere far above me through the crystal water, I could hear the children distantly singing. In that paradise on earth where the pines sighed, I heard the moving Czech national anthem, 'Where Is My Home?'

As if in reply, they sang the *Hatikvah* in perfect harmony, Helga's sweet notes rising above the rest like a songbird in flight until their voices slowly faded. Those precious fragments of verse transported me back to nights under the stars sitting around campfires.

'*Within a Jewish breast, beats true a Jewish heart,*' the children had sang as the orange glow of flames reflected in their eyes.

'*Our hope is not dead – our ancient hope and true – to be a nation free forevermore.*'

Mouthing the words as air from my lips rose in a glistening stream of silver bubbles, I closed my eyes for ever. '*Hope is not dead. Our ancient hope and true.*'

Epilogue

MY NAME WAS *Alfred Hirsch, although my friends called me Fredy. Please, be so kind as to remember my name. There is no one left alive who can bear witness to how and why my life ebbed away.*

Until my final breath, I fought to brighten the days of those who would die alongside me and save any who'd survive. They are my true legacy.

My name was Fredy Hirsch. I was twenty-eight years old. I was a teacher. I was a dreamer. I loved and laughed, cried and almost died a thousand times.

My name was Fredy Hirsch. Millions of names have been forgotten so, please, be so kind as to remember mine.

Survivor Testimonials

'Fredy was the most beautiful man I ever saw ... He was absolutely moral as a human being; almost puritan ... He was unique. He was goodness ... we all learned from Fredy a sort of hope that even in a terrible situation you can arise from the dead.' **Zuzana Růžičková**

'Fredy Hirsch was an amazing man, very intelligent and courageous. Even the Germans paid attention to him because he had this direct way of staring and looking so unafraid ... He accomplished a real miracle, he stood his ground and managed to wring a children's home out of them. He had the courage to stand up to the SS.' **Jirí Franek**

'The spirit of that place was Fredy Hirsch ... He was a beautiful man – the ideal specimen of a man. He was an example to us. Somebody to follow. We wanted to be like him.' **Dita Kraus**

'He was a wonderful, wonderful man ... he looked like a toothpaste advertisement. He had this shiny black, slicked back hair, a very handsome face, and an incredible grin with white, white teeth.' **Dina Gottliebová**

'He was an almost mythological figure. This was some kind of other world.' **Otto Dov Kulka**

'*His love for youngsters was to help them, to encourage them. To forget as far as possible their daily life and also to shield them from the negative things that were happening.*' **Yehuda Bacon**

'*Fredy Hirsh became a very respected figure . . . he knew each child by name . . . he soon became very popular among the whole camp; a very respectable personality . . . by his upright behaviour and obvious human dignity.*' **Rudolf Vrba**

'*Laughter was around him always . . . how he created this out of nothing in this really terrible place and to protect the children . . . was really the highest of achievements.*' **Michael Honey (Misha Honiwags)**

'*He built a wall in our hearts against suffering.*' **Eva Gross**

Author's Note

The idea to write a book about Fredy Hirsch first came to me in the autumn of 2017 when I was living and working in Prague, researching a book called *One Hundred Miracles* about the Holocaust survivor and world-renowned musician Zuzana Ružičková.

Aged ninety and tiny like a bird, this indomitable survivor of three camps cried only twice throughout our extensive interviews. First when she recounted how her father died in Terezín and secondly when she told me about Fredy Hirsch. On her desk she kept a photo of him beside pictures of her mother and father, referring to them as her three guiding lights.

'This beautiful man was like some sort of vision,' Zuzana said. 'I'd fainted not long after we arrived and, when I came to, he was leaning over me with a warm smile on his face. From that moment on, he became the most important person in my life.'

Every child survivor of Terezín or Auschwitz that I met, or whose testimonies I have examined, had the same reaction. Their faces immediately lit up with affectionate memories of the kind, brave, young man who – impossibly – gave them some of the best days of their lives in the worst places imaginable. Remarkably, Fredy was able to create a little piece of heaven in Auschwitz: children could escape the horrors to sing, dance, put on shows, even meditate to stave off their hunger and the constant fear of death.

All those who survived him still missed him terribly and swore that the physical and mental resilience he instilled in them remained with them their whole lives. It also saved them: when the December transport was due to be liquidated when their six months ran out, the children that survived did so because of Fredy. Not only did Dr Josef Mengele, the so-called 'Angel of Death', save almost ninety teenage boys because he'd come to know them personally in Block 31 but his decision to select younger people for slave labour also saved Zuzi – and her mother – by default.

Paraded naked before senior SS officers who were deciding who should be gassed and who was suitable for slave labour, Zuzana watched in horror as her middle-aged mother was sent to the left, which meant death. Panicking, when it was Zuzi's turn, she decided to tell them she was a gymnastics teacher rather than a pianist in the hope that might save her. Until she met Fredy, she'd never done any gymnastics in her life as she was too frail and spoiled but she hoped he had taught her enough.

'Show us some gymnastics, then,' she was told by the inspecting SS officer. Taking a breath, Zuzi performed a perfect somersault. Impressed, they told her to go to the right. Lifting her chin in defiance, she stepped left.

The *Obersturmführer* frowned and scolded, 'You silly goose, you're going to your death.'

Zuzana replied, 'My father died in the ghetto. My mother is going to be killed. I have no reason to live.' He sighed and said her to her mother, 'You, old goat, go to the right with your daughter.' With that split-second decision, the fate of both were sealed. Zuzana lived until the age of ninety after a career as one of the world's greatest baroque musicians and her mother had lived until eighty-seven.

Fredy wasn't allowed the privilege of the life he longed for but he lived by his principles until his death in Auschwitz at the age of twenty-eight. Faced with an impossible dilemma and having been found unconscious on the night of the massacre of the September transport, many believed he'd committed suicide. But few of the children ever accepted that, declaring that he would never leave his charges.

Years later another possible scenario unfolded. A pharmacist saved from the gas chamber confessed that the doctors had asked him for Luminal, a strong drug used to stop seizures in epileptics. This they gave to Fredy to knock him out cold and prevent him from leading the uprising they feared would have resulted in their deaths, too.

In the decades since that fateful night, Fredy's memory was either forgotten or denigrated by Communists and homophobes who accused him of being a coward and a collaborator, accusations that felt to the survivors like a terrible betrayal. No monuments were ever erected to their beloved Fredy until, after decades of obscurity, Zuzana and others had a memorial plaque to his memory installed in Terezín. Bearing his face carved in stone, the inscription reads, *Fredy Hirsch – gratefully, children of Terezín, Birkenau BIIb*. As Zuzana later told me, 'Fredy was the spirit of morality, an ideological figure. In giving us a spark of hope, he not only saved our lives but he also saved our souls.'

From the moment I first heard her speak his name and saw how deeply etched it was in her psyche, I was determined to give Fredy a voice. I hope I have done so in this book, fictionalising parts of his story to fill in the gaps and make it more accessible. It is my fervent wish that no one who reads this will ever forget the name of Fredy Hirsch.

This novel wouldn't have been possible, however, without all those survivors who refused to give up on Fredy. Special thanks to Zuzana Ružičková, Frank Bright and Dagmar Lieblová, who spoke to me of Fredy in the weeks before they died. May their memories be a blessing. There is no surviving documentation about the children's block so their testimonies and those of others from the Shoah Foundation and other organisations (including the United States Holocaust Museum, the Imperial War Museum, Yad Vashem, the European Holocaust Research Infrastructure and the Terezín Memorial) proved invaluable.

I am also grateful to the countless authors and academics who researched and archived so much of the historical information on which this book is based and to those who digitised it. As a Fellow of the Royal Historical Society, I am indebted to all the historians whose diligence put invaluable resources about this period into the public domain. I would also like to thank director Aaron Cohen for giving me access to his wonderful film *Heaven in Auschwitz*, and to director Rubi Gat for making the animated *Dear Fredy* movie.

Among those whose archives were most useful to me were the Auschwitz-Birkenau Memorial and Museum, Beit Theresienstadt Archives, The Holocaust Museum of Jewish Virtual Library, The Fortunoff Video Archive for Holocaust Testimonies, The Institute of Terezín Initiative, Deutschlandfunk, The Imperial War Museum, Holocaust CZ, Memory of Nations archive. I am also grateful to Haaretz magazine, Ceska TV, Tablet magazine, Geni.com, New Yorker magazine, Remember.org, Jewishgen, Medical Review Auschwitz, Jerusalem Post, Patmatnik Terezin, the European Holocaust Research Infrastructure, Attitude magazine, Lide Mesta journal, Centropa.org and too many more to list. Special thanks must go to the UK Holocaust Educational Trust and the United States Holocaust Memorial Museum, both organisations I frequently speak for.

Piotr Setkiewicz, the inimitable Director of the Centre for Research at the Auschwitz-Birkenau State Museum, was as kind and patient as ever in answering my many questions, and Professor Elizabeth R. Baer, Senior Researcher with the United States Holocaust Memorial Museum and Scholar in Holocaust Studies, kindly read and verified the historical accuracy of my work and gave me a glowing endorsement.

There was one person who believed in this book long before it was even written and her name is Sarah Benton. She and her outstanding team at Bonnier, especially Rights Director Stella Giatrakou, have supported and encouraged me from the start and their passion for Fredy and understanding of the importance of bringing his story to the world kept me going. If it weren't for them and for my husband Chris, the singular human being who has been by my side for more than four decades, reading every one of my books before anyone else, I might well have gone under.

Thanks to their spiritual and physical sustenance, Fredy has finally been brought out of the shadows and into the light he deserves. Thank you all.

Wendy Holden, 2025

Cast of Characters

✦ *Perished at the hands of the Nazis*

✦ **Fredy Hirsch** (1916–1944) *After Fredy went into a coma in Birkenau on 7ᵗʰ March, all attempts to revive him failed and he was carried unconscious to the crematorium. Those left in the Family Camp wept when they heard trucks arrive to force the September transport out of camp BIIa. Several resisted and were shot. As the prisoners were driven away, many started to sing the Czech national anthem and then the Hatikvah as a final act of defiance. Apart from a few scuffles, some kept singing as they walked into the gas chamber, holding the hands of Fredy's beloved children. It took several hours on that dark night of 8ᵗʰ March but when it was over all 3,972 people had perished, including Fredy Hirsch who was with them to the end. He was 28 years old.*

✦ **Alfred Heinemann** (1886–1942) *Fredy's uncle was transported from Germany to Chełmno in Poland along with his wife and two children, all of whom were murdered in the back of sealed vans pumped with exhaust fumes. He was 56.*

✦ **Jakob Edelstein** (1903–1944), also **Miriam** (1908–1944) **and Arieh Edelstein** (1931–1944)*In June 1944 Jakob was briefly reunited with his wife Miriam, son Arieh and mother-in-law in Auschwitz I, just as Adolf Eichmann had promised. He was then forced to watch his son be shot and then his wife and mother-in-law, before he too was murdered. He was 41.*

✱ Egon 'Gonda' Redlich (1916–1944) *In October 1944 Gonda, his wife Gerta and their baby boy Dan were transported to Auschwitz and sent straight to the gas chamber. His diary was discovered hidden in a loft in 1967 and published in 1992. Like Fredy, Gonda was 28.*

✱ Leo Janowitz (1911–1944) *Fredy's stoic friend and supporter was gassed in Birkenau as part of the September transport on 8 March 1944. He was 33.*

✱ Friedl Dicker-Brandeis (1898–1944) *The compassionate art teacher of Terezín was murdered in the gas chamber of Birkenau in October 1944. More than 4,000 drawings that she inspired the children to create were saved in her suitcases and entrusted to a friend. After the war, the drawings were donated to the Jewish Museum in Prague and the Pinkas Synagogue and many have travelled the world in exhibitions. 550 of the more than 650 children who drew for her were murdered or died in the Holocaust. Their pictures are their legacy. Friedl was 46.*

✱ Bernd Nathan (1904–1945) *A German set designer and member of the* ghettowache *in Terezín, Bernd was transported to Auschwitz in September 1944 and survived almost to the end of the war before being shot on a death march in January 1945, just days before the camp was liberated. His wife Anka and their baby Eva, conceived in Terezín and born at the gates of Mauthausen concentration camp in April 1945, both survived and are the subject of the book* Born Survivors. *Bernd was 41.*

✱ Ottilie 'Ottla' Kafkova (1892–1943) *Sister to the writer Franz Kafka, Ottla volunteered to travel with the Bialystok children when they were transported to Auschwitz from Terezín in October 1944. They were all sent straight to the gas chambers. Ottla was 50.*

✱ **Max Mautner** (1879–1942) *Jenda's father was murdered in Auschwitz after being transported there from Terezín. He was 62.*

✱ **Jenni Mautner** (1880–1942) *Jenda's mother was murdered in Auschwitz after being transported there from Terezín. She was 62.*

✱ **Jaroslav Ruzicka** (1893–1943) *Zuzana's father perished in Terezín from an untreated bowel condition. He was 50.*

✱ **Heinz 'Heinzek' Prossnitz** (1926–1944) *After doing so much for so many prisoners with his thousands of parcels, Heinz and his parents* **Fritz and Marie** *were all murdered in Auschwitz in 1944. Heinz was 18.*

✱ **Hanka Epsteinová** (1904–1944) *The woman affectionately called Auntie who'd devoted her life to children was murdered in the gas chamber on 8ᵗʰ March with Fredy and their young charges. She was 39.*

✱ **Erik** (Date unknown–1944) *A troubled boy named Erik was transported from Terezín to Auschwitz and became the* piepel *of Böhm. When he was saved from the list of those going to the gas chamber, he refused to leave his parents and was gassed alongside them. He was in his mid-teens.*

✱ **Viktor Pestek** (1924–1944) *Less than a month after Fredy died,* Rottenführer *Pestek helped a prisoner named Lederer escape from Auschwitz-Birkenau wearing an SS uniform. Accompanying him out of the camp, Pestek planned to secure false papers for Renée and her mother and to return. Lederer travelled to Terezín to warn the Elders about Auschwitz but wasn't taken seriously. When he and Pestek returned to free Renée, Pestek was captured, tortured and executed. Lederer evaded detection and spent the rest of the war in the Resistance attempting to get news of Auschwitz to the world. Renée survived the war with her mother and emigrated to New York where she married, had a son and died in her sixties. Pestek died at the age of 20.*

✷ **The December transport** *After another transport of over 7,000 prisoners from Terezín arrived in the Family Camp in May 1944, the Nazis carried out a selection of the remaining members of the camp. Some 3,500 were sent to slave labour and the remaining 6,500 were sent to the gas chamber. Almost 90 boys aged between 14 and 16 were saved by Mengele, a rare act of mercy attributed to Fredy Hirsch: the boys, including Misha and Yehuda, had been in the children's block and were known to the SS. Collectively they became known as 'The Birkenau Boys' and approximately half survived the war. In total 17,500 men, women and children were sent to the Family Camp from Terezín between 1943 and 1944. Of those only 1,294 survived. Auschwitz was liberated by the Red Army on 27th January, 1945, which is now marked worldwide as Holocaust Memorial Day. An estimated 1.1 million people were slaughtered there.*

✷ **The Prisoners of the Gypsy Camp** *An estimated 20,000 Romany gypsies perished in the camp between February 1943 and August 1944 before it was liquidated and as many as 5,000 men, women and children were sent to the gas chambers. This massacre is remembered in the Romani language as 'The Devouring'.*

✷ **Josef (Seppl) Lichtenstein** (1915–1945) *The young man Fredy appointed as his successor in Block 31 was given Fredy's whistle by members of the* Sonderkommando *who'd salvaged it from his body after they'd tried to revive him. It was said that Seppl rarely used it, as it would have felt like sacrilege. When the December transport was liquidated in the summer of 1944, Seppl was sent to a labour camp and died on a death march back to Terezín, which was liberated not long after in May 1945. He was 29.*

✷ **'Grandma'** *Fate unknown but is believed to have perished.*

- **Heinrich Hirsch** (1881–1926) *Fredy's father died at his home in Germany of an unknown disease, aged 45.*

- **Olga Hirsch** (1887–1957) *Fredy's mother escaped to South America where she died aged 70.*

- **Paul Hirsch** (1914–1979) *Fredy's brother Paul fled with his mother and stepfather to South America and remained there until his death. He became a respected and much-loved rabbi. Paul married and had a daughter. He was 65.*

- **Jan 'Jenda' Mautner** (1912–1951) *After being sent to Auschwitz and on to a satellite branch of Sachsenhausen concentration camp where half the inmates were worked to death, Jenda was one of the few who survived the brutal conditions and the death march back to Terezín. Even though he suffered from chronic TB, he completed his medical training to become a doctor and found happiness with a new partner. Having never fully recovered his health, Jenda died of TB in Prague aged 39.*

- **Dinah Gottliebová** (1923–2009) *After Dinah and her mother were saved from the gas chamber along with medical staff and a few other privileged prisoners, she continued working for Mengele as an artist until liberation. She later moved to Paris where she married one of the animators of Walt Disney's Snow White, the film she'd recreated on the walls of the children's block. The couple emigrated to California in the United States where she became a mother and an animator for various film studios. She died aged 86.*

- **Marianne 'Mausi' Hermannová** (1921–2017) *A member of the December transport, Mausi's paintings of children of the world also brought her to the attention of Mengele who had her paint dwarfs and twins. In July 1944 she was sent to Germany for slave labour and then to Bergen-Belsen, where she and her mother were liberated. After living in Sweden for several years she married a German refugee and moved to Scotland where she had* *three children. Later, she reproduced her wall paintings in the block for the Yad Vashem Holocaust memorial in Israel. She died aged 86.*

- **Shragga Honigwachs** (1919–1970s) *Shragga, who drew the long match against Fredy to see who would go to the Promised Land, reached his destination and remained there until his death.*

- **'Misha' Honigwachs** (later Michael Honey) (1929–2014) *Shragga's younger brother Misha was one of approximately forty boys who survived the war as one of the 'Birkenau Boys'. After the war he moved to Britain where he gave invaluable testimonies to Holocaust organisations about his wartime experiences, insisting that he would never have survived if it hadn't been for Fredy Hirsch. He died at the age of 85.*

- **Avi Fischer** *and* **Hugo Lengsfeld** *Fredy's successors in the children's block both survived the war. Avid emigrated to Israel, and Hugo took the name Pavel Lenek and became a theatre director.*

- **Rudolf 'Rudi' Verba** (1924–2006) *After failing to save Fredy Hirsch and witnessing the liquidation of the September transport, Rudi resolved to escape before his own time there came to an end. A month to the day later, on the eve of Passover, he and a fellow prisoner escaped and walked 80km to Slovakia. Once rescued, they wrote a comprehensive report about Auschwitz that was first published in Switzerland in May 1944, one year before the end of the war. After training as a chemist, Rudi settled in Canada where he became a professor of pharmacology and gave multiple testimonies of his experiences. He died at the age of 81.*

- **Zuzana Ružicková** (1927–2017) *Zuzana not only survived Auschwitz-Birkenau with her mother but also survived in Hamburg and then typhus and starvation in Bergen-Belsen. Her piano playing hands ruined, and with most of her family murdered, she tried to kill herself but was discovered in time. Resuming her musical studies, she switched to the harpsichord: her love of the* *music of J S Bach saved her psychologically. Even though she was Jewish and living under a Communist anti-Semitic regime, she went on to become one of the world's leading Baroque musicians and the only person to record the entire works of Bach. She married the Czech composer Viktor Kalabis and the couple remained in Prague until their deaths. In 1996 she unveiled a plaque in Fredy's memory in Terezín, saying of him, 'We Jews have no saints. Instead, we have 'tzaddikim', which means a righteous leader or guide. Fredy Hirsch was not a saint. He was a fallible human being ... But he was a* tzaddik; *a good, brave and beautiful person. Many children would not have survived without his great sacrifice.' Having completed the interviews for her memoir,* One Hundred Miracles, *Zuzana died before it was published. She was 90.*

- **Frank Brichta** (later Frank Bright) (1928–2023) *After studying physical education under Fredy in Prague, where he learned how to shot putt, Frank and his parents arrived in Terezín not long before Fredy was deported. His father was sent away and he and his mother were sent to Auschwitz in October 1944 where she was gassed. Sent as a labourer to Sudetenland aged 16, he survived and was invited to Britain by a relative. He trained as a civil and municipal engineer, married an Englishwoman and had a daughter. He died in England aged 95.*

- **Wilhelm (Willi) Brachmann** (1903–1982) *After Böhm was sent to the front in March 1944, Willi took over as camp elder and remained there until July when the December transport was liquidated. He was then sent to the Gleiwitz and Gross-Rosen camps. Having escaped from a death march to Bergen-Belsen in March 1945, he moved to Hamburg, Germany, where he died aged 78.*

- **Arno Böhm** (1913–1962) *After the liquidation of the September transport in March 1944, Böhm was sent to the front in an SS unit of criminals to fight Polish partisans. At the end of the war,* *he was taken prisoner by the Soviets and released five years later. He lived in Frankfurt until his death aged 49.*

- **Ada Fisher,** the hangman of Terezín. *Fate unknown.*

- **Fritz Klein** (1888–1945) *The doctor who assisted Mengele ended up at Bergen-Belsen. When it was liberated by the British, he was among many SS officers ordered to bury the hundreds of corpses before being tried and sentenced to death. At his trial he described the Jews as 'the gangrenous appendix of mankind'. He was hanged at the age of 58.*

- **Adolf Eichmann** (1906–1962) *The senior SS officer who had been pivotal in organising Hitler's 'Final Solution' which led to the Holocaust was captured but escaped and lived as a forestry worker in Germany until 1950 before fleeing to Argentina with his family, where he worked for Mercedes-Benz. He was captured by Mossad agents in 1960 and taken to Israel for trial, where he was hanged two years later and his ashes scattered in the Mediterranean Sea. He was 56.*

- **Josef Mengele** (1911–1979) *In January 1945 Mengele, 'The Angel of Death', escaped and fled west where he was arrested by the Americans. When they failed to identify him as a war criminal, he was released. With false papers and the help of an SS network, he fled to Argentina in 1949. His wife refused to accompany him. Working in a number of occupations, he eventually became a salesman for his family firm of farming equipment and practised medicine without a licence. After returning to Europe for a holiday in the 1950s he married his sister-in-law and took her and her son back to Argentina. When Nazi-hunters tracked him down and sought his extradition, he fled to Paraguay and then Brazil. There he established several businesses and evaded capture until his death of a stroke while swimming in 1979. He was 67.*

*

Fictional Characters

In order of appearance:

- *Herr* Steil, the teacher
- Ilse, the temptress
- Hana and her brother Pavel who were sent east
- Tomáš, Petr and their friends
- Many of the named children Fredy taught
- Wilhelm
- Carl, Fredy's protégée
- Walter, the bully
- Jan
- SS officer Müller
- The people in the food queue
- The children in the attic
- Miloš, known as 'Sparrow'
- Mordechai, team leader
- Anna, the girlfriend of Ernst
- Miroslav, Fredy's friend
- Olga and Berta who had crushes on Fredy
- Werner, the physical trainer
- *Untersturmführer* Scholz
- Franka
- Andrej and Arno
- Father Marek
- Franz at the Maccabis
- Michal at the Maccabis
- Bohdan, the bully
- Dirk, the toymaker
- Dr Heller
- Alice, the cat lover

- Ze'ev and Ari, counsellors
- Kurt, Fredy's lover
- Wolfgang, the butcher's assistant
- The clerk who was a Jehovah's Witness
- Aleš, the gendarme
- Łukas, Mr Fox
- The SS thug who beat Fredy
- Ladislav, the prisoner in the Small Fortress
- 'The Bookseller' prisoner
- 'Eyebrows', SS officer
- Jana and Martina, sisters

Timeline

11th February, 1916: Aachen, Germany: Fredy Hirsch born

February 1925: Aachen, Germany: Fredy's father Heinrich dies

Summer 1932: Fredy leaves home and works with youths in Dusseldorf and then Frankfurt

September 1935: Fredy flees to Prague

Autumn 1936: In Brno, Czechoslovakia: Fredy meets Jenda Mautner

Summer 1937: Fredy supervises Maccabiah Games in Slovakia

Autumn 1938: Fredy's family flee to Bolivia where Paul becomes a rabbi in Argentina

15th March, 1939: Germany invades Czechoslovakia

1st September, 1939: Germany invades Poland and WWII is declared

December 1941: Fredy Hirsch arrives Terezín ghetto, Czechoslovakia

March 1942: Fredy opens the first of the *Kinderheims* for children

July 1942: Jenda arrives in Terezín

24ᵗʰ August, 1943: Białystok ghetto children arrive Terezín, Czechoslovakia

6ᵗʰ September, 1943: Fredy is deported to Auschwitz-Birkenau along with Leo Janowitz

September 1943: Fredy establishes the children's block

November 1943: Jakob Edelstein arrested and sent to Small Fortress

December 1943: 5,000 more inmates from Terezín arrive in the Family Camp including Jakob, his wife and child, but Jakob incarcerated in a Gestapo prison cell in Auschwitz I

February 1944: A delegation led by senior Nazi Adolf Eichmann visits the Family Camp and inspects the children's block

February 1944: A beautification programme begins in Terezín in anticipation of Red Cross inspection, which takes place later that year

March 1944: With their six months allotted time in BIIb running out and liquidation imminent, the *Sonderkommando* urge the Czechs to rebel, asking Fredy to lead it

8th March, 1944: Auschwitz II-Birkenau: Fredy Hirsch perishes in the gas chamber along with Leo and some 3,800 Czechs, including almost all the children

June 1944: The Red Cross visit Terezín and declare it a haven for the Jews. They never visit Auschwitz

20ᵗʰ June, 1944: Jakob Edelstein, his mother-in-law, wife and son all executed in Auschwitz

2ⁿᵈ September, 1951: Jenda Mautner dies of tuberculosis contracted in the camps, aged 38

1957: Fredy's mother Olga dies in Buenos Aires, aged 70

1979: Fredy's brother Paul dies in Buenos Aires, aged 65

1996: Plaque erected to Fredy in Terezín that reads, *Fredy Hirsch – gratefully, children of Terezín, Birkenau BIIb*

2016: Fredy's 100ᵗʰ birthday was marked in Aachen with his name on a *stolperstein* or 'stumbling stone' designed by a German artist to trip people up and remind them of Jews who were murdered. Embedded in the ground outside the site where he had once lived, it reads: *Here Lies Fredy Hirsh. Born 1916 Deported to Auschwitz September 6, 1943*. The final line read, *Flucht in den Tod* – Escaped to Death – *March 8, 1944*. There is also a communal garden named after him in the town, as well as a school cafeteria and a boy scout troop

February 2021: On what would have been Fredy's 105ᵗʰ birthday, Google honours him with a 'Google Doodle' on their home page, depicting him in an athletic pose

2017: Survivor Zuzana Růžičková dies aged 90 in Prague

Bibliography

- *One Hundred Miracles*, Zuzana Ružičková with Wendy Holden, Bloomsbury, 2019
- *Born Survivors*, Wendy Holden, Little, Brown Book Group, 2015
- *Theresienstadt 1941–45*, H.G. Adler, Cambridge University Press, 2017
- *Fredy Hirsch*, Lucie Ondrichová, Hartung-Gorre Verlag, 2017
- *Erinnern in Auschwitz*, Lutz van Dijk, Joanna Ostrowska et al, Quer Verlag GmbH, 2020
- *Fredy Hirsch und die Kinder des Holocaust*, Dirk Kamper, Orell Füssli Verlag, 2015
- *I Never Saw Another Butterfly*, edited Hana Volavková, Random House, 1994
- 'Block 31: The Children's Block in Birkenau' in *Yad Vashem Studies, Volume XXIV*, Shimon Adler, Yad Vashem, 1994
- *The Pink Triangle*, Richard Plant, St Martin's Press, 2000
- *In Memory's Kitchen: A Legacy from the Women of Terezín*, edited Cara de Silva, Jason Arondsen, 2006
- *Elder of the Jews – Jakob Edelstein of Theresienstadt*, Ruth Bondy, Grove Press, 1989
- *Women of Theresienstadt – Voices from a Concentration Camp*, Ruth Schwertfeger, Berg, 1988
- *We're Alive and Life Goes on; A Theresienstadt Diary*, Eva Roubicková, Henry Holt, 1998
- *As Messengers of the Victims. From Theresienstadt to Theresienstadt. With a stop in Auschwitz-Birkenau and Schwarzheide*, Pavel Stransky, Rekan Publishing, 2004

- *The Terezín Diary of Gonda Redlich*, edited by Saul S Friedman, University Press of Kentucky, 1992
- *The Terezín Ghetto*, Ludmila Chldková, Památník Terezin, 2005
- *The Terezín Requiem*, Josef Bor, Knopf, 1963
- *University Over The Abyss*, Elena Makarova, Sergei Makarov, Viktor Kuperman, Verba Press, 2000
- *People in Auschwitz*, Herman Langbein, University of North Carolina Press, 2004
- *Shoah*, Claude Lanzmann, De Capo Press, 1995
- *I Escaped from Auschwitz*, Rudolf Vrba, Robson Books, 2006
- *The Search: The Birkenau Boys*, Gerhard Durlacher, Serpents Tail, 1998
- *The Painted Wall*, Otto B. Kraus, Random House, 1994
- *The Jews of Białystok During WWII and the Holocaust*, Sara Bender, Brandeis University Press, 2010
- *Boy 30529*, Felix Weinberg, Verso Books, 2013
- *Survival in Auschwitz*, Primo Levi, Bnpublishing, 2007
- *Trapped*, Ruth Bondy, Yad Vashem Publications, 2008
- *Mengele*, Gerald Posner and John Ware, Cooper Square Press, 2000
- *Survival: Holocaust Survivors Tell Their Story*, edited Wendy Whitworth, Quill Press, 2003
- *Fireflies in the Dark*, Susan Goldman Rubin, Holiday House, 2000
- *We Are Children Just the Same*, Marie Rut Krisková, Kurt Jiri Kotouc, Zdenek Ornest, Jewish Publication Society, 1995
- *Piepel*, Ka-Tzetnik 135633, Anthony Blond, 1961
- *Triumph of Hope*, Ruth Elias, Wiley, 1998
- *Five Chimneys*, Olga Lengyel, Academy Chicago Publishers, 1947
- *Night and Hope*, Arnošt Lustig, Northwestern University Press, 1976

- *Helga's Diary*, Helga Weiss, Penguin, 2014
- *The Tin Ring*, Zenka Fantlová, Northumbria Press, 2010
- *Spring's End*, John Freund, Holocaust Survivors Memoir Program, 2007
- *A Time to Speak*, Helen Lewis, The Blackstaff Press, 1992
- *A Delayed Life*, Dita Kraus, Ebury, 2020
- *As If It Were Life*, Philip Manes, St. Martin's Press, 2009
- *A Garden of Eden in Hell*, Melissa Muller, Macmillan, 2007
- *The Holocaust Sites of Europe*, Martin Winstone, I.B. Tauris, 2010
- *Threshold of Pain*, Vera Miesels, Speaking Words, 2017
- *Hope is the Last to Die*, Halina Birenbaum, Routledge, 1996
- *Poetry of the Second World War*, edited Desmond Graham, Pimlico, 1998
- *Landscapes of Memory*, Ruth Kluger, Bloomsbury, 2004
- *Inherit the Truth 1939–1945*, Anita Lasker Wallfisch, Giles de La Mere, 1996
- *Witness to the Holocaust*, Michael Berenbaum, HarperCollins, 1997
- *People In Auschwitz*, Hermann Langbein, University of North Carolina Press, 2004
- *The Boys*, Martin Gilbert, Wiedenfeld & Nicholson, 1996
- *The Holocaust: The Jewish Tragedy*, Martin Gilbert, William Collins, 1986
- *The Unloved*, Arnošt Lustig, Northwestern University Press, 1996
- *The Cap*, Roman Frister, Wiedenfeld & Nicholson, 1999
- *Life with A Star*, Jirí Weil, Daunt Books, 2012
- *Doctor 117641*, Louis J. Micheels, Yale University, 1989
- *Against All Hope*, Hermann Langbein, Paragon House, 1994
- *Smoke Over Birkenau*, Seweryna Szmaglewska and Jadwiga Rynas, The Auschwitz-Birkenau State Museum, 2015

- *It Kept Us Alive: Humour in the Holocaust*, Chaya Ostrower, Yad Vashem Publications, 2014
- *Children and Play in the Holocaust*, George Eisen, University of Massachusetts Press, 1988
- *A Day at Bunny School*, Albert Sixtus, Edition Tintenfass, 2012
- *The Cat with the Yellow Star*, Susan Goldman Rubin with Ela Weissberger, Holiday House, 2006

The stólperstein (stumbling stone) commemorating
Fredy Hirsch in Aachen

The plaque unveiled by Zuzana Ružičková in Terezín

Wendy Holden was a respected journalist and war correspondent for the *Daily Telegraph*, covering news stories around the world. A Fellow of the Royal Historical Society, she is the author of more than forty non-fiction titles featuring inspirational men and women, many of which are international bestsellers. They include *Born Survivors*, the true story of three young mothers who hid their pregnancies from the Nazis and gave birth in the camps, published in twenty-four countries, and *One Hundred Miracles* the memoir of musician Zuzana Ružičková who survived three concentration camps.

She also wrote the No.1 bestseller *Tomorrow Will Be a Good Day*, the memoir of British centenarian Captain Sir Tom Moore, and *Tomorrow to Be Brave* about the only woman in the French Foreign Legion in WWII. Other books include *Behind Enemy Lines* about a French Jewish spy; *A Woman of Firsts* the memoir of the 'Muslim Mother Teresa'; and *I Give You My Heart* about a Catholic couple in Poland who paid the ultimate price for hiding a Jewish child.

She lives in Suffolk, England, with her husband and two dogs.

www.wendyholden.com